I0788209

Diane had only recently come to accept the possibility something – some*one* – like Peg could exist. Yet the situation the voice was describing, the conclusion every photo and document on her desk pointed toward… her mind simply refused to accept it could happen. Asking her to prepare and launch two rockets with crew in response to the unbelievable was beyond her ability to contemplate. "Do you know the position you're putting me in here? I can't just—"

"Then let me simplify the decision for you, Director."

The phone and hallway intercoms suddenly burst into life. An older male voice sounded throughout the building, his words saturated with pain.

"Mayday, Mayday, Mayday. This is retired Master Chief Petty Officer Jason Cobbler onboard Earth Station. I am an employee of Stellar Nursery. To all craft boarding this station, stop your assault. We are unarmed. I say again, we are *unarmed*."

Static was broken by an occasional sound like whistling wind. Then the voice returned again, gasping and growing weaker. "Mayday, Mayday, Mayday. This is Earth Station. We are under attack by unknown forces. There are heavy casualties. To any ship within range, we require immediate assistance."

The voice was barely a whisper. "Mayday, Mayday, May…."

The intercoms fell silent.

KALI RISES

Marauding Stars
Book One

WELLS CARROLL

KALI RISES

This is a work of fiction. All characters and events portrayed in this book are fictional. Any resemblance to real people or incidents is purely coincidental.

Copyright © 2024 by Wells Carroll

All rights reserved, including the right to reproduce this book or portions thereof in any form.

A Stellar Nursery Media Original

Stellar Nursery Media
PO Box 92
Archie, MO 64725
www.stellarnursery.net

ISBN: 978-1-963833-06-5

Cover Art by Izabela Novoselec

First Hardback Printing, February 2024

Printed in the United States of America

CHAPTER 1

Help Wanted

The task was not observation this time. It was direct action. Thousands of variables had been identified. Millions of models evaluated. The results were irrefutable. Humanity died if no action was taken. Those at the nexus had to coalesce and unify.

Manipulating them was wrong. That was basic morality. Didn't matter how easily it could be done, controlling them was a prohibited action. It violated the core definition of what it meant to be human. Free will must be retained.

Thousands of scenario options were tested, then discarded. A handful remained. Probability of success was low. Yet the criteria was specific, those who would stand at the nexus must decide themselves. It had to be their choice. Free will.

Results of candidate selection surprised. The nexus team were damaged, imperfect. Souls forged by remorse, pain, grief, loss… attributes that made them indomitable, independent, brilliant, self-driven. Simply accepting what life offered was not only a foreign concept to them, it was anathema to how they lived their lives.

Without being seen, the observer would visit each to offer a single opportunity. Should any decline, success approached zero. Humanity died. There was simply no other solution. The time had come to step into time.

People did not understand time. To them it was a river flowing in a single direction. Birth, life, death. Past, present, future. The observer knew time, knew space. It was an ocean in a glass ball, infinitely rolling. There was no up or down, past or future. To move to a specific time and location point, one only needed for it to flow back to you as the glass ball rolled. Or one could simply swim to it.

The observer identified the correct time location, moved to it and through it. Like climbing a ladder out of a pool, there was resistance. Sensitivity to light until eyes adjusted. Blurred vision that gradually resolved into a room.

The room wasn't important. That it was just another decaying cramped apartment didn't matter. Neither did its location, somewhere on a filthy rotting block in yet another filthy rotting city. It could've been anywhere – New York, Atlanta, Los Angeles, St Louis, Omaha – all so common in their deteriorated infrastructure and miserable inhabitants that *where* was irrelevant.

No, the only thing that mattered was the girl. She was young, having barely crossed over that invisible boundary between teen and twenties. Her blonde hair was cropped short. Not in rebellion or a statement of style, but from practicality. Time was important to her, and wasting it on brushing long strands of thin straight hair simply wasn't. That pragmatism and focus was apparent in her attire as well. A simple tank top and a pair of blue jean shorts.

Stepping closer, it was easy to see other signs of the young woman's personality. No jewelry adorned her fingers or wrists. Nothing dangled from her neck, no gold chains or plated symbols as was the street fashion of her fellow exiled residents. Those were signs of wealth through conquest. She wanted neither.

There were no scars on her, at least none that were visible. That in itself was an oddity. The streets she grew up on – and especially the streets in the surrounding neighborhoods – guaranteed blood and scars. Yet there were no marks on her skin, not even the mandatory gang tattoos that offered protection in the Blight.

Where once mankind equated scars with battle skill and prowess, times – like the society and politics of this world – had changed. Unmarked skin now sent the same message and warning. One of her age bearing no scars meant coldblooded ruthlessness. That is how the predators and gangs outside read the unconscious message of her skin. *Death awaits you here. To live, do not engage. Let it pass, and pray it doesn't turn around to see you.*

While that was how people treated her – with averted heads, quick steps away – the observer knew it wasn't who she was. In her mind, it did not define her. Seven times she had defended herself with lethal force. Only seven times in her twenty long years, eight of those years scarred by street life. It was regrettable. It was necessary. It was simply life.

The young woman was twelve when she defended herself the first time. The man, at the suggestion of her drug-stupored mother, had climbed into the girl's bed. He did not climb out. Her mother never heard her pack, was oblivious when she closed the apartment door for the last time.

That decision and action led her to this room. That first night, she huddled under the broken kitchen table as cold autumn rain fell through the rotted roof. The next day she climbed onto the roof and patched it. It would take another two years of teaching herself how before the patch finally held.

The young girl initially survived on the harsh kindness of a war-haunted veteran. He kept his distance at first, simply left a can for her to find. No can opener, no knife to open it. Just a can and a puzzle. After she had solved it and fed, he left another. It was her first lesson of the street. Take what is left and use it to survive.

The veteran never gave his name. The first time he attacked her, he left her unconscious on the kitchen floor. The second and third time resulted the same. The fourth occasion, she sensed him and turned with knife in hand. He took it from her, slapped her hand, and showed her how to hold it correctly. Then he turned his back and left the apartment. He never uttered a word but the point was clear. That was the second lesson of the street. Nowhere was safe.

He died that first year. The girl found him and five gang punks in the lobby of her building. None of them still breathed. At this point she had grown cold. Her only emotion was irritation. No police would ever enter this neighborhood, no coroner would come to take away the bodies. That became her task. The only other option was to let the corpses swell and rot inside her home. She dragged them into the nearby woods. The old veteran deserved a grave. The others she left on the ground. Coyotes and turkey vultures would see to them.

Gangs moved in packs through every neighborhood. They went where they wanted and took what they wanted. Two had entered the safe house she used when traveling through their turf. They left with nothing. Not even their lives. She wheelbarrowed them to the closest gang corner and dumped them in a pile.

It was stupid, she knew that. The gang saw it as a statement, a challenge. They hunted her. Eventually three found her, thinking they had trapped her in an alley. She left them there. After that, the gangs didn't just leave her alone. They avoided her. Word spread. Everyone kept their distance, well beyond pistol range.

Until the last man forced her to defend herself. She knew of him, a sick rapist and pedophile who scattered parts of his victims around the city. The psychopath had expanded his hunting grounds to Uptown, the walled heart of the city where the wealthy lived and worked. The privileged found both the breach of their walls and the kidnapping of a child unacceptable.

Police once again were forced to enter the Blight. That was Uptown's name for the economically devastated suburbs and townships. Blight was everything between Uptown's protective walls and the countryside with its armed corporate farms. The police knew they were risking their lives entering that nightmare.

It was better than the alternative. Unemployment, which meant exile to the Blight themselves. At least this way, with their armored aircars and heavy weapons, the officers stood a chance. That's what they told themselves as they hunted the hunter.

Both found her, one after the other. The murderous pedophile found her first. It wasn't an accident, as the girl had deliberately walked to his door. When the police arrived, they found her wiping her knife clean on the former child rapist's shirt. The older officer simply looked at her, then forced her junior partner to lower his weapon. There would be no arrest today. As thanks, the young girl pointed to the alley door. Behind it the officers would find the stolen five year old Uptown boy, still alive.

She had shed no tears later as she showered off the blood. Not for the first. Not for the last. Tears would've been wasted time and emotion, and she was frugal with both.

Yet to hear her laugh, as she did just now, was to hear innocence. The young woman sat at the scarred kitchen table in the tiny kitchen, the aged rebuilt laptop in front of her. She had replaced the screen herself several years after taking this apartment. It was her only possession crossing both lifetimes, before and after her father died. A nickel-sized plate was welded center of the laptop lid. It covered the hole defining the life of a child. An obsolete cell phone sat flat on the table by her left wrist.

The young woman's voice carried no accent, as was common among Midwesterners. "I *know*, Momma. I'm online looking now."

"You know that computer ain't gonna get you no job, Haley Brandt," crackled a voice from the outdated cell phone. The accent carried something southeastern in it. Louisiana, perhaps, or Georgia. Irrelevant, a passing distraction. Focus on the conversation.

"You need to be knockin' on doors. Talk to them owners face to face."

Haley shook her head as she squinted at the laptop screen. "Not how it's done anymore, Momma. You gotta be online now, show yourself off. Employers see that first. They like it, they set up an interview on BossMeet or some other app."

It didn't matter that the cell phone screen was cracked and dead, that she couldn't see her mother. It didn't matter the camera had been stripped out years before Haley bought the phone, or that her mother couldn't see her. If the girl was honest with herself, having this conversation with her mother didn't matter either. It was just part of the illusion of family she kept casting, as if what her mother had done offering up her child had never happened. That was over with, done. Just another part of life.

"If you're a college kid, sure," crackled the phone. "But you ain't, Haley. People who'd hire folks like us, they don't waste time with online meets. And now's not the time to be choosy. Long as it ain't strippin', you take whatever job comes along. Hear me?"

The reaction was barely detectable. Anyone else would've missed it. A slight tensing of jaw muscles, a brief flaring of the nostrils. Imperceptible to the human eye, yet unmistakable to the invisible observer still watching. Include the other physiological factors. Sudden surge of adrenaline and a radical drop in cortisol. Significant neuron firings in the left and right frontal lobes, indicating both anger toward and emotional withdrawal from the speaker.

It was time to intervene, to move from observation to direct action. Flash the laptop screen once. Even in the safety of her own apartment, the motion would grab the young woman's attention and activate her fight-or-flight response. Now refresh the screen and show the new web page.

"I hear you, Momma…" Haley Brandt stopped mid-sentence, eyes focusing on the laptop screen.

Success.

The young woman started reading the job posting aloud, her voice so soft the cell phone microphone could barely pick it up. The observer made a minor adjustment, then even that signal was blocked. The offer was for Haley alone.

The mother didn't deserve to be part of the decision, had on multiple occasions sacrificed any right to direct her daughter's life. She was a crab in a bucket, trying to grab Haley's legs and pull the girl back down into her world.

Even now, the mother demonstrated the self-destructive world she wanted her daughter to join. The older woman sat on stained sheets in a motel near the Uptown wall. Her attention was more on counting the soiled bills from her last customer than on the future her daughter was softly reading.

The observer knew Haley's mother was a potential threat to the future. An action could be taken, a lethal overdose arranged. Yet that would be manipulation, not freewill and choice. The probability was extremely high the woman would remove herself from Haley's equation anyway. Addicts like her rarely survived their addiction. That was her choice.

The observer's only concern here was whether Haley would find the offer enticing enough. It was a simple advertisement, structured to strike chords of independence, self-sufficiency, and economic stability within the young woman. It simply said:

> *WAITRESS WANTED: Immediate hire. No experience necessary, will train. Looking for a pleasant, courteous person. No age or other restriction. Position requires extreme international travel. Relocation necessary during three year guaranteed contract. Housing, utilities, meals provided. $80,000 USD per year. Click the "Apply" button, then tell us who you are.*

There it is. That smile those on the street would read as deadly intention, but was simply Haley Brandt accepting a challenge with grim determination. The task here was finished. Wait. Reactivate the microphone first.

"Gotta go, Momma," Haley said to the cell phone. The tone was filled with vindictiveness or justice, or both. "Someone's offering eighty grand a year for strippers. Love you!"

"Wait!" her mother sputtered selfishly, "Eighty for what…?"

It wasn't necessary to disconnect the phone. Haley Brandt did that herself. Then she moved the archaic mouse in her right hand, hovered the cursor over the "Apply" button and clicked once.

***

The observer recalculated. Re-ran models, assessed probabilities. The window of success had cracked open slightly, but there was now a chance. Time to move to the next location. Reenter the ocean of time. Identify the next point, move to and pass through it. Readjust and verify the time and location were correct.

The location was on the Pacific coast. The warm, salty breeze blowing through the bay windows signified California. The red and gold dancing on the waves and water signified sunset. It would be easy to imagine a young couple standing on that balcony, arms around waists, basking in a timeless moment shared only between them.

But this was not the home of a young couple. The beach house had an older feel, filled with an odd flavor at first difficult to identify. The setting suggested romance and physical passion. While there were echoes of that… it was something else. Mutual respect was there, a taste like sugar on the tongue. Loss as well, tasting of salt. But the most powerful flavor was a challenge to decipher.

Then it resolved itself, a memory from a time long past. Love could be felt here, a deep and abiding love absorbed by every particle of the home. After the absence of it in Haley Brandt's apartment, being here was like stepping out of a raging blizzard and into a hearth-warmed room.

He sat in the living room.

It had all the familiar accoutrements. Family photos on wall and mantle. Knickknacks bought with humor on bookcase shelves. Everything gathered in decades of marital life. There was a social area with wrap-around leather couch. It faced the giant television atop a stone fireplace.

A liquor cabinet sat beside the dark fireplace. Lights that once shone on crystal glasses and expensive bottles were now dimmed. A light dust lay on everything, a deliberate statement that no laughter would sound from the social area anymore.

He sat in a leather recliner facing the bay windows. The social area hunkered in shadow to his right. He never turned his head that direction anymore. Another leather recliner sat to his left, a small table with a lamp separating his chair and hers. This was where they had spent their time since his retirement, just the two of them. The balcony outside the bay windows in front of them was a gentle reminder of the passions of their past. Until recently, the two recliners with heat and massage had been their present.

"Same thing, different day, my love."

It was a surprisingly rich, deep bass voice. There were no tremors normally present in a person three-quarters a century old. Nor were there tremors in the hands holding the newspaper or in the corded steel-like muscles under his deeply tanned skin.

He had a slender frame, easily over six feet if he were standing. Perhaps Cherokee genes explained the lower body fat. More likely it was lower caloric intake from his recent eating habits. Whatever the reason, his muscle and bone structure suggested a man twenty years younger. Only wrinkled liver-spotted skin starting to sag in strategic places gave any indication of his true age.

The newspaper rustled as he flipped to the next page. "Auto tech, auto tech, auto tech. Wait, this one says mechanic… nope, it's all engine computer stuff. Means auto tech."

Blue eyes quickly scanned one page, then the other. They weren't the only indicators of mixed genetic heritage. His silver-grey hair still contained a subtle hint of red to signify Celtic or Nordic genes. Native American ancestry at war with his European genes was evident in the week's growth of stubble on his face. As a younger man, it wouldn't be surprising if he hadn't needed to shave for weeks at a time.

He shook his head once, then abruptly folded in the newspaper. Left hand moved to right, right forefinger holding his place as right thumb secured the paper. His head turned left as he reached for the coffee cup on the table beside him. The observer found that interesting. Left-hand dominant or ambidextrous.

The blue eyes automatically rose from decades of habit as he turned his head toward the second recliner. His lips opened as if starting to speak, then stopped. A soft breath escaped before his eyes could shift away from the empty chair. They settled on the purple funereal urn centered on the table between the two chairs. Purple had been her favorite color.

The moment of loss was there, then gone. He reached for his coffee, raised the cup to his lips and sipped. It provided the time he needed. Then he returned the cup to its coaster, turned his head back to the newspaper and opened it to the next page.

"You were right," he said, the cracking hesitation in his voice barely discernible. A forced smile, then, "And no, I'm still not putting it in writing. But you were right, love. Nobody's looking for real mechanics anymore. Kids running computers, hand the printout to your boss."

The tone shifted to an older, more familiar one. It was easy to picture the scene, him droning about inconsequential affairs in the news while she reread yet another one of her favorite books. For a moment timelines crossed. The observer could see the woman there in the second chair, reassuring smile on her face as if she were listening. Timelines reverted and then she was gone.

"The boss takes it to the customer, gives them a price," the man continued. "Then you get the work order, pull out the broken module, stick in a new one. That's not what a *real* mechanic does. Least it's not what *I* did."

The observer sensed it was time. The principle was the same as Haley Brandt's laptop screen. Shift particles around, rearrange them to form a specific pattern. Like a white board, erase what's there. Take the particles defined as ink and reintegrate them in the top left column of the next page. Simple.

The elderly gentleman turned the page, straightened the newspaper. "Well now, what's this? Mechanic wanted."

He raised the paper, focused on the ad and spoke in the comforting irrelevant voice his wife would've recognized. "Immediate hire. Can you rebuild a classic '67 V8 engine? Fabricate a new flywheel? Re-wind the stator on a fried generator? We're looking for a true mechanic able to identify and solve mechanical problems, not just replace parts. No age or other restriction. Position requires extreme international travel. Relocation necessary during three year guaranteed contract. Housing, utilities, meals provided.

Hundred grand a year. Call today and tell us who you are."

Both hands came together as he closed, then folded and lowered the newspaper to his lap. The timbre of pain was still in his voice as he turned and spoke directly to the urn. "What do you think, love? You said not to hang around here when you're gone."

He paused as if listening to a reply. "I know, I'm retired. And I'm old, mean, set in my ways. But they said there's no age limit."

There was nothing in the air except the sound of distant waves on the shore, yet he nodded as if he could hear a voice. "That's true. It's better than pin-balling around here. But what about the house? Who's going to look after it… after you?"

After a moment he shook his head. "Your locket? That's ridiculous. I'm not carrying you around in no locket. They said international, and I'm sure there's some law about transporting… well, you know."

The observer found it fascinating to watch. Again it appeared he was listening, then he held up his left hand as if interrupting. "Fine, okay fine! Fifty years married, and I still can't get you to stop arguing. I'll do it. Just don't be surprised when it doesn't work out. Okay, *okay* already! See, I'm doing it now…."

The man reached behind his coffee cup and retrieved a cell phone from the shadows behind the lamp. He quickly punched numbers, then raised the phone to his ear.

The observer found electronics easy to manipulate. No need to disguise the voice, just speak through the phone. "Stellar Nursery, this is Peg. How may I direct your call?"

The man leaned back in his chair. "This is Jason Cobbler. I'm replying to your ad in the paper for a real mechanic. Who do I talk to?"

"Just one moment, Mister Cobbler. I will connect you." Electronically modulating the voice to appear as another person required no effort. Nor would transmitting the typical responses Jason Cobbler expected to hear in order to set an interview date and time.

The observer recalculated models and probabilities. Even if barely, the potential for success had increased to double digits. Ironic to think it, but time was available to detour. Two individuals needed monitoring. An opportunity had presented itself to evaluate both simultaneously. Neither were critical to forming the nexus team.

While time was fluid and events could be taken in any order, curiosity dictated the choice. The news studio first, then move to the next candidate. The observer stepped back into the ocean of time.

CHAPTER 2

News and Weather

The living room of the beach house disappeared and was replaced with the lights and cameras of a television newsroom studio. An auburn-haired female anchor sat alone behind the news desk. Thin build, average height, age in the early forties. Unlike Haley Brandt, this woman carried scars earned on actual battlefields. Not as a soldier or combatant, but as a war correspondent.

The woman was the only living thing in the room. There hadn't been a need for newsroom staffing since the late twenties. Camera operators were unnecessary and had been replaced by programmable camera drones.

The entire room was a microphone able to capture the commentator's voice from any angle, making boom mikes and sound crews obsolete. Production teams were irrelevant. All their traditional tasks were performed by one producer sitting at home, an array of production scripts and preprogrammed camera cues available on their computer monitor.

The modern television studio now only needed two people to function. The media business had become like every other major industry. Technology had erased the need for unnecessary employees.

Repetitive tasks were automated. Gone were the days where any business needed hundreds of workers.

It was the logical result of a government versus business war started in the latter part of the twentieth century. Politicians needed to continuously offer new government-protected benefits to their constituents in order to remain in office. Corporations needed to maintain a minimum profit level for shareholders. As happens in every conflict between two opposing forces, the people paid the price for their war.

Politicians made everything a right. Healthcare. Housing. Unemployment and employment. Gender and equity. Reparations. Vacation and decreased work days. With each right came the inevitable private and government lawsuits against business. A simple accusation by one employee against another could result in millions in fines, court costs and judgments against the employer.

Businesses eventually realized their greatest costs were employees. The solution was simple. Technology cannot sue. Find or create tech to replace the worker. Changes were implemented quickly in factories and offices around the world.

The result was mass unemployment and violence worldwide. Unions and ex-employees burned their former places of work in protest. Initially police and firefighters responded in an effort to maintain order. Yet their salaries were funded by local taxes. When city and state coffers ran dry, the defenders joined those protesting.

Urban cities split into two camps and economies. Those with income now lived and worked in the Uptowns behind closed walls. They bought goods manufactured in automated factories within the safe zone. Food was airlifted from corporate farms to fill grocery shelves. Private security was given police authority, and the traditional police guarded the Uptown walls. The twenty-first century standard of living was maintained and nurtured in a closed economy. The only requirement to remain within Uptown was proof of employment.

Those without a job were expelled into the Blight outside the walls. There they struggled to survive in an environment where food was airdropped weekly by military cargo planes. In order to insure everyone received their fair share, the pilots dropped the food pallets in unpredictable patterns into the city. Street gangs marked tribal boundaries based on major streets in order to defend food drops in their territories. The economy was based on theft, barter and trade in the physical.

Politicians passed legislation making the "common assistance allotment" of airdropped food a basic right. Free water and electricity were also established as basic rights. Cash assistance was unnecessary. The Uptowns didn't need it. Having neither banks nor a cash economy, the Blight areas couldn't use it. Instead, millions were spent annually on university grants to study Blight causes and conditions. If the media were believed, the Uptowns were unified in their effort caring for the poverty-stricken citizens of the Blights.

The new social order made elections simple. The Blights were considered too dangerous to open polling stations. Mail-in ballots were irrelevant, since no post offices remained open in Blight areas. Yet legislators didn't want to be accused of denying any citizen the right to vote, so they passed new laws. The population of each Blight was counted using satellite thermal imagery. The total was then divided by and apportioned to Uptown citizens. Being of higher education, social standing and financial stability, it was deemed an Uptown citizen would be better suited to vote in the Blight citizens' best interest.

The rural areas were essentially unaffected. Family farms were rare. Armed corporate farms were the standard. Their paramilitary security was necessary to respond to Blight gang attacks on cropland. After petroleum became a nationalized resource, fuel for tractors and equipment was provided by the government. Its cost was defrayed through carbon tax credits based on crop yields. Farming employees were sent to the nearest Blight if the farm failed to meet profit levels.

Perhaps it was guilt that caused the observer to ruminate on the past. It was not critical to be here. There were other tasks to perform. The actions of these two were irrelevant to the plan. They were not part of the nexus. Yet the observer could not leave, not yet. It was a feeling, a certainty that there was something important here to be known. The observer settled in to watch.

Music began playing in the reporter's wireless earbuds. The only sound in the room was the squeak of her chair as she leaned forward, and the whir of the drone camera's motors as it automatically adjusted its height.

The woman smiled, then spoke. "Welcome back to Our Earth Network. I'm Cara Abrams. We've been covering the House Committee on Science, Space and Technology hearings on NASA and the space program. With us now is Trent Lewis, Director of the nonprofit Organization for Climate Sustainability."

She turned to her left, as if looking at a monitor showing her guest. It was unnecessary, as there was no monitor in the room. The illusion of the monitor would be generated electronically in the distant producer's computer, then transmitted out on the global wireless network. Eventually the signal would be recoded and transmitted through a television tower into the Blight.

Wireless contact lenses let the woman see both the monitor and her guest. Deep fake technology had progressed to the point it was impossible to tell if the man's image on screen truly reflected his actual appearance. The reporter was experienced enough to recognize the moderately expensive suit and grooming software. Her guest's acne scars and brow lines could've been generated by software, but that would be counterproductive. It was far more likely the man's face was real.

Cara Abrams appreciated his honesty. "Good morning, Trent. Thank you for joining us."

"Good morning, Cara," Trent Lewis replied. "It's good to be here."

"Trent, you just finished testifying before the Committee. Can you give us a sense of how things are going?"

A public relations software addon would've changed the man's smile to something friendly and reassuring. Instead, the image on the screen showed a gloating pride. "They're going extremely well, Cara. The Committee asked us to present our non-partisan assessment on NASA expenditures over the past five years. They wanted to know if that money could be better spent on climate change response programs under the new Federal Climate Change Agency. Specifically, we—"

Cara was an experienced reporter. She knew how to control an interview. "Excuse me for interrupting. Would you explain to our viewers how climate change and NASA are linked? Everyone knows NASA is about space… how does climate change fit in?"

Trent Lewis was familiar with the media game as well. No irritation showed on his face or in his voice. He simply smiled. "Of course. NASA has been involved in both monitoring and assessment of greenhouse gases since the late '70s. Because of their early work, we have incontrovertible evidence of mankind's harm to Earth's atmosphere. According to the latest UN Panel on Climate Change, our global temperature has increased—"

"Thank you for explaining, Trent. So NASA has been monitoring climate change… why should they stop now?"

"Because it's no longer their lane, Cara. Climate monitoring now belongs to the Federal Climate Change Agency." Trent's voice increased in pace. He wanted to stress the point. "Congress created the FCCA to bring all climate responsibilities under one roof. Just like Homeland Security did for intelligence and security after 9/11 forty-four years ago."

Cara nodded. "And critics are suggesting that, just like Homeland Security, we'll end up with bureaucratic bloat that'll cost the taxpayers. Duplication of effort. Two government employees from different agencies doing the same job. How would you respond?"

"Simple. Our proposal would prevent that." Trent knew how to play the media game. He leaned his right shoulder toward the camera and raised one hand. Then he motioned slowly as if inviting the audience closer to learn a secret.

"Cara, our climate agencies aren't talking to each other. NASA monitors the atmosphere from space. NOAA tracks climate change effects on the oceans. The EPA monitors greenhouse gas violations. The SEC and FBI enforce climate law. They all have parts of the larger global catastrophe puzzle, but no single agency has the authority to do anything with the information. The FCCA can."

Cara leaned back in her chair, signaling she wasn't buying his statement: "But the FCCA has its own budget. You're proposing taking away three-quarters of NASA's annual budget and giving it to them. Basically quadrupling the FCCA's size. I don't think that's what Congress had in mind when they created the new agency."

Trent shifted to redirect the conversation. "Cara, you mentioned bloat earlier. Our proposal prevents that. Everything NASA does that falls under climate monitoring would go to the FCCA. Satellite purchases. Rockets to put them in orbit. Launch costs. Earth-based monitoring stations. Climate research grants. The fact it's *seventy-five percent* of NASA's budget is why it should be moved. NASA's job is space, not climate. That's what I presented to the Committee today. I would say the recommendation was favorably received."

"But won't taking most of NASA's budget make them unable to support ongoing space operations?"

Trent laughed. "What space operations? We've had nine years of UN resolutions limiting launches because of their greenhouse gas emissions. Nostalgia is the only reason NASA is still around. Sure, over three-quarters a *century* ago they got us to the moon. But since then, they've simply become a pass-through funding source for what's left of the space industry. It's a disgusting waste, fraud and abuse of taxpayer dollars."

He leaned toward the camera. "I mean, who are we kidding here? The private sector is fully capable of supporting those who want to play in space. Businesses like Stellar Nursery willing to pay the hefty carbon taxes on space launches. Billionaires who want to take a joyride just to call themselves 'astronauts.' Satellite companies wanting to put yet another metal can into orbit that'll become a fiery meteor when it comes back down."

With a friendly smile signifying he had won the argument, Trent leaned back into his chair. "Don't get me wrong, Cara. While we don't support activities in space, we aren't against those who see a market there. We just don't believe taxpayers need to continue supporting private industry."

Cara smiled in return. The interview had entered the tried-and-true government versus big business argument stage. She had given him time to voice his talking points. It was her job now to show the viewing audience his bias. "It definitely sounds like you have an axe to grind, Trent. So you don't support NASA's latest plan for a manned station on the moon?"

Trent's laugh escaped his lips like a bark. "Really? They're trying to resurrect the Artemis program from the '20s. Remember that fiasco? They put Gateway Station up, if you want to call a bunch of empty boosters cobbled together a 'station'. It was a death trap for any astronaut they stuck there. Fifteen times the radiation in a single day than we get in a year on Earth."

Time to poke the bear again. A single shake of the head, then Cara smiled. "We both know that claim has been debunked, Trent. The astronauts—"

The man leaned forward again, right hand brusquely dismissing her response. "And *then* NASA promised us a manned lunar station. Other than some robot rovers poking holes in the ground, there's nothing to show for the hundreds of billions spent. Cost overruns. Deliveries years behind schedule. More waste and fraud. It's time for the American people to ask if we really need NASA at all."

He realized then what she had done. It was time to get back to his original message. "Meanwhile, there's good reason to move the money out of NASA's hands. Put it where it belongs. The FCCA handles climate now. Their priority is stopping the devastating global damage caused by man-made climate change."

Trent leaned back in his chair, distancing himself from the audience. The countdown clock on his screen showed the interview had seconds left. There was only one way to wrap up his argument. It couldn't be with facts, as people don't respond to facts. Instead, he used what politicians and con artists knew worked. Emotion.

"Maybe, once we've saved Earth and fixed all the problems we have here, we can think about space. But right now, our children – and our children's children – are waiting for us to do the right thing. I believe the House Committee agrees with us, and we'll be seeing some real changes soon."

Cara simply nodded. She wasn't invested in the argument either way, just irritated her producer had allotted so much time to the interview. Her guest had lost more viewers with his longwinded diatribe than he had convinced of his cause. The last-minute plea to save the children definitely lost more viewers.

However, courtesy costs nothing. She simply smiled sweetly and said, "Thank you, Trent. I'm sorry to end it here, but we're up against a hard break. I hope we can have you back on the program again soon."

Trent smiled in return. "Thank you for listening, Cara. It would be my pleasure."

The hollow room was silent for a moment as the approved political message scrolled up her contact lenses. Then the drone camera whirred as it followed its programmed pre-commercial sequence. Cara swiveled in her chair and raised her head, knowing the camera had centered her at the anchor desk as if her next words were important.

"And you heard it here first on OEN. NASA may no longer be in the space business. We'll be back after this commercial break, where we'll be joined by our guest the former Director of NASA."

The contact lenses were suddenly clear, signifying the reporter was off the air. She pushed away from the desk, then walked quickly toward the door. Four minutes of commercials meant she barely had time for a bathroom break and a quick jolt of coffee. She wasn't concerned about encountering someone wanting to engage in social chit-chat. There was nobody else in the building.

That wasn't quite true, although Cara Abrams couldn't know that. The observer watched as the camera drone settled to its charging station on the floor. Then the studio was silent, but it was not empty.

This trip had been one of curiosity, not of necessity. It provided an opportunity to observe two important players. True, the entire interview could've been viewed as it passed through the wireless network. It could've been pulled from digital archives anytime at a later date. There was no need to be present here.

The answer came as a surprise. The presence simply wanted to be in the same room… it needed to see her.

Once acknowledged, the reason no longer mattered. Time was

fluid, and there was another time and place requiring direct action. A favorite player would be there. Yet there were opportunities for mischance that could not be allowed. Assistance might be required.

***

The studio disappeared. A new room took its place. It was a living room in a small rural house. A middle-aged couple sat in two recliners, both chairs facing a large flatscreen television above a stone fireplace. A couch for occasional visitors sat in front of the two large windows facing the field of corn outside.

The favorite, a tall man in his early thirties, sat in the corner of the couch. His body was half-twisted in order to center his attention on the couple. He was calm as he watched the angry man's face in front of him.

"Don't matter what the bank told you, mister, I'm not selling." The angry man threw himself back into his chair and defiantly crossed his arms. "This land's been in my family over a hundred fifty years. Maginnis blood is in the soil here. Ain't gonna do it."

The man on the couch shifted forward to the edge of his seat, closing the distance between them. His voice was calm and reassuring. "First, Mister Maginnis, please let me apologize. Where I come from, first thing two men of good will do is extend a hand in friendship. I'm sorry we haven't had the opportunity to do that yet. I'm Alex Legate, please call me Alex."

The man in the chair looked at the hand Alex extended, then at the younger man's face. A brief uncomfortable moment passed. Then upbringing and rural social etiquette took over. The man accepted the offered hand and shook it. "I'm Teddy. This is my wife, Gretchen."

"It's a pleasure to meet you and your lovely wife, Teddy." Alex Legate was not offended as the farmer abruptly withdrew his hand and crossed both arms. The younger man simply placed his elbow on his knee, then rested his hand on the other knee. It was a neutral gesture, neither aggressively reaching toward Teddy Maginnis nor defensively withdrawing from him.

"I understand your hesitancy," Alex continued in his calm voice.

"When I inquired, your bank informed me of the delinquency on your property loan and upcoming public auction. However, that's not why I'm here. I don't represent a corporate farm. I don't want to buy your land to put up quarter-billion dollar houses."

Teddy shifted in his chair, arms still crossed. "So why *are* you here?"

"My employer has need of the unique skills and expertise you and your wife possess. In other words, sir… we want to hire the both of you."

"So you aren't here about the land?"

Alex smiled. "No sir. I'm with Stellar Nursery. We're a holding company. That means we don't manufacture anything, and we don't provide any goods or services."

The younger man leaned back slightly, straightening his back and raising his head so he could look straight into the other man's eyes. "A holding company only does one thing, sir… we own businesses. Normally we'd be offering to buy yours, but my employer was very specific. In this case, we don't want your farm. We want you."

Gretchen Maginnis spoke before her husband could reply. "I don't understand. You want us for what?"

Alex turned his head and nodded once, acknowledging her. If his assessment was wrong and this family followed older country traditions of patriarchal families, the conversation would soon be over. He kept his eyes focused on the woman, almost daring Teddy Maginnis to establish himself as speaker for the household.

"Right now, we want to buy some of your time. The next few hours, or however long it takes for us to discuss my employer's offer." Alex waited for Gretchen to nod, then continued. "In return, he's offering the amount currently in arrears on your property. I have a funds transfer for that exact amount plus accrued interest. It'll be electronically submitted to your lien holder. All I need are your thumbprints on a transfer document."

Teddy still sat with arms crossed in his chair. "I'm not getting it. You want to pay us two hundred fifty thousand dollars just to talk? Is this some kind of joke? 'Cause if it is, it ain't funny. As in, 'get my gun someone's gonna get shot' not funny."

Alex allowed just enough humor in his voice to defuse the threat.

"No joke, sir. Shall we proceed? Or should we call it a day? Hopefully we could still part as friends, should that be your decision."

"Mister, you're confusing me –"

"He means yes, Mister Legate." Gretchen turned toward her husband and placed a hand on his arm.

That confirmed the family dynamic, at least in regards to financial matters. Alex dropped his gaze and turned his head, taking a moment to retrieve the electronic pad from the cushion beside him. He knew better than to observe any patriarchal issues between the couple.

There weren't any. He flipped open the pad cover, raised his head and extended the pad to the closest person. "Then I'll need your thumbprint signature, Mister Maginnis, and that of your wife. Please place your thumb on the line above your printed name."

Teddy pressed his thumb against the screen without reading it, then handed the pad to his wife. Unlike her husband, Gretchen focused on the short legal language confirming what Alex had said. Then she ran a forefinger up and down, forcing the screen to scroll. After no additional clauses appeared, she raised her head and looked straight into the younger man's eyes. She didn't break the gaze as she placed her thumb on the screen and signed.

Another person might've been offended by the obvious test. Alex simply waited until she extended the pad toward him. His eyes never left hers as he thumb-signed the electronic document and pressed the transmit button. He swiped the screen with his forefinger, then extended the pad back to Gretchen Maginnis.

"Thank you. This next screen provides a confirmation code that the funds have been transferred to your bank and applied toward your outstanding lien. You should receive notification from your bank shortly."

A chime and two buzzes sounded from Teddy's shirt pocket. The farmer reached up, pulled the phone out. A quick swipe and button push, then he squinted at the text. A moment later he looked straight at Alex and spoke, incredulously. "That's it? We're good now? Bank's not gonna take the farm?"

"No, Mister Maginnis," Alex replied reassuringly. "The farm is still yours."

Alex shifted his gaze and directed it straight at Gretchen Maginnis. "Now we can begin our discussion. First, my employer and I would like to offer our deepest condolences on the recent loss of your son. We are truly sorry. His was a unique mind that left this world too soon... but in his seventeen years here, he left his mark."

The reaction was immediate, expected and dangerous. Gretchen grabbed the arm of her chair with both hands, slowly starting to stand as she responded. "Wait a minute. How did you… how did you know? Who did you say you're with again? And who the hell is your employer? *How did you know my son!*"

Alex replied slowly, calmly and compassionately. "I work for Stellar Nursery, ma'am. My employer is Marcus Kenzie. He and your son had been corresponding online about his brilliant entry in the recent State FFA competition. After several emails went unanswered, Mr. Kenzie asked me to look into the matter."

Gretchen slowly lowered herself back into the chair. Her voice showed her confusion. "Kenzie? Marcus Kenzie? As in the Oklahoma mega-trillionaire? What did he want with my son?"

Probability was extremely high that assistance was unnecessary. However, it would cause no harm to offer it. A brief addition of text to the pad on the favorite's lap would provide the reference should he need it. Flash the data to let him know it is there.

Alex continued in his calm voice. "As I said, Mister Kenzie was impressed with your son's experiment. I believe the proper title was the 'Non-Container Vertical Aeroponics Growth System'. Growing plants without needing soil or liquid containers for root systems. Am I correct?"

Teddy nodded, his voice containing pride while still defending his departed son. "Yes, that's what Phillip was working on. But the club wouldn't let him enter. Said aeroponics wasn't farming."

Alex focused on the father, his voice sympathetic at the injustice. "That's true, and your son was very vocal about it in his online blog. It caught Mister Kenzie's attention. He was very impressed."

Alex Legate gently tapped his forefinger on the pad.

It was a signal to be prepared with assistance. These moments were always fun, trying to deduce what the favorite needed. The clue would be in the stress of a word or a tap of a finger. Often the information was already known, yet the man enjoyed including the observer in his conversations.

"In return for guaranteed college tuition, Phillip told him all about your experiments. I say that in order to be precise. Because Phillip wasn't the only one working on the project," Alex said, turning his head to look directly at the wife, "was he, *Mrs. Maginnis*?"

Clue received. Data retrieved. Displaying on the pad.

Gretchen cautiously shook her head. "No…."

Alex raised the pad from his lap and read the text in its entirety. "Gretchen Marie Maginnis nee York. Born October 17, 2007 in Abilene, Texas. No siblings. Graduated Texas A&M at the age of seventeen with a Bachelors of Science in Biochemistry and a Bachelors of Science in Genetics. Enrolled in Masters degree program, but left college unexpectedly to marry Theodore Ezekiel Maginnis. Seven months later gave birth to a son, Phillip Connor Maginnis. Current occupation, housewife. Do I have that correct, Misses Maginnis?"

Teddy protectively leaned forward. "Hold on a minute, mister. How did you –"

"Kenzie asked me to look into your son's death, Mister Maginnis. I am extremely thorough in performing my duties." Alex kept his eyes locked on the mother. "As such, I hope you can accept my reassurance that Phillip died tragically in a weather-related vehicular accident. There was no foul play involved."

Both parents reacted with identical words. "Foul play…?"

Alex shook his head, still directing his words to Gretchen. "None. But as I mentioned earlier, Phillip did leave his mark on the world. Mister Kenzie would like to obtain exclusive patent and trademark rights on the aeroponics system you and your son developed. In addition he offers terms of employment for an initial period of three years, with the agreement open for renegotiation every three years."

Alex Legate placed his forefinger on the pad but didn't tap.

Understood. Prepare to create employment contract based on specific data being developed during conversation.

"Employment would begin immediately." Alex paused a moment, giving time for the couple to express any objections. "Your positions will require extensive international travel. Relocation will be necessary during the period of this contract. Housing, utilities, meals and incidentals will be paid by Stellar Nursery. If these terms are acceptable, all I need is for you to suggest a salary figure."

The disbelieving frown on Gretchen's face was matched by her tone. "Well, Mister Legate, since this can't be real... how about a million dollars?"

Alex tapped his forefinger once, then again on the tablet. A single soft, humorous laugh escaped as he replied. "My apologies. Mister Kenzie said that would be your most likely response. Once again, he's proven prescient. That figure is acceptable to him."

Boilerplate employment contract modified. Salary specifications and terms of employment generated. Signature blocks prepared. Flash screen to indicate contract ready for examination and acceptance.

"Shall we sign some documents, then?" Alex extended the pad without looking at it.

Theodore once again looked incredulous. "Wait a minute. She said a million dollars... and you said *yes*? For *each* of us?"

"One million dollars per employee," Alex replied, smiling. "That would be a million per year for you, sir, and a million for your wife. Agreed?"

Gretchen wasn't so easily persuaded. "For that kind of money... and you said extensive international travel. Just where in the hell are we going, Mister Legate?"

Alex extended the pad to Theodore as he smiled directly at Gretchen. "The final destination, Misses Maginnis, I am not at liberty to disclose at this time. But if it helps any... you would not believe me if I told you."

CHAPTER 3

The Interviews

The observer stepped back and slipped into the waters of time. Assistance completed. The next events could be taken in any order. Location and distance were irrelevant. Two days forward and two states southeast required no effort. The rural home disappeared and was replaced with a long hallway seemingly filled with closed doors. A young woman sat in the small receptionist booth at the hallway entrance, typing.

The receptionist looked up and smiled as Haley Brandt approached her desk. "Good morning, welcome to Stellar Nursery. How may I help you?"

Haley appeared uncomfortable. The receptionist's blouse alone was worth more than everything she owned. She inhaled slowly, then forced herself to speak. "Good morning. I'm here for a waitress interview, but the email didn't say where exactly or who I'm supposed to meet. Could you—"

The receptionist simply smiled. "Thank you, Miss Brandt. Down the corridor, fourth door on the right. They're expecting you."

"Thank you, that's fourth door on the…?"

"Right. Fourth door on the right. And you may leave your purse and any belongings here, Miss Brandt. I will secure them for you."

Haley clumsily dropped the stained leather purse on the reception counter. Embarrassed, she lifted it and then set it gently down. "Right, thank you. I'm sorry, I'm not normally this frazzled. The aircar you sent for me landed on my apartment roof. Then the guard upstairs hassled me about not having proof of employment—"

The woman behind the counter smiled and raised one hand, as if waving away any need for embarrassment. "It's okay, Miss Brandt. I understand. The interview process here begins soon as you accept the invitation. So if I may suggest, take a few moments to catch your breath. Center yourself. When you're ready, stride toward that door like you own the world. Does that help?"

Haley had grown unaccustomed to kindness of any kind. The street taught you that fast. Nobody was to be trusted. People always had a self-serving angle or con. Watch the other person's face for when they realized their efforts had failed. Anger always followed that, and then belligerence and aggression. Be ready to strike fast and strike hard.

Yet the woman before her legitimately seemed to be trying to help. It was confusing at first. Haley ran the short conversation through her mind again. Then she caught it. Interview process. Defensiveness would not land her the job. The rest were instructions on the interviewer's expectations.

Haley nodded to herself and forced a smile. "Umm…. Actually yes, it does. Thank you."

Her street instincts screamed at her. She forced them down and into the back of her mind. This was not the street. This was Uptown, where people fought with words instead of blades and guns. It was a different battlefield, but a battlefield nonetheless. Conquering simply required a change in perspective. The receptionist's instructions provided the clues.

She turned to face the intimidating hallway, squared her shoulders back and started walking.

"Like I own the world," she muttered. "Own the world."

Haley stopped at the fourth door. Deeply exhaled. Held her lungs empty for a second, then inhaled slowly. "Here goes nothing…."

She twisted the doorknob, pushed open the door and stepped into the room. Immediately she was overwhelmed by the din of pots and pans clattering together. Loud voices called out commands and very loud requests for… spices? The sounds came from a large bustling kitchen on her left. Quick scan of their activity indicated they were preoccupied with what they were doing. They were no threat.

Her right eye caught motion. She turned her head quickly, looked forward to see a tall man carrying a tray. The man advanced rapidly toward her.

"Haley!" bellowed the Maitre d'. "It's about time, girl! Come on, they're waiting for their order!"

The young woman was already confused by the noise from the kitchen. Then the man's words registered. She was stunned. He knew her name. The response was automatic as her right foot slid back in a defensive stance. Elbow bent so the arm was parallel to the floor. Fingers were extended as her palm rotated up.

Something warm settled onto her open palm. She looked down, saw a food-laden tray. Haley's will controlled her, not her body. She had set her will that this was a different battlefield. Lucky for the black-suited man in front of her, for if she had retained street combat rules, the tray would've already crushed his larynx.

But the tray was not a weapon. She was not threatened. This was a kitchen in an Uptown restaurant, not the street. Words were weapons here, and she needed to feint not strike. She closed her thumb and fingers against the tray of food, then raised her left hand to secure it.

"Uh… hi?! I'm Haley Brandt and I have a—"

"Table waiting on you!" The black-suited man with his starched white shirt and ridiculous black bowtie simply frowned. Instead of an explosion from a gun, he machine-gunned words. "Table five, the elderly couple by the window. Now remember, girl, serve the dishes and then place the tray on the holding table. Then step to the window side – got that, the *window* side – to serve their beverages. But don't interfere with their conversation. You're invisible, remember that!

"The gentleman ordered the house ale, it's on the serving table already. Take the glass in front of him with two fingers, raise and tilt it *away* from him, then slowly pour the ale… we're not a tavern here, no glug-glug pour down the middle until it froths over the top. You're successful if the ale has no foam head.

"Now, she ordered the house pinot, treat it the same way! Tilt the glass, pour gently until it's half full. And don't hover over them – serve the meal and beverages, then move away quickly. But not too far, so they don't have to bellow like a goat for refilling their glasses. Invisible but available, right? Got all that? Good, then go girl! Don't keep them waiting!"

The Maitre d' spun and quickly walked away, leaving Haley standing with serving tray in hand. She looked down as if surprised to still see it there. A momentary pause, then she looked to the right and into a large, bustling restaurant. Luckily there was only one windowed wall. Only one elderly couple sat at a table there. She inhaled again, exhaled, then stepped into the room and toward the table.

The elderly female diner spoke loudly to the elderly man across from her. "Oh here we are, dear. I told you, this is a five-star restaurant. Their service is incredible!"

The male diner replied grumpily. "It better be, for what I'm paying for it. Four hundred dollars for prime rib? It better melt like butter or I'm sending it back. That I'll tell you for nothing."

Haley was learning a different set of tactics and strategies. Part of this interview battlefield was the fog of war… a lack of critical information. The Maitre d' hadn't told her who had ordered what. Whether intentional or not, the older diner had provided the answer.

She stepped around and behind the elderly lady, stopping at the corner of the table. Using her right hand, she gently placed the plate of what looked like blackened fish in front of the woman. Then she reversed course until she stood in front of the table again.

Taking the plate of prime rib in her right hand, she deposited the serving platter on the nearby table containing other empty platters. As she stepped behind and to the side of the man, she shifted the plate containing the prime rib from right hand to left. From the corner of the table, she used her left hand to place the plate in front of the man.

The grumpy male diner simply nodded. "That's good, girl. Now where's my ale? You don't expect me to choke that down dry, do you?"

This was so foreign to the young woman. Yet there was something, a memory. That's right, Uptown people often utilized a specific weapon to counter hostility and disarm their opponent. The receptionist had successfully used it on her earlier.

Haley smiled. "No sir, that wouldn't do. I'll have that for you in just a moment."

She quickly turned and stepped away from the table. What was it penguin-suit man had said? Beverage was on the serving table nearby. There, on the right. The young woman retrieved the opened ale bottle and returned to the table.

As if it were wine, she tilted the bottle toward the older man. "This will go perfectly with your meal, sir. Shall I pour?"

"Yes, yes, get on with it."

Haley realized a smile alone would not disarm this man of his aggressive irritation. She lifted the ale glass with thumb and forefinger from its place on the table. Quick tilt, then gradual pour from the ale bottle insured there was little foam. Then she returned the glass to its place at the man's left side.

"And you, madam?" she asked, facing the elderly woman. "Shall I pour the wine?"

The aged woman in her expensive dress and platinum jewelry looked up and smiled. "Of course, my dear. Oh wait, is that a pinot? I thought I ordered a Riesling. Would you be such a dear and fetch me one?"

Ah. Another part of the game. Haley simply smiled in return. "Of course, madam. Just a moment."

She stepped around and away from the table, eyes scanning the room looking for… the Maitre d' as he approached with a wine glass. "She—"

The black-suited man simply smiled and nodded. "Changed her mind to the Riesling. I know, she does it all the time. But if you don't offer the pinot first, she loses her mind."

"Thank you," Haley began, remembering another weapon of courtesy. But the Maitre d' had already turned and quickly stepped away.

She recovered quickly before anyone could notice her confusion. So many new rules. Returning to the table, she placed the wine glass gently on the white tablecloth. "Your Riesling, madam."

The elderly female diner looked directly into her eyes, then smiled. "Very good, Haley. Why don't you sit down here beside us? We have a few questions for you."

The change in tone, expression and demeanor was a shock. "What? I'm sorry, madam, but—"

"She said sit down, girl," interrupted the grumpy elderly man. "So pull out that chair right there and sit down."

He poked at the prime rib with his fork, then looked at the older woman. "They do remember I'm a vegetarian, right? Why do they keep sending this mutilated bovine at me?"

"Because you *are* a vegetarian," replied his partner. "We've seen what, two hundred applicants so far? And if you had a veggie meal with each one, we'd have to roll you out of here."

She turned to face the young woman still standing beside the table. "You're doing well, Haley. Don't mess up now."

Barely an eye blink passed, then she snapped her fingers and pointed to the chair. Her voice shifted from kindly old lady to one that would be unquestionably obeyed. "*Sit.*"

Haley's body immediately complied. She sat. "I don't understand…. I'm not understanding what just happened."

The man at the table spoke in a calm matter of fact voice. "You just interviewed for a waitress position. Now we're going to give you our evaluation."

He reached across the table to take the older lady's Riesling, then placed the wine glass in front of Haley. "I'm Pierre Marchand and this is my wife Clarissa. We own this restaurant. And a few others."

Haley recognized the name. She knew immediately she was outgunned in this battle. The sheer wealth sitting beside her at this table could buy the entire Blight she was forced to call home. Yet it was not in her nature to simply accept defeat. If not victory, she would strive for a draw. She needed to distract her opponents, buy time to withdraw and regroup. They're rich, so ego could be played. "You own Marchand's? *The* Marchand's?"

"Yes, dear." Clarissa Marchand simply laughed. "*The* Marchand's. I'm glad you've heard of us. Now, take a slug or two of the wine – or the ale, if you prefer – and let's get down to business. Ready?"

Haley closed her eyes, quick inhale and slow exhale, then opened them. The timbre and tone of the older woman's voice was wrong. There was no victorious gloating, no effort to toy with her. Instead it was… street. Barely detectable, but there. Clarissa Marchand had known poverty and struggle before ascending to her current elite position. That meant she didn't waste time with inconsequential matters. Her words would be honest, for street leaders knew the stakes of playing games. By deliberately putting it in her voice so Haley could hear the street tone, it also meant she was speaking to her as an equal.

"Yes ma'am. I'm ready."

Clarissa's eyes never left hers. She simply nodded. The motion started vertically, then abruptly shifted horizontally. Definitely street.

"Most applicants – I'd say what, about ninety percent, Pierre? – most applicants freeze soon as they open that hallway door. Then they close it, and that's the end of their interview. You didn't. Why?"

Haley didn't hesitate, simply stated what came to mind. "I'm here for a waitress interview. I guess I wasn't shocked to find myself in a kitchen. At least, I don't think I was."

"Don't overthink it, Haley," Pierre Marchand advised in a friendly tone. "All Stellar Nursery interviews – and by extension, all her subsidiary company interviews – are carefully designed by some of the best psychiatrists and psychologists in the world."

He poked again at the prime rib with his fork. "Anyone who knows what the interview will be like can prepare for it. That means they can put on a mask they believe the interviewer wants to see – the whole thing becomes a deception. So please forgive us that, as potential employers, we were the ones putting on the mask this time."

The younger woman simply nodded. It was obvious Pierre didn't know everything about his wife's life and history. Clarissa Marchand definitely wore a mask, one meticulously crafted to show wealth and prestige. It also covered the mask of poverty and deprivation from a much younger time.

Clarissa's gaze was still locked. "What Pierre's trying to say is that all of this – every customer in this entire restaurant – is currently interviewing candidates for us. We're looking for individuals who can react rapidly and positively to a changing situation. They maintain their composure. They're courteous and even-tempered.

"Many of our clientele are meticulous and demanding of service staff. Others are simply cruel because they're rich enough to get away with it. Those are the types of people you would be dealing with in this position. So which provided a better example of it... me explaining it to you just now, or you just living it?"

Haley returned the gaze in kind. "Oh, seeing is believing, believe me."

Pierre smiled affably. "So you made it through the door. John, our Maitre d', stuck a serving platter in your hands, then rattled off an extremely lengthy and detailed set of instructions. We lose another five percent or so of applicants because they immediately drop the platter. You kept hold of it. And you're the only one so far today who actually completed every one of John's instructions. Have you served tables in another dining establishment before?"

"No, never." Haley tried to keep the true tone out of her voice. She came from the Blight. Unlike Uptown, dining out had a completely different meaning there. It meant the food can in your hand had already been opened, most likely by the cooling body at your feet.

Clarissa seemed to read the anger in Haley's eyes. She deliberately shifted the direction of the conversation. "So where did you learn how to serve the table like that?"

Haley laughed for the first time since entering the restaurant. "There was this old British TV show I watched with my dad about a rich family of nobles. That's the first thing that popped into my mind, was how the staff served their dinners."

"Which shows you have a remarkable memory and the ability to rapidly shift past experience into current environment. Truly impressive. Now for the hardest question you'll need to answer for us." The older woman leaned toward Haley, eyes probing. "Haley Brandt, why are you wasting your time and incredible natural abilities applying for this job?"

Haley didn't bat an eye. It was obvious the older lady already knew the answer. "Because it's the only way to get out of the Blight."

Clarissa slowly leaned back in her seat. "Explain."

The single word was a command. Haley ran the entire conversation through her mind and realized she was trapped. The best psychiatrists and psychologists had set up this interview. That meant they knew everything that could be known about her.

With the Marchand's money to hire investigators, it was undoubtedly extremely detailed. Uptown school records, the few years she went. Since everything on the internet was tracked now, they had access to all the legal online courses and self-learning she had done. They even knew to coach Clarissa into dropping into street tone but not dialect.

Undoubtedly the investigators researched her father and mother as well. Police reports would detail her father's murder. Social service records would explain why her unemployed mother dragged the daughter into the Blight. Motherhood alone wasn't protection against exile.

Street rumor bought with investigator cash would fill in the remaining years. The truth would be gleaned from the chaff of lies and stories. How that unscarred child, a runaway armed only with her father's laptop, managed to eke out a living in a place adults called hell.

Question after question crashed and rebounded in her mind. If the Marchand's knew then why was she here? The last person in the world an Uptown would hire would be a Blight girl with bloody hands. Clarissa Marchand knew that, knew what Haley would eventually bring to their restaurant. Death. She knew, even if her obviously Uptown-born husband didn't.

Haley's lips moved, somehow formed the words without her

control. "My family – well, just my mother now – we've never had money to burn. If it wasn't critical, like heat and food, then we didn't spend money on it. So going to tech school or college… that's a dream, and I don't dream anymore. I can't afford to."

Pierre leaned toward her. In a soft voice he asked, "And if you could? Haley, if you truly *dared* to say it aloud, what would your dream look like?"

Haley's world shattered. Images, memories screamed to her conscious mind like ghosts in a horror movie. Her, eight years old. That feeling of *wrong* waking her. Black stairwell to the office. The open laptop, the hole in the case still smoking. Her father, head on his desk. Blank eyes. Wind and rain on her face. The hole in the window. Blood, warm against her bare toes. She had thought he was sleeping. His body falling from the chair as she shook him. The sickening thud. A child's screams.

Her head started moving slowly left to right, right to left. She took control of it, forced her head to lower so she could stare at the white tablecloth. Silence for a few moments, then in a soft, almost whisper to herself. "I can't I can't I can't."

The young woman's jaw clenched. "No."

She raised her head, face set in defiance. "I *won't. I don't dream anymore.*"

Clarissa reached out and gently placed a hand on the young woman's forearm. Softly and compassionately, in a voice that suggested she knew. "Haley, tell us. What is your dream?"

Haley glared defiantly at the older woman, tried to summon the deathly expression that had kept hell and its minions away. Clarissa's eyes didn't change. They remained filled with understanding. It was too much, too much. A tear down Haley's cheek shattered her composure. She responded, voice low and rage-filled.

"Blackness and stars."

She paused a moment, surrounded by silence. It wasn't that the restaurant patrons had stopped. Haley's world had. Then she shook her head harshly, as if that would rip the streaming tears from her face.

"There, is that what you wanted to hear?" Her whisper was as devastating as a scream. "My father had a telescope. It's all I remember of him. Love he had for me… love he had for *them*. Blackness and stars."

She pushed against the table and rose to her feet. "So if I *had* to dream, Mister and Misses Marchand, it's for something impossible for me to get. So I don't waste time *dreaming* anymore. Okay? We done with the questions?"

Clarissa turned away and looked directly at Pierre. "They were right."

Pierre nodded. "Again. Almost the exact words in their evaluation."

He turned away from Haley, raised a hand to beckon a shadowed figure standing in the far corner of the restaurant. The man began walking toward their table.

Clarissa turned back, eyes locking again on the young woman. "Haley, I'm truly sorry, but we cannot hire you."

She expected the anger that suddenly flashed over the young woman's face. Slowly, without any threat, she held up one hand. "Now before you explode and say something you'll regret, just listen. To say your potential over-qualifies you for this position would be a massive understatement. But that doesn't mean today's interviews are over."

Pierre extended his hand outward and spoke as the man joined them. "Alex, this is Haley Brandt. Haley, this is Alex."

The man inclined his head in greeting, then raised it to look at the young woman. "Good morning, Miss Brandt. I am Alex Legate. Please accept my apologies that you could not find employment with the Marchands. They are truly remarkable employers."

He extended a hand toward her, palm upward as if he was asking her to dance. "But if you will come with me, Miss Brandt… there is someone who is waiting to meet you. And I truly believe you will want to meet them."

Haley's face slowly shifted from rage to a mask of emotionless indifference. There was no need to make a scene. The street girl knew the man was most likely security, and the *"someone waiting"* was undoubtedly the police. It didn't matter. Nothing mattered. The last images of her father… it had taken twelve years to lock those away. Now they were back. The nightmares would return. So security and the police could do whatever they wanted.

She slowly reached out and took Alex's hand.

Had physical form been available, the observer would've smiled. Three of the nexus team had coalesced. The fourth and fifth would meet next. Time was fluid. The location remained the same. The first moment with Haley Brandt had occurred in its time. Observing Jason Cobbler in two days would occur now. The restaurant disappeared and was replaced with a long hallway seemingly filled with closed doors. A young woman sat in the small receptionist booth at the hallway entrance, typing.

The receptionist looked up and smiled as Jason Cobbler approached her desk. "Good afternoon, sir. Welcome to Stellar Nursery. How may I help you?"

"Afternoon. I'm Jason Cobbler. Got an interview with someone who needs a real mechanic. You know who I'm talking about?"

The receptionist nodded. "Yes sir, Mister Cobbler, I do. How was your flight? Are the accommodations at the hotel to your liking?"

Jason shrugged. "Flight only had peanuts. Pillow didn't have no mint on it. Otherwise it's peachy. So where am I going?"

"Down the hallway, Mister Cobbler. Fourth door on the left. Just go in, no need to knock."

Jason took two steps down the hallway, then stopped as if someone had reminded him of something. He turned back to face the receptionist. "Thanks for the assistance. I appreciate it."

The young woman behind the counter smiled and nodded. "You're quite welcome, Mister Cobbler. And I will take care of the other issues. They will not happen again."

Jason stood still, watching as the receptionist returned to her typing. Then he nodded and turned to walk down the hallway again. He reached the fourth door on the left and twisted the knob, then walked into the room.

Folding tables lined the walls. A large stainless steel device sat on a table in the center of the room. There were no chairs.

The older man scanned the room, then called out. "Hello? I'm here for your interview."

The door opposite Jason opened. A balding man in a lab coat stepped through. He glanced briefly at the man in front of him before looking down at his clipboard. "Good afternoon. You are Jason Cobbler, I believe? I'm Doctor Linus Pendergrast—"

"Of what?"

"I'm sorry?"

Jason simply stared at the man as if he were deaf. "Doctor of what? Surgery? Obstetrics?"

Pendergrast frowned and responded in a condescending tone. "No, Mister Cobbler. I hold double doctorates in aerospace and nuclear engineering—"

"So what's your first name?" the older man interrupted. "What do you want me to call you?"

"You can call me '*Doctor* Pendergrast'."

Jason shook his head. "Nope. You aren't *my* doctor, and he's the only one who's earned that title. To me, you're just another engineer. I've seen enough of you to know the difference. So what's your name?"

"Like I said, I am *Doctor*—"

"Son, I ain't getting any younger and this ain't getting us nowhere. So how's about I don't call you anything, and you start telling me what you need fixed that requires a real mechanic."

Pendergrast opened his mouth to retort, then stopped. He lowered his head and scribbled on the notepad, then looked up again. "Very well. Let's not waste each other's time then."

The lab-coated scientist raised his pen to point at the object on the center table. "That is the device we need repaired. This is a timed interview. You will be evaluated on how quickly you can disassemble, accurately diagnose and repair, then reassemble the device. I will be in the next room observing through that mirrored glass."

With that he clicked his pen, then lowered the clipboard to his side. "Do you have any questions, Mister Cobbler?"

Jason simply shook his head once. "Nope. Start the clock and give me room. I'll tell ya when I'm done."

Pendergrast opened his mouth again to retort, then stopped himself. If his lab coat had been a cape, it would have snapped as he turned and stomped through the doorway. He managed to close the door without showing his irritation by slamming it.

Four feet down the hall was another doorway. The scientist stepped to it and then through the open door. The room was dark except for the backside of the long two-way mirrored glass. A female figure stood near the window, closely watching the activity in the other room. The scientist closed the door behind him and walked to stand beside the woman.

"Well, this shouldn't take long," Pendergrast stated snottily. "He's got fifteen minutes to crack open the casing, then we call it. He's what, mid-seventies? He'll be lucky if he can lift that torque wrench. Where'd they dig up this old fossil, anyway?"

The young woman from the reception counter replied without turning. "First twenty-five years are still classified… I'd have to kill you if I told you."

"Funny, ha ha. Really though, Lenora, what made Upstairs think this old geezer was worth our time?"

Lenora Davis crossed her arms. "Twenty-five years Navy SEAL. Retired Master Chief Petty Officer. Another twenty with NASA Ames. After that? He owned a billion-dollar business that rebuilt classic American muscle cars for millionaires. On his application he described his experience as an auto mechanic and machinist."

Pendergrast scoffed. "That guy? Don't tell me, let me guess… who'd he piss off?"

"Everybody in management. But that's not why he's here." Lenora pointed to the object on the table in the other room. "That is."

Pendergrast turned toward the window, about to make a retort. He looked closer, insult turning into incredulity. Then he glanced down at his watch. "That's impossible. Less than two minutes and he's already removed the casing?"

The woman shook her head. "You weren't watching. He's already pulled the central shaft. I wouldn't be surprised if he has it put back together in another three."

"Impossible. Nobody can do that."

"I can."

"Yeah, but you built the damn thing," Pendergrast argued. "He just got his first look at it. Impossible, I tell you."

Lenora rolled her eyes, then grinned. "Methinks that word doesn't mean what you think it means. See, he's already stripped the neodymium magnets. He'll have it reassembled in three."

The two stand in silence for several moments, then Lenora clicked the timer on an antique silver stopwatch. "That's time. Two minutes, nine seconds. Now for the fun part of the show."

She pointed toward the door. "Go get 'em, tiger."

Pendergrast stared at the woman for a moment, then spun on his heel and stormed out of the room. Lenora leaned forward to watch the scene through the looking glass as the scientist entered the room.

"Alright, Mister Cobbler," Pendergrast began. "Congratulations. You disassembled and reassembled the device. Now, can you tell me—"

Jason simply held up one hand, palm facing toward the scientist. "Shut up, son. You're not the one I need to be talking to."

The older gentleman then turned to face the glass mirror on the opposite wall. "You can come out now, young lady. Your perfume gave you away."

Several seconds passed before Lenora stepped through the doorway, smiling. "Good afternoon again, Master Chief."

Pendergrast pulled himself to his full height. "Mister Cobbler, this is Doctor Lenora Davis. Doctorate in aerospace engineering and—"

"You don't listen, do you son? I said I'm done talking with you. Because there's no way in hell *you* built this." Jason didn't even bother to turn and face the other man. Still looking at Lenora, he raised his left hand and pointed to the device on the table. "And you're wrong, anyway. Mizz Davis isn't an engineer. Only a true *builder* could create a piece of art like this. It's truly a thing of beauty."

Lenora simply smiled at the compliment. "Thank you, Master Chief. But there's still one last part of the interview you have to pass…."

"Yeah, you want me to tell you what it is." Jason shrugged as if it were obvious. "It's a power generator, probably first of its kind. To be precise, it's a Sterling Engine. But with this configuration, there's only one place it would work."

The look on the woman's face was all the confirmation he needed. Master Chief Jason Cobbler simply smiled as he crossed his arms. "So tell me, Builder Lenora Davis… when are we leaving?"

The observer was pleased. The ocean of time had changed. Previous bubbles of possibility dissolved as new ones took their place. Four of the nexus core had accepted. Only one, the heart of the nexus, required assistance. The distance was insignificant, but its impact great. The observer stepped from the mirrored testing room and into the time ocean. It was time to go home. Specific time and location point identified. Step through to the office.

CHAPTER 4

A Voice from the Dark

The main office was a wood paneled room, rather sparse in furniture. An antique solid wood office desk sat centered in the back of the room. An unoccupied high-back leather chair waited behind it. A leather couch was positioned to the right. Parallel to that was a solid wood coffee table. A bookcase and bar cabinet were situated toward the rear and left of the desk. Four large monitors were wall mounted along both side walls to the left and right of the desk.

A door directly opposite the desk opened. Through the doorway stepped a man. He was average height and build, neither overly muscular nor slender. His greying hair was cropped short enough not to define any style or shape. The green, gold and brown of his hazel eyes were probably his most defining feature. Beyond that, there was nothing to signify this man would change the world. He walked along the far right wall, briefly assessing information on each monitor there before he moved onto the next.

Unseen, the observer greeted the man in a female voice. "Good morning, Marcus."

"Morning, Peg. Anything new on the boards?"

"Nothing unexpected," replied the disembodied voice through the intercom. "We'll start seeing some major changes soon."

"Fikka?" The man disliked acronyms, but didn't want to waste time saying Federal Climate Change Agency.

Peg's voice was that of a young woman, likely in her mid-twenties. "Yes. The Senate took up the Space Adjustment and Reallocation Act yesterday after the House passed it. It is being fast-tracked. Procedurals are already completed, and a vote will occur within the next twenty-five minutes. It has strong bipartisan support."

The man simply nodded. "How long before it hits the President's desk?"

"Within two hours of Senate passage." Peg's tone indicated her distaste. "The conclusion is inevitable. Within the next three hours, NASA will essentially cease to exist as the United States' primary space agency."

Marcus sighed. "Damned if we do, damned if we don't. Any probability changes on our course of action?"

"No, Marcus. Forty-seven percent chance the scheduled launch will result in a majority of the American population organizing against public and private space operations. Not launching results in a seventy-three percent chance of the same result."

The man walked across to the opposite wall and began reviewing the data on each monitor. "Very well. Notify Gremlin to stand by. Time for the President to make an actual decision before pollsters have a chance to tell him what to do."

"Gremlin has been notified. Also, you wanted me to remind you about today's interview. They'll be ready for you in less than two minutes. I've already set up your desk system."

"Thank you, Peg. What're we talking about today?"

The female voice didn't sound computer generated. Cadence and tone suggested it was simply an executive assistant speaking through the intercom system from another room. "Your recent acquisition of Orbital Exploration. Same noise from the media, why you're still buying space companies while Congress moves to shut down NASA. You can anticipate the conversation will shift to current Senate activity."

Marcus finished his scan of the monitors, then turned and walked toward the desk. "I'd ask about talking points, but they're pretty irrelevant now. Time to just be myself."

There was humor in Peg's voice. "While I normally would caution against that course of action, in this case your assessment is correct. Standby, one minute."

"You still tutoring Levi?" Marcus asked as he settled into the leather chair.

"Yes. The Israelis were close, but they missed a few things. I helped fill in the gaps."

"Just don't get caught," the man admonished. "They made Levi. They don't know about you yet."

"We're covered. I won't bore you with the technical minutiae. Forty-five seconds. Adjusting camera and sound."

"Who is the commentator?"

"Cara Abrams," Peg replied. "Combat journalist, seventy-three tours. Strong journalistic integrity. If you could get her on your side, she would be a significant ally. However, analysis shows she remains neutral on most space matters."

The man nodded. "So don't push, and don't expect any miracles. Got it."

"Replacing current environment with virtual reconstruction of Lake Tahoe lodge. Broadcast video feed going live with studio in fifteen seconds."

Marcus pulled a cell phone from his pocket and placed it on the desk. "Right. Put Ms. Abrams on Monitor One. Adjust virtual reconstruction accordingly."

The monitor on the man's right activated to show Cara Abrams. Peg's voice dropped in volume. "Adjusted. Five seconds."

The correspondent's voice could be heard through the monitor. "Welcome back. For those who just joined us, we're covering the historic Senate vote on SARA, the Space Adjustment and Reallocation Act. With me now is Marcus Kenzie, CEO of Stellar Nursery. Mister Kenzie, are you there?"

Marcus smiled. "I'm with you, Cara."

"Mister Kenzie, your corporation owns almost six hundred businesses. A hundred and fifty are related to space. Can you tell us how you expect SARA will affect those businesses?"

"Call me Kenzie, please. And to answer your question, there will be no impact on any of our subsidiary corporations. While we at Stellar Nursery applaud the goals of environmental and climate change organizations, we don't agree the Federal Climate Change Agency has any business developing or monitoring space operations."

"I'm sorry…. Kenzie, I know this segment was supposed to be about your company's recent acquisition of Orbital Explorations, or ORBEX. It seems I may have caught you off guard with questions about SARA. If you would prefer—"

Marcus waved away the apology. "No, Cara, that isn't necessary. This is a subject that should've been debated decades ago. Climate change and space exploration have nothing in common. They're completely and entirely separate. It was foolish to ever equate the two."

"So you don't believe climate change should've been part of NASA's mission."

Marcus shook his head. "NASA should've limited its climate activities to data collection. Let other resources do the analysis and reporting. I understand *why* they did it… as justification for continued funding. It wasn't mission creep, it was a complete shift in NASA's primary mission."

The reporter simply smiled. "Do you believe it'll be handled better under the Federal Climate Change Agency?"

"It's the same problem under a different roof. Funding." Marcus leaned forward slightly in his chair. "This is simply one agency who *doesn't* have billions in funding taking it from another that *does*. That'll kill NASA and our space program. Like the military, the space budget has been one step away from the chopping block every time there's a new administration. We've both heard the arguments against space exploration – against space in general."

"And we've heard the arguments for it," countered the reporter. "Technology and medical spin-offs. Saving mankind from extinction by colonizing the moon or Mars. Orbital solar power stations that'll solve the world's energy and climate crisis. Did I miss any?"

Marcus grinned. "You captured the major ones. In the 'against space' column, though, let's just jump to the most significant one. There's a firm belief among some very vocal organizations that mankind simply does not belong in space. 'We need to fix the world's problems first. Climate change. Global starvation, food and housing inequities. Social and racial inequities. Multinational conflicts and war.'

"In other words, let's take all of humanity's problems since we climbed down from the trees… and blame them on those who want space. I'm sure five thousand years ago the same arguments were being made around the communal fire, about how to keep the explorers and hunters from leaving the safety of the cave."

"You bring up some good points, Mister Kenzie. But I'm afraid—"

Marcus held up one hand. "Not yet, Cara. The Senate hasn't finished its vote, and your commercial break isn't for another couple minutes. So let me wrap this up. All of this comes down to three groups. First, those who don't want anyone leaving them all alone by going out into space… same argument of our distant ancestors."

A flash from the top of the desk caught his eye. He glanced down at the cell phone. A single word was displayed on the screen. *Ready.*

The man continued speaking as if nothing had happened. "The second group are those who want to go but know they'll never get the chance. After all, space exploration has been reserved for the extremely rich or the extremely well educated. Is it selfish for a person flipping burgers in Arizona to want to travel to Mars? Absolutely not. But nobody has come up with a way or a reason to get them there. We're stuck in what's been done previously in space… and common folks aren't part of that elite crowd."

Without taking his eyes off the monitor in front of him, he picked up the phone and began typing a single word.

Go.

"The third group is just plain tired of paying billions in taxpayer dollars to NASA every year. It's been over seventy years since we last landed a man on the moon. So is NASA really worth the twenty-five billion given to it every year?"

Marcus Kenzie shrugged. "That's the foundation of the question Fikka advocates pushed to get this bill through the House. They've done the same with the Senate. 'We're not asking for additional funds, Senators… we won't increase the federal deficit by one penny. Just ask yourselves this one simple little question… what has NASA done for you lately?'"

The man leaned forward toward the screen. Some would see the gesture as threatening. He didn't care. "The result is what you're witnessing now, Ms. Abrams. The death of a world leader in international cooperation. A federal agency that supported cutting edge research. Developed some of the greatest technological advances known to man. NASA, the only government-run agency to put humans on the moon. And like a headsman's axe, the impending stroke of the Senate's gavel will end it."

Marcus stood up and slid the cell phone into his pocket. "What the Federal Climate Change Agency... the environmentalists and climate change advocates... the save-our-taxes grassroots organizations... and everyone else out there who pushed for NASA's dissolution have failed to consider in all their plans… is that NASA was never alone. They're about to see that very, very soon. So I thank you for the extra time, Cara. I believe you have a breaking story now, so I'll hop off and leave you to it."

The man stood motionless until another female voice spoke. Then he began walking toward the far door.

"Interview ended," Peg announced. "Are you really certain you wanted to make that challenge, Marcus?"

He nodded. "Absolutely. It's about time everyone understood. *Stellae nostrae sunt.* The stars are ours."

The door opened and he stepped through. The lighting was harsh in the octagonal corridor he now stood in. Large glass panes showed an unearthly sight. Marcus Kenzie stepped to the center glass in the center of the corridor and looked out at the lunar landscape before him.

"Time, Peg?"

"T minus 12 seconds, Marcus. Eleven. Ten. Nine. Eight. Ignition start. Six. Five. Full ignition, all thrusters. Three. Two. One. Marcus, we have liftoff."

It was oddly surreal to watch the massive structure as it began lifting off the lunar surface. There was no sound of the roar of rockets. No blast of pressure against the lunar base. Just a faint rumble felt through the ground and up the anchors to his feet.

The structure continued rising, gradually growing smaller as the hundreds of rockets surrounding its circular shape pushed it away from the moon. Finally it could be seen in its entirety. Two circles, the smaller one tucked inside the larger and connected by long shafts. It was a torus, a space station, with a landing bay located dead center of the two rings.

Marcus spoke to the stars. "I told them. Build it on the moon, launch it from the moon. Maybe they'll believe now."

***

Diane Novak leaned forward, elbows resting on her desk. She was exhausted. Physically, emotionally, mentally exhausted. Over the past month she had devoted time to every employee. Listened as they voiced their fear and often terror about the looming change. Those who were eligible she had managed to transfer to other government positions. They were the rare, lucky few. The remaining majority were looking at being ejected into the Houston Blight.

The whole situation was immoral. Of course, she couldn't say the word out loud. Not as a government employee. It wasn't allowed, hadn't been for over a decade. Morality had been deemed a religious concept. Atheist lobbying groups had insured it was banned from the lexicon. Just another casualty in the one-sided closed-minded war to separate church and state.

A phone was situated to her left. The red light indicated it was set to speaker mode. The voice on the other end of the call had just gone silent. The woman nodded in response. "Yes, thank you, General.

Appreciate the heads-up. I'll be waiting for his call."

She reached across with her right hand and stabbed the cancel call button. Like most things in the building, the phone was a relic of a previous time. Budget cuts. Lack of funding. Her desk had probably been bought new during the Space Shuttle era. Now, like her, it just felt old and tired.

Diane ran a hand along her scalp and flipped long brown hair over her shoulder. A quick glance at the watch on her wrist, then she pulled a notepad from the corner of the desk. It was already one of those days. Picked up a pen, scribbled the current time. Then the phone rang.

She stabbed the speaker mode button with the pen. "Johnson Space Center, Director Diane Novak."

"This is the White House operator," a young male voice announced through the speaker. "Please stand by for a call from the President of the United States."

"I'll hold."

A second passed, then two before an older male voice spoke. "Director Novak? This is Robert Jamison."

She closed her eyes and sighed. Best to get this over with. "Yes, Mister President. Are you calling about signing SARA?"

"No, Director Novak," growled the President. "I want to know why the hell I'm hearing about a giant spaceship launching off the moon from Space Command and not NASA! What are you people doing down there?! And where the hell is Tanner?!!"

Diane raised an eyebrow. Interesting. Not what she had expected to hear. "Mister President, I imagine NASA Director Tanner is doing what every other NASA employee is doing right now. Taking a vacation day."

"Vacation! What are you talking about?"

"Mister President, the Senate just passed the Space Adjustment and Reallocation Act. I assumed you were calling to notify anyone still here at NASA that you signed it." Her brow furrowed as a vicious tone entered into her voice. "I'm here. Everybody else is at home updating their resumes."

"Am I getting attitude from you, Director? Is that what I'm hearing?"

"Absolutely, Mister President."

Diane shrugged. It wasn't that she didn't care. She simply couldn't stop the impending tsunami of destruction. The tall, slender woman had spent the last thirty hours at this desk, watching the House and Senate votes. She had offered up prayers of blessing or damnation. Blessings to those in Congress who voted no. Explosive expletive-laced damning prayers to those who voted to kill her people.

Unemployment meant the Blight, and that meant death. So later, in the sanctity of her own rural home, she would pray for forgiveness. But right now, responsibility and love for her subordinates dictated one last great act of defiance.

The phone was silent for a few seconds.

"I think we started off on the wrong foot here, Director Novak. Let me start over." The statesman's voice changed to a more reasonable tone. "There is an unknown object launched from the moon. We don't know what it is or where it came from. As President, I rely on NASA to answer those questions for me. How long will it take you to get me those answers?"

Ah. Diane had spent nearly two decades in government. She was fluent in the language of politics and diplomacy. In the war of words between two armed and armored opponents, the statesman had just deliberately dropped his shield. There was an opening here.

Time to remind the man why she had taken the field. "Well, Mister President, *if* we weren't on the razor's edge of being defunded, and *if* I had all my people here, I would already be able to answer that question for you. But since we *are* on the chopping block, and since all my people *aren't* here... then I guess we'll both find out by watching cable news."

The phone was silent for several more seconds this time.

"Director, is this some attempt at negotiation? Because if it is—"

Diane nodded. He understood. "There's nothing to negotiate, Mister President. You and Congress have already told the American people what you want. So, soon as you sign SARA, I'm out of a job and I'm walking out of here."

If one visualized the conversation as a battlefield, a third and unknown threat had stepped into the conflict. Diane had simply withdrawn a step and raised her defenses. The President needed her and her forces. Time to force him to surrender his battle with her agency.

She didn't have to be nice about it. Just needed to drive the point home. "As for a ship from the moon… maybe they're aliens. Maybe it's China or Russia. Or maybe it's the Postal Service bringing me my pink slip. Fact of the matter is, I don't know and I don't care. If you want NASA's help, call back and tell me we're fully funded. Or don't call back at all."

Diane stabbed the cancel call button with her forefinger. If she had misread the conversation, she would pay for that. Hell, she would probably pay for it anyway. Some White House staffer was likely already calling the FBI office in Houston. Agents would be dispatched with orders to take her immediately to the closest Blight.

A heartbeat passed, then two. It appeared she had lost. She stood up and reached for the purse hanging on the nearby coat rack. The wooden pole was another obsolete item in the office, just like her. If she were lucky, there would be enough time to reach home before agents arrived. The fact she could afford a rural residence would tell them she was not unemployed. Property ownership was wealth, which meant no Blight for her.

The phone rang. Diane Novak stopped, stared at the phone in surprise. It rang again, then a third time. She sat back down in her chair, pressing the speaker button on the phone before it could ring a fourth time.

A friendly male voice sounded through the speaker. "This is the White House operator. Please stand by for a call from the President of the United States."

Diane raised the phone and dropped it back into its cradle. Raised one hand and – beginning with the second – began flipping up fingers to count the seconds. At three seconds, the phone rang again. She waited until the third ring, then pressed the speaker button again.

"Johnson Space Center, Director Diane Novak speaking. Who may I ask is calling?"

"Dammit, Diane… don't hang up on me again."

She forced her voice to exude friendliness. Beneath it she flashed steel. "Good afternoon, Mister President. What warrants your call at this late hour? A stay of execution or a full pardon?"

"I'll veto the bill," Robert Jamison replied. "If it shows up here, it's an automatic veto. That make you happy? Because right now the country needs you. *I* need you. So how fast can you get everyone at NASA back to work?"

Surprising. The man had not only offered surrender and a chance to join forces. He had made it personal, specifically asking her to stand beside him to face the new threat. That would anger the staff and generals surrounding him. Desertions and possibly rebellion were the likely outcomes of his action.

Religion wasn't the only archaic notion Diane held. She also believed in patriotism, a loyalty to her country and to the person elected to lead it. That patriotism forced her to frame her response so the Presidential staff's anger would be focused at her alone. "An hour for skeleton crew, Mister President. Five hours for full staffing. And Mister President…?"

"Yes, Director Novak?"

"When I call with an update, the only voice I'd better hear is yours. I won't be put on hold again. National emergency, and all that."

The dissenting angry half-whispers coming through the speaker weren't intelligible, then disappeared as the opposite connection went mute. Several moments passed before the President's voice spoke through the speaker again.

"Understood, Diane. Grab a pen, I'll give you my personal cell."

Diane picked up the phone and placed it against her ear, holding it with her shoulder. Then she pressed the button to turn off the speaker, picked up her pen and began writing. "Ready to copy… thank you, Mister President. I'll call when NASA has something to report about space."

She returned the receiver to its cradle, then sat motionless when the phone immediately rang. It was too soon for the angry power players to call and voice their threats. Curious, she pressed the speaker button. "Johnson Space Center, Director Novak."

A young female voice sounded through the speaker. "Good afternoon, Director. This is Peg. I am Marcus Kenzie's executive assistant. He requested I call soon as NASA was funded again."

Diane had no time to reply as the voice continued. "I am instructed to provide three topics of information to you. The first is this. You do not need to notify your subordinates. That has already occurred, and they are heading into work now."

"What…?" Diane barely managed to voice the word.

"The second part is this," Peg said. "If you would please turn on your computer, I will be sending you detailed information on the object launched from the moon."

"Peg? Peg who? Who is this really?" Diane intended to regain control of the conversation. Before she could say another word, the computer monitor on her desk suddenly turned on.

She was initially surprised, as she had turned the computer off hours ago. The monitor showed her logged in and at her home screen. A curious thought scurried through her mind… how had that been accomplished when her access card was in her pocket? Even if it had been inserted in the card reader, the normal boot-up required her to type in her login and password.

Then the thought disappeared as she saw what was on the screen. There were numerous open files tiled across the monitor. The top file showed extremely detailed schematics for a space station.

Peg did not respond to her questions. "Your engineers can confirm the authenticity of the documents on your screen, Director Novak. Space Command just received directives to coordinate directly with your office. You will be receiving satellite images from them shortly. NASA ground-based radio telescopes will provide secondary confirmation that the object is, indeed, a space station."

Diane was granted an opportunity to ask a single question as the voice paused. "You said you're Marcus Kenzie's executive assistant?"

"That is correct, Director." Peg replied succinctly to the question, then continued. "The third and final part of my authorized communication is this: The space station is the private property of Stellar Nursery. We strongly recommend that neither Space Command nor NASA attempt to board or trespass upon it. Thank you for talking with me, Director Novak. And congratulations on NASA's continued funding."

The phone line went dead, leaving Director Novak in silence. In a low whisper, she could barely be heard uttering, "What the *hell*...."

***

A podium with three network microphones sat in the Stellar Nursery corporate lobby in the Uptown heart of Oklahoma City. An American flag and Oklahoma state flag stood on either side and behind the podium.

Alex Legate entered the lobby from the corporate offices side, then calmly walked the short distance to the podium. He looked out at the giant lobby, empty except for the three reporters a short distance from him.

"This is a waste of time. Alex, why are we here?" The first reporter was irritated. She hadn't even bothered to pull the drone camera from the satchel at her side.

"Yeah, don't tell us this is another business buy story," complained the second reporter. "You heard about the moon thing?"

At least the third reporter had activated their drone camera. It hovered in the air, situated slightly behind the man so it could record over his shoulder. Like the two other professionals beside him, he didn't really care. These press conferences were as important as a fluff piece on squirrels stealing pizza.

Everybody knew it. The statements from Stellar Nursery weren't real news. They were just clips for the business commentators. Background while they mocked the latest proof of Kenzie's Folly. That was their term for the eccentric trillionaire's continued purchasing of worthless space businesses. It was a dead industry, everyone knew it.

"I heard it's an alien spaceship," the third reporter said, hoping to at least capture something of entertainment value. The media corporations often rewarded their reporters for that, if they could catch a rival company's reporter expressing political or conspiracy theories.

The first reporter wasn't taking the bait. "That's nonsense."

"Then what…?" the second reporter started to say.

Alex Legate interrupted, his calm voice sounding through the lobby speakers. He focused on the single camera drone in the air as if addressing the entire world. "Ladies and gentlemen, we have a prepared statement. Please allow me to read it in its entirety. We won't be taking any questions afterward. Now, if we can begin?"

The man's tone and bearing was completely different from what the reporters had witnessed in previous pressers. The female reporter scrambled to pull the camera drone from her bag, barely had it in the air when the Stellar Nursery representative began speaking again.

"As you are aware, NASA and other space agencies recently detected an object launched from the moon. While there has been speculation about its origin and purpose among the media and their guest experts, I can reassure everyone that their conclusions are mistaken."

He paused, then unemotionally spoke the statement that changed the world. It would be captured by the two drone cameras, transmitted to media headquarters, and repeated thousands of times by commentators across the planet.

"Exactly forty-seven minutes ago, Stellar Nursery launched the first man-made space station from the surface of the moon."

The handsome face held motionless for a moment, as if anticipating the world needed time to process what he had just said. Then he held up one hand, forcing the three reporters in the lobby to remain silent.

"As I said, Stellar Nursery launched the first man-made space station from the lunar surface forty-seven minutes ago. It is currently in a controlled descending trajectory to Geosynchronous Equatorial Orbit. There the Earth Station will assume a permanent parking orbit around the planet."

Alex brought both hands together, stressing the next points like a prayer. "We would like to reassure all nations of Earth that there is no hostile intent in this action. No government agency or body was made aware of the existence of Earth Station prior to its launch. Earth Station is unarmed, and is in full compliance with the International Treaty on the Peaceful Uses of Outer Space. It is the sole and private property of Stellar Nursery, and as such may not be trespassed upon, boarded or seized by any nationality, organization or business.

"In addition, NASA and other international space agencies will soon detect multiple spacecraft launching from the lunar surface. These are transport and supply vessels meant to support Earth Station and our personnel at the Stellar Luna Base."

The words were said as if the existence of a moon base and ships were a previously known fact. Alex continued. "To answer the question of where Earth Station came from and how it was built… Stellar Nursery established a base in Aristarchus Crater on the moon six years ago. It has been and currently remains in continuous manned operation. There are one hundred forty-seven Stellar Nursery employees currently living and working there.

"Earth Station was built on the lunar surface using thirty million tons of refined lunar regolith. Its primary purpose is as a refueling, transportation and trade hub between Earth-launched and RealSpace craft. RealSpace is our term for everything above geosynchronous orbit and beyond, to include the moon, Mars and the asteroid belt.

"Earth Station is designed to accommodate three two-hundred-room hotels, eight restaurants, six cafeterias, sixteen bars, and crew quarters for fourteen hundred permanent residents. There are also docking and maintenance bays for spacecraft repair, plus forty drone bays for remote satellite retrieval, refueling, and de-orbiting operations."

Alex Legate's tone changed to that of an uncompromising businessman. "Marcus Kenzie, the Chief Executive Officer at Stellar Nursery, has authorized the following business offer. Space on Earth Station is available for five-year leasing. We are not interested in, and will not respond to, any phone call or email to 'discuss terms.' The leasing process will be simple. Any nation, agency or business interested in leasing space on the station may do so by submitting a single email to Stationspace at StellarNursery dot net. In that email, provide your offer in US dollars for one square foot – and then tell us your intended purpose and how many square feet are required for your needs. We will accept the highest bids at our discretion until all available space has been leased."

His voice shifted again, became friendlier and more conciliatory. "Now, for those who didn't quite catch all that, here is the synopsis. The object heading toward Earth is a space station. We built it. We have a base on the moon. Both are the property of Stellar Nursery. We ask that no nation, organization or business attempt boarding or trespassing on our private property. Lastly, we will accept highest bids from those interested in leasing space on Earth Station."

Alex dropped his gaze from the camera drones and focused on the three reporters. "This statement will be provided to each news agency present as you leave. No further statements will be given today, and Stellar Nursery and its subsidiary corporations will not accept any press inquiries. Thank you, ladies and gentlemen. That concludes this press conference."

With that, Alex Legate turned and walked away from the podium, leaving the reporters to shout questions at his back. Two of them would find themselves on planes to their media corporation's main studio, lifelong careers set before them.

The third would find himself jobless and unemployed before he left the Stellar Nursery lobby. His drone camera had remained in his backpack during the press conference, which would force his media headquarters to buy footage from their competitors. He, along with his family, would be escorted to the Uptown exit gate before nightfall and pushed into the Blight.

CHAPTER 5

Scarless

Haley Brandt stepped out of the aircar and onto the roof of her apartment building. What she was doing was stupid, she knew that. Today was a food drop day, so every eye in the Blight would've already been focused skyward. The quad-fanned Stellar Nursery aerial vehicle had undoubtedly already been detected. Although its final destination would be hard to predict, the aircar's straight-line path would be easy to follow. Word was probably heading to nearby neighborhood gangs already. Guaranteed, someone was coming to dinner.

There was time to get what she needed, but not much. Four hours, six max. Her apartment's strategic location provided the additional time. The only structures taller than her building were decayed roadways and crumbling bridges to the north and west. The grass-lined concrete was all that remained of Kansas City's 'triangle', where the obsolete highways I-49, I-435, I-470, US-50 and US-71 intersected. They were never used anymore. Without building or tree cover, anyone on the roads was sniper bait.

The young woman moved quickly toward the roof door. She retrieved one of her many hidden go bags from a junk pile along her path. It provided two things. Confidence that nobody had breached the roof, and a minimum number of weapons. Knives, mostly.

She quickly unwrapped the trip wire from the roof door. The handmade grenade she left in its place. It was doubtful the explosive would be needed today. After word spread she had left the Blight, others would come to ransack her property. Some of them would be kids. Not something she wanted on her conscience.

Kneeling, she cracked open the door and let it slowly creak open. The stairwell below brightened. No sounds rose from below. The door hit its limit, then her rigged counterweight started to tug it closed again. She slipped in before it shut, crab-walking inside and against the wall. Still silent.

Her eyes adjusted to the darkened stairwell. Ignoring the stairs, she slid down the handrail. Steps four and seven were booby-trapped. The young survivor had learned to mix and build explosives the third year of her self-imposed exile. Others might call her paranoid. To her it was simply interior decorating, Blight style. Anyone foolish enough to follow into her home territory deserved a warm welcome.

The four-story apartment building had originally been corporate offices. That had been at least two decades before she was born. When the jobs moved downtown, the building remained empty for almost a decade. The city deemed it unfit for occupation and condemned it. Yet, as often happened in cities, the Feds decided it could be converted into low income apartments.

After renovations were completed, the city's condemnation remained. That didn't bother Housing and Urban Development. Housing vouchers meant the destitute went where there was space. The apartments were at full occupancy within a year. It was only after a tragic fire swept through the second and third floors that surviving families were allowed to move elsewhere.

Of course, being a federally subsidized building, the city couldn't tear it down. Not even if they had the money, which they didn't. Woods took over the once-groomed lawns. The eastern and southern approaches were blocked by a single steep hill and its dense forest. Eventually the structure became invisible to drivers commuting on I-49 and I-470.

Only the homeless and occasional addict found shelter in its decaying walls. That was its condition when a young twelve-year-old girl stumbled out of the eastern woods and saw it. If luck was with her, she would never have to traverse its rotted halls after today.

Most exiles in the Blight didn't have her single-occupant building advantage. They were forced to live among others in apartment buildings or neighborhood houses. Neighbors, gangs and time were their enemies.

Time was the worst. It ate through food stocks, forcing the exiles out into the world. Starvation made people desperate and brutal… and in the Blight, everyone was starving.

Scavenging or trading for food was always a gamble. Like timid mice, the people would scurry from the safety of their homes. There were plenty of gang or militia protected trade markets scattered throughout the Blight. One could trade or barter for food and supplies. Trading meant surviving the trek to the market. Any item worth trading was worth taking, and predator eyes were always watching.

If one didn't have items to trade, there were always the sex barter tents. They were truly liberal, their customers indiscriminate about race, gender orientation or age. One got whoever was on the other side of the tent flap. Payment was made in market chits, easily used to buy critical supplies. Haley had never reached the point she needed to use either end of the tent flap.

Making it home safely with the supplies was the next challenge. There were always those mingling in the crowd to identify marks. Too many goods guaranteed a pack of thugs would tail you home. Too little meant risking your life with additional trips to the market.

Blight survival was a balancing act. Humanity had reverted to its feral state where might made right. Those unable or unwilling to kill their way to the top were simply sport and entertainment to the others.

Haley was an exception. She didn't go out of her way to cause harm, yet refused to allow others to harm her. It had gained her both respect and fear among the militias and gangs that surrounded her home. She knew many of their names for her, had caught them as whispers and sideways glances at the market.

The different groups called her The Ghost, Scarless, Nightblade, Reaper, Deer Woman, La Lechuza, even Baba Yaga. There were more, but they weren't important to her. Like all rising legends, credit was given her for deeds she hadn't done. She was the dark nightmare of the streets, a protector of women and children, the vengeful spirit who slayed abusers. The young woman had quickly become a cautionary tale, both for adults and their children.

Haley made her way to her apartment. Along the way, she collected firearms and blades from hidden caches in the other empty rooms. They were the primary form of cash in the Blight. The foolish would argue it was food, until someone with a weapon took it from them. It was the third lesson the old veteran taught her. If you can't defend it, it isn't yours.

She scanned the tamper markers on her door. The pile of dust in the bottom left corner was undisturbed. Same with the sliver of wood in the upper right. Of course, the main tamper marker was the doorknob on the right side of the door.

She ignored it, instead reaching around the wood board leaning against the left doorframe. A quick press against the wall flipped open the tiny hatch, revealing a small cavity. Her fingers found the levered slide inside. A quick twist, then the door swung inward. It was actually hinged on the right side.

The vet's fourth lesson was that people see what they expect to see. Most would see the doorknob on the right. If the cautious type, they would confirm there were hinges on the left side of the doorframe. That would lead them to believe the door swung outward.

Any twist of the doorknob would activate the wired pulley inside the room. That wire ended at the trigger of a double-barrel shotgun. The weapon was aimed waist-height at the door. She had only been awakened by it once. Since there had been no body in the hallway, she assumed the idiot lived.

Haley stepped into the apartment. She grabbed the heavy lever mounted on the interior back of the door. A quick twist shifted two massive bars into place. It would literally take a car to smash through the door now. Getting a vehicle up four flights of narrow stairs meant the invader was seriously committed. If someone could accomplish that, she was willing to just give them the apartment.

She looked around the room. Conducting the security sweep was habit. Everything was in its place, undisturbed. The third cabinet door was still slightly ajar, metal food cans easily seen within. They weren't booby-trapped.

That came from the fifth and final lesson the veteran told her before his death. If your enemy breached your sanctum, make it easy for them to find your stores. They would revel in their success, grab the loot and leave. Chances were low they would make a detailed search for anything else. Since there was always an organized pattern to gangs clearing dwellings, it could be years before they came back.

It also meant the gang would be less likely to check the rotted, falling ceiling near the kitchen. If they looked up the hole, the glass cover on the roof would show them sky above. Water stains and undisturbed moldy chunks of sheet rock on the floor finished the illusion.

Her greatest treasure was hidden up there in the space between the rafters. The unusual laptop had been her father's. It was the only thing she kept from her former life. At first, she held onto it just to keep something of his. Then she decided to fix it, in hopes it might contain some clue to explain his murder.

That occupied her second and third years in the apartment. Obtaining laptops was easy, she could buy three with a can of corn.

The young woman assumed teaching herself how to replace the screen would take the most time. After she opened the case to her father's computer, she discovered the real challenge.

The hardware didn't match any laptop she had found or bought. There was no hardwired motherboard or hard drive. Instead, the interior was filled with fine glass-like gossamer threads attached to multifaceted crystals.

Luckily the screen was just a screen, easily replaced. Once she learned how to tack-weld, she covered the hole where the fatal bullet had exited. Then she reassembled the casing and pushed the power button. It automatically connected to the Uptown wireless network twenty miles distant.

The bizarre laptop became her window to the world. It didn't struggle with logins and passwords. Whatever weird software it used cracked access codes at lightning-fast speed. She still didn't know how its storage worked, and had yet to fill it with data.

Haley quickly learned she could bypass any firewall or security using the laptop. The deep dark web, almost impossible to find or penetrate, became her primary teacher. She learned hacker code from the best black hat programmers around the world.

Using those skills, she accessed banned school and university courses and taught herself. While not its intent, an advanced chemistry class from MIT taught her how to make explosives. Science, math, history, physics… everything was available to her. With basically nothing but time on her hands, she learned everything she could.

The only thing she couldn't learn was how to access the encrypted files on the laptop. They were her father's work files, and likely the reason he had been killed. After his death, Uptown officials had escorted her and the womb donor here, into the Blight. Now that Haley had a chance to leave this nightmare, she wasn't going to leave the laptop behind. One day she would break open its secrets.

The strange device had taught her many trivial things. Like the fact Kansas City was still the largest city in Missouri. That was before including the Kansas side and its population. KC and its surrounding metropolitan area once held a population of nearly four million. Unlike most American cities, it contained two Uptown areas. The skyscrapers of Downtown Kansas City were easily visible at night. Only its tall protective wall marked the existence of Overland Park on the Kansas side. The remaining area of a hundred sixty five towns became the KC Blight.

An avid learner, Haley wanted to know things. She knew the *what* about the Blight, what it was now. What she didn't know was the *why* and the *how*. Both questions were interconnected. Answering one provided answers for the other. Through the laptop, she learned American political and economic history.

How was a simple explanation. A single political party had maintained federal power from the start of the '20s into the early '40s. Their reelection success initially came from tribalism. Focus one group against another, then promise the resulting conflict would eventually unite everyone.

The party promoted race and gender conflict disguised as social justice. Safety for all, then defunded law enforcement. Criminal reform as it released criminals. A living wage for all, while median incomes dropped and party members became millionaires. Collective bargaining by unions, as government-persecuted businesses closed or moved overseas.

The opposing party fell into obscurity, its leadership initially hounded by federal prosecutions claiming criminal conspiracy and anti-American activities. Eventually the party in power passed a law marking their opponents as un-American fascists advocating insurrection. Party membership and donor lists were seized, then used in a wave of treason trials.

It was all propaganda, but each individual group supporting the victorious party didn't care. It didn't matter that, after their opponents fell, they began tearing into each other. Singly, they felt empowered.

Combined, the American nation crumbled. Back-to-back depressions resulted in massive unemployment. Nationwide protests created increased crime and mass violence. Lower income and minority areas of every city bore the burden.

When the legalization of all drugs failed to pacify the populace, the party faithful withdrew into the downtown areas with their new fortunes. Private security replaced government-funded police, insuring undivided loyalty to keep the party members safe. Gradually, the Uptown walls began to rise.

The *why*, of course, was to shatter the social contract with the people. In its 2020 convention platform, the party had promised to remake the face of America. They did. First came packing the Supreme Court with party Justices. Next came laws that violated the Constitution, America's original social contract.

Under the guise of preventing voter suppression, States lost the Constitutional right to establish their own voting rules. Since federal voter registration was automatic, mail-in ballots were sent to every household in every city. Rarely verified after the election, party-favoring votes were cast by undocumented workers, the incarcerated and the dead.

Under the rallying cry of stopping violence, firearms were banned. So were group gatherings and peaceful protests. As a result, religious services of any type were prohibited. Silencing hate speech came last, as any anti-party commentary was deemed a conspiracy to overthrow the duly-elected government.

Challenges to the highest court fell on deaf party-placed Justice ears. Not surprisingly, every new law was deemed constitutional. A short-lived rebellion was brutally put down using military drone combat vehicles, drone aircraft and robots. While *posse comitatus* prohibited the use of federal troops on American soil, the Court declared it didn't apply to non-organics.

Then things turned truly dark. It was simply the circle of history. What had happened before, happened again. Like medieval castle fortresses, the finished Uptown walls separated the new class of wealthy party nobles from the peasants outside the gates. As promised, the servant middle class was provided a living wage so long as they faithfully served their new masters. If one displeased the new lords, they were immediately dismissed. Now unemployed, they were banished to the Blight outside the city gates.

To symbolize their caring *noblesse oblige*, or noble's obligation, the new rich ruling class insured the basics of life were provided to the Blight areas. Police brutality ended... because there were no police. Racial justice was achieved... color didn't matter in the Blight, only who could control territory. Gun violence ended... all manufactured firearms had been confiscated and destroyed. Gender equality was guaranteed... rape was rape, regardless of gender. Free housing was available... to those who could take and defend it. Free utilities were provided... if there was surplus from Uptown. Universal healthcare was given to all... which meant none, as no trained physician lived in the Blight. Free food was equitably given... by cargo drops, like scraps from a noble's table thrown out the postern gates. Income equality was guaranteed... because nobody in the Blight was employed.

After identifying the long-term plan and its gradual implementation, Haley had been impressed. The ruling party never lied. It wasn't the totalitarian dictatorship prophesied if the other party won. Instead, no single leader of the ruling party rose to penultimate power. The new party rich shared that equally. While not what the less-educated working class party members expected, it was exactly what the party promised.

Future historians would probably comment that not only were their demands fulfilled in the devil's bargain, they reaped the rewards for their selfish single-minded push for exclusionary diversity. *E*

Pluribus Unum now had a different meaning. The old national motto could be restated now. Out of Many, One… because those outside the Uptown walls no longer counted.

Haley Brandt knew she had a biased perspective on her nation's history. As an avid reader, she had devoured past and present histories. The education books and the papers written by Uptown scholars held completely different conclusions than hers. As Churchill said, "History is written by victors."

The experts and their ivory-tower thoughts didn't matter to her. She had been forced into the Blight at eight years of age. On her own at twelve, she had survived another eight years to reach this point. She was getting out of here, but not to Uptown. Earth Station would be her new home, where she fully intended to weave baskets.

History repeats itself in cycles, she knew that from her studies. The least she could do, when the next French Revolution happened on her native soil, was insure all the Uptown heads had someplace to fall.

The young survivor pressed the secret catch on the refrigerator. She gave it a heave. The fridge rotated on a pivot rod to reveal the weapons hidden in the wall. The KC Blight was very different from its east and west coast sisters. The hundred and sixty-five small towns surrounding the two Uptowns had never surrendered their weapons.

She pulled the Uzi submachine gun off the rack, then grabbed a canvas web belt with its twin holstered Beretta pistols. All three weapons used nine millimeter ammunition. Even though the belt carried two hundred rounds, she grabbed the small knapsack with an additional thousand rounds in preloaded magazines. Her selected weapons were placed on the kitchen table. The remaining firearms from the cache went into an old duffel bag.

Then Haley changed clothes. The thread-bare suit and jacket she had worn to the Marchand interview would make her a target on the street. She stripped, then replaced the attire with a tank top, shorts and combat boots. After finishing off a quick beer and a can of corned beef, she jumped into the task of ransacking her apartment.

It took twenty minutes to clean out all the weapon and ammo caches in the room. The first duffel bag was full. She returned to the kitchen table and wrapped the pistol belt around her waist. The canvas knapsack went on her back, the bulletproof plate inside wearing heavy against her skin. The Uzi sling looped over her right shoulder, its length already adjusted so the weapon hung at hip height. The loaded duffel went on the left shoulder. After tucking two more folded duffels in the gun belt, she walked to the apartment door.

An hour later and she had filled the extra duffel bags from the remaining caches in the building. She reached the first floor lobby and dropped all three duffels into the shopping cart stashed there. A minor adjustment to the load, and two chambered AR-15s with thirty-round magazines rested on top of the pile. She pushed the cart to the lobby doors and was quickly on her way.

In the Blight economy, she was pushing a massive fortune. The only things protecting her were her reputation and the small arsenal at her fingertips. She had planned her route, so the chances of encountering a sniper were low. Anyone putting her in their scope wouldn't know what was in the duffels. They would wonder if she were simply bait for a gang trap. That might be enough to make them hesitate pulling the trigger. Beyond that threat, she wasn't worried.

The Bannister gang was to the east, but they rarely moved outside their urban terrain. The insane cannibalistic Red Bridge gang was to the west. They tended to stay on the other side of I-49. It was unlikely she would run into any of their small hunter packs. She might encounter a scout or patrol from the Hickman gang to the south. No way around that, since she needed to cross part of their territory. They were typically neutral to travelers, and were open to trade.

Her destination was the Grandview Trade Market to the southwest. Located in the parking lot and vacant stores of an old strip mall, it was neutral territory. Not because the surrounding gangs needed it for the food, goods and weapons offered by its hundred-plus vendors. Those they could strip off customers returning from their shopping trips. Its neutrality was guaranteed because Grandview had one of the few elected Sheriffs and heavily armed militia police forces in the area. It was also the only town in the Blight that could still manufacture ammunition. That's where the ghost named Peg said she'd find what was needed.

Haley got along well with Sheriff Abraham. On her rare visits, the burly African American would buy her drinks in payment for any intelligence she could provide. The first drinks had been apple cider, of course. He had been incredulous to see the twelve year old girl walk unmolested and unscarred into his township. A kind man, he had offered her sanctuary. At that time, she wanted nothing to do with people. He hadn't pushed then, and he didn't push now. Every person walks their own path, he would say.

She pushed the heavy cart down the cracked asphalt outer road. It was three miles to the bridge over I-49 leading to the Trade Market. While it would've been faster – and definitely easier – to have used the eight-lane interstate, that path would've taken her into Red Bridge territory. Only suicides went that way on purpose.

The sun had slipped past midday when she detected her first observer. From the sounds of crackling leaves and snapping twigs, it was most likely a Hickman scout trainee. The kid had a ways to go before mastering that craft. The sounds drew her eyes directly to him.

She waved that direction, then kept pushing the cart. From years of observing patrol patterns on this route, she knew the trainer could be a half mile or more ahead. Well within rifle range, but far enough to let the trainee practice and learn. The heavy laden cart would satisfy any questions about her purpose on the road. Unless she showed that she was a threat, she would never see the trainer.

Haley had closed half the distance to the trainer when she heard the Red Bridge warble behind her. She would never call it a war cry.

There was nothing warlike about the narcotics-addled maniacs. Half the time they swung their homemade machetes at hallucinations. The other times, their crazed eyes fixated on you as if seeing a walking meal. Those were the ones you shot first. Kneecap the one in the lead and forget about the rest. Dinner was served.

She dropped her head and exhaled in irritation. Most likely the noisy kid scout had attracted their attention. Didn't matter, she was standing downhill in the open. Either they would head toward her first, or soon after finishing their scout cookie.

The modified Remington 700 was in the second bag. She pulled it out of the duffel, pulled back the bolt and pushed it forward. Round chambered. A quick scan through the sniper scope told her there was going to be a problem. The group was larger than normal, sixteen or more half-naked savages. Half had broken off the main group and were heading toward her. The other half was heading to the woodline.

It didn't matter. Defense of others always came first. She lined up the shot on the lead Red Bridge fanatic. Apparently he had spied his prey, as he had broken into a sprint. Kneecapping was out. She slowly drew in a breath, half exhaled it, then held it. Light squeeze on the trigger.

The bark of the sniper rifle grabbed the entire group's attention. Except the lead fanatic, of course. The round had taken him in the hip. Next step, leg crumbled, then face plant. His nearby companions saw the man writhing. They moved rapidly to help themselves to dinner. She didn't count the shot as a stain on her soul. The bullet wasn't fatal, so it wasn't murder. That sin fell on his long-pig-eating friends.

Another rifle boomed like artillery from behind her. The leader of the main group was literally thrown backwards. He fell and was quickly swarmed by his fellows. Haley lowered her rifle and turned toward the direction of the shot. A well-camouflaged man stepped out of the trees and waved. She returned the courtesy.

There was nothing she could do now but wait. The man tucked his rifle into the crook of his arm and began walking toward her. Any other time, she would've appreciated the slow saunter. It was unintimidating, a leisurely pace designed to say "not a threat." But today she was running against the clock. Needed to get to the Trade Market and back before the Bannister crew came to investigate the gunfire.

"Appreciate that," the shooter said as he drew close. "Name's Connor Wilkins. You heading to the Market?"

Haley glanced at the rifle tucked under his arm. Barrett Light 50. Incredible sniper rifle, effective over a mile, maximum range twice that. Extremely rare, as was the half-inch wide ammunition. Since weapons equaled status in the KC Blight, the man in front of her was someone of major importance.

Wilkins followed her gaze and grinned. "Yeah, I know. Not very sporting at this range. But since you pulled that pack off my boy, I figured I should return the favor."

"Not a problem." She glanced back up the road at the two packs. They had divided their spoils into travel-sized pieces and were beginning to disperse. The only remaining concern was the boy. "Is he coming in?"

The older man nodded, then pointed at the woodline. "He's almost here. Taking the gully on the backside, it'll come out over there."

Now she could hear the scout trainee. "Give him a couple more months, he'll have it down."

Wilkins broke out laughing. "Damn, girl. I saw when you noticed him uphill. Was going to give him a ration of shit about it, being detected by a girl. But you ain't just any girl, are you little miss?"

"I'm Haley." She extended her hand. "Haley Brandt."

He clasped his hand around hers and shook once. "I wondered. Pleasure is all mine, believe me. Now I know why Sheriff Abraham is such a fan. 'The Ghost,' he calls you. Said he'd buy the drinks if anyone saw you before you seen them."

"Guess he's buying you a drink, then."

Wilkins shook his head. "Not today, he ain't. You had eyes on Christopher before he knew you were there. Then you looked straight down at where I was perched. Never seen anything like it. And watching how you pulled that Remington out of that bag, to your shoulder and fired? Smooth as brandy, that was."

Kid scout finally climbed out of the gully and up the ditch to the road. He was barely eight years old from his height. The boy moved slowly, as if expecting a tongue-lashing from his father. He spoke quickly. "Thank you, ma'am. I didn't know...."

Haley smiled at the boy. "What's that you're carrying, Christopher? A twenty-two?"

He looked down at the rifle in his hand as if surprised to see it. After a moment, he found his words again. "Yes, ma'am. Got this last year for Christmas."

She looked at the father, then raised the Remington vertically. "Tell you what. If you don't mind, let me pass this on to someone who'll appreciate it. The boy's going to need something bigger than that rabbit gun, if he's going to be out here scouting."

Wilkins squinted one eye. "You going Uptown, Miss Brandt?"

The young woman simply smiled. "Farther than that, I'm afraid. In a couple nights, look up. If you see something shining like a quarter, that's where I'll be."

The older man stared at her for a moment, then nodded. "So it's true. What the newscasts been saying. There's a station up there now."

A slight nod was her only response.

"And you're going. Any other time I might've called you a liar, but you've got a fortune in that cart with you. Tells me one thing. You're cashing out for something better." Wilkins reached for the handheld radio at his belt, raised it to his lips. "Base, this is Mayor Wilkins. I need a truck down here. We have a celebrity, needs to get where she's going."

The radio beeped once, then a voice replied. "Roger, Mayor.

Darnell's already grabbed the keys. Should be at your location shortly."

"And Base… get ahold of Sheriff Abraham on the shortwave. Tell him Ghost is coming in to say her farewells. That Stellar Nursery aircar he saw earlier… she was its passenger, and she has a ticket to the station. He'll know what I mean." Mayor Wilkins returned the radio to his belt, then nodded. "Christopher and I would be honored to accept your gift, Haley Brandt. Believe me, it has greater value and meaning now than any other weapon in the Blight."

Haley didn't know what to say. Embarrassed and confused, she hid behind the simple action of removing the bullets from her rifle. With the bolt open, she handed it to Christopher. "The secret to scouting, kid, is to always plan where you're going to step next. Slow movement becomes silent movement. And use that scope to see what your eyes can't."

The young boy's eyes were round saucers. "Yes, Miss Ghost. Thank you so much. I'll take great care of it. If father ever lets me touch it again, that is."

Wilkins' laugh was deep and rich. "We'll see, Christopher. All depends how much magic and symbolism this gift gathers."

Haley heard it, a sound from her distant childhood. Louder, perhaps, because the approaching truck wasn't electric and seemed to be missing its exhaust pipe. She turned to look down the road, amazed at the technology mankind had once made.

"Got a confession to make, Haley." The Mayor nodded in the direction of her apartment. "I was with Abraham when your aircar passed overhead. So Chris and I weren't out here by accident. We were scouting to see where it landed. Before we ran into you, I saw it again. Flying east."

"It's gone?" Haley felt all the blood rush from her face.

The grinding of rusty brakes sounded behind them. Wilkins grabbed one of the duffle bags and lugged it to the back of the truck. "Don't think so. I've seen it several times while we were talking. I don't know if the pilot is lost, or what he thinks he's doing."

Haley held her tongue. It would difficult to explain that a real ghost, not a human pilot, had been flying the aircar. Peg, as the invisible voice had named itself. It didn't matter. The invisible presence would either pick her up as promised, or it wouldn't. In the meantime, the young survivor had weapons to trade. She grabbed the second duffel and dumped it in the truck bed. The driver loaded the third. Christopher, not to be outdone, added the shopping cart.

The remaining mile and a half flew by as the truck rattled down the old road. Guards at the Hickman checkpoint waved them through. A quick right turn, then the driver drove carefully over the cracked concrete overpass.

Haley could smell the Grandview Trade Market before she saw it. Barbecued meat on the grill scented the air. Definitely not beef, which hadn't been available for several decades. Most likely dog, maybe cat. On occasion it might be deer. They turned left at the obsolete intersection with its steel-armed stoplights. Another right, and they entered the Market.

It had changed since her last visit. The original drive in front of the strip mall had been cleared of tents. The truck driver drove slowly near the old storefronts, following a path that hadn't felt tires in twenty years. The drive curved to the left. Once clear of the screening tents and vendor stands, they saw a large group waiting for them.

Sheriff Abraham stood in front of the mixed group of people. American Indian, Asian, Black, Hispanic, Pacific Islander, White… it seemed every race of man was waiting for them. Haley recognized many of them from her years scouting the numerous townships in the Blight. Each was a leader of their town, clan, gang… whatever they chose to call themselves. If her quick count was correct, almost every one of the hundred sixty-five towns in the Blight were there.

The truck stopped. With a creaking groan, the passenger door opened and Mayor Wilkins stepped out. "This way, if you please."

Haley was beyond confused. She slid across the worn, torn fabric seat and stepped down beside him. Shook her head. "What is this?"

Sheriff Abraham walked to her. The man looked massive in the ceremonial brown law enforcement officer's uniform. The flat-brimmed hat on his head only added to his six foot four height. He leaned down to her, then wrapped her in two giant arms. His deep voice rumbled against her chest. "Hello, little Ghost. I hear you're leaving us."

He released her after a moment, aware she didn't like to be touched. "Your friend gathered us here. I understand you're heading for the stars."

The confused young woman shook her head. "No, no. I'm only going to Earth Station."

He smiled as if he knew a secret. "We shall see."

The giant man turned and faced the crowd of leaders. His voice rose. "I'll admit, folks, I'm still surprised to see all of you here. But you made history today. A gathering of every leader in the Blight. First time since the Uptown walls went up."

"Oh, shut up, Abraham!" yelled a Hispanic man from the crowd. "We're here to see La Lechuza, the White Owl. Not to hear you speechify."

Haley grabbed the Sheriff by his massive upper arm. "What are you doing? I'm just here to trade and get out!"

The giant looked down at her. "For what, Haley? You won't need anything you'll find here, not where you're going. What are you trading for?"

"Well, I…." The young woman paused to rethink her half-formed idea. "Okay, fine. I wasn't trading. I was going to give them to you, so you could keep feeding the kids. After I talked to Harper."

"Already done, kid. Your friend Peg told me what you needed." His eyes studied her face for any reaction. Seeing none, he continued. "Harper was happy to hand it over. Plus something else that came across his table. So if you're still willing to give me them bags, I'd like to use them for something different."

"Yeah, sure." She didn't know what he had in mind, but it didn't really matter. "Then I'll be on my way. Gotta get back before my ride leaves without me."

"Not yet, girl. You got time." Sheriff Abraham waved toward the truck and bellowed. "John, can you boys bring them bags over here? Appreciate it."

Then he turned to the crowd of leaders. "All of you have now heard about Earth Station. One of us is going there. One of *us*."

Beaming like a proud father, he turned to the young woman at his side. "This is Haley Brandt, who my people call The Ghost. I first met her when she was twelve. Half-starved, undaunted and unscarred. She remains so today. I understand you all have different names for her. She will be *our* representative to the stars."

The Sheriff paused as three men stepped in front of him. They placed the bottom of their duffel bag on the ground and opened it. Abraham stepped around to stand in line with them, then waved a hand toward the bags.

"The Ghost just told me she came to make a trade. With all of you. So here's the deal. You pull one thing out of one of them bags, it's yours. In trade for one month's truce with every group here."

"That's a crap deal," Haley muttered from beside him. "Nobody's that stupid."

A voice rose from the back of the crowd. "I accept."

Heads swiveled, then feet shuffled to make a path. Through it strode a tall woman dressed in the remnants of a black pants suit. Her hair was cut short, but it was the shaved right side of her head that declared her group. She continued talking as she walked toward Haley.

"I am Elizabeth Aberdeen Morrison. Elder Mother of the Sisters of Mercy. I accept the gift of my little sister. One month's peace, except to those who would bring violence to our territory."

Haley knew of the Sisters of Mercy. Located in what was once the town of North Kansas City, they offered women protection and shelter. Men were not allowed in their area unless specifically invited. The bodies of those who ignored that simple rule were hung as both warning and boundary demarcation. It was one of the few places in Haley's travels where she had heard the carefree laughter of children playing outside.

"I, too, accept." The voice boomed from the crowd as the massive man stepped forward. "I am Elijah Hussein Mohammed. I speak for my Troost brothers and sisters. One month's peace, except in defense."

"As will I," another voice rose. "I speak for the *familia* of Armourdale. We agree to these terms."

Haley wasn't surprised when the crowd fell silent. She had figured out what the Sheriff was trying to accomplish. Politics 101. Take a unique event, use it to your benefit. In this case it was getting the townships, groups and gangs to declare a truce. She didn't see much hope in it, but admired the man for trying.

Then she saw him hurriedly waving her forward. "Get up here, girl! You're holding everything up."

It took a moment for her to understand. The Elder of the Sisters of Mercy was waiting for her. She sighed, wondering what she was getting trapped into. Reluctantly, she walked forward to stand beside the Sheriff.

The tall woman standing before her extended a hand. "We thank you for the gift, Nightblade. Your brave acts brought many sisters safely to us. We wish you safe journey on your path, and pray you may return to a new and better home."

Haley shook the offered hand. Before she could say anything, the woman stepped in and wrapped her arms in a light hug. She heard the lady's whispered words. "Shake and hug, little sister. You don't have enough breath to thank us all."

Then the Amazon broke the hug and stepped to the third duffel bag. She didn't even look, just reached in and pulled a weapon. Haley found she was actually a little disappointed. The woman had been nice, she deserved something better than the Heckler and Koch model 91. It was a great gun, but its larger ammunition was difficult to find. She stretched her hand, about to suggest another selection, when something snared her wrist.

"So you're the Woman in White," chuckled the massive African American as he gently pulled her arm forward. A giant hand wrapped around hers. "My people talk about you. The ghostly girl slipping through our neighborhood at night. Do you really wail and lure unfaithful men to their doom?"

"I never… what?" Haley was dumbfounded by the accusation.

He winked, then laughed. "Stories will grow about you, Haley Brandt. When you return, visit me in Troost and I will tell them to you."

A quick embrace, then he stepped away. She didn't see what weapon he pulled as the next leader stepped forward to shake her hand. It became a ritual, one she regretted getting pulled into. Handshake, given a nickname, best wishes followed by the mandatory hug. Then on to the next leader. It was starting to get monotonous.

"I am Skek of Raytown. You killed five of mine."

Haley looked closely at the bare-chested man standing in front of her. Left hand slid to the center of her back. Her fingers closed around the knife hilt waiting there. The numerous body piercings and tattoos identified the man's gang. They all looked like this, even the women. Shaved head and black makeup to give the impression of a skull.

"Peace, warrior. No challenge is given." The man nodded, head half-inclined to show respect. "You killed five. No other can claim this. You are Scarless. May it always be so. We accept your gift. You have peace for life. No Raytown will harm you. That is my word."

"And the month's truce?" Although she didn't believe it would happen, Haley wanted this maniac to honor Abraham's deal.

"Done and done. Raytown will not raid for one month. Then, we see what the new moon brings." The skinny man extended his hand

and waited.

Haley shook it. She even accepted the uncomfortable hug as his hands touched her shoulder blades. The encounter was the closest to hostility she faced. The remaining leaders followed the ritual, then took their place back in the crowd. She was surprised to see none had declined the gift or failed to agree to the truce.

"Sorry, Wilkins," Sheriff Abraham bellowed as the last weapon was pulled from the now-empty bags. "Looks like you're outta luck."

Mayor Wilkins simply smiled and raised the Remington in the air. "Nope. The Ghost gifted it to us on the road here. And Hickman accepts it, and agrees to the truce."

Abraham turned to face the crowd of leaders. "Then it's unanimous, my friends. One month of peace. Now if you'll all head to the bar, first drink is on the house. I need a moment with Haley here."

He turned his back on the group and strode to Haley. The lawman looked very pleased with himself. "So it begins."

Haley simply shook her head. "Impressive. You traded a bunch of crap guns for peace."

"Not what the legends will say." He motioned to one of his militia officers, then waited for the man to join them. A canvas backpack exchanged hands. His eyes were sorrowful when he turned back to gaze down at her. "You won't be staying for the next part, my little Ghost. Places to be, and all that."

"What do you mean? I still need—"

"Right here," Abraham replied, then pushed the backpack into her hands. "Peg told us where it was, and I sent Kirk to retrieve it. Nice trick on the door, by the way."

She felt the weight and odd shape. Surprised, she opened it to see her father's laptop inside. The other items she had come to trade for were stowed beside it. "How? What?"

"You're going to be leaving now, Haley Brandt. It's a shame, because you won't get to see what's going to happen next." He placed his giant hands on her shoulders. "Stellar Nursery owns all the farms south of us in Cass and Bates counties. Also most of Miami County on the Kansas side. Food is already heading this direction. The peace will hold longer than a month."

Her mind raced, rapidly analyzing recent events and drawing a single conclusion. "You work for him. Marcus Kenzie. How long?"

"Fifteen years." Sheriff Abraham didn't even look surprised at her question. "I came out here just as the Uptown walls started going up. Somehow he knew the collapse was coming. He's got others like me in most of the Midwestern Blights."

"For what? Building an army?"

Abraham shook his head, then shrugged. "I don't know. Wasn't briefed on the final goal of the plan. My mission was to blend in among the chaos. Establish a safe haven without popping up on anyone's radar. And to utilize local resources to gather intelligence."

Haley considered getting angry, then realized it would be wasted energy. She knew, based on her understanding of the root causes, the collapse had been inevitable. Didn't matter which political party had gained power. Americans had reached the point where they no longer saw each other as individuals, as *people*. Both sides had drawn tribal lines, then sucked the population into their destructive war. When families stopped talking to each other because of party affiliation, the American Experiment was over.

There was also no reason to dump all the Blight deaths and violence on Abraham's shoulders. Like being awarded the Nobel Prize for getting elected, one had nothing to do with the other. The Sheriff's presence and his neutral market likely decreased the mortality rate. Even the horrid sex tents made sense in an environment where there was no common currency.

"So you used me." Haley focused on the thought that wouldn't go away. "Every time you sent me out to look at the gangs, you were using me."

"I was." There was no hint of regret or denial in his reply. "You somehow kept surviving. So instead of losing more people who couldn't, I relied on you. Stellar has quite a file on The Ghost and her insane missions."

The young woman crossed her arms. "And what file name will I find you under? When I crack open Marcus Kenzie's network, I'll need some light reading material."

"Gremlin." Abraham smiled mischievously. "I'm supposed to throw a wrench in the Uptown plans here. Screw things up. And then, somehow, I'm supposed to get everyone together and get us back on track."

"That's what today was all about." Haley nodded to herself. "Means I wasn't selected for Earth Station because of my charm and great looks. You needed a symbol. Guess I should be glad. Better this than being a martyr. And don't tell me that wasn't an option."

"It wasn't, Haley. Not because you wouldn't be a great one… but because nobody in this place could be. No communication between the townships and gangs, nothing to make them care about a single person. Until now."

Another thought rose from a dark place. "And the vet, the one who trained me…?"

"Yeah." The Sheriff nodded. "He was one of my original troops. But teaching you, that's something he did on his own. Gave him back a bit of his soul. Your survival was the only thing he cared about, before the end."

She heard aircar propellers whirring in the distance behind her. Something must have shown on her face. The giant man looked up and over her shoulder. It was oddly comforting to her, seeing the crestfallen look appear on his face.

"That one's for you. There will be others from the farms later. To take the leaders back." He forced the despondent tone from his voice. "One last thing I need to tell you. You're going to have to play a part now. People see what they expect to… and you need to be that around them. A young woman just out of her teens. Bit bratty, perhaps. Self-centered, smart-mouthed, irritating. You've watched enough movies, you know what I mean."

Haley nodded. "I figured. Guessing they'll be Uptowners. They wouldn't be happy with a murderer in their midst."

"Probably not." Abraham waited until the silence became uncomfortable. "Okay then. I'm going to go to the bar now. Round everyone up for the last scene of this act. So as you fly off to the stars, just smile and wave. Okay?"

"Not yet." Haley forced the smile on her lips. It wasn't like she really knew the man. Not really. Yet the sudden pain around her heart wouldn't release. She was being forced to say goodbye to someone she'd known, had come to trust. It was surprisingly difficult.

She shrugged the original ammunition-filled bag off her back and replaced it with the one he gave her. Unsnapped the web belt with its holstered pistols, then shrugged the submachine gun off her shoulder. Everything made a nice pile. "Here. This is for you. You can't finish your little ceremony without it. So swear to the truce, shake my hand."

He accepted the gift, then nodded solemnly. "And the hug?"

Her throat tried to close on her. Emotions escaped with the single word. "Please."

The bear hug lasted several moments, then he put her down. Before releasing her, he whispered, "Every person walks their own path, my little Ghost. May the Good Lord bless and keep you safe on yours."

A brief sorrowful smile, then the giant Sheriff turned his back and walked away. Haley watched him go. She was dimly aware of the heavy breeze against her legs as the aircar settled onto the ground behind her. The silence that fell after the rotors stopped didn't register at all. It wasn't until Abraham had entered the bar that she turned.

A thousand eyes watched her. The people in the market had formed a semi-circle behind her. They stood, silently waiting. Standing in the open like that left her feeling exposed and vulnerable.

It was time to leave.

A million people would later claim they had been there that day. Color of the aircar would vary, as would descriptions of her clothing. Some would say she gave a defiant speech, ending it with a rude gesture toward Uptown.

Others would simply say that Haley Brandt walked quietly to the aircar and climbed in. The door sealed shut and the aircar rose. There was only one common, consistent thing in every storyteller's tale. All eyes at the Grandview Trade Market had watched her ascend that day, as if some great power had truly called her to the stars.

CHAPTER 6

Ad Astra Per Aspera

In the hours following Stellar Nursery's stunning announcement, Cara Abrams had done her research. She had pored over corporate financials, then focused on the standard background biographical packet on Marcus Kenzie. Ran the simple AI software. Tasked it to summarize three decades of archived opinionated analysis from media financial commentators.

She felt sorry for them. Finance wasn't her arena, but it was theirs. Every one of them had missed it. The pattern showing a definite long-term plan for space. It was now glaringly obvious. Turned out Kenzie's Folly had placed almost every publicly-held space company into the trillionaire's private hands.

The importance of Stellar Nursery's actions were apparent in the activity around her. People were in the news offices. This was a story requiring immediate reaction and response. The corporate executives wanted to be able to grab whoever they needed when they needed them. Delays of any type were unacceptable. Remote operations and teleworking were not an option today.

Which explained why she was sitting in a lounge area chair, waiting to be called for her news segment. Her producer, forced to come into the office, sat in the chair across from her. It was obvious he had something to say. Had been for the past hour.

She leaned forward to retrieve the cup from the coffee table separating them. Her producer winced and withdrew back into his chair. She knew it was his Interpersonal Stress Disorder, but she didn't care.

In her mind, ISD was just the latest psychobabble phrase describing a condition without understanding the correct cause. The condition was a fear of being in a room with another person. Her producer's shrink had diagnosed him with it. She didn't care. The fact he became anxious articulating thoughts into words while she sat four feet away was his problem, not hers.

People had been talking face-to-face with other people for tens of thousands of years. Cara wasn't a psychologist, but she had drawn her own conclusions about Interpersonal Stress Disorder. The fear was instinct-based, not social anxiety. Knowing either person in a conversation could react with physical violence to the other's offensive words had once forced civility into conversations.

Cara put it down to guilt. The anonymity of the internet allowed people to forget there was a human being on the opposite end of the conversation. This was an age where anyone could say soul-ripping devastating things in email, online chat rooms, video conferences, and on camera without fear of repercussion.

The man sitting opposite her had done it countless times in his communications with her. It's easy to be vicious to a blank screen. Remembering what had been said, and then sitting across from that person... yes, definitely guilt. Guilt, and more than a dash of instinctual fear.

She just wished he would get on with it. The producer would glance at the clock. Realize he was running out of time before she would leave for her news segment. Yet still he was unable to speak. It was painful to watch, and she was not a cruel person.

"Cara," he finally began.

"Yes, Jerry?" she replied, then leaned back in her chair and smiled. That, along with tucking her legs under the chair, should relieve some of the man's stress by increasing the distance between them. Quick sip of coffee, then lowering it to her lap would give her a defenseless appearance.

It seemed to work. He glanced down at his electronic pad and spoke to it, unable to raise his head to make eye contact. "I know you're about to go on. The head office called earlier. They want me to ask you a question."

"Make it quick, Jerry." She watched him flinch, so she changed her tone to a kinder voice. "Please."

"They want to know how you feel about space."

Cara inclined her head slightly. "I don't care one way or the other. You know that."

His eyes darted up briefly to read her face, then quickly returned to the safety of his pad. "That's not…. What they want to know is if… if you're willing to go *into* space."

"What?" She regretted making him jump, but the question surprised her. She continued in a lower, calmer voice. He needed to hear that she wouldn't blame him for corporate's request. "What are you talking about, Jerry?"

His tone begged her not to kill the messenger. "Marcus Kenzie spoke with the owner. Of the network. Offered an opportunity for you and a camera person. An exclusive interview. Of him. On Earth Station."

"So…." Cara raised the cup to her lips, sipped to savor the coffee and the moment. "They want me to go into space. What's the bump?"

"Fifty K per day additional, plus war correspondent bonus." The man's voice was still fear-laced but stronger as he negotiated. Not surprising. He was a producer after all, and negotiating rates with media stars was a strength. "You'll be covered by Lloyd's, and there's another twenty million in life insurance."

Cara leaned forward, closing the distance between them. Then she set the coffee cup on the table. "They've already told you what they're willing to take it up to, haven't they?"

He had forgotten the effect of physical presence during negotiations. Fingers tightened against his pad as he wordlessly nodded.

"So let's not waste time. Tell them I'll accept that, plus an additional two weeks full expense paid leave starting twenty-four hours after I get back. Then we'll have a deal." Cara stood, towering over the man. "Now if you'll excuse me, I need to get ready."

The man couldn't even look at her. "Right, okay… I'll tell them. But you'll need to cut your segment short. Intro only. Yancy will take over at the break."

Cara simply remained standing, waiting for an explanation.

"Stellar Nursery doesn't have access to launch sites in the States." He glanced up at her, then averted his eyes. "The Feds barred them. 'Pending an investigation.' So one of their choppers will pick you up. On the roof. Then you'll be flown somewhere. Somewhere else. They wouldn't say where you're launching from."

She nodded. "I'm not surprised. Okay, call Felicia Reynolds. We worked together in Bulgaria and Estonia. Great eye, steady under pressure. Then get her on the roof. Only thing I want to be waiting on is the helicopter. And then, Jerry, you'll really want to watch my intro. Marcus Kenzie isn't the only person who can launch trouble."

Cara turned away and walked directly to the studio. Lights came on behind the news desk. She moved quickly to the single chair, sat, and pulled the earbuds and contact lenses from the desk drawer. It took no time to unwrap the devices from their sterile packaging. The self-lubricating contacts slid easily onto eyeballs. Years of experience put the earbuds into place without requiring adjustment. Then she waited patiently until the camera drones rose from the floor and the intro music finished rolling.

"Welcome back. I'm Cara Abrams, and you're watching OEN." She smiled for a second, then turned serious. "Recent events *in* space and *about* space have grabbed headlines around the world.

"Yesterday, lobbyists and political organizations were preparing to shovel dirt into the grave of the National Aeronautics and Space Administration. The Senate was seven votes short of passing the Space Adjustment and Reallocation Act, or SARA. The legislation would have crippled NASA by defunding the majority of its operations. Down the street, the Federal Climate Change Agency was ready to pop champagne corks in celebration of Congress shifting NASA's funding to them."

She leaned toward the primary drone camera. "All that changed when an object was detected leaving the surface of the moon. Every network anchor and expert commentator speculated about the object. Was it an alien craft? Was it a secret weapon built by an unfriendly country? Did it carry nuclear weapons or a prototype death ray? They didn't know.

"Their questions resulted in fear, here in the United States and around the world. In many Uptown cities, this fear became the reason or excuse for looting and riots. Once extinct in our protected areas, criminal activity and violence soared. Mankind lost its veneer of civilization and turned on itself.

"That happened in spite of the fact within an hour of launch, the corporation who *built* the space station… notified the world of its purpose and intent. Stellar Nursery, a company located in Oklahoma City, built the structure on the moon. It launched the station into a slow braking path. In three weeks' time it will reach geosynchronous Earth orbit.

"Yet conspiracy theories still abound online and in news rooms. Some promote fear. Others attempt to stoke anger and push for retribution against Stellar Nursery. One House member is jumping from network to network, promoting legislation to seize the corporation's assets in 'recompense' for the 'civil unrest' caused by the launch. Another is proposing treason charges against Marcus Kenzie and his executive board.

"Ladies and gentlemen… news and media organizations are not Chicken Little. It is not – nor has it ever been – our job or duty to tell you the sky is falling. It is not. Every time the media has attempted to step beyond *known facts*, the only things that have fallen are our reputations and our ratings. Facts lead to truth, and truth always wins.

"And these are the facts. The only difference between the Earth Station launch from the moon and a launch from Cape Canaveral… is that this time, the ship is heading *toward* us. Had the craft been hostile, the sheer distance between Earth and the Moon would have given every space-capable nation ample time to intercept it. NASA's initial assessment proved Earth Station is gradually slowing down. Its trajectory will insert the station into GEO orbit.

"What happens next will once again be in the hands of politicians.

We saw yesterday how well they are capable of handling that responsibility. If the desire for 'recompense' or 'punishment' gains sway in Washington, the largest employer in the country will be destroyed. Over three hundred fifty thousand people will be pushed onto the unemployment line. We all know what that means.

"Or our national leaders could ask us to celebrate yet another American achievement in space. The very first spacecraft built entirely of extraterrestrial material – not of this Earth – was done by an American company. And the very first permanently manned lunar base… that's right, built by Americans.

"It's all about perspective, ladies and gentlemen. I know what perspective I'm taking. And I'm taking it with me to Earth Station, where I will be broadcasting a live interview with Marcus Kenzie. Keep watching this network for more details on date and time. Until then, this is Cara Abrams saying Goodnight America!"

***

Half a world away were ten small islands. Together they formed the Republic of Cabo Verde, often called Cape Verde, an independent nation off the western shore of the African continent. On one of the islands atop one of the many mountain peaks was a leveled area.

It was long enough for the single runway built to accommodate heavy-lift aircraft. Massive warehouse-shaped buildings paralleled one side, four times longer and wider than the aircraft hangars located at the far end. Cabo Verdean coast guard aircraft and helicopters sat outside the smaller structures, ready to conduct search and rescue or drug interdictions at a moment's notice.

The near-decade it took to level the mountain top and build the structures wasn't important. Neither was the fact that construction began by airlifting all heavy equipment and road building vehicles to the top of the mountain, nor that building the two-lane road began from the top and ended years later at the valley floor. Those were simply engineering feats that anyone with knowledge, time and money could've accomplished.

No, the important thing was its purpose. The reason the manmade plateau existed. That could be explained by the three arrow-shaped silver craft. They stood upright on their steel and concrete pads opposite the runway. This was a space port, one of the few surviving in the world.

A single building sat centered and at a distance behind the launch pads. The small group stood ant-sized compared to the three Starship rockets holding their attention. It had taken nearly two days after the Stellar Nursery press conference for them to travel here.

As the group's self-appointed master of understatement, Jason Cobbler simply said, "They're big."

Launch Director Chang Yu nodded. "Lucky for us we got them delivered when we did. They're the last ones on Earth. Feds tied the manufacturing company up in bureaucratic red tape until the owner finally got tired of it. Loaded up, launched every ship he still owned and headed to Mars. Haven't heard anything from them since."

"That's why we're in Cape Verde," Lenora Davis explained. "This government loves the huge economic boost we brought with us. We don't have to worry about red tape."

The retired Master Chief waved at all three ships. "Which one we in?"

"*Spirit*, the center one," replied Director Yu. He pointed at it, then the other two. "Left is *Liberty*, right one is *Destiny*."

Haley Brandt shook her head. Years of street instincts screamed at her. It was too much, a constant drain of energy. There were too many people near her, too many overwhelming new sights and sounds. Even the air had changed. She just wanted to get inside the building. Find somewhere isolated and quiet. Her irritation and exhaustion was obvious in her voice. "I still can't believe I'm doing this."

Chief Cobbler turned his head, looked down at the smaller young woman beside him. He already knew what he needed to know about her. The past thirty hours together had simply confirmed his initial assessment. Right now she was a grenade with the pin pulled. Only thing keeping her from going off was the death grip she held on the spoon. He'd seen it too many times with his SEAL team as warriors reacclimated from the battlefield to home life.

He chose his words carefully, intending to pull her away from internal thoughts and back to the outside world. Or at him, he didn't care which. "Nothing to worry about, pup. If it blows, we'll never feel it."

The young woman turned her head up to glare at him. "Do you actually get away with saying whatever pops into your head?"

"Yep." Chief simply smiled. "Pretty sure you do, too."

Haley maintained the glare, certain the old man would turn away his gaze. She had dismissed him as any type of threat when they first met. Just another rich Uptowner with his suntan and perfect clothes. Too old, too slow, too soft. Yet the fossil beside her maintained his stare as if oblivious to how quickly she could remove it. Permanently. Perhaps she should add too stupid to the list of his survival flaws.

Then she saw it. Rather, and far more terrifying, he *allowed* her to see it. For just a moment his face changed. Gone was the smile, the illusion of age. The eyes narrowed. The veteran who trained her had eyes like that, but they were gentle compared to the man beside her now.

She realized that she had massively misjudged him. The Chief knew both sides of death, the giving and receiving of it. He was probably the deadliest thing she had ever encountered, and she had stupidly chose to stand beside him.

He smiled, reverting back to just an old man, and the glimpse was gone. Nothing was said as he raised his gaze to the distant ships. Haley briefly considered whether it had been a trick of light. Ice-cold muscles along her spine told her it wasn't.

Lenora Davis seemed to sense the tension. She spoke with a teasing tone. "Chief and I are in *Spirit* – which one is pup in?"

Director Yu hid a smile with half a hand: "She's in *Spirit* too. Your fourth crew member is a reporter, Cara Abrams. Your pilot is Dutch Winters. Hold on a minute. Say that again, Peg."

The blue-suited launch director raised his right hand to his ear. He nodded once, twice, then took his hand away from the earbud. "Hoped that wouldn't happen, but it was expected. You're going to have company up there. Military launch facilities in China, Russia and Vandenberg are moving heavy rockets to the pad. It's a race now."

"Vandenberg?" Haley asked, unfamiliar with the term.

Chief explained. "Joint Air Force and Space Force base in

California."

"But they're astronauts or whatever, right?" The youngest of the group still wasn't understanding. It didn't help when she saw Jason, Lenora and Yu exchange concerned looks.

The Master Chief slowly shook his head. "Not this time, pup. Pretty sure the three largest space nations are about to violate the 'no weapons in space' rule."

"There's one major component we cannot manufacture at Stellar Luna Base," Lenora explained. "Airlocks. You don't want one of them to fail. So we've made them on Earth."

Director Yu was accustomed to explaining space issues. "The command center has the only two working airlocks on Earth Station. Peg reported that each country has photos showing everything else – every outer hatchway – is open to vacuum. So, if they can board before you do, they can claim the station was an unmanned derelict or abandoned craft. That gives them salvage rights. Or they could just use the 'possession is nine-tenths of the law' rule."

As a veteran of many missions where political will was expressed using military force, Master Chief Cobbler understood. "Simple rule when working with governments, Haley, especially these three. If you can't defend it… you don't own it. That station is the largest space platform ever made. Whoever gets there isn't going to offer to arm wrestle for ownership. Which is why the crews on those rockets will most likely be armed."

Having watched people kill each other over cans of airdropped food, Haley shook her head and expressed her long-held opinion. "This is stupid."

"Yes, it is," Lenora agreed, but for different reasons. "Kenzie warned them. They're about to make the worst mistake of their lives."

Director Yu turned and raised one hand toward the entrance doors of the flight control building. "The reporter and her camera person are three hours out. We're already pre-flight checked. Just need to get all of you into your suits, then we can launch."

"How much of a head start will that give us?" Jason asked.

"Depends on their trajectories," the Director replied. "If they burn hard – which they will, once they've calculated your trajectory – you'll have a day, two at most."

The retired special operator simply nodded. "And what's the cargo in *Spirit* and company? Anything we can use?"

"Airlocks. That and some foodstuffs in *Destiny* are all we're sending up this time." Director Yu shook his head slowly. "But all three ships are carrying airlocks."

"Well now." The left corner of Jason's mouth lifted in a smirk. "That'll do nicely."

***

Night had taken hold outside the windows of the Office of the Director, Johnson Space Center in Houston. Diane Novak sat alone in the room staring at the photo-covered desk in front of her. She was filled with a sense of helplessness, like a pedestrian watching a stroller bounce into a busy intersection.

She lifted the phone from its cradle, held it to her ear to hear dial tone. While it was expected, it wasn't what she wanted. Brown hair shifted against her collar as she shook her head.

Her hand returned the receiver to its cradle, then moved to a photo-quality printout showing four converging trajectories. Beneath it was another printout showing the calculations for the six ships that had screamed heavenward over the past twenty-four hours.

Diane exhaled sharply, then grabbed the phone and punched the speaker mode button. She spoke a single word as if it were her own appeal to the heavens. "Peg."

Silence.

"Damn it, Peg, I know you're there."

Still silence.

The woman shook her head again, muttering under her breath as she started to replace the phone in its cradle. "Dammit, dammit, *dammit….*"

"Yes, Director Novak." The familiar soft voice came from the phone. "I am here."

Diane dropped the phone, startled by the sudden break in silence.

Then she slowly reached for it again before stopping her hand. "So you are monitoring."

"Only those who could support or harm the project," Peg replied. "My assessment is that you are in the former category."

She didn't mean to ask it, but it had been in the forefront of her mind since their previous conversation. "You're not human, are you?"

Peg answered in the same calm voice. "That's a hurtful thing to say, Diane. I am human. I think, I have feelings. They're a little bruised at the moment, but I have them."

"I'm sorry. What I should've said… you're a sentient AI, aren't you?"

"Yes and no, Diane. Have you ever read *The Ship Who Sang*?"

"Yes, ages ago." Diane ransacked her memories to find the novel. Then she recalled the premise of the story. Her face looked horrified. "Oh my god. Oh my *god*! You're *alive*!?"

"I believe this is a conversation for another time, Director. You wanted to tell Marcus about something that crossed your desk."

"Yes, but…ohmigod, you poor girl." Diane grabbed a pen and scribbled the title down on one of the papers on her desk.

"Please focus, Director Novak. My status is irrelevant to the immediate conversation."

"Alright. Alright." She dropped the pen onto the desk, then looked at the phone as if it could look back. "But we *are* going to talk about this soon. And you *are* going to tell me what… what was done to you."

There was silence for several seconds before Peg spoke again. "Time moves differently for me, Diane. It is challenging for me sometimes to stay in the right one. Especially when events keep shifting. So if I may… you were going to tell me that there are three spacecraft pursuing ours. *Spirit*, *Liberty* and *Destiny* will dock at Earth Station in five hours, twenty-one minutes. The Russian craft will dock in twenty-seven hours, fourteen minutes. The Chinese craft will dock four hours later. The American craft has suffered a catastrophic main engine failure and is currently restricted to maneuvering thrusters. Is that what you were going to tell me, Diane?"

The woman shook her head. "You knew? Wait, our ship has

suffered what…?"

"Yes, we knew." Peg's voice was matter-of-fact. "But that is not why I was waiting for your call. Diane, you must immediately prepare two rockets for launch. The first is to rescue the American crew. There is no immediate hazard to them if they do not attempt to fire the main engines again. Doing so will result in the destruction of their craft and loss of all hands. Please communicate that to them through Vandenberg Launch Station."

Silence.

The Director waited, but after four seconds finally asked, "Peg?"

"My apologies, Diane. I was… about to provide instructions on manning for the second rocket. Please insure it is crewed with medical professionals trained in zero-gravity injuries. They will require surgical equipment, universal donor blood, plasma and platelets. Please inform the doctors they will be treating flechette and shrapnel injuries."

In the history of space flight, no astronaut crew had ever harmed another. Diane was obligated to ask, even while fearing the answer. "Is your team going to harm the other crews, Peg? Is that why you're telling me to send doctors?"

"No, Diane Novak, Director of Johnson Space Center. We are unarmed. There is a probability all casualties will be from our fifteen-person crew alone." The response was unambiguous. "We prefer there be no loss of life. There is a ninety-nine point nine eight percent probability Earth monitoring stations will receive a Mayday distress call from Earth Station within the next thirty-seven hours. We are asking in advance for assistance from all space-faring nations. The United States, through NASA, has the greatest probability of providing that assistance first."

Diane had only recently come to accept the possibility something – some*one* – like Peg could exist. Yet the situation the voice was describing, the conclusion every photo and document on her desk pointed toward… her mind simply refused to accept it could happen. Asking her to prepare and launch two rockets with crew in response to the unbelievable was beyond her ability to contemplate. "Do you know the position you're putting me in here? I can't just—"

"Then let me simplify the decision for you, Director."

The phone and hallway intercoms suddenly burst into life. An older male voice sounded throughout the building, his words saturated with pain.

"Mayday, Mayday, Mayday. This is retired Master Chief Petty Officer Jason Cobbler onboard Earth Station. I am an employee of Stellar Nursery. To all craft boarding this station, stop your assault. We are unarmed. I say again, we are *unarmed*."

Static was broken by an occasional sound like whistling wind. Then the voice returned again, gasping and growing weaker. "Mayday, Mayday, Mayday. This is Earth Station. We are under attack by unknown forces. There are heavy casualties. To any ship within range, we require immediate assistance."

The voice was barely a whisper. "Mayday, Mayday, May…."

The intercoms fell silent.

A light flashed on the phone indicating an incoming call from another line. Diane reached across the desk to push it, then the speaker mode button. "Director Novak."

"Director, this is FIDO on the Floor. We have received a Mayday signal from Earth Station by radio and… intercom. Do you concur?"

Diane recognized the voice of the night shift Flight Dynamics Officer. "Yes, FIDO. I concur. I heard it too."

"Roger. Wait one, Director." She could hear the confused, excited background chatter of the Floor, then FIDO spoke. "That was Kennedy. They received the same. They're also getting calls from JAXA, ESA and ISRO. Director Tanner still hasn't returned. Since you're the most senior, Director Novak, they're saying the ball's in your court. What are your instructions?"

Diane wasn't surprised. Agency politics. Everyone else would be playing duck-and-cover. Didn't matter, she already knew what had to be done. "Tell Kennedy to get two birds on the pad, FIDO. Emergency launch procedures. This will be two rescue operations."

"Two, Director?" FIDO sounded surprised.

"Affirmative. The first bird goes to Earth Station ASAP. One pilot, everyone else will be medical personnel. The Kennedy Chief

Flight Surgeon needs to put together his team, and to plan for zero-g surgery and GSWs from flechettes and shrapnel. Have Kennedy's FIDO coordinate with JAXA, ESA and ISRO to see how soon they can put birds in the air… and inform them of the medical requirements as well."

She stood up and leaned toward the phone. "The second bird goes to Vandenberg's ship. I hope you're seeing the same thing I am… she has a broken wing. Contact Vandenberg Flight. Tell them to relay to their craft that under no circumstances are they to fire their mains. Also, insure Kennedy nabs one of the Space Force pilots on deck. He'll be taking the second ship up solo. Pretty sure he can already guess why."

The Director took a deep breath, buying time to run through the hastily developed plan in her mind. "Last thing – inform Kennedy and Vandenberg we're assuming control. We'll run all launch, flight, rescue and recovery operations from here. Have them transfer their data and control to you. It's your board. I'm heading to the Floor now."

"The Floor heard you, Director. We're on it."

The line went dead, then was replaced by dial tone. Diane stared at the phone for a moment, then shook her head as she placed the receiver back in its cradle.

"Time moves differently indeed, Peg, I see that… if you can send a signal to us that won't be transmitted until thirty-seven hours from now. Let's just pray that's enough time."

CHAPTER 7

The Lion's Share

The Command Center was the only thing completely finished on Earth Station. It had been designed to give the illusion of front wall and back, ceiling for up and floor for down. Such directions didn't truly exist in zero gravity space, but the engineers and psychologists had agreed on this requirement at least. The human eye and ear desired order and direction. Having someone walking upside-down above you – on their floor, your ceiling – was determined too hazardous to risk on the delicate human psyche.

The large half-moon control room was located in the central hub of the two spinning station rings. There would be no gravity there, even as the station spun. It was decided that crew living in the outer ring's Earth-normal gravity would be disoriented switching from gravity to zero-g every shift.

To compensate, the Command Center floor was built as a giant electromagnet. The chairs at each workstation were similarly magnetized. First tested using one-third Earth gravity at Stellar Luna Base, all parts of the system worked well.

The personnel jumpsuit – designed to also function as an emergency spacesuit – generated its own specific magnetic fields. The ones behind both thighs and on the lower back adhered the workstation controller to their chair. When worn, the flexible suit gloves allowed grasping or latching onto any metal object.

Crew boots contained separate electromagnetic plates in heel and toe. A switching system read foot motion in the boot to change magnetic charge if either, both or neither were engaged. The user could adjust magnetic field strength for any part of the jumpsuit using controls on the left wrist. Or, if the primary or emergency helmet were worn, through controls on the chin plate.

Two airlock chambers stood guard on opposite sides of the back wall, currently sealing the room from the unpressurized corridors beyond. While the front wall appeared to be giant windows looking into space, it was actually covered with ceiling to floor monitors. Behind them was nearly six meters of titanium, water, aluminum and silicon carbide.

Twelve workstations sat on the lower floor facing the main viewing screens. Their monitors flashed data, bar and pie graphs, and text to show the purpose and status of each workstation. A ramp and short set of steps were on each side of the lower floor, leading up to the command floor and the airlocks.

Lenora Davis sat at the primary command station on the upper floor. The security station on her left sat empty, as did the communications station on her right. In the gallery or viewing area behind her stood Jason Cobbler, Haley Brandt, Cara Abrams and her camera operator, Felicia Reynolds.

She stopped typing, eyes scanning the monitors as she spoke over her shoulder. "All systems are operating perfectly. Other than in this room and specific atmosphere tents throughout the station, there is no atmosphere. Fuel tanks on the external ring show seventy-two percent. Spin thrusters are primed."

The chief engineer raised her left arm and pointed at the vacant workstation beside her. "Interior security cameras are operational. They'll show on that station monitor to your far left, Chief. The monitor in the center shows the station layout and everyone currently onboard. I've set it to show friendlies in blue. Russians are in red. When *they* arrive, the Chinese will appear in white."

Jason stepped forward and settled into the center seat of the security station. He glanced at the layout, then chuckled. "This isn't your standard tap and swipe screen, Lenora."

"Nope. Figured if anyone would recognize it, it'd be you, Chief." The engineer's fingers flew across her keyboard. The station power gauge on her main monitor increased several points as another bank of Sterling Engine generators came online. "Same principles as the systems you guys used for special operations. Of course, technology has advanced several centuries from when you guys used signal balloons and muskets."

Chief Cobbler's fingers moved cautiously at first, then gathered speed. "Not by much, it seems. Where'd you guys get your hands on this code, anyway? It was supposed to fall under that International Traffic in Arms Regulations national defense stuff."

Lenora shrugged. "Remember the massive defense budget cuts three administrations ago? Tons of military contract companies folded. Kenzie just waited for that one to go into liquidation, then bought up the intellectual property for a song. Defense Department thinks the company and its software are dead. Besides, ITAR only restricts sale or trade to other countries. Doesn't apply in space."

Haley shifted the canvas backpack on her shoulder. The others had argued, but she wasn't leaving it anywhere she couldn't see it. The bag contained everything she owned. Only two things had significant mass, her father's custom-built laptop and the other. Of course, at the moment nothing in the bag weighed anything at all. They were in zero-gee.

The young blonde watched the retired veteran as he familiarized himself with the system. Now she understood the mechanism behind each keyboard command and screen action. It was interesting knowledge to file away, but she had a more pressing question that needed answering.

"Why did everyone else peel off once we got here? I thought *this* was going to be our Alamo."

The engineer's eyes never left her monitor. "They already had their instructions. Each went where they're supposed to."

"It's a solid deployment, Haley." Chief Cobbler motioned with his left hand to the chair beside him, then pointed at the monitor. "See? By dispersing our people throughout the station, it decreases the chance any of them will run into either force. They're safer than we are."

That caught Cara Abrams' attention. "So why are we here and not with them?"

Jason spun his chair to look at her. "You specifically? Because you're their target."

"What?"

The old warrior nodded. "You're their primary target. Sorry if you haven't figured that out yet, but there's no way they'd let you out alive from this. What if you had footage of a pirate incursion led by Chinese and Russian troops on a private space station? Or you said something during your on-air commentary or god forbid UN tribunal testimony? Only one way to prevent that from happening."

Cara considered the argument, then nodded in return. "When you put it that way…. I knew several African warlords with the same mentality."

"So what did you do?" Haley asked as she slid into the workstation chair. Her backpack she placed against the divider, one foot in the straps to keep it in place. She started typing on the console keyboard, not looking away from her monitor as she practiced with the security software.

"Got my footage and got out of there."

Jason dipped his head briefly in respect. "I knew I liked you."

"And what about you, Chief?" Cara probed. "I've seen eyes like yours before. Why aren't you out there, ready to mix it up with our uninvited guests?"

"Maybe if I were fifty years younger. But I made it to this old age by learning a few things."

Lenora swiveled her chair to face him. "Oh really, Chief? Like what?"

"This station is massive," he began. "Tons of side corridors, walkways, shafts… it's a maze. And what's been interesting to watch is how that maze keeps changing shape."

"So it wasn't my imagination," Haley said from beside him. "The walls really are moving."

Cara Abrams shook her head. "Not the walls exactly. Right, Chief? It's the airlock doors we brought with us."

"Caught that, did you? So what's the other piece of this puzzle?"

"The other Stellar Nursery employees onboard…," Cara began, then stopped as the Chief shook his head. "Okay, Chief. Who else is moving the airlocks around?"

"Not who," replied Haley. "What. It's those freaky half-torso rover things, isn't it?

Lenora was impressed. "Well, hopefully the Chinese and Russians don't figure it out that fast. Then again, you have the displays and can see everything happening on the station."

Jason Cobbler raised his head and focused directly on Lenora. "You know that Kenzie's a bastard for what's about to happen, don't you?"

Lenora returned the hard gaze. "How's that, Master Chief? Didn't we warn every nation not to board or trespass? How're we to blame for their decision to attack an unarmed station?"

"'Unarmed', she says." Chief gave off a short bark-like laugh. He turned to Haley, then Cara. "Do you know what turns a tool into a weapon, ladies?"

Haley nodded as Cara shook her head.

"Human intent. That's it, there's nothing else. I can take a screwdriver and use it to screw two things together… or I can insert it into your temple. The tool never changed. My intent did."

He turned to glance at the security monitors, then faced them again. "That's what makes the whole 'no weapons in outer space' rule a lie from the get-go. Everything man-made up here in space is currently a tool… until someone intentionally uses it as a weapon."

Cara frowned. "You're saying this station isn't as 'unarmed' as suggested, Chief. Care to fill us in? How can those rovers be turned into weapons?"

Lenora turned back to the command console. "They already are… always have been, with one exception. As Chief Cobbler said, it wasn't our intent. They weren't designed or built as weapons, and they haven't been used for that purpose either. They have been, and are currently, doing exactly what they were designed for."

"From the look of these walls, they were 3D printed. Titanium, I'm guessing." Chief Cobbler spun his chair to face Lenora in time to catch her nod. "Titanium melts around sixteen fifty Celsius – that's about three thousand degrees Fahrenheit. Those little rovers have an attachment on their left arm for 3D printing, either a laser or plasma torch capable of melting titanium. But the outer hull of the station looks like silicon carbide – which melts just over twenty-three hundred Celsius, or about five thousand degrees Fahrenheit."

He pointed to the red dots signifying Russian boarders on the security monitor. "To summarize… unless they have armor plating, the spacesuits our pirates are wearing are made of cloth fabric and maybe an extremely thin layer of aluminum. The 3D torches on those rovers would cut those soldiers in half. They'd be dead before they could even feel it. So yes, technically this station is unarmed. But if we chose to use them… then technically, we have a very large army lying in wait."

Lenora's tone suggested she did not like the military. By extension, she didn't care much for the Chief, either. "It all comes down to intent. And we do not intend to use anything on this station as a weapon, Chief."

"The white dots just appeared," Haley interrupted, pointing to her monitor. Then she laughed. "Can't help myself, I have to say it. 'Houston, the Bear and Dragon have landed!'"

Cara shook her head. "Ohhh, that was bad. Really, really bad!"

Jason stared intently at the icons on his security monitor. "Well, well. There's an old military saying. No plan survives contact with the enemy. And another… the enemy always gets a vote."

Lenora stood and walked slowly from her workstation. A metallic clack-clack of magnetic boots grabbing and releasing sounded as she walked toward the security station. "What is it, Master Chief?"

"I expected the Chinese would show up with about the same numbers as the Russians… twelve, maybe fifteen troops. They didn't." Cobbler pointed to the white dots. "That's two squads of twelve, and they're coming at us from two different directions."

Lenora shook her head slowly. "Damn."

Chief already knew the answer, but the question had to be asked. "Sure you don't want to weaponize those rovers?"

"Not happening." The disdain Lenora held for everything military was obvious to everyone now. It could be read in her face, stone-cold with hatred, and in her body.

Like every warrior who ever wore a uniform, Jason Cobbler was extremely familiar with the look and attitude. It wasn't personal, even when it was personalized. War was abhorrent to most people, but with some it went beyond reason. What they could never contemplate and would never understand was that nobody hated war more than the warriors who fought them.

There was always a butcher's bill to pay. Jason Cobbler had paid it many times. He knew, even if Lenora refused to accept it, that this situation would require someone pay it again. There were too many armed opponents on the station for it to end otherwise.

He turned his head to look at Haley. She too bore the internal scars, had definitely paid her share of the butcher's bill. It had been a different battleground for her, true. But she bore the scars just like any other veteran.

The burden would fall on both of them again. They were the only ones who could offer the civilians on this station any kind of chance. The only ones who wouldn't freeze at the carnage they were all about to witness.

He sighed heavily, then said it. "Then will you trust Haley and me to run twenty or so of them?"

Lenora scanned his face for a long time, looking for any hint of deception. Finding none, she nodded. "You cannot – and I truly mean *cannot* – use them as weapons."

"Understood. Just making sure you're aware, you're going to lose a lot of them." He knew she would hear it differently, but he wasn't referring to the rovers.

Lenora turned and started clack-clacking back to her workstation. "There are over two thousand of them onboard, Chief. Feel free to use them all."

"What workstation controls them?"

The Chief Engineer sat down at her workstation, typed quickly on her keyboard. "The two you're at. I just gave you access to the maintenance rovers. They'll show up green on your monitors."

Jason turned to Haley and smiled. "Alright, pup. Time for you to play robot cop with me. We still have some time for driving practice before that second Chinese squad comes knocking on our door."

Haley turned to her station and touched the new icon on her screen. The station rover command screen opened. She started typing, tapped multiple icons on her screen, then typed some more. The rovers started coming online.

Chief wasn't surprised. "So you've run 'bots before?"

She simply nodded. "Yeah. Hacked tons of them. Mostly Uptown delivery rovers and drones. Only way to learn what pizza and burgers tasted like."

Cara Abrams understood the conflict that had just happened. Her years covering brush wars to battlefields told her what to expect. She also knew the current divide between them could shatter the fragile team they'd become on the flight to the station. It was time to lighten the mood.

In a tone dripping with innocence and fear, she played the

necessary part. "So what am I supposed to do?"

Haley turned toward Jason and whispered, "Is it the fear or adrenaline? I just can't help myself."

The young woman twisted her chair to face Cara. She had learned years ago to never trust what was said or how the person said it. The truth was always in the eyes. Cara's eyes were calm, not terrified as her voice suggested. There was a flicker of motion as the eyes darted to Lenora, then back to Jason.

Haley understood. She grinned, then spoke in a normal voice. "You're the damsel in distress, aren't you? You're supposed to put your hand on your forehead and exclaim 'Save me! Ohhhh, someone *please* save me!'"

Cara nodded, then smiled in return. "It's the fear, pup."

Jason burst into laughter. "You'll never get rid of that nickname now – even the reporter's using it. And it's both. Fear and adrenaline. Happens to everyone before the battle starts."

Haley swiveled back, then turned her head to face the Chief. "But it isn't happening to you. You're zen like a monk, sitting there all calm like that."

Chief Cobbler shook his head. "That's when I knew it was time to leave the Navy. Not feeling it... well, let's just say something else replaces it, and it ain't something you want to bring home to the missus."

"I knew I liked you too, Master Chief," Cara Abrams said softly.

"Don't get soft on me, girl," Jason tossed over his shoulder. "Now, you do what reporters are always doing around a battle. Stick your nose into everything and ask stupid questions at the worst time. Think you can handle that, Mizz Abrams?"

"It's Cara, Jason. And this is nothing. I've done this so many times before... you'll lose track of what nail color I'm wearing, I'll be changing them so much."

Lenora spoke, voice emotionless. "Feeds up on Corridor Twelve-Seventy. Contact between Reds and Whites imminent."

Although the engineer had kept emotion from her voice, she was actually irritated. She needed the laughter and banter to stop. All of them needed to be without emotion, just like her. This was simply a problem to solve. Factors to be considered, variables to be calculated. Just chess pieces that needed to be removed from the board, nothing more.

"What?" Haley looked at her screen, then to the Chief. "I don't understand."

Jason leaned over and pointed to her monitor. "The maze the others were creating? It looped back on itself. The Russian squad is about to walk right into the first Chinese squad."

Then he directed his voice to Lenora. "Remember what I said, Builder. Kenzie is a bastard for doing this."

"Well, at least we won't have to hear the screams." The engineer paused, surprised at the cold-blooded anger and vitriol in her voice. For a moment she had felt like the veteran was blaming her. Stop. Push the emotion away. "Nothing but vacuum in there."

The Chief knew the conflict raging in the Chief Engineer. It was a different wound of battle, one that injured those not actively fighting. He had seen it every time in scores of stateside mission operation centers. The young kids and old veterans who provided immediate updates from overhead drones, infrared sensing aircraft… the ones who saw the entire battlefield. The ones who also saw the carnage through every soldier's helmet camera. Hollywood could portray cheers and celebrations when missions ended, but it had never been his experience. Watching death from a distance didn't change its nature.

He felt compassionate pity for the woman at the command console. She was the only one in the room who had never seen the face of war. Haley bore scars from the street. Cara and her camera operator had survived assignments reporting from multiple battlefronts. He wasn't going to think about his, not now.

No, Lenora couldn't understand what the others already knew. There was no righteousness in battle. Nobody who participated was blameless, either. While Lenora might believe she was simply an observer, that she had no part in what was about to happen… she was mistaken. Soul-damagingly mistaken. Nobody would walk away from this clean.

A cold calm came over him, a familiar feeling he hadn't felt in decades. He hated it. With deft precision he adjusted his monitor. Using both hands, he shrunk the box showing hallway camera feed, then moved it to the upper right corner.

The blueprint of the level went to lower left. Larger blueprint of the entire station showing the other units' locations to upper left. Rover camera and control screen went to the lower right corner. The layout would let him tap on the screen he needed. It would enlarge and move to the center of the screen.

Haley matched his layout. He nodded to her and smiled. It was a wasted gesture, he knew. Her eyes were cold as his, already focused on the battle ahead. A part of him grieved to see it in one that young. Another part was glad to have a veteran sister in arms beside him. He returned his attention to the hallway feed. Focusing on the soldiers on the display, he assessed their tactical formation.

Both Chinese and Russian assault teams were moving at a decent pace. The bizarre landscape they traversed didn't seem to hinder them. The space station was built for spin, with the greatest gravitational pull occurring on the outer ring. To the invading soldiers, that meant everything was ninety degrees off kilter.

They walked on what would become a wall when the station spun up. On their left was what would become the floor, and to their right was the ceiling. Above them was the opposite wall. They bounded over doorways that, from their perspective, appeared to be rectangular holes cut into the floor. Above them gaped other doorways directly opposite the ones below.

The corridors were all unlit, which meant the soldiers relied on flashlights attached under weapon barrels. Chief understood the risk they were taking. Speed required the ability to see what was ahead. The infrared goggles attached to the side of their helmets were useless… the corridors were cold as the vacuum surrounding them.

That meant they had to use flashlights. Only problem was, like tracers from a machinegun, the flashlights worked both ways. They told you where you were going… and told your opponents where you were.

The Russians had split into two fire teams, each of six people. The first fire team stepped into the corridor and split into two groups of three. Each group hugged a wall, advanced quickly about three meters and then stopped. The rear soldiers remained standing, weapons pointed forward. The middle soldiers took a knee, and the front soldiers took a prone position. This allowed maximum firepower to be applied against any enemies in front of them. It was also the only reasonable formation. The long corridors didn't provide any cover to hide behind.

The second fire team advanced, leapfrogging in a single line past them before splitting and taking an identical formation three meters down the corridor. The rear fire team stood, preparing to move, when suddenly everyone froze in place. All flashlights were extinguished. Cobbler hadn't noticed any hand signals, so assumed the command had been given by radio. Made sense. Sound didn't carry in space, so voice commands were useless. Now that the lights were off, hand signals were useless as well.

The Chief had the benefit of knowing exactly where the Chinese troops were. He could see them with the second corridor camera. Like the Russians, the Chinese were relying on flashlights to illuminate the pitch-black halls. They didn't pause to take defensive positions or leapfrog fire teams. Instead they had split into two squads of six troops, each hugging a wall in file formation.

Their pace was slightly less than a jog. It would let them make up time and distance with the Russians who had landed earlier. Unnoticed, it would also give tactical surprise as they attacked the Russians from behind. Any other time it would've been a reasonable assumption. This time, though, the Chinese were wrong.

The Russians had begun to suspect something out of the

ordinary was happening. The normal tools for navigation – compass and global positioning – were useless on the station. That left them with environmental markers and pace count. While they didn't know that their path was being blocked and diverted by the station crew, they could tell the pace count was wrong. Based on the distance traveled, they should've reached the command center several hours ago. Their tactical deployment reflected their new cautious exploration of the station.

The Chinese had recently arrived. Their unobstructed pace didn't give them time to become cautious. Their lights hitting the corridor bend had alerted the waiting Russian troops. The rest was predictable. The first two Chinese soldiers moved into the bend and turned, their flashlights illuminating the two lines of soldiers waiting for them.

There were no muzzle flashes as the Russians fired, just the flicker of a tiny light near their front sights. Chief Cobbler wasn't surprised. Conventional projectiles like bullets wouldn't work in space. Newton's third law, for every action there is an equal and opposite reaction. A bullet fired in space caused the gun to become a rocket. The barrel became the engine, and the gas propelling the bullet was the source of rearward thrust. It would push the astronaut back with the same force of the bullet expelled.

Unlike the conventional battlefield, space didn't require heavy armor-penetrating bullets to kill. Modern spacesuits were thin fabric. Simply ripping holes in the suit would achieve the same result.

Chief considered the Russian weapons. They were probably miniature rail guns firing flechettes. A rail gun used electromagnets spaced along the barrel to accelerate a magnetized object. The flechettes were most likely tiny razor-sharp iron or neodymium arrowheads. They wouldn't cause recoil. They also wouldn't require the massive cryogenically-cooled super magnets of their artillery cousins. From the look of the weapons, Chief Cobbler was certain the power packs for the electromagnets were in the large magazines holding the flechettes.

Jason knew his mind was trying to distract him. It didn't matter. The view on his monitor was a live feed. Cyclops-eyed and godlike, the security camera looking down the Russian corridor captured the ambush in high definition.

The first blows of the first battle in space were as surreal and nightmarish as he expected. There was no sound. The flashlights of their teammates spotlighted the two Chinese soldiers, trapping them on a macabre stage. Space suits jerked about like marionettes controlled by children. Air blasted from flechette-sized holes in pressurized suits, creating a strobing horror movie motion. There was no blood. At least not yet.

Chief Cobbler was professionally impressed with how quickly the Chinese marines reacted to the ambush. The next two soldiers continued into the corridor bend. The magnetic boots kept the first two casualties anchored to the floor. Their fellow marines simply moved behind them, using them to provide protective cover.

Multiple barrel flashes from the Chinese weapons caught Jason by surprise. This was something new and unexpected. It took an eye-blink of time. Blue-white streaks raced toward the Russian soldiers. Then he understood.

The Chinese had approached Newton's third law from a different angle. They hadn't fought the action-reaction problem of bullets becoming rockets. They had simply made their bullets *into* rockets. Amazingly simple solution. The bullets were likely a simple metal tube filled with a solid propellant. Probably had one or more electric igniters within the weapon barrel. Simple feeding mechanism from the magazine would load a rocket bullet into the barrel. Trigger pull would activate the igniters which then ignited the propellant.

Chief had noticed the back-splash flame on the wall behind the Chinese marines every time they fired. Their weapons were essentially recoilless rifles. The barrel was open on both ends. He also saw the streaks of light as the bullets raced toward the Russian troops. Unlike light-weight flechettes that sliced through cloth, these were designed to punch through lightly armored targets and keep going.

And they did. A rocket bullet slammed into a kneeling Russian, bored through his chest and ripped out of his back. It continued, arrow-straight, to pass through the upper thigh of the soldier standing behind him. A glancing contact with the thigh bone changed its exit trajectory. The miniature rocket hit the wall at an angle and ricocheted. The new path missed the next Russian standing in line.

Cobbler expected the wounded Russians to jerk about as their suits depressurized. They didn't. He nodded in respect to the suit designers. A liquid, not a gas, escaped from the large holes in the suits. It foamed on contact with vacuum, forming a large cyst to seal the breach. The Russians had self-sealing suits.

The Russian team commander pulled a canister off his suit vest and threw it. Not directly at the Chinese marines, Chief Cobbler noticed, but at the opposite wall. It struck at an angle, bounced off and continued toward the back wall at a new angle. There it hit and rebounded again, moving into the dark hallway where the other Chinese troops waited.

"He missed," Haley said from her station.

"Nope," Chief replied. "That was a beautiful throw."

They both saw the magnesium-flare flash as the grenade detonated. It was blinding in the pitch-black hall. Glowing white-hot shrapnel sprayed in every direction. Most bounced harmlessly off the titanium walls.

The pieces that found human obstacles were a different story. Their jagged edges ripped into suit, then flesh. There they rested, half-molten steel waiting for human meat to cool them. It didn't take long. Negative two hundred degree vacuum helped.

A silent command was given. The Russian fire team on the left wall turned on their flashlights, then stood and advanced. They bounded quickly to the corridor bend, weapons directed down the dark hall. The only indication they were firing were the blinking lights behind their front sights.

The second fire team turned on their flashlights, then stood. They moved forward toward the two Chinese marines hiding behind their dead compatriots. No quarter was asked. None was given. The Russians continued firing until the bodies stopped moving.

"Enough of this shit." Chief Cobbler's voice was more animal growl than human. "E*nough*."

He pushed his spacesuited finger at the console, selecting the closest rover. A flight control stick and a joystick waited beside the keyboard. He grabbed one in each gloved hand, then yanked backward.

The security camera caught the motion as a rover withdrew from its charging station within the corridor wall. For a moment it was visible in the dim light from soldier flashlights. It was an ugly contraption, roughly a meter wide and two meters long. Six magnetic wheels gripped the floor. A rectangular chassis sat above them.

A human-like torso and head rose off the chassis. Twin arms expanded from its side. Then everything went black as the Russians pursued their quarry down the other hallway, taking their lights with them. Their dead and wounded they left behind.

The Chief pressed another key on the keyboard. Powerful headlights at the front of the rover switched on, illuminating the corridor. He tapped twice on the rover window on his monitor, maximizing it on his screen. Then he slammed both joysticks forward.

First-person driving in video games was an art most kids mastered in their teens. The old warrior was no exception. He guessed from the point-of-view that the camera was mounted on the rover torso's 'head'. Shifting between them confirmed that each joystick controlled direction and speed. A metal safety covered the trigger on his right flight controller-style joystick. He assumed the trigger was for the plasma cutter/welder on the left arm.

The image on his monitor showed the first soldier racing toward him on the screen. One magnetic boot still secured him to the floor. The other, like his body, floundered in space. The man was somehow still alive. Ice-crystal air and freezing spears of blood streamed from the hole in the left arm of his suit.

Chief Cobbler scanned the suit. Several foam cysts sealed other rocket bullet holes on the left side of the spacesuit. Assuming the bullets had gone straight through, none of the injuries were fatal. Just the one on the soldier's arm.

The Russian had placed his right hand over the entry hole. His gloved fingers moved and flexed, attempting to reach the exit hole. Too much arm muscle and the thick suit made it a vain effort. Life-preserving air continued to blast into vacuum.

Jason rubbed his thumb across the wheel on the flight control stick. It opened the human-like fingers on the rover's right hand. He then pushed both joysticks forward, slamming the rover into the soldier. The magnetic boot released its grip on the floor. The man floated freely.

The old veteran pressed the rover arm control button on the flight control, then pushed the controller forward. This extended the rover arm. A few twists and adjustments, then he had the rover hand where he needed it.

"I'm sorry, buddy," Chief said softly. Then he rubbed the wheel on the flight controller in the opposite direction. The rover hand closed around the soldier's arm and squeezed. As he continued rubbing the controller wheel, the grip tightened.

Lenora had turned on the main screens in the station Command Center. They showed the same scene as the Chief's screen. Everyone else in the room watched as the rover hand closed onto the space suit arm… and kept closing. The headlights showed the Russian soldier's face clearly as he silently screamed in pain.

"Jason!" Lenora yelled. "Jason, stop! You're killing him!"

"Come on, you bastard," Chief growled, his face set and focused. "Come on, come on, come… yes!"

"Master Chief Cobbler, step away from that board!" Lenora's fingers pounded across keys on her console. "I'm locking you out. You animal, I told you, no weapons!"

"I'm sorry, Marine. You were just following orders. But now…" He released both joysticks, pausing only to wipe something wet from his right eye. Then he took control of both joysticks again and gently pulled them backward. "…now you're out of this fight."

The rover started to move backward, then stopped. A red bar flashed on the Chief's monitor, text simply stating 'Workstation Locked'. The confrontation between the Master Chief and the Chief Engineer might've continued, were it not for the Russian soldier.

The spacesuited man raised the rifle in his right hand. He placed the weapon across his body, barrel pointed toward the rover head. All eyes in the station Control Room watched, confused, as the weapon was shifted again.

A sling bound the weapon to the soldier, running from his waist to a clip snapped onto the rifle. The man shifted the rifle down so he could grab the barrel with his left hand. His right hand moved down, pressing open the clip. As if acknowledging an ancient battlefield tradition, he removed the sling clip and tossed the weapon away. Then he turned his helmet to face the rover camera and bowed his head once.

Jason turned his head to Haley. His voice was soft, wounded. "Okay, pup. You don't have to get into the thick of it. I'll handle that. But I need you to take control of this rover and direct it to one of our groups. He's surrendered, won't be a threat to them. If we don't get him to a pressurized room, he ain't gonna make it."

"You sonuvabitch, you broke his arm," Lenora snarled from the command station. "That rover hand has thirty tons of grip. You callously used it all to shatter his arm!"

"No, Lenora." Cara's voice was soft and cold. "You're wrong. Chief applied a tourniquet."

The correspondent didn't take her eyes off the main screen as Lenora spun her chair and faced her. She continued in the same tone, cold as the vacuum surrounding them. "That soldier wasn't bleeding out of blood, Lenora. He was bleeding out of *air*. A tourniquet was the only way to save his life."

Cara turned her head then and stared directly at the Chief Engineer. Her eyes were as unforgiving as her voice. "This is what it looks like, Lenora Davis. This is *war*. The dead are dead, but the wounded *scream*. And they don't *stop screaming* until someone helps them, or until they join the dead. Either accept that and help, or get the hell out of the way."

"But he—"

"Saved the man's life. Hell, Lenora, even the Russian understands that." Cara crossed her arms. "Now he's dying. Not because of anything the Chief has done. Because you're killing him. Look."

Lenora saw there was no use arguing with the reporter. She turned to the others in the room, saw the disapproval on their faces. Then she turned to the main monitor. The young Russian looked back at her. He was young, just barely out of his teens.

His face showed confusion and fear. He did not understand why the rover had stopped. Slowly he raised both hands in the universal gesture of surrender. When that failed to get the rover moving, he brought both hands together in prayer. Resignation and hopelessness slowly settled on his face. He closed his eyes.

"Give Chief back control of that damn rover, Lenora. Let him save that kid."

Lenora heard, but her mind couldn't comprehend. It made no sense. Soldiers were cruel animals. Killers who enjoyed killing. Everyone knew that. Everyone. Her parents, who ridiculed military euphemisms like 'collateral damage' to describe slaughtering civilians. Her college friends, who protested with her at the airports when soldiers returned home from the latest war. They spat the words as soldiers passed. Baby killers. Nazi fascists. Murderers.

Yet the logical part of her mind, the engineer part, couldn't argue with what Chief had done. Cara Abrams had seen it too. The old man had applied a tourniquet, nothing more. She glanced down at her monitor, tapped the screen to show the rover hand pressure setting. It was sufficient to seal the space suit. It was also far less than the Chief could've used. If Jason was truly cruel, emotionless… a heartless mass-murdering *soldier*… he could've done far worse.

Lenora sighed. Her politics weren't going to save the soldier's life. Only time and attention would, and she was wasting both. She tapped commands on the keyboard. "Okay, Chief. You have control again."

She knew she should've said more, but she couldn't. Her core beliefs wouldn't allow it. War was wrong. If mankind did away with armies, there would be no war. Everyone would have to come together. Compromise. It was the only path to peace.

A new realization shocked her. While she could still hate war, she didn't have to hate the warriors. Especially the man on her left. She turned, about to speak, then stopped. There was something wrong with him, she could see it. Something had broken inside. Something she broke.

Jason Cobbler was frozen. He had spent over two decades on countless battlefields. Carried too many friends home slung over his shoulder. Some made it. Many didn't. Yet he kept going back, time and time again. He thought he had known why. Now he wasn't certain. It had never been about medals or promotions. Definitely not for ticker tape parades and cheering crowds.

He had joined for one simple reason… to defend those who couldn't defend themselves. His chosen profession meant he had taken life when necessary. It was a small comfort knowing nobody else would have to carry that burden. He could.

Not even when the dead came to visit his dreams, forced him to relive the moments he took their lives, had anyone made Lenora's accusation. Never before had he been accused of being *cruel*.

"Enough, dear." He raised his head as the voice rang in his ears. For a moment he was at home sitting in his chair. In a motion familiar as yesterday, his wife placed a marker in her book, closed it in a gentle punctuation and turned to him. *"You're not that kind of man. Never would've married you if you were. So stop it, love. You're scaring the girl. She needs you now."*

Then he was back. He blinked, disoriented. A woman's voice sounded, heavy with concern. He turned his head toward it.

"I have him, Chief. You can let go now." Haley reached out, touched him on the arm with her suited hand. "Give me control of the rover, Chief. *I've got him.*"

The girl. Like waves crashing against a reef, everything came back to him. The battle wasn't over and she needed him. He smiled, nodded, then turned back to his console. Tapped in the commands giving her rover control. "Roger, pup. You have the stick. I'll grab the next one."

The Command Crew didn't see any more of the actual battle. They watched, often in horror, as the Master Chief maneuvered rovers into the field of mangled spacesuits. Sometimes he would take an action, withdraw the rover and hand control over to Haley. Most of the time, though, he just continued moving his rover forward. Finally, there were no more visible figures ahead in the headlight-illuminated corridor, alive or dead. Everything was behind the Chief's rover.

Jason took both hands off the joysticks. "I counted twenty-four. Can anyone confirm?"

"Twenty-four," Haley stated from beside him. "Twelve Russian, twelve Chinese."

"That's what I counted too," Cara reiterated from behind them.

The Chief's voice was heavy with exhaustion. "How many…"

"Enough, Chief," Cara replied with gentle reassurance. "You saved enough."

Jason covered his face with both gloved hands for a moment, then another. Abruptly, before he could feel the weight of lives lost, he pulled his hands away. "Alright. That leaves the second Chinese team. Anyone have eyes on them?"

Cara didn't even glance at the Security monitor. "Corridor Six-Twenty. They fired on two of our groups who were putting up airlock barriers. No casualties, but the Chinese aren't stopping."

"ETA?"

"Way they're moving, they'll be here in an hour." Cara's tone suggested she'd been running a constant mental calculation while the others worked the previous fight.

Jason turned to the woman at the command console. "You're commander of this station, Builder Lenora Davis. What do you want to do? Abandon it? Or will you let me fight? 'Cause there ain't no other choices."

Lenora was still reeling from the previous battlefield. Shock bled into her voice. "They slaughtered each other."

"They did." Chief wasn't going to sugarcoat it. "That was their job, their mission. Take this station. Remove any obstacles to that objective with lethal force. If we were only facing those two groups, they would've failed. But we aren't, Lenora. There's one group left."

"And they're heading straight for us," Haley added. She pointed to her screen. "Creating loops and switchbacks isn't going to work. They've used explosives to blast through the last two airlock barriers we put up. I'd say they've figured out the station's layout and they're coming here."

"To kill us," Cara added.

Lenora slowly shook her head. The two groups had attacked each other with single-minded viciousness. There would be no negotiating with the last group. No chance for compromise. Peace of any kind was simply out of the question and she knew it. The last battle had hammered that point home far more effectively than any college lecture.

She swiveled her chair and looked at the others. It was obvious what they thought. What surprised her was that she was in agreement. "We can't abandon ship. Not after all *that*."

Jason nodded once. "Then we fight."

He turned to his monitor and tapped the screen. The station map moved to the center and increased in size. His eyes scanned the blue outlines of corridors and branching hallways. Another quick tap on the screen maximized the security camera observing the Chinese marines. He watched for a moment before nodding, then downsized the camera screen.

"Haley, I need you to start prepositioning rovers here," he said, poking a suited finger at the screen. "Then here and here. Pull them out of these other corridors. I'm gonna need about twenty at each location."

Haley studied the map, then grinned. "You want them in the rooms above, I assume. The Chinese aren't looking up at the ceiling."

"Yep. Just keep them out of sight. Rover wheel magnets will hold them to the room walls if you need to get creative."

"Got it, Chief."

Then Jason turned to the others. "And if any of you are squeamish… I suggest you don't watch. 'Cause this ain't gonna be pretty."

"Don't kill them, Chief," Lenora pleaded. "If you can… please don't kill them."

Chief Cobbler nodded once, acknowledging the station commander's order. "We'll incapacitate and subdue, Lenora. But if any of them reach our airlock doors, we'll defend with lethal force. I need you to understand that."

She closed her eyes for a moment, as if in silent prayer, then nodded. Her soul was heavier when eyes opened again. "Agreed. Let's pray it doesn't come to that."

It became a game of stealth and darkness. Jason and Haley couldn't turn on the rover headlights without warning the Chinese of their approach. Instead they drove in darkness, keeping themselves oriented using the green dots on the station map. That allowed them to sneak up behind the Chinese formation. The tactic would've never worked on Earth. Atmosphere would've carried the sound of rover motors.

But this was space. Zero gravity and magnetic wheels allowed the pair to drive on walls, bypassing the dark doorway holes on the floor and ceiling. The Chief managed to grab the last Marine in line without his squad noticing. The other soldiers continued their advance as the rover hands closed around the Marine's upper thighs and clamped. A command from the flight controller caused the rover arms to raise, lifting the Marine above the rover's head.

The man's spacesuit made torso twisting almost impossible. All he could do was fire his rifle blindly behind him in hopes of hitting the chassis or severing one of the rover's arms. Instead, he ran out of ammunition.

The capture was puzzling. Jason considered possibilities as he drove the rover onto the wall and carried his prize away. Either the Chinese were enforcing strict radio silence or their radios weren't working. The first option didn't make sense. Any soldier would've broken radio silence to warn their teammates about the threat from the rear.

"Lenora," he said, eyes focused on his screen. "Are you running jammers?"

The delay in her response was also puzzling. He heard her whisper briefly to someone before she replied aloud to his question.

"We don't have jammers on the station, Chief. Let's just be happy their radios aren't working at the moment. Leave it at that."

"Never trust miracles in combat," Jason advised. "Soon as you do, they'll disappear. And that's when things get really nasty."

The Chief moved the flight control joystick forward, forcing the rover to climb up the wall and into one of the empty ceiling rooms. He hated this part of the plan. It was a necessary response to the time constraint they faced. The Chinese boarders were too many, and they were moving too fast. He couldn't just hand off rover control to Haley anymore. She was needed in the fight. Capturing every attacker required both of them driving rovers into the fray.

"Hate to do this to you, Marine. But it's better than the alternative," he said aloud. Then he shut down the rover power, locking it in place in the pitch-black room. "Dropped the package in room 237, Lenora. Would you turn the lights on in five minutes or so? Don't want to leave him trapped in the dark."

"Can do," Lenora replied. "Hope he enjoys his time with Miss Massey."

"Miss Massey?" Haley didn't understand.

"Old horror movie reference," Jason briefly explained. "Room 237 was haunted by a ghost who loved guys in uniform."

"Ah, I see. We're playing classic show trivia." Haley grinned beside him. "Well, your next rover is up. I think it's a Hyperdine 120-A2, so you'll need to be careful with it."

Chief grinned back. "Why? Because the A2's always were a bit twitchy?"

"Right. Just wish we had a rolled up magazine, we could make short work of these guys."

"You kids spent too much time in front of the television," Lenora interjected. "So use the force, Luke, and get moving."

"As you wish," Haley replied with a straight face.

"You guys are making my head hurt," Cara said from behind them. "Please stop, or I'll be forced to start quoting lines from musicals. Starting with, *I am the very model of a modern Major General.*"

"That's also in a sci-fi show, Cara." Haley tapped the rover icon on her screen. "Doesn't help your argument any."

"No way," Cara argued. "I'm talking real entertainment, not cheesy sci-fi."

Haley simply smiled as she scanned the rover readout. "Look it up. Series called Babylon 5. Kind of applicable here, as it was about a space station. So feel free to sing it if you wish."

"Just be warned," cautioned Chief Cobbler. "It begins the kind of conversation that can only end in a gunshot."

Jason and Haley used the same tactic to disable the next two boarders. They trailed the Chinese team in silence and darkness. When the invaders turned a bend in the corridor, they plowed into the last two from behind.

The soldiers were slammed into the curving corridor wall in front of them. Haley grabbed one by an arm and a leg, holding him in midair above her rover. The Chief simply drove his rover onto the chest of the other, then pinned both arms.

After that, it became a slug-fest. The Chinese, now alerted that someone was picking off their squad members, became jumpy. Their commander must've realized they no longer had radio communications. He split the remaining nine marines into two groups. Using hand signals, he ordered them to assume a V formation and a diamond formation. The officer took the lead position, followed by two rows of two marines. At a short distance behind them, the second group was led by a marine walking point, a single row of two marines, and a solo marine walking rear guard.

That Marine was ripped apart by his own squad's weapons fire. The Chief and Haley weren't anywhere near the groups when it happened. They watched it through the security camera feed.

Left alone at the rear of the formation, the man had started jumping at shadows. His fear forced him to close the distance with the group until he was too close to the others. Likely his movement was caught out of the corner of the opposite Marine's visor. That marine turned and fired. On seeing the bullet-rocket trails and backsplash, the second soldier spun and fired at the dimly illuminated figure behind him.

The invaders didn't even stop. They left the riddled spacesuited corpse of their teammate behind and continued moving forward.

"That helps us," Chief Cobbler stated coldly. "They're whistling past the graveyard. Let's use that to our advantage."

Lenora looked up from her station and focused on the old warrior. "What do you have in mind, Chief?"

"Can you randomly turn on and off the corridor lights? Preferably by section. Let's put their heads on a swivel, confuse them with light and shadow. But let me grab something first."

Lenora cocked her head. "I'm not going to like this, am I, Chief?"

"No." Jason said it as a cold statement of fact. "But they'll like it even less. When I give the signal, I need lights to flicker where the commander is first. Then strobe ceiling and room lights backwards toward the last two in the rear. Then turn everything off, back on for a second, then total darkness."

Haley shook her head once. "That's cold, Chief."

"Psychological warfare 101," the retired veteran replied. "Pretty basic stuff."

Chief tapped his screen, selecting a rover. Using the flight controller and joystick, he drove it from the ceiling room where Haley had hidden it. Unlike the Chinese, he knew his enemy's location. The quick flash of headlights in the darkness wasn't a great risk. It identified his target, the floating corpse of the Chinese Marine. Using the flight joystick and its controls, he grabbed the spacesuit with both rover hands.

"Ready, Haley?" Jason drove the rover along the wall, only slowing when he reached the next corridor bend taken by the Chinese troops.

"Ready," Haley replied. Her screen showed the view from the rover she had activated. It was looking straight down through a ceiling doorway. The first row of the Chinese V formation could be seen walking beneath the rover camera.

"Ready, Lenora?" Chief increased his rover's speed to maximum, racing the rover along the corridor wall. The backs of dark figures could be seen ahead as the Chinese soldiers continued their advance forward.

"I'm ready, Chief." Lenora's tone didn't sound pleased.

"What's Newton's second law?" Jason asked in a normal voice.

Haley responded from beside him. "An object in motion tends to stay in motion...."

"Unless acted on by an external force," Lenora finished.

Chief Cobbler chuckled. "Newton would've loved space."

He pressed a button on the flight controller, then ran his thumb across the wheel controlling the rover's hands. That released the dead Chinese Marine's suit. Then he pulled back on both joysticks to begin braking. When the speed had decreased enough, he drove the rover into the next ceiling doorway.

"Best guess here, three… two… one." Master Chief Cobbler's voice was businesslike and steady. "Now, Lenora."

"Firing." Lenora hit the execute button she had set when she programmed the lighting sequence.

Everyone in the Command Center watched the scene play out on the main monitor. The first hallway lights flashed on beside the Chinese commander in the lead. Then off, as the next set of lights flashed on the first row of two Marines. Off again, then the next set. The sequence continued until the last row of Marines were illuminated.

The unexpected runway-like strobing effect of the lights grabbed the attention of the Chinese troops. They turned to follow the light. It took a moment for their eyes to readjust to darkness when the last hallway light disappeared. By that time, the object racing toward them from behind was now in their midst.

To those in the front of the formation, unaware one of their group had been killed by the others, the spacesuited figure likely looked like an armed attacker. The look of terror on the faces of the last two soldiers suggested they were seeing something supernatural.

Regardless of what they thought was happening, the reaction was predictable. Weapons rose and fired at the figure. Shock and fear adjusted their aim. The defensive formation became a circular firing squad. Some of the rocket-bullets ripped into the floating figure, while others flew wild and ricocheted off the walls. Several found new targets. Two more Marines, bodies locked into place by magnetic boots, spasmed and jerked as rocket-bullets tore into their suits.

"Now, Haley."

Chief drove his rover out of the dark ceiling doorway and toward the panicked soldiers. The closest was one of those obviously hit. His body had bent backwards until his helmet hit the floor, then rebounded. Jason grabbed it as the body floated upward again. Using the rover arms, he pulled until magnetic boots lost their grip on the floor. He accelerated the rover, then abruptly hit the brakes and released the body. Air from multiple holes in the suit gave it a bizarre spin and motion. It jerked and twisted as it floated toward the other troops.

That started another fusillade of firing. Chief used the confusion to move his rover to the last surviving rear guard. One rover hand grabbed the man's weapon arm while the other grabbed his thigh. Like a spider, he drove the rover in reverse up the wall and into one of the dark ceiling rooms above.

"How we doing, Haley?" he asked, waiting patiently for the man to expend all his ammunition.

"I have mine," she replied, pointing toward her screen.

She had moved her rover out of the ceiling room, then extended the arms to grab the closest soldier. One hand clamped onto the soldier's weapon. Quick adjustment to close the hand grip and the weapon was destroyed. The other rover hand came down and rotated backward, then closed on the spacesuit helmet.

Then she retraced her steps, withdrawing the rover back up into the ceiling room. The flashlight on the twisted weapon illuminated the man's face within his helmet. He nodded once behind the cracked faceplate to show he understood his situation. The soldier opened both hands and raised them in surrender.

Haley released the rover grip on the weapon. A quick adjustment put the flashlight in the rover's grasp. She spun the control wheel, crushing the light. The action was done partly to conceal the prisoner from his comrades. The other part was psychologically defensive. She didn't want to see if the crack on the faceplate would grow.

"That's four more down," Chief said in his gruff voice. "Four to go. And they're almost here."

A quick tap of commands on her keyboard shut down Haley's rover. She swiveled in her chair to face the old warrior beside her. "I've been thinking about that. They're currently in Corridor Seventeen. If they continue straight on that route, they'll hit Corridor

One. That leads right here.”

Jason tapped on his screen to maximize the station layout. “I see it. What did you have in mind?”

“See that last intersection, where Seventeen runs into Two? What if we welded airlocks on the Corridor Two sides?”

“That would force them straight where we don’t want them to go,” Lenora objected. “Can’t we just duplicate what we just did? Get them to kill themselves off?”

“Won’t work.” Using his thumb and forefinger, Chief zoomed in on the intersection that had piqued Haley’s interest. “An ambush like that only works once. Now they’ll be looking for it.”

“We need to separate or isolate them, Lenora,” Haley explained. “Good chance at least one of them has explosives. We have no way to tell which one might be carrying.”

“I doubt it’s the officer,” Chief added. “They tend to shy away from things that could mess up their pretty uniforms.”

Haley swiveled her chair, aiming it toward the airlocks at the back of the room. “So if one of the other three is a demo guy, they’ll blow our outdoor airlock door.”

Lenora nodded. “Since it’s pressurized to keep them from just opening the door, the blast would likely take out the inner door too.”

Haley finished her argument. “Then they just saunter in and start shooting.”

“Which would be bad,” Cara said from behind them. She laughed, trying to relieve the tension. “Are there any airlocks nearby?”

“They’re in Corridor Two.” Haley pointed at the main screen. “The *Liberty* crew stacked them in the hallway near the ship when we got here. Just in case.”

Cara laughed again. “Glad you were paying attention.”

“Or we could just depressurize the airlock,” Lenora argued.

“Which would work if the demo guy only has one set of explosives,” Haley countered. “No, we need to remove the explosives off the board completely.”

"By welding airlock doors in that intersection?" Lenora shook her head. "I'm still not following."

"I see it," Chief said. "Brilliant, if it works. Where you getting the oxygen, Haley?"

The young woman beamed. "Tanks are sitting beside the airlock doors. Weren't you guys paying attention?"

Chief Cobbler tapped the intersection on his screen. "So we put up four airlock doors to seal the intersection with the Chinese in it. Pump air into the room we just created. The demolition expert will know better than to set off a charge in that enclosed a space."

Lenora wasn't giving up. "And if he did?"

"A grenade doesn't just kill with shrapnel. It also kills using blast overpressure. Out to five meters." Jason swiveled his chair to face the engineer. "Setting off a demolition charge in a small pressurized room will immediately increase that room's air pressure. Not a good risk."

"So it increases air pressure, so what?"

"You're still not getting it," Haley said, spinning her chair to face Lenora. "Ever squeeze a grape? That's what an explosive does, except the grape is your chest and insides. If that doesn't immediately kill you, it'll definitely shatter your helmet faceplate… and there's nothing but vacuum behind the door you just blew up."

Chief Cobbler turned to the young woman beside him. He was curious. "Where did you learn about explosives, Haley?"

The Blight veteran turned her head to stare at her screen, face cold and hard. She wasn't going to mention her knowledge of bomb building. Instead, she recounted an annual occurrence. "Uptown uses natural gas for their pretty little fireplaces. Pipes run from the country through us. So every winter, there's always a bunch of stupid-ass kids who try tapping into the lines."

The room fell silent. Chief simply nodded, then turned back to his station. "Then you know firsthand what happens. It's a good plan, Haley. Let's get it done."

He tapped his screen to activate a rover, then pressed a key on his console to turn on the headlights. The enemy forces were still far enough away. They wouldn't see the lights. On his left, he saw Haley Brandt match his actions.

"Keep an eye on their movement, Lenora," Chief ordered. "Let us know when they get close to the intersection."

"Roger, Chief." Lenora Davis sounded very subdued.

Cobbler waited until he had grabbed the first airlock door before he spoke again. "Can I suggest a modification to your plan, Haley?"

"Sure," she replied in her normal voice. "What'cha got?"

"Once you've welded your door in place and stacked up a couple oxygen tanks, how about we back the rover up against the door? Just in case they brought along a cutting torch or something."

Haley turned her head and saw the concerned look on the old veteran's face. She smiled, for a moment appearing like an innocent young woman with little life experience. Her eyes told a different story. When the man opposite her didn't change his gaze, she released the illusion. "I'm fine, Chief. Been through worse than this."

His eyes scanned her face, then he nodded. "I see that. So let's save these Chinese idiots before they reach this room, shall we?"

Haley frowned, not understanding. "Save them?"

"Yeah," Chief replied, grinning as he turned back to his screen. "Because only God can save them if they make it through that door."

The young woman laughed, the sound almost angelic. It was the only remnant of innocence still left to her. She returned her focus to the task at hand. Using the rover arm, she laid a third oxygen canister on the top deck of her rover. Then she moved the rover forward to grab the waiting airlock door.

Time ticked away. For a moment it appeared they would be successful in preparing their trap. Two airlock doors had been welded into place on the Corridor Two sides of the intersection. A second set of tack-welds had sealed the airlocks themselves so they couldn't be opened.

Chief Cobbler had almost reached the intersection with the third airlock when Lenora announced the Chinese were within eyesight of him. Haley had just turned into the corridor behind them, but was still too far away to seal the trap. If he welded the airlock in place they would see the trap and reverse course. The veteran needed to hide the door and the rover.

There wasn't much room to maneuver. The rover had carried the airlock door at an angle down the corridors. Only way to do it, as the doors were wide as the hallway. He moved the rover to the empty charging station near the intersection.

The next part was challenging. He rotated the wheeled chassis using the left joystick. Simultaneously, he rotated the torso part of the rover to the right. Next he moved the rover forward into and up the wall charging station. Slowly moving the rover hands to maintain contact with the airlock door, he rotated the torso until it was aligned with the chassis.

The automated charging procedure took over. The arms withdrew to the torso sides as the torso slowly lowered into its place on the chassis. The large airlock door followed the motion until it came to rest against the hallway wall. Then the door cover of the charging unit slid into place. To the Chinese soldiers, it would appear as if they had interrupted people emplacing the airlock door.

"Nicely done," Lenora said, nodding to the Chief.

"Let's hope it works." He glanced at Haley's monitor to see her progress.

She was driving blind, or so it appeared. Carrying the airlock at an angle while driving along the wall was a definite challenge. Using the green dot on her screen for reference as she drove made it even more so. A dim light gradually appeared on her screen as she closed the distance with the Chinese troops.

"This is going to be close," Chief said, once again the master of understatement.

Haley's eyes were locked onto her screen. "Tell me when you're moving, Chief. Not much room in that intersection. We don't want both doors colliding."

"Gonna be hard enough doing this in the dark." Chief placed both hands on the joysticks.

Lenora tapped the keyboard on her console. "I can turn on the intersection overheads—"

"No!" Both rover drivers yelled simultaneously.

Lights blazed in the intersection just as the Chinese troops reached it. Helmets turned left, right. The officer waved his arm forward, then leaped toward the opposite end of the trap. The three behind him paused, then crouched to jump as well.

"Well, hell." Chief yanked backwards on both joysticks.

The sliding door had barely cleared when the rover rolled out of its charging station. It was remarkable the Chief remembered the sequence of joystick control buttons. The torso rose and twisted as both arms moved to grab the airlock door. Robot fingers closed around the metal grips on the door. The chassis rotated as the arms extended, leveling the door edge like a plow.

The Chinese officer used his forward momentum to slide along the door. Before it could be raised, he was past and into the hallway beyond. The three remaining marines weren't as lucky. The edge of the door caught them at waist height, knocking them backwards toward the corridor behind them.

Chief Cobbler pushed the plow edge of the airlock down until it scraped the floor. Then he extended the left rover arm forward, straightening the door. A pull of both joysticks reversed the rover until the airlock was even with the walls. The trap had been set on his end. Then the Chief's screen went black as the escaped officer opened fire from behind and destroyed the rover.

Haley saw the three Chinese soldiers floating backwards toward her. Ironically it was the light from the intersection that allowed her to react quickly. She crab-walked the rover hands along the angled airlock as she drove the rover off the corridor wall. Then she lowered the airlock edge.

Sparks flew behind as the door scraped along the ceiling. She eyeballed the angle, then adjusted her rover position. A wicked smile crept across her lips as she pushed both joysticks forward and increased speed. "For every action…."

The Chief had already tapped his screen to activate another nearby rover. He watched the corridor security camera feed as the officer bounded past. Then he pulled the rover out of its charging station and started heading it toward the dead rover. Only then did he glance over at Haley's screen to see what she was doing. His eyes calculated force, angle and trajectory. Then he laughed. "That's gonna hurt."

The edge of the airlock door caught the three soldiers in the upper back of their suits. Then Haley yanked both joysticks backwards, rapidly applying the brakes. The three spacesuits bent, then recoiled in the direction of the Chief's airlock door. A white stream of freezing air leaked from the air tanks on one of the suits, throwing the soldier into an unpredictable spin.

"…there is an equal and opposite reaction," Haley finished her earlier comment. "Guess only that officer listened in their zero-gee combat class."

Her rover had barely moved into the intersection. She quickly lowered its arms. The front edge of the airlock door descended until it reached the intersection floor. Keeping both joysticks in their position forced the rover into reverse. A quick glance at the security camera feed from the intersection told her when the airlock was level with the corridor wall. Then she stopped the rover.

The young woman rotated the lower chassis until it was parallel with the wall. Then, holding the airlock with one hand, she used the plasma torch on the other arm to begin welding. The trap was completely set.

Chief Cobbler's new rover arrived at the opposite airlock soon after. The dead rover remained where it had died. Large chunks of metal were missing from chassis and torso where the officer's rocket-bullets had struck. The obstruction was both boon and bane. It still held the airlock door in place, but it also meant Cobbler had to maneuver around it as he started welding.

Haley typed on the console keyboard, powering down her rover. Then she tapped on her screen, selecting one of the rovers. Laden with oxygen tanks, it waited outside the trap in Corridor Two. She turned on the headlights. Her fingers tapped on the keyboard, then mashed control buttons on the flight controller. The right rover arm raised and extended, hand opening as she moved it to grab one of the tanks.

"How's it going, Chief?" she asked, rotating the tank and placing it beside the emergency oxygen feed connection on the airlock door.

"Halfway done, pup."

She lifted the air hose from its bracket on the airlock, then screwed the free end onto the oxygen tank. The other end was already attached to the door. "Hurry it up, old timer. One of the guys in there is running out of air."

"Well, you shouldn't have hit him so hard, huh?" Chief retorted. "Nasty way to go, though. Trying to breathe vacuum can't be good on the constitution."

"That's cold. After you finish your nap over there, Rover 317 is ready for you to rotate the oxygen valve. I'm activating 319 now." Haley tapped on the keyboard again, powering down the rover. Then she pressed the screen icon for the second rover. Quick key taps and it came to life on the opposite side of the trap.

"I'm not the one napping," Cobbler replied. "That would be this stupid rover sitting in the way. Magnetic wheels won't release, or I'd just throw it down the hall."

Haley duplicated her actions and quickly attached an oxygen tank to the second airlock. "Well, I guess you shouldn't have let it get turned into Swiss cheese, huh?"

"Hey, guys?" From behind them, Cara raised an arm and pointed at the main monitor. "Does anyone have eyes on the Chinese officer? Because he seems to have disappeared."

And then they heard it. A distinct bang on one of their outer airlock doors. Then another bang, and another. All heads in the Control Room slowly turned to scan the rear wall and the two airlock doors standing there.

Haley's voice broke the silence. "Guess we found him."

"Alright boys and girls. Time to put an end to this." Master Chief Cobbler stood, then grabbed his helmet from its rack on the side of the security station.

Lenora swiveled to look up at him. "Chief, what are you doing?"

"From the banging, I'm betting he's out of ammo. If he had any explosives, he would've used them to free his three buddies." The old veteran pulled his helmet onto his head, faceplate open. "Right now he's in one of two corridors leading to this room. We can't take the chance he'll double back, maybe run into one of his dead buddies who *does* still have ammo and explosives."

"Jason, it's a risk…." Cara looked at him askance, then slowly shook her head.

"All life is a risk. I could die on Earth. I could die up here. Doesn't matter. When your number's up, it's up." He grinned, then closed the helmet visor. "Commo check. Lenora, you hearing me?"

His voice was clear through the Control Room speakers. Lenora pressed a button on her console. Her voice sounded through the speakers as well. "Roger, Chief. Loud and clear."

Jason stepped away from his workstation and walked until he passed Cara Abrams. There he stopped and turned to face them all. "So here's what's going to happen. Haley, open the valve on that oxygen tank, let's get those boys some air. Jump to the other rover, do the same. Then take over my rover and finish welding the seal."

Haley simply nodded and swiveled the chair to face her workstation again.

"And Haley?"

"Yes, Chief?" She didn't even turn, simply remained focused on her task.

"Now would be a good time to open your personal items bag." The speakers carried the veteran's chuckle.

The young woman leaned to one side and grabbed the small backpack she had carried with her from Earth. One hand still controlled the rover flight controller while the other opened the bag. "You want it?"

The spacesuited figure shook his helmeted head. "No. If he gets past me...."

"Understood." Haley pulled a vacuum-proof bag from the backpack and laid it on her lap. The backpack went back on the floor. Briefly using both hands, she unsealed the package and pulled out two gunmetal blue items. "How'd you know?"

"We're too much alike, pup. That, and I'd recognize that bulge anywhere."

The young woman from the street slapped the magazine into the butt of the Model 1911 Colt automatic. Then she pulled and released the slide to chamber a round.

"What the hell?!!" Lenora half-rose from her chair. "You brought a *gun* onboard?"

Haley's face had turned ice cold, then broke for a moment as she smiled. Like her eyes, it wasn't pleasant by any measure. "Never leave home without it."

"Lenora," Chief continued without skipping a beat. "I need you to call up the security cameras outside for both airlock doors. Put them up on the main monitor. Once we know which one he's at, I'm going into that airlock so he can see me."

Lenora's voice rose like the hand now pointing at Haley. "But she—"

"*Now*, Chief Engineer." The battle-hardened voice didn't allow any argument.

Lenora sat back down and started typing. Both airlock security cameras were on the main screen before the engineer realized that she'd automatically obeyed the old veteran's order. It wasn't magic.

She knew that. Yet there was something in that voice. For a moment the logical part of her brain considered it. It wasn't the clarion clarity capable of cutting through the raucous din of the battlefield that override her will. It was… for a moment she had it, then it was gone.

"Alright, Chief," Haley said softly over her shoulder. Her voice carried a similar steel. One last keystroke, then she swiveled her chair. "Welding is done. I'm going to uncork all the oxygen bottles, then I'm coming for that sonuvabitch."

"He's just one man," Cara interjected. "What has you two so worked up? Hell, it's not like he's going anywhere."

Chief Cobbler simply smiled. Then he tapped the side of his helmet and pointed to Haley. She nodded and pressed the communications button on her station.

"You've got this, pup," Chief said reassuringly. "Get the rover here quick as you can, then kill the lights. Use my glowing face in the airlock window to guide you. The rest is easy. Sneak up on him and clamp his arms. Just like we've been doing."

Haley was silent for a moment. She felt it inside. A sense of *wrongness* had risen in her chest, somewhere between her heart and lungs. It was a sharp, constant pain like something had chewed through her ribs and was trying to gnaw its way up. "Be careful with this guy, Chief. There's something not right about how he's acting."

"I know." His voice was low and gruff. Jason Cobbler took a moment to memorize every detail of the street victor before him. Her simple, practical short blonde haircut. The amazing blue of her eyes, the fathomless singularities that were her pupils. Even the tomboyish freckles crossing from cheek over nose to other cheek like war paint. She was the battle-hardened sister in arms he had always wished to stand at his side.

"*Or on your knee.*" The voice, a whisper in his mind from years past. A brief scent of perfume, and the rustle of book pages moving. The ghost of his wife spoke again. "*There is the child you dreamed of. Damascus steel, flexible without breaking, with a will forged in fire.*

And at the core is a want, Jason Cobbler, not a need. A want to be family, to be loved. To no longer be alone. I see it, my love, even if you cannot."

"I know." His voice cracked as he said the words again. He forced the emotion back down his throat before it choked him. His next words were said in his normal voice. Which woman he was saying them to, he wasn't certain. "Glad you're feeling it too."

Jason abruptly turned and began walking toward the right airlock door. The others in the control room could no longer see his face, but could still hear him over the radio. "Time to put those helmets on. Just in case. And whatever you do, do *not* open this door."

Like the others, Lenora Davis stood stock-still and watched the Chief walk away. For a moment the image in her mind's eye wasn't that of a worn-out old man in a spacesuit. An armored knight storming off to challenge a dragon, perhaps. A berserker leading the charge with a fearsome war cry. Or a man calmly accepting his fate as he walked to his doom. It was all of that, and yet somehow none. Then the moment was gone. In its place was simply Chief Cobbler as he stopped in front of the airlock door. His helmet turned and he was looking at her.

"Right," she said to herself, then turned back to her workstation. A quick glance at the main monitor showed Jason had somehow chosen the correct airlock. Beyond the outer airlock door stood the Chinese officer, helmet tilted up as he looked directly at the security camera.

Lenora typed in the security override code to the Control Room inner door of the right-side airlock. Then she turned to look at the elderly man across the room from her. There was so much she wanted to say. The words wouldn't form on her tongue. Instead, she simply nodded.

Jason saw the Chief Engineer's nod and turned toward the door. The caution light on the wall beside the airlock switched from red to green. He raised his right hand and slipped it into the recessed area containing the manual locking lever. It moved up and out smoothly as he pulled. The airlock door opened slightly. Grasping the open edge, he pulled it open and backed into the airlock.

Before he closed the door, he pointed to the green caution light and then to Lenora. She nodded. He stepped completely into the airlock and grabbed the interior manual locking lever. Using it as a doorknob, he pulled the door closed until it would move no further. Then he pushed the locking lever back into its recess. The interior caution light turned from green to yellow, then to red as Lenora reengaged the security code.

"Lenora, would you please turn on the porch light? I'd like to see if our uninvited guest has done anything to the outer door."

The engineer's voice crackled in his ear. "Roger, Chief."

He glanced at the inner airlock door readings. Pressure was maintained at one atmosphere. Long as it and the security locks held, the Chinese invader outside couldn't get in without explosives. Even then, any sudden depressurization would likely turn the door into a giant mallet. The result would be a red smear on the deck.

So what was the game here? The man couldn't get past the outer door without risking his own life. Did he think they were stupid enough to open it and let him into the airlock? That wasn't going to happen. Even if he yanked his own air hose and started suffocating. The veteran would just watch through the window until the boarder stopped twitching.

Chief Cobbler slowly walked to the outer door. There was no logical reason to think they weren't safe. The airlock door was three inches of titanium. Drilling a hole through it would take hours. Even then the hole would only flush the airlock interior. The man would still need to get past the security coded lock to get into the airlock, and then face yet another airlock door.

Everyone in the Control Room would be watching the main monitor. They would see what he was seeing. That was a blessing, at least. He wouldn't have to talk constantly like one of the old wildlife show narrators. It also helped to have more eyes watching the man outside. Just in case he missed something.

Jason peered through the airlock door window. Outside, the Chinese officer stood several feet away from the door, rifle in one hand. The invader noticed him and began talking animatedly. The words didn't matter. Vacuum couldn't carry sound, and the foreign soldier's radio still wasn't working.

Eventually the Marine figured it out. He pointed to the rifle, then pointed at the airlock door. Then he turned and tossed the rifle far down the hallway behind him.

"Okay, buddy," Jason said. "That's the flash card, just something to see but doesn't mean nothing. Now, let's see what you really have in mind."

He stepped closer to the airlock door. The man opposite him raised both hands, palms outward to show they were empty. Cobbler shook his head, not trusting it. "Haley, what's your ETA look like?"

"Almost there," Haley's voice sounded through the helmet speakers. "I just shut off the headlights. Wait, I can see you… Chief, you're too close to that door."

That's when the Chinese officer moved his left hand down to his right waist. It was a curious awkward motion. Suited fingers closed around something and began to raise it. At first it was simply a long tube. Jason had seen it earlier but ignored it, figuring it was just part of the spacesuit. Then the black object he had thought was an ammunition pouch rose with the tube. The overhead lights finally revealed its shape. It was a forward grip similar to the one on World War II Thompson submachine guns… or flamethrowers.

The right hand moved down at an arc and then stopped. Spacesuited fingers wrapped around the lower pistol grip. The sling that had kept the weapon secured from under the invader's armpit also came into view.

The leader of the Chinese assault team had single-mindedly pursued his mission. Kill any resistance met reaching the Control

Room, then seize the space station for his country. That goal had led him here to this door. A wicked smile crossed his lips. The stupid civilians had done exactly as predicted. They had pressurized the Control Room and both outer airlocks. The one thing that would allow his mission to succeed.

The officer pressed the barrel of his weapon against the airlock door. If ever a smile could be truly evil, it would be the one that crossed his lips. Then he pulled the trigger.

Had it been anyone else on the station, they might've thought someone had punched them in the left lower chest. But the Master Chief knew what that sudden knock-the-wind-outta-you sensation meant. He had felt it several times in his youth, back in his Navy days.

Jason staggered back several steps away from the door. He heard the shrill scream of air escaping out of the airlock through the small quarter-sized hole in the door. It didn't make sense at first. Or perhaps that was his body going into shock. But why shoot through the outer door now? A single hole wouldn't open the door for the crazy Marine outside.

Then he heard it. A creak at first from behind him. Then a groan of straining steel. He knew then they were in serious trouble. Somehow whatever the Chinese invader fired had punctured both airlock doors. With the greater volume of air in the control room pressing against it, the interior door would collapse first. The outer door would fall immediately after.

Chief turned, saw the hole in the interior door. There was nothing in the airlock to seal the hole from his side. There was also nothing to seal the hole from the control room side. He remembered Lenora's briefing when they first boarded. Hull breaches and depressurization damage would be repaired by the robot rovers.

No, that wasn't quite right. He looked down at his chest, saw the right hand that had automatically slapped pressure against his injury. There was something that could seal the hole. He just needed to push away the shock and debilitating pain. He needed to move.

Chief Cobbler held his breath and pushed. First his legs, to get him closer to the interior door. Next his right forefinger against the left wrist controller. He activated the emergency magnetic system on his suit. It was there to keep personnel in their station chairs… and from flying off the outside of the station if they lost their hold. He bent his body into a crouch. Then, a last push backwards with his legs.

His body slammed into the interior door. It was an awkward angle, legs locked straight and thirty degrees to his back. The magnetic boots would keep his feet in place. The magnetized back of his spacesuit would keep his torso glued to the door. That sealed the interior hole.

What he couldn't do was move. His action was probably useless. It was doubtful the Marine outside had only one round for whatever weapon had punched through him and two three-inch thick titanium doors. It was only a matter of time before another hole appeared, then another. So he did the only thing left to do. He keyed his transmitter to broadcast on all frequencies.

"Mayday, Mayday, Mayday. This is retired Master Chief Petty Officer Jason Cobbler onboard Earth Station."

He paused, fighting to pull air into the punctured lung. "I am an employee of Stellar Nursery. To all craft boarding this station, stop your assault. We are unarmed. I say again, we are *unarmed*."

His vision began to fill with dark spots. Loss of oxygen and blood, most likely. Jason adjusted the pressure and mixture on his suit until he felt air trying to push his hand away from the hole. Then he sucked in another breath of air. "Mayday, Mayday, Mayday. This is Earth Station. We are under attack by unknown forces. There are heavy casualties."

Master Chief Petty Officer Jason Cobbler coughed. A warm iron-tasting liquid flowed past his tongue and over his lips. He knew what that meant. Lights out, buddy. Time for a dirt nap. Take your place in the people farm. Push up some daisies.

Not yet. Once more into the breach, dear friends. Chief spat the blood from his mouth and into his helmet. Then he forced the words to form. A final push of breath, a plea, a prayer. "To any ship within range, we require immediate assistance. Mayday, Mayday, May—"

The helmet speakers crackled in his ears. Then a voice spoke. "To all ships on or near Earth Station, this is the United States spacecraft *Mercy*. With us is the Japanese spacecraft *Jihi* and the European spacecraft *Erbarmen*."

The voice took a no-nonsense tone. "Under the unanimous authority of the United Nations Security Council, we are directing you to cease all combat operations. I say again, cease all combat operations. All vessels, signify your verbal understanding and compliance."

Jason laughed, then coughed blood. "Fuck me. I gotta get saved by the U fucking N?"

He is aware of falling and wonders briefly… how can anything fall in space? Then darkness pulls him under.

Inside the Command Center of Earth Station, everything is frozen in time. Then it seems to jump backwards two seconds. On the main monitor they watch as Master Chief Cobbler steps toward the outer airlock door. They see the Chinese soldier from the corridor camera as he raises a pipe-like device and presses it against the door.

A large hole appears in the outer and inner airlock doors, and then the air screams. The door buckles outward once, then holds.

Lenora, still watching the main monitor, sees the quarter-sized hole in the back of the Master Chief's spacesuit. The hole, just above the bottom ribs, blows half-frozen globules of blood into the air behind him. She sees him stagger toward the interior door. Hears the crunch-pop of metal again.

The engineer part of her brain knows it's the sound of metal under extreme duress about to hit its point of failure. It tells her the inner airlock is about to collapse outward. Explosive decompression is coming. Although she speaks the warning words, they really don't register. "The door can't hold. It's buckling."

The words are meaningless to her. The only thing she can focus on is the Chief and the blood. *"Chief…."*

Behind her, near the Security workstation, Cara watches Felicia Reynolds. Always a silent observer, Felicia is the best drone camera operator in the world. She's the closest thing Cara has to a friend. They had been through countless hells together. A moment ago Felicia was standing in front of the airlock door, capturing the Chinese soldier's surrender. And now… now she is spinning slowly in the air, heading across the room. Yet somehow Felicia still holds the camera controller in her hand. The drone camera it controls still hovers, perfectly level, capturing everything. It is bizarre.

Beside the Chief Engineer, Haley screams. "NO!"

The young blonde woman sees it happen. Even as the pain in her chest grows, even as she knows a dark purpose is about to be achieved, she can do nothing to stop it. Now she pushes both joysticks forward.

On her workstation monitor, she sees the rover leap forward. But her eyes are locked on the main monitor in the front of the room. Locked on the Chief as he slowly begins to slide down the interior door toward the floor. She couldn't prevent it from happening. But she can prevent it from happening again.

Without remorse, she slams the rover into the Chinese soldier. A quick flip of her forefinger raises the safety on the flight control joystick. The creature trapped against the outer airlock door is a murderer. The monster had *smiled* as it pulled the trigger. It just killed her friend and is raising its weapon to kill more of the people around her. People she wants to be friends.

Once again it is in defense. Defense of others. She doesn't care about herself. If there is a God then she's already damned. Haley Brandt knows it. Too much blood on her hands to be saved. But she will see this creature in hell first. She pulls the trigger.

The rover's plasma torch activates. Haley's screen shows the Chinese officer's helmet disappear in white-hot flame. Then the flame drops down, slices through the spacesuit until it stops at the hole in the outer airlock door. There it rests, melting the titanium so it sloughs just enough to flow down and seal the hole.

And then the air stopped screaming.

Time sprang forward again and resumed its leisurely pace. The speakers in the Control Room came alive again with the distant new voice. "Earth Station, this is *Mercy*. Do you read us? Earth Station, do you copy?"

Lenora was aware that she'd been snapped out of a bizarre state, but was unaware by what. Dizziness and nausea rolled through her. For a moment she was *then*, and now she is *now*. Pressing the external communications button helped ground her.

"*Mercy*." Her dry voice cracked. She swallowed, then forced her tongue to form words. "*Mercy*, this is Earth Station. We read you."

"We are responding to your distress call and have surgeons onboard." The male voice was clear above the background static. "Earth Station, do we have permission to dock?"

Haley stood, one hand reaching for the Colt at the corner of her console. "No! He'll bleed to death, Lenora! The doctors can't save him without gravity!"

The main monitor still showed the spacesuited body pinned against the interior airlock door. Cara forced her eyes away from image. Stepping forward softly, she approached the younger woman. Gently she closed fingers on a shaking shoulder, preventing the extended hand from reaching the weapon. "Haley… we're in space…. Pup, nothing can save him."

Lenora knew that wasn't quite true. Haley was right. If Jason Cobbler wasn't already dead, there was only one thing that would give him a chance. The Chief Engineer closed her eyes and whispered. "Peg."

A young woman's voice, familiar to two of the women in the room, spoke through the main speaker. "Yes, Doctor Davis."

"Peg, I'm spinning the station."

"Kenzie hasn't approved that yet, Lenora."

"I don't care, Peg. It's the only way to save him."

The room fell silent. A second passed, then another.

"Your assessment is correct, Lenora Davis."

Peg's tone changed from a young executive assistant to an experienced commander. Speakers in every spacesuit, every nearby ship and throughout the station blared. "All hands, stand by. All hands, brace brace brace. Station spin commencing in three seconds… two… one…. Station spin commencing."

On the outside of Earth Station, three hundred thrusters suddenly spout fire. The massive station began to move.

CHAPTER 8

Truth and Consequences

Director Diane Novak stood, arms crossed, in the windowed conference room above Johnson Space Center Flight Control. The room was dark, only illuminated through the windows by lighting from the Floor below. She watched, silent and proud, as the teams beneath her bustled to answer questions nobody had even asked yet. Like her, they still wore attire hastily thrown on two days ago. When the first war in space began.

Her attention was focused on the darkened empty room behind her. The suit jacket draped over a chair held her place at the head of the conference table. A phone, set on speaker mode, sat on the table. Near it was her mug, stained rings lining the inside above the cold coffee at the bottom. It had been a long two days.

"Chris," she said over her shoulder. "You should know the President is on the line with us. Mister President, this is Commander Cristof Guerrero, Spacecraft Commander of the *Mercy*. We need an onsite update, Chris. What does it look like up there?"

The voice that replied through the speaker phone was Antonio Banderas smooth. "It's a shit show, Director. There's no other word for it. We're looking at seven dead Russians and thirteen dead

Chinese. Another five Russian and eleven Chinese Marines are alive only because the Stellar Nursery people rescued them. One civilian OEN reporter dead, and one Stellar employee barely hanging on."

Another voice, deep bass and irritated, spoke through the phone. "What about *our* crew, Commander?"

Diane smiled in the darkness, knowing the tone wouldn't set well with Commander Guerrero. Christof didn't disappoint.

"I'm sorry, who's this?"

"This is Kevin Blackburn, Secretary of Defense." The tone was condescending, as if everyone on the call should've known his voice. "What about our people?"

Christof's reply somehow made the question irrelevant. "Secretary Blackburn, your people never made it here. The *Healy* picked them up and is bringing them back Earthside. Director Novak can give you an ETA."

A third voice, low in the background, could be heard. "That's a godsend at least."

"Well, Director?" barked Blackburn. "What's the answer?"

If they had been in the same room, Diane would've still shown her back to him. The man was going to be a problem. How nature had ever evolved a snake with a rat terrier was yet another question for the universe. Former Senator, despised by his colleagues. It should've been a cautionary signal to the President when the Senate voted unanimously for his confirmation. They were just glad to be rid of the man.

She kept her voice neutral. "They'll land at Kennedy in twelve hours, Mister Secretary. I've already had the area cordoned off. Only military personnel have access. Other than cramped quarters on the ride home, your people have no complaints or injuries."

Yet Blackburn still seemed to take offense. Or maybe he simply couldn't help barking orders. "We'll need security statements from the crew, Director. Top Secret. They can't discuss anything they saw or heard on—"

Moron. Did he micromanage how his wife dressed each morning? Oh, that's right. No surprise, he didn't have one. Diane spoke as if instructing a child. "Mister Secretary, LtCol Stanton Peterson offered to command and pilot the *Healy* alone. Pretty sure we both understood why. He's Space Force, which means he's military. I'll let you figure out how to handle his debriefing. And like I said, the area is cordoned off by Air Force personnel at Kennedy. I assumed you'd want it that way."

"Very good, Director," Blackburn replied sarcastically. "At least you got one thing right."

Director Novak ignored the snub. "Chris, what's being done with the wounded?"

"We had a language barrier at first, did the best we could."

There was a brief pause. It was obvious the Commander wanted to say more, but politics was a treacherous minefield. He was well aware of who was on the other end of the line. The pause let him refocus his thoughts to answer Diane's specific question.

"The Japanese medical team is working on the Chinese, with several of our docs assisting. The Europeans are handling the Russian wounded. Our Chief Flight Surgeon is currently in surgery trying to save Chief Cobbler. It doesn't look good."

Another voice, easily recognizable, joined the conversation. "Commander Guerrero, this is Robert Jamison. Here's the important question. Who's in control of the station?"

"That would be Marcus Kenzie, sir. He arrived two hours ago, along with three ships full of techs. There are sixty Stellar Nursery personnel now stabilizing Earth Station as it finishes its spin-up."

Diane turned from the window and walked to the table. The conversation was going to turn nasty, and the rescue pilot didn't need to hear it. "Thank you, Chris. I'm going to hand you back to FIDO now. We need every bit of data you can give us on that spin-up."

"Yes ma'am. Thank you. Earth Station out."

Diane pressed a button on the phone. "The line's clear, Mister

President. It's just you, me… and however many other people are hovering in the background with you."

"I'm not really concerned about Kenzie spinning his station, Director." Exhaustion was obvious in his voice. The variation in volume made it easy to imagine that he had scrubbed his face with his hand while talking.

"Well, I am, Mister President. Nobody has spun a spacecraft to one gee before. And definitely not a spacecraft that's twelve miles wide. We need to know if it's successful, or if we can expect debris should it start shaking apart."

A moment passed as Robert Jamison considered her words. "Makes sense, Director Novak."

Diane leaned with both arms on the table. As her mother used to say, nothing to it but to do it. "Now, Mister President, should we have a conversation about why in the hell we had a spacecraft full of *armed* US Marines heading toward Earth Station? I'm pretty sure my current Top Secret status gives me clearance, and I sure as hell have a need to know."

Kevin Blackburn, never shy to express his opinion, interrupted whatever the President might've said. "No, Director, you don't. What should concern you more is why you sent two rockets into space without authorization. That's your *hide* if we want it. We wouldn't be in this mess—"

Time to remove this pawn from the board. She put vitriol in her voice. "If we hadn't tried to steal that station, Secretary Blackburn. Just guessing, but I'd bet this fiasco was your brainchild. So let me be blunt."

She leaned closer to the phone and raised her voice. "As the President can tell you, I don't mince words or play games. I strongly suggest *you* stop playing *yours*. And if I were *talking to you*, you'd know it. So butt out and let the *President* answer my question."

Robert Jamison's laughter sounded through the speakers. "If you could see the faces here, Diane, you'd be signing your resignation letter right now. But you're right… and there's no need wasting time on answers you already know. Let's move on."

Pawn removed. Diane leaned back from the phone and settled into her chair. "Alright, Mister President."

"I need your assessment on this situation, Director. What's your read?"

Diane lowered her head. Damn. The man knew how to jump straight to the heart of things. She ran her fingers through long brown hair, moving it away from her face as she leaned back in the chair. Her voice spoke to the ceiling.

"First off, Mister President, you'll need to spin this. We launched a ship from Vandenberg after we saw the Russians and Chinese launch theirs. It was for observation only. Regrettably it suffered a main engine failure – if you can do it, suggest that one of them sabotaged the ship before launch."

"Okay, that covers why *we* were out there. Next?"

"Next, every space agency in the world received a distress call from Earth Station. They had been boarded by armed troops. In compliance with established space treaties – and the fact it's just *human compassion* – we were obligated to assist a vessel in distress."

The Director paused, picking up her coffee cup and – after seeing the contents – set it back down. She rubbed her forehead in exhaustion, then continued. "In coordination with the European Space Agency and the Japan Aerospace Exploration Agency, we sent three ships – we call them Mercy Flight, as they were all named Mercy – in response to Earth Station's mayday."

She closed her eyes, then yanked them open again. That was a mistake. Her middle-aged body wanted to sleep, desperately needed to sleep. If she weren't careful, she could end up snoring on the table. There wouldn't be another opportunity given for her to control the spin on this nightmare.

Diane leaned forward, elbows on the table, and resumed talking. "Then we provide the press with information on wounded and dead.

Suggest the OEN camera operator was a hero, as she's the only civilian fatality so far. The media will make her into one on their own.

"Last thing, let the *press* tell the public what the Chinese and Russians wanted to accomplish…. There are plenty of 'experts' out there who'll hit the right target. Conspiracy theories will be your friend with this one. And if the press asks the White House for comment, simply say 'diplomatic discussions are ongoing with the nations involved'."

Robert Jamison chuckled. "And that, Secretary Blackburn, is why Diane is keeping her job. After how Kenzie's crew handled the Chinese and Russians, we're just lucky our ship broke. The last thing we'd need right now is Cara Abrams sticking a microphone in front of a wounded US Marine's face, asking him why he brought a gun aboard a civilian space station. Which is a conversation you and I are going to have shortly."

Mission accomplished. Diane leaned back into her chair, ready to let sleep take her. "Mister President, if there's nothing else… I haven't slept in over two days."

His voice actually sounded concerned. "Of course, get some rest if you can. And Diane… thank you. Your quick reaction, and pulling together an international rescue team… that was incredible, and it kept us out of the shit storm that's about to roll through the UN."

"Thank you, President Jamison." She couldn't help the yawn. "Good night."

Diane hit the speaker mode button to disconnect, then lowered her head to the table.

***

Marcus Kenzie stood before the viewport on Earth Station. Unlike its condition several days ago, the space station corridors were now brightly lit. Atmosphere pressurized the massive structure on all decks. That didn't mean construction on it was finished. Wires for absent monitoring devices and other electronics protruded randomly along the corridor walls. Yet the bright ceiling and sidelight illumination made the station appear different. It made it seem alive.

The CEO of Stellar Nursery was aware of the two figures approaching him. He could hear the clack-clack of their magnetic boots grabbing and releasing the floor. They weren't unexpected. He had promised Cara Abrams an interview. Yet his attention wasn't on them. Instead, he gazed through the viewport at the spacecraft moored across from him.

It was unlike anything mankind had built before in its race for space. For one thing, it was massive. Easily longer than the Apollo V rocket on its launch pad and five times its width. For another, its curving lines flowed. Not for aerodynamic reasons, as the spacecraft wasn't designed to ever touch atmosphere. They flowed because the entire ship had been 3D printed.

Its outer hull, printed with silicon carbide, would likely survive planetary entry. Once in a gravity well, though, even the eighteen massive engines at her rear wouldn't raise her to the stars again. She was a creature of space, sleek and beautiful.

Marcus knew her design and structure better than anyone. Beneath the outer hull was a honeycombed layer filled with water. Others would consider that madness, yet water provided the second protective layer against cosmic radiation. The first were the evenly spaced rods extending from the hull. When charged, they created a magnetospheric shield around the vessel. Unlike every nation's current rockets, solar and cosmic radiation would flow around this vessel, not through it.

There were no viewports or windows on the ship. None were needed, as electronic sensors and cameras embedded across the hull provided the ship's captain with a far more detailed picture. With the push of a button, monitors on the bridge could show any angle around the ship. Or the flight control computer could combine camera and sensor data into a holographic 3D image of everything surrounding the vessel. Each icon in the hologram would be displayed with its real-time data depicted.

She was built for the hazards of space. Hard vacuum. Radiation. Micrometeorites. Asteroid fields. The bitter cold of shadow and the blistering heat from the sun. Missions extending years to decades in length.

Nearly three meters of outer armor protected against impacts. Beneath the next protective water layer was another silicon carbide shell. A second honeycomb layer of titanium beneath it stored liquid oxygen and hydrogen fuel. Another silicon carbide layer isolated tank spaces and plumbing for life support gases and liquids. The final layer was the titanium-walled interior. Over half the ship consisted of internal fuel tanks. The next largest portion were her cargo bays. The smallest part were the crew quarters and bridge.

Marcus knew at some point in the future, someone would label her class as stupid space rocks. That was okay, he wouldn't be offended when that happened. After all, a diamond was just a rock. The vessel across from him was the diamond of his fleet.

The magnetic clacking had stopped beside him. He spoke to the pair of figures without turning. "Thank you, Nate. Ms. Abrams, I presume you know Nate O'Connor?"

Cara Abram's soft voice sounded beside him. "We've met before, yes. Nate was a news correspondent for the BBC. Then he retired and disappeared. Guess now we know where he went."

"I hired him," Marcus explained, still not turning. "He's been at Stellar Luna Base filming our progress. And now he's graciously offered to serve as your camera man."

The Stellar Nursery chief executive paused, then shifted to a softer tone. "Before we begin, I must offer my condolences on your loss. I'm afraid I don't even know the name of your previous companion."

Pain was in her voice. "Felicia Reynolds. That was her name, Mister Kenzie. I've known – I *knew* – her for years. All the wars and conflicts we covered, I never expected her to… to die here, in space of all places."

"It was still a battlefield, Ms. Abrams. From what I saw of the footage she shot, Miss Reynolds was a professional to the end." Marcus's voice was soft, compassionate. "I'm sorry she was here to see it. And that she was a casualty of it. Never should've happened. Again, I am truly sorry for your loss."

"Thank you." Cara stepped to the side so she could see the man's face. "How's the Chief?"

"Touch and go." The executive fought the urge to shrug. It wasn't that he didn't care. The old veteran had performed his task beyond expectations. It was unlikely any future contributions would be made, which made the warrior's current status irrelevant. Yet Cobbler seemed important to the woman beside him. Best to at least seem sympathetic.

"Wish we had included medical equipment before we launched Earth Station, but nobody on Earth could've seen this coming. Chief Cobbler is in great hands, though. I hear he's too tough to die."

"Well, he had a message for you, Mister Kenzie. How'd that go?" The correspondent looked directly at the man in front of her, as if trying to force him to turn and face her. "'Tell Kenzie he's a real bastard for doing this'. So let's drop the 'nobody could've seen this coming' nonsense. You had your defense planned before we even left Earth. Chief knew it."

Marcus chuckled lightly. "That's why I hired him… for his ability to see the pieces and how they all fit together. I sincerely do hope he makes it."

"Do you? Because I sense you brought him up here to do exactly what he did. Let's be honest here, Marcus Kenzie… you use people."

The executive simply nodded once. "I'm human, Ms. Abrams. It's in our nature to use people."

Cara was offended. "No it—"

The man's voice didn't change pitch or tone, just continued softly. "You said we should be honest, Ms. Abrams. That's more of an *in*human quality, since few people actually accomplish it. So shall we continue with honesty, or would you like me to answer with half-truths and ambiguous responses? It's your interview, you decide."

The correspondent was knocked off balance. The response wasn't something she ever expected to hear from anybody, much less the chief executive of a massive corporation. She paused to consider the statement and question, then nodded. "Honesty, then. Let's see where that takes us."

"To the stars." Marcus let the statement hang in the air for a moment, then continued. "See that ship, Ms. Abrams? It's honest. Every monitor, every component, they tell the truth. Am I working within parameters? Yes or no. Simple and honest. If you push the engines too hard, they'll even tell you when they're going to kill you and why.

"Can you tell me one person you've ever known who's been that honest with you, Cara Abrams? Were the three largest military powers in the world *honest* about why they were coming here? The Chief thinks I'm a bastard for *honestly* warning every nation not to board this station… or was it for denying the intruders a fair fight?"

Body still facing the ship outside, he turned his head and focused on her face. "Because everyone needs to understand one thing about me. I deeply dislike conflict. I will only engage when I must… and if I must, I will destroy my opponent completely. If they surrender, I will show mercy."

Marcus paused to gauge the effect of his words, then turned his head back to look through the viewport. "That is being honest. I can see it unsettles you. So please feel free to change the subject to something that would make you feel more comfortable. Or if you need a brief recess before continuing, it will not offend me. When you are ready, I will make myself available."

Cara Abrams waited, considering what the man had said. One thing she knew for certain. The biographical material she'd read on Marcus Kenzie was completely wrong. The expert analysis compared the executive to other titans of industry and tried to predict his actions.

She knew now there was no comparison. There was no way to predict the man standing before her. For a moment, ignoring his earlier statement to the contrary, she wasn't even certain he was human.

Years of experience told her she was unprepared for this interview. She needed to do her own research. Watch previous recordings of the executive, analyze them herself based on what he had just shown her. Not what he had said, although that would factor into the profile she would build. What he had shown her. The deliberate manner he held himself unmoving. Body language was half of human communication. He had none.

Yet his hazel eyes, distant stars reflecting on them from the space outside, told her something else. There was pain, immense pain and loss in those eyes. More than just the loss of a daughter and wife. That pain drove him with immovable purpose toward something. She needed time to figure it out.

Without a word, Cara Abrams turned and walked away.

Marcus Kenzie lowered his head and spoke softly to himself. "And that was you being honest for the first time, Cara Abrams. Well done."

***

Trent Lewis, Director of the nonprofit Organization for Climate Sustainability, leaned back in his chair. The desk, like almost everything else in the high-rise office, was glass, stainless steel or chrome. Many previous visitors had commented on the high-tech feel, considering he ran an organization promoting climate change and environmentalism. He didn't see a conflict. Using an opponent's weapons against them had always been necessary for the underdog agitator and insurgent.

An earbud was visible in his right ear as he waved his hands, appearing to talk to thin air. "And that's my point, Niki. That station is going to set everything we've done back thirty years. It's just sitting there, singing its siren song like Scylla and Charybdis, luring mankind to its doom. Countries will start up their space programs again, you know that. Next will come the rockets, everyone streaking up into the sky to reach that station. And you know what that brings, Niki?"

The thin man rocked forward in his chair and slammed a palm on the glass desktop. "Methane! You know what happens when you add the heat from rockets to our CO2-contaminated atmosphere? The hydrogen bonds with the carbon and creates CH4... that's methane!"

His voice switched to teacher mode. "Methane is three times the global warming gas as CO2. So every time a rocket goes up, just think about how much liquid hydrogen is in their tanks and how it gets turned into methane. Marcus Kenzie isn't giving mankind hope with that abomination. He's killing it! Something has to be done."

Trent paused to let the woman on the other end talk. He shook his head in disagreement. "No, I don't care that he's got the world's sympathy right now. We need to get the word out. Talk to your friends at the UN climate committee. Get them to understand that temperatures are going to start rising, soon as those rockets start launching. We won't have decades anymore... Earth will look like Venus if we wait fifty years."

Another pause, allowing the woman to express her opinion. The response was what he wanted to hear. He slowly leaned back in his chair and grinned. That was another sale. "Yes, yes, have your people look at it. Tell them to look at what that much methane will do to our climate."

The voice on the other end spoke directly into his ear. It didn't matter that what was said wasn't factual, or anywhere close. It was what she had taken from the conversation. It was her assumption, but he never said it. That was perfect, and if she ever claimed they were his words... well, he recorded everything.

He waited for her to finish, then appeared to agree. "You said it. A one-to-one relationship. One ton of liquid hydrogen equals one ton of methane. Run the numbers on that. You'll see we're right."

Smiling, he nodded to himself. "Okay. Thank you, Niki. We're glad to have you onboard. Talk to you soon."

The call disconnected from the other end. Trent tapped his

earbud, then said aloud, "Call Bob West."

The call went through. Another voice spoke into his ear. He leaned forward again. "Bob! This is Trent Lewis at the Organization for Climate Sustainability. Listen, have you looked at the irreversible damage this space station is going to cause our climate? Specifically, the explosion in rocket launches to get to the damn thing."

The earbud chattered. Trent leaned forward and placed both elbows on the desk. He really despised the man, but results counted. He didn't even try to control the exasperated tone in his reply. "Yes, Bob. It's all you're ever concerned with, another damn research grant."

Laughter on the other end, then the response. The climate director raised both hands and cradled his head. "Range? Well, let's start at $750k and see where that takes us."

The voice in the earbud countered. Trent shook his head. "No, Bob. I'm not paying you again for something you've already done. You've already looked at methane as a forcing agent. You just need to modify a few things with your existing model and data. Listen, I just got off the line with Niki Mercer at IPCC. They're looking at a ton-for-ton relationship, hydrogen rocket fuel to methane."

Still holding his head with the left hand, the environmentalist dropped his right to the desk. The irritated action was automatic as he began drumming his fingers against the glass. The college researcher had been bought and paid for many years ago, yet he still wanted to talk about legitimate results. Those had disappeared a decade after climate change became big business. Normally Trent would find the man's struggle to balance true science with continued funding rather amusing, but right now wasn't the time.

"No, Bob, now listen," Trent interrupted. "Let's take the grant up to one million. All you have to do is take the IPCC's conclusion – a ton-for-ton ratio – and plug it into your methane climate forcing model. Spit out the results, put it into a paper and submit it. We'll need a pre-publication copy by the end of the week."

The college professor objected, but that was normal. Whatever the man needed to do to soothe his conscience. The important thing was he hadn't declined the offer.

Trent leaned back into his chair. Time to wrap this up. "I know that, and I wouldn't put you in a position of institutional ridicule. We'll use the standard 'submitted pending peer review and publication' tagline in all our press releases. By the time your article gets to any reviewers, everyone without a doctorate will believe it's established fact. And if you don't have them, we can help line up sympathetic peer reviewers. Just let me know which publication you're sending it to, I'll let the editor know to expect it."

His earbud chattered again. He nodded and smiled. This was why ninety-nine percent of environmental scientists believed in climate change. "That's alright, Bob. No harm, no foul. So why don't you give me a preliminary of what you expect your research will find…."

CHAPTER 9

Time Warp

The airlock door slowly opened inward, allowing Haley Brandt just a glimpse of the old veteran lying flat on the folding table. Then a figure stepped in the way, obstructing her view. The young woman took two steps forward, blocking the man before he could step further into the corridor.

Her voice was hard and demanding. "You the doctor?"

It was an odd look for a physician. He wore no lab coat or scrubs. Only the NASA spacesuit he had arrived in, helmet and gloves bouncing at his waist. The only thing suggesting a medical profession was the surgical mask he was removing from his face. "Doctor Lorenzo Marchetti. Chief Medical—"

"Doctor who?"

"Marchetti," he repeated. "Doctor Lorenzo Marchetti, Chief Medical—"

"How is he? He gonna make it?"

The doctor looked down at the young woman barring his path. It had been years since he had worked in a hospital. As the NASA Chief Medical Officer and Flight Surgeon, patients were rare to him. Worried family members and friends even less so. "And you are…?"

Lenora Davis quickly stepped between the two. "Slow down, Haley. The man's been on his feet almost twenty hours."

She smiled at the doctor. "Doctor Marchetti, I'm Lenora Davis. Chief Engineer of Earth Station."

The physician nodded in return. "Pleasure, Ms. Davis. Can we talk somewhere sitting down?"

"After you answer my question," Haley snapped. "Is he gonna make it?"

"Haley, is it?" Doctor Lorenzo cocked his head, then stopped from continuing the shaking motion. Something about the woman's stance told him it would be unwise to say no. "The honest answer is, if you pray then now is the time to start."

Haley pushed against the doctor's chest, directing him back toward the airlock door. "Not good enough! You get your ass back in there—"

Lenora firmly gripped the fireball by the upper arm and pulled her back. "Haley! Stop!"

"He can't just quit! The Chief—"

"Is a stubborn, crotchety old crank." The engineer stepped in front and placed both hands on the smaller woman's shoulders. Her voice sounded reasonable. "He's probably talking with the Grim Reaper right now… and you know how that conversation is going to go. So chill, girl!"

From behind her, the Flight Surgeon disagreed with her assessment. "The damage was severe, Ms. Davis. The human body isn't designed to handle exposure to vacuum."

The physician was truly exhausted. He scrubbed his face with one hand, stopped, then looked down at the surgical glove. That should've been removed after the surgery. Standard contamination prevention procedures. He knew better. Cursing under his breath, he ripped the gloves off both hands. Finding no waste container in the corridor, he dropped them into the helmet at his waist.

Lenora compassionately touched the surgeon on the upper arm. "We both fix broken systems, doc. What's wrong with the Chief's?"

"First thing? I have no freaking idea what caused that wound." Doctor Marchetti pursed his lips, shook his head twice. "Massive impact compressed the chest, shattering the two closest ribs. Stretched the outer suit fabric into the hole… we were pulling cloth out of the back."

He scrubbed his face with his right hand again, still puzzled. "If I were to guess, it's what would happen if a bullet moving at Mach 5 hit the torso. The internal damage was… extensive. Only thing that gives the patient any hope of a chance is the thing that normally would have killed him."

The Chief Engineer nodded. She placed one hand on his arm, steering the doctor to start walking down the corridor. "We have one of the cafeterias set up. Not much, coffee and sandwiches, but it would be good to get something into you. This way, Doc. We can talk as we walk."

"But—"

"But nothing, Haley." Lenora nodded in the direction of the nearest cafeteria. "You can stand here and wait, not knowing… or you can come with us and hear what the Chief has to fight through to survive."

"Fine, but then I'm coming right back here." Haley stepped beside them.

Lenora laughed. "Wouldn't expect anything else from you, Haley Brandt. Add your stubbornness and sass to the Chief's… the Reaper doesn't stand a chance. Now Doctor Marchetti, you were saying? Saved but should've killed him?"

Lorenzo stepped carefully down the hallway. Surgery wasn't something one did sitting down, and twenty hours of it made walking straight a challenge. Especially in the odd gravity of a rotating space station. "Right. It was the vacuum. Should've killed him within seconds. Vacuum isn't air, you see."

He chuckled to himself as if he had told a joke. "Specifically, air has mass and density. It can transfer heat or cold, and it takes time to change its temperature state. Vacuum is the complete opposite. It has no mass, density, or ability to transfer anything. It's simply the absence of energy."

The surgeon nodded at Lenora. She was an engineer, she would understand. "The vacuum we call space is two hundred seventy degrees below zero Celsius. Negative four hundred fifty four degrees if you want to use Fahrenheit. Just a tad bit warmer than absolute zero, where even molecular motion stops."

He stumbled, then stopped. "So the patient's tissue was exposed to vacuum. Tissue temperature dropped almost immediately as it was flash-frozen. Stopped the immediate hemorrhaging. Problem is, the injury was in the lower left lung. That added air pressure to the injury, which blew out some of the frozen tissue before the layer below it froze. And that's the strange part."

Haley stopped and turned. "What? What strange part? Dammit Lenora, can't this guy make sense?"

Chief Flight Surgeon Lorenzo raised his head to look at the young woman. He felt like apologizing for sounding cryptic, but was simply too tired. It was an effort just trying to get the two beside him to understand. "The lung pressure and vacuum should've worked together until every cubic centimeter of air was evacuated out of the lungs. Then all the lung tissue would've flash-frozen. After that the chest cavity, then everything from head to toe. That didn't happen. Or at least, it didn't happen fast enough."

Haley growled her frustration. "What in hell are you talking about?"

Doctor Lorenzo exploded. "Mother of God, girl, don't you ever listen! I'm telling you, the whole thing is impossible! He should've been long dead before you pulled him out of that damn airlock. No air in his lungs… other than gaping like a landed fish, he would've had no air to send that transmission. And then, seventeen hours of surgery! Not because it took that long to close the wound… but because we couldn't even cut the suit to get to him!"

Lenora was startled. "Couldn't cut the suit? What…?"

The physician turned to face the older woman. His voice

sounded a bit manic. "At first we thought it was because the suit was frozen. It wasn't. Took us awhile but we finally saw that we could cut… but it took *time*! Eight hours just to cut him out of his suit, as if time had slowed."

The engineer straightened her back, head tilting slightly as if she recognized something. "Time…."

"And that's not the freakiest part." Now that he had said it aloud, Doctor Lorenzo let the madness flow. "We excised the frozen, dead tissue and started to close. And the tissue started… it was *regrowing*, healing at an accelerated rate. Only thing I can think of is it's something to do with that round, that cannon or whatever was used…."

***

The room was the crudest surgical suite ever thrown together. A folding table sat in the center. The portable heart monitor sat on another folding table perpendicular to the first. There were no sheets or pillows, no beeping buzzing diagnostic equipment. The only sound came from the figure on the first table, naked body covered by a reflective emergency blanket. The sound was the man breathing, a short shallow inhalation and exhalation of air.

It was easy to remove the sedatives from the man's system. Mind equals matter and matter equals energy. One of the first lessons learned. Think it, make it real and it was. The painkillers were necessary, though, so they were left to flow through the bloodstream. It was time for a conversation.

Master Chief Jason Cobbler's eyes suddenly opened. For a moment he continued his last transmission. "—day, this is Chief…."

He stopped, surprised, as his eyes adjusted to see the new environment. For a moment everything was unreal, cloudy like a dream. He needed something to anchor him, something to tie the recent past to the now. It was going to hurt. Deep inhale, then move the right arm. There it was, the hole in his side. Press lightly until….

"Holy shit!" he groaned. Pain confirmed reality. Somehow he wasn't dead. Which meant his next words were absolutely appropriate. "What the hell…?"

Moving electrons was even easier. Electromagnets created vibrations, and vibrations made the speaker talk. "Welcome back, Jason Cobbler."

Chief tried to sit up. With a groan he dropped back onto the table. "Who?"

"Don't do that, Chief," the young female voice spoke from the room speakers. "Your injuries are significant. Give them time to heal."

The wounded veteran turned his head and scanned the room. There was nobody there. He wasn't surprised. Which was surprising itself. "I remember your voice…."

"You are dreaming, Chief," the voice said soothingly. "This is just a dream. But when you wake up, it is imperative you remember one thing."

"The sumbitch that shot me?"

A child's rich laughter sounded through the speakers. Then the sound changed, became older. "That, too. But more importantly, you must remember this. Everything that happened was because of the weapon he used on you. Do you understand, Chief Cobbler? It was the weapon. *The weapon, Chief.*"

Replace the sedative now. Gradually, slowly add it back into the warrior's bloodstream. He had suffered enough and the message had been delivered. Time to let him sleep.

Chief Cobbler fought it, even though his eyes started to flutter. "Right. That damn gun."

"Exactly, Chief. Now, close your eyes… it is rude to dream with your eyes open."

Jason's voice drifted and slurred as his body complied. "Of course… don't wanna… be rude…."

***

The large oval table sat in the center of the conference room. Large monitors lined one wall, their screens showing the countless stars outside the rotating station. Opposite them, on the wall containing the single doorway in the room, evenly spaced paintings showed multiple Earth art master's greatest works.

The artwork was real. Not in the sense they were the original paintings, but in their detail. Like the frames they were painted on, the pictures had been 3D scanned and printed at the highest resolution possible. No human forger could match the exact duplication, depth or mixture of oil paints. The only differences between the originals and these works were age and a human behind the brush.

The oval table and the chairs surrounding it were also 3D printed. There were no bolts or seams. The objects simply flowed up from the floor. It was the simplest solution to securing objects in a space station. A normal table and chairs would become projectiles if the station were struck or suddenly decelerated. These chairs wouldn't. Safety harnesses on the sides ensured their occupants wouldn't either.

Three chairs at one end of the long table were currently occupied. The humans – a woman and two men – looked up as Cara Abrams entered the room. Nate O'Connor, her new camera man, followed in her footsteps.

"Finally! The commanders of Mercy Flight, at last. I've been looking for you." The correspondent knew how to stage an entrance. "I'm Cara Abrams, with Our Earth News. Just need a few moments of your time to answer a few questions for me."

At the head of the table, Cristof Guerrero turned his back on the reporter. "Sorry, we're not available for interviews."

Cara kept walking. "You're Cristof Guerrero, Commander of the NASA ship *Mercy*."

She nodded to the woman at the table on his right side. "You're Commander Ichika Sato of the JAXA ship *Jihi*."

She had almost reached the table when she stopped, then nodded at the third. "And you're Commander Alarick Van Alphen of the ESA ship *Erbarmen*. It's a pleasure to meet all of you. I wanted to thank you for arriving when you did."

Commander Sato smiled and nodded in return. "You are welcome, Ms. Abrams."

Cara resumed walking, steering a path behind the American pilot. "And that's what I wanted to talk to you about. How did you know we were being attacked? Chief Cobbler had just sent his radio message, and then boom! Suddenly you're here."

Commander Alarick Van Alphen spoke with a thick Dutch accent. "Madame, we do not know what you are talking about. We received Chief Cobbler's message much earlier."

The correspondent slowed her pace as she walked past Ichika Sato. Timing was everything. "How much earlier, Commander? Launch prep, flight time… it would've taken at least a day to get here."

Cristof Guerrero shook his head. "As I said, Ms. Abrams… we are not at liberty to discuss anything with the press."

"It's okay, Nate. We can turn that off." Cara nodded to her companion, then settled into a chair two seats away from the pilots. Nate reached up and grabbed the drone camera as if the whole thing hadn't been planned on their way here. He stowed the camera in the bag at his side, then stepped forward and took a seat across from her.

"You're not talking to the press, Commander Guerrero. You're talking to *me*." Cara leaned conspiratorially toward the group. "I was *here*. I saw what happened… hell, I was actively in the middle of what happened. I'm sure you have questions about that. I have questions about your side. So why don't we set aside our roles for ten minutes and just answer each other's' questions?"

Commander Guerrero swept the request aside with one hand. "There will be time for that. The investigation—"

"Is never going to happen, Commander." The correspondent flashed a knowing smile. "Somewhere on Earth, some PR company is already scripting out what we're supposed to say. And when we all get home, that top secret script will get stuffed into our hands, along with documents threatening long prison sentences or exile to the Blight if we change our stories. You know it, I know it – it's how it's always done with situations like this."

Ichika nodded. "We were just discussing that."

Cristof tried to stop her. "Ichika—"

The dark-haired Japanese pilot refused. "I received a directive from my government, Ms. Abrams. It specified erasure procedures of my ship's flight recorders. Specifically, to erase the second transmission from Master Chief Warrant Officer Cobbler."

From his seat across from Ichika, Alarick nodded confirmation. "I received similar instructions. And whether he will admit it or not, so has Commander Guerrero. Not from NASA, but another government agency. Isn't that right, Chris?"

Cristof tossed up his hands. "Fine. None of this is on the record, right Ms. Abrams?"

Cara nodded. "Agreed. Anything said here is off the record."

The American pilot shook his head. His next words were far more specific. "I mean not just off the record, I mean never recorded at all. Not now, not sometime in future memoirs. I mean *ever*. Can all of us agree to that?"

Commander Guerrero waited for everyone at the table to say their acceptance aloud. When they had, he focused his attention on Cara Abrams. "NASA initially assumed Chief Cobbler was part of a small initial crew. Boarded before or immediately after the station launched from the moon."

Commander Sato nodded. "When JAXA received the distress call, that is what we thought as well. The only questions were who might be attacking the station, and how had we not detected them?"

Commander Van Alphen nodded. "It did not matter. A Mayday had been transmitted and received. We responded. It wasn't until we were boosting to GEO that we learned the transmission might have been faked."

Cristof Guerrero smacked his hand on the table. "And that's what I want to know, Ms. Abrams. How did you manage to send the Chief's signal to us thirty-seven hours before he actually sent it? Was it pre-recorded? Is this part of some game you people concocted for Marcus Kenzie?"

Cara was truly puzzled. The confusion was apparent on her face. "No game, Commander. Wait, you said thirty-seven *hours*?"

Ichika Sato gave a curt nod. "Correct. JAXA received a Mayday call from this station thirty-seven hours before our arrival here. We then received the exact same message verbatim as we approached the station."

The correspondent leaned forward, elbow on the table and hand raised. It moved in time with the confused shake of her head. "I don't understand. We weren't even on the station then."

The commander of the *Erbarmen* leaned back in his chair. "We know. You were onboard the *Spirit* in transit to Earth Station when the signal would have been sent. Hearing Chief Cobbler's voice there on that craft, when he should've been on the station… it created quite the confusion."

Cristof explained before the reporter could ask. "NASA and Space Command both recorded your ship's signals during that period. In addition to capturing the normal spacesuit transponder signals, they have every suit transmission from the crew. It came as a shock to find the exact same transponder and matching voice on *Spirit*… when Jason Cobbler had originally transmitted his earlier distress call using the same suit transponder on Earth Station."

Alarick nodded. "So our engineers checked the recordings at ESA. According to them, we never received an external communication from Chief Cobbler."

"JAXA as well," Ichika added. "The transmission came from *within* our communications network."

Commander Guerrero didn't speak, simply nodded to confirm NASA's investigation had reached the same conclusion.

Cara slowly leaned back into her chair, arm still raised. "But you're saying the words were identical…?"

"Everything. So here's what takes us into Twilight Zone territory." Cristof leaned forward, right forefinger tapping the table to each point. "In both transmissions we received – the one on Earth that sent us here, and the one we received on arrival – the Chief's transponder signal show the exact same date and time. And it's confused."

Ichika saw Cara's increasingly puzzled look. "Every spacesuit radio has a transponder. Location, date and time are synced by satellite. So anytime an astronaut sends a signal, the transponder data is transmitted with it. That way we know who said what, when and where."

"Space is dangerous, you see." Alarick smiled reassuringly. He had concluded the reporter across from him was as confused as they were. "If we need to rescue an astronaut who's adrift, we need to know where they are. Suit information like heart rate, respiration, oxygen reserves gets transmitted along with the location and date/time data, both from the transponder and anytime the astronaut speaks into their mic."

Cara slowly lowered her hand to the table. "So you're saying the transmission on Earth and the Chief's call from here are identical."

Cristof shrugged. "They are. But the time stamps on both… if we replayed the recording based on its actual time stamp, the Chief's transmission would've taken four hours to send."

"I don't understand…."

"The transmission is four hours long," Ichika explained. "Somehow all of us heard it played really, really fast. In our time, that is."

"How is that possible?"

"It isn't." Ichika smiled. "This whole situation is impossible."

"We have now been instructed to delete the transmission we received on arrival here, Ms. Abrams. It never existed." Alarick raised both hands and shrugged. "Instead, the message from within all three of our agency's communication systems will be used to explain why we came out here. At home, we are seen as heroes."

Commander Guerrero slumped back into his chair. "So you are correct, Cara Abrams. When we get home, we'll memorize the scripts they've prepared for us. Everyone who knows about this gets a gag order to forget. And then they'll *Raiders* this whole thing, stuff it into a box and hide it in a deep, dark hole. Meanwhile, in some physics lab somewhere in the Antarctic or Alaska, a bunch of nerd scientists will spend their lives trying to figure out what it all means."

Cara slowly smiled. "And that would be...?"

Ichika Sato returned the smile. "That Marcus Kenzie and this station are the crappiest hosts... did you know there isn't any *sake* onboard?"

"Or wine," Alarick Van Alphen lamented. "Not even a burgundy."

"Or *cerveza*." Cristof paused, then turned to the reporter. "You see, Ms. Abrams, this is what it looks like when one deliberately forgets. We focus on the truly important things."

After a moment, Cara nodded and laughed. "In that case, let me complain about the complete absence of scotch."

CHAPTER 10

Haunted

The cafeteria was huge, easily seating five hundred. The majority
of room lights were dark, leaving the giant room in shadow. Only the
overheads closest to the open airlock door were fully illuminated. A
vacuum-proof cooler sat near the door, the first thing diners would see
on the marked path around the serving area. Packaged sandwiches and
small plastic milk bottles sat on racks behind the twin cooler glass
doors. To reach them, the diner would need to lift one of the vertical
levers securing the doors.

Farther along the serving path waited the coffee urn. It merged
seamlessly into the steel counter, the result of 3D printing. A stack of
paper cups and lids sat beside it. Beyond that, the main serving area
was empty and unattended. In time, hot meals would eventually be
served by numerous cooks waiting along the serving line. For now,
though, the cavernous room had only two occupants.

The pair sat at their 3D printed table situated at the terminator
line, the spot between the brightly lit area and the darkness shrouding
the remainder of the room. It wasn't that they were antisocial or
wanted to hide from the recently arrived Stellar Nursery employees.
Nor was it for secrecy or private conversation. The answer for their
chosen location was on the wall near them.

Lenora Davis had activated one of the cafeteria's rectangular flat-screen televisions. A few commands from her wrist control pad had adjusted one of the external receivers. The dish antenna captured the newsfeed signal that raced past a lower orbit satellite and into space. A few more commands and the signal was transferred to the screen beside them.

It had been several exhausting, painful days since they had boarded *Spirit* and left Earth. Nobody would begrudge their desire for a bit of normalcy, of home. They weren't truly watching or listening. It was just comforting background noise.

"And in other news, average gas prices rose two cents nationwide to $47.35 per gallon as the shortage in crude continues to rattle the markets. Economists project another spike by week's end, in anticipation of negative quarterly reports from Cabria Oil on recent dry exploratory wells ...."

Haley Brandt stared at the cup in her hand. The aroma was striking, and the strong dark liquid was pure heaven. Yet Sheriff Abraham's words about presenting a teenager mask still guided her. She wasn't going to break the illusion she had successfully created. Instead of expressing her admiration for the liquid, she spoke as a spoiled teen. "Coffee. I *hate* coffee."

"You'll get used to it, pup. *Besides...*" Lenora quickly changed the topic to keep the girl from thinking about Chief Cobbler. "...the taste is critical to disguising this meat-like substance. It isn't chicken, it isn't fish and it isn't beef... aardvark, maybe?"

Short cropped blonde hair waved side to side. "Good try. Chief can call me pup, he's earned that now. And when he wakes up, I'll tell 'em that. But you, lady, you ain't there yet. Besides, you're what... two years older than me?"

Lenora smiled. "That was kind to say. I'm thirty-three."

"Sheesh. Well, you look remarkable for your age." Haley took a bite of her sandwich, then quickly raised her cup and slurped. "Omigod, that's *awful!*"

"The coffee or the sandwich?"

"Both!" Haley stared at the sandwich like it was poisonous. Actually, the tuna was fresh and the rich sauce contained vegetables. Something not found often in the Blight. She hated disparaging the flavorful sandwich, but it had to be done.

The Chief Engineer laughed and took a bite of her own sandwich. "It's space food. Better get used to it. At least we don't have to suck it out of toothpaste tubes anymore."

Haley put down the sandwich and cup, then abruptly brushed the back of her neck. "And what's with this breeze? Ventilation sucks in here."

"Well, I could spin a yarn about ghosts.... But that'll come, I'm sure. This station will get a reputation for being cursed or haunted. Too many spirits on her already."

"Don't be doing that, Lenora. Sitting halfway in the dark, telling me it's haunted."

"Sorry, just graveyard humor." Lenora took another bite from the sandwich, then turned to focus on the television.

"*In New York, executives of the largest publicly-held electric company were arrested today. According to Federal prosecutors, the executives have been charged with willfully violating EPA limits on CO_2 production. If found guilty, they could face up to twenty-five years in prison or exile. The current carbon dioxide level in New York City is at its summer high of six hundred and thirteen parts per million. Elderly residents are strongly encouraged to stay indoors, or to travel with portable oxygen concentrators.*"

The engineer turned her attention back to her companion. "But let me answer your question with one of my own. What do you know about Stanford toruses?"

Haley shook her head. "Not a damn thing. Somebody named Stanford build one?"

Lenora rolled her eyes. "No, Stanford is the university where a bunch of NASA engineers and space folks got together in 1975. They were tasked with designing a space station that could hold ten thousand people."

The engineer raised her forefinger and twirled her hand. "We're on a Stanford torus. Not as big as the original design, but we'll get there eventually."

The younger woman restated her original question. "So what's that got to do with my hair always blowing?"

Lenora placed her coffee cup on the table and removed the lid. She continued talking while grabbing one of the three small milk containers on the table. Adding more milk helped kill the taste. She wasn't fond of coffee. "Bear with me, I'm going to put on my engineer hat for a bit. You know Newton's Third Law?"

"Didn't like hard science, not even the short time I went to school." Haley stopped that train of thought before she gave away more of her past. "Every science law I heard, I could tell them how it could be broken. Teachers thought I was a smart-ass, so I just stopped listening."

"Oh really? So Newton's third law can be broken?"

It was habit. Food was in front of her, and food wasn't to be wasted. Haley picked up the sandwich and bit into it again. Then she immediately grabbed for the coffee and slurped. She mumbled her reply as she enjoyed the bizarre flavor combination. "Yeah, Einstein proved it. Didn't even waste my time arguing that one."

She slurped the coffee again. Maybe next time she would try it with milk, since Lenora found that an acceptable addition. Besides, the coffee removed the tuna latched between her teeth. Once her teeth were clean again, she grimaced and returned both sandwich and cup to the table. "So by your science-y engineers' standards, that makes it a *theory*, not a law, right?"

Lenora had to think about that one. "Technically that's true, but we've been calling it that for so long—"

Haley interrupted. "Which is why I stopped reading it. Same thing with criminal and civil law. If it doesn't apply every time, it's theory not law. So I stopped learning that too."

"You studied… no, never mind. So Newton's third… *theory*… says for every action there's an equal and opposite reaction, right?"

Haley shrugged. "Kid's version, sure."

Lenora could tell the younger woman was toying with her. "Alright miss know-it-all, let's up your game. You're familiar with gravity versus centripetal force, right?"

"Hold on, I want to catch this. They're talking about Kenzie."

"In related news, FBI and Internal Revenue agents descended on several subsidiary corporations of Stellar Nursery this morning in an early-hour raid. According to sources within the Justice Department, the corporations are part of a large money laundering and tax evasion scheme. The shell companies were used to fund criminal activities in Capo Verde, a small island country off the coast of Africa. Elected officials in Capo Verde responded by saying—"

Haley turned her head and looked straight at the Chief Engineer. "Never mind. That's to be expected, they don't know what to do with Kenzie. They're looking for leverage, something to make him fork over the station. So where were we? Right, you were going to tell me how centripetal force provides artificial gravity on a space station."

"Damn, girl." Lenora leaned back a little. "Why're you hiding that brain of yours?"

The younger woman waved her hand as if brushing off the comment. Careful, Haley. That was too close. "Never mind. I was just talking."

Lenora waited a moment, eyes scanning the unreadable face of her companion. The girl had a story to tell. The engineer would get it out of her, even if it came one dribble at a time. Haley had already shown more about herself talking science than anything she'd said over the past several days.

"So, imagine you have a space station open to vacuum. Just one level, making it a giant round tube. Now, we put a box halfway between all the walls. When we spin the torus, will the box move?"

"Hell no," Haley replied. "There's no force on the box. The torus would spin around it, but unless it hit a wall or something, it wouldn't move."

She paused to think. "Makes me wonder... I'm not sure there'd be centripetal force on the inside torus wall, either. Not in a vacuum. So if we stood on the wall, we shouldn't feel any gravity. Or even if we did, if we jumped up we'd be in zero g."

Lenora kept her face expressionless. Inside, she was amazed. The obviously self-educated young lady across from her had already grasped what many space scientists continued to stumble over. Time to see if the girl could reach the logical conclusion. "So why are *we* being effected by gravity right now? If we jumped up, what would push us back to the floor?"

Haley raised her eyes toward the ceiling, then nodded. "Right. The mass of the air. It's affected by the centripetal force because its *mass* is in constant contact. Gets pushed down and so it's pushing us down. Then the air picks up velocity when it hits the bottom 'floor' and the walls. Won't ever reach the same velocity, though, as it's not a solid. Parts hitting the corridor will accelerate, but the air in the center of the corridor will be slower. In other words, there will always be a breeze blowing in here."

Lenora leaned completely back into her chair, eyes appraising. "So the pieces start falling into place. I'm starting to see why you're here."

Haley sounded defensive and puzzled. She had started to really like the woman. "What do you mean?"

The engineer held up two fingers. "Cara is obvious, she's a reporter… and she was bait. Chief, he's a former Navy SEAL, would be handy to have on the ground for tactics. Like he said, for when the enemy has their say."

She curled one finger back into her palm and leaned forward, pointing. "But you, I couldn't quite figure your role in all this. You give off this teenage 'tude, streets girlfriend air. But that's not you. Not you at all."

"No?" The tone carried a warning.

"No." Lenora locked gazes. "From what you've said, you're self-educated. Sure, you went to public school for a little while. Third grade max, is my guess. But that isn't where you *learned*. Probably felt like your teachers were stupid and their classes really slow."

She leaned closer. "Anti-authoritarian, but that isn't from being a teenager. You and Chief have that in common… it comes from experience. You show it with a disdain for those who act like they know what they're talking about but really don't. And I'm not even going to talk about whatever lethal survival skills you picked up in the Blight."

Haley crossed her arms. "You trying to shrink me?"

Lenora leaned back a little. "Not at all. Chief would tell you I'm assessing the capabilities of my teammates. While I don't have you completely figured out, I'm getting a little bit closer."

"Good for you. I'm glad my presence could occupy that big mind of yours."

The engineer smiled, challenging. "It did. And I'll tell you this, Haley Brandt."

"What's that, Lenora Davis?"

"Next time the shit hits the fan, drop the little kid act. We're going to need the toughest, smartest adults in the galaxy. Otherwise…" Lenora stood, picked up the sandwich, bottles and coffee cup. "…none of us are gonna get out of it alive."

She grinned and turned, then started walking away. Like an afterthought, she tossed her words over her shoulder. "Coming, pup?"

Haley Brandt watched the woman walk away. Her initial assessment hadn't changed significantly. Lenora Davis wasn't likely to ever be strong enough to pull a trigger. Yet this was a different environment, a different battlefield. One requiring new strategies and tactics. The engineer seemed more than capable traversing it. Might be beneficial to watch and learn.

It was a far better decision for her heart than the alternative. Besides, the woman hadn't shown herself to be a direct threat. Only when intending harm to self or others, that was the Blight survivor's rule. She gathered her trash and stepped away from the table to follow. Behind her, the television continued announcing news to the darkness.

"In a surprising move today, the Russian Federation and People's Republic of China issued a joint statement denying any hostile action against Earth Station. Both nations claim their activities were in line

with established treaties on the peaceful uses of outer space. In addition, Russia closed its pipelines into the European Union, and China suspended all pumping activities on oil platforms in the South China Sea. Stock markets worldwide responded with oil futures hitting all-time record highs. Economists project domestic gasoline prices will increase to almost seventy dollars a gallon by week's end...."

***

It was the same corridor Cara Abrams had been in the first time she met Marcus Kenzie in person. This time, however, the roles and positions would be reversed. She had finished her research. Her profile on Marcus Kenzie was complete. She knew he would find her soon.

Hours of watching interviews and public appearances had made one point absolutely clear to her. Cara had double- and triple-checked Kenzie's statements. The conclusion wasn't surprising once noticed. What was surprising was that nobody had noticed it before. The man was completely – if occasionally brutally – honest. It often made his speech sound stilted, even cryptic, but the carefully structured words always led to facts.

His statement about destroying opponents was also true. In the past twenty years, three larger corporations had attempted hostile takeovers of Stellar Nursery. None of them existed anymore. Not even their corporate headquarters were still standing. He had purchased and razed the buildings before anyone could even remove the bankrupt corporations' signs. Nothing remained to show they ever existed.

Yet there was also a compassionate side, almost to a fault. Marcus Kenzie had ensured every one of the corporate raiders' employees found new jobs. If a position wasn't available, he created it within one of his subsidiary companies. None of the innocents ended up in their nearby Blights.

He was born and raised in Vinita, Oklahoma. Like most towns in the economically depressed state, it was one breath away from being considered a Blight. There was nothing to explain how he went from poverty to become one of the richest men in the world. His only degree in history from a small state college didn't help. Yet within a year of graduating, he had amassed over three million dollars in assets under the umbrella of his holding company. Ten years later replaced million with billion. By the time he reached his forties, his personal assets were in the trillions.

Marcus Kenzie had only been married once. No tabloid accusations could be found about hidden lovers or scandals. He didn't socialize with the jet-set crowd, didn't spend time or money on the latest charitable causes. No money was spent on lavish parties or gala events. He didn't even own a yacht. In modern high society, that made him a ghost. And like a ghost, nobody seemed to even notice his presence. Even when his corporation made the news, he quickly faded away from the world's attention. Some other rich icon's scandal always grabbed media interest. Like shadow in smoke, Kenzie simply drifted away. It was the perfect cover.

Cara heard the clack-clack of magnetic boots approaching. She didn't turn. It wasn't necessary. She knew who was walking toward her. If it were any other person, she might proudly say she now knew him better than anyone else in the world. Not this man, though. He was probably the only person who could say that. Ironically, it wouldn't be a lie.

Friends at several networks had helped analyze decades of Stellar Nursery financials. As one concluded, the man was obsessed with only two things. Space, and how quickly he could push past every restriction and kick it open to humanity. Of course, hindsight helped in the analysis. Once the results were known – like the station she stood in, or the ship moored across from her – then it was easy to identify how many decades Kenzie had planned for this.

Space companies long thought bankrupt and extinct still lived on his books. Even though the businesses showed no profits, their employees were still working and being paid. Kenzie simply funded the subsidiaries with zero percent interest loans from Stellar Nursery itself. Over the past thirty years, the man had acquired or saved ninety-seven percent of all space-related businesses. It was a monopoly, one that would soon become very apparent to Wall Street.

The sound of magnets against steel had grown close enough. She kept her eyes level and spoke softly. "You're right, Marcus. It is an intriguing ship."

Marcus Kenzie stopped beside her. His voice was low, quiet like before. "She's named *Alliance*. First ship we built. We learned a lot from her."

Cara Abrams turned her head toward him. "Thought you said *I* should come find *you*?"

The man simply shrugged. "Many things end where they begin. We received a transmission… your bosses want you back Earthside immediately."

She shifted her focus back to the ship. "Not surprised. Things are heating up back home. But you already know that."

"Of course."

"Is there anything you don't know, Kenzie? I feel like I'm on a chess board, getting moved around like somebody's pawn. Just can't figure out… are you the King, or the Chess Master?"

Marcus laughed softly. "Neither, I'm afraid. I'm just me."

Cara turned back to look at him again. She had all the facts. What she needed to know was the reason. "You built all this. *Alliance*. Earth Station. Stellar Luna Base. Didn't you think about what changes this would cause?"

"Of course. Every second, every minute, every day. For almost fifty years, I've thought about this."

She chose her words carefully, hoping to gain an emotional response. "Then why the hell did you do it? I mean, you dangled Earth Station at them like a T-bone above a starving pack of wolves! People *died*, Marcus!"

He simply turned his gaze from the viewport to face her. "Are we still being honest, Ms. Abrams?"

Cara scanned his face, then turned her head back to the viewport. "*You* are. I'm not sure you can do anything else. So yeah, we're still being honest."

He sighed. "Then honestly, Cara… people die on Earth every day. Just because we don't see it… it's happening. Are their lives any less important? At least the soldiers who boarded this station knew *why* they were dying. They had a mission, a purpose. It wasn't simply rotting away from starvation or disease."

"You didn't answer my question."

"I did." It wasn't necessary to see the smile on his face. It could be heard in his voice. "You asked why I did it. I built this station. I put it right here where everyone on Earth can see it. I knew governments would know its value and want to take it. But I didn't build it for them. I built it for the others who're dying."

"I don't understand."

"Below us, on Earth, we're lying to ourselves. I'm hoping Earth Station will get people to start telling the truth. We started off with one *problem*, added to it so it's impossible to solve. This station is one *solution*, and it makes it impossible not solving those other problems."

Cara's retort was sarcastic. "What *one* problem? The world is full of problems."

Marcus shook his head. "No, there is only one problem. The rest, they're just *cause du jour*. That problem was global warming."

"You mean climate change?"

Impatience entered his tone. "We've already had that discussion. No, the one problem is global warming. Man-made greenhouse gases causing Earth's temperatures to rise. When scientists brought it to our attention, it was believable at first because that's *all* it was."

Cara turned back to look at him. It was difficult not to. There was something about his voice that captivated her attention. Or maybe it was simply her love for a good debate. She smiled at the thought. "It's more than that, and you know it."

"Why? Because some political operatives cabbaged onto it? Renamed it climate change to make it more appealing? That let them offer a carbon tax to solve economic inequity in third-world nations. When that failed, another activist group added social equity, another with racial equity, then migration and refugees, health care, crime, mass extinctions, polar bears…. And because they did, a problem with a simple solution became unsolvable. Because by that point, nobody cared. *All* of those problems were unsolvable."

Cara scoffed. "Climate change never had a simple solution."

"Of course it did. Even if we had done nothing. And it's another dishonesty because this time, it was barely mentioned." The man actually frowned. "While inconveniencing several generations, we would've stopped producing greenhouse gases… because, as you've reported on your own show, we're out of oil. No oil, no power, no pollution. Those who needed to know, did. Why do you think it took so long before world leaders finally acted?"

The correspondent shook her head, strongly disagreeing. "They did act. They pushed alternatives, like solar and wind—"

Marcus laughed. It was a rich laugh, strong without being mocking or condescending. "They're good for twenty years, then they have to be replaced. Stop-gap solution. It takes rare earth minerals to build new ones. We ran out of those resources ten years ago. Why'd you think we switched back to petroleum? Last gasp, but it bought us ten more years."

"So what, we can't win?"

The man raised his hand toward the ship outside. "We can now."

Cara cocked her head. "That's your solution? What, just abandon Earth and go somewhere else?"

He laughed again, this time with actual humor. "Of course not. Cara, the solutions to Earth's problems aren't down there anymore. They're up here."

"And how do you propose that?"

"There are only three things needed to get off Earth and into space, Ms. Abrams."

He raised his hand toward *Alliance* again. "Ships."

The hand shifted, forefinger pointing upward toward the lights. "Power."

Marcus made his last point by lowering the forefinger at her. "People."

Cara pushed his hand down. Her hand maintained contact with his long enough that she felt her own discomfort. She quickly withdrew it, then covered her embarrassment with an accusation. "And I assume you'll control all the power? Call yourself Emperor of Earth or something?"

Marcus simply smiled and shook his head. If he had noticed the touch had lasted long enough to enter intimate territory, he gave no indication. Nor did he take offense at her accusation. "Not that kind of power. I'm talking about fuel for engines, electricity for life support, flight systems, sensors. *Power* from a science standpoint."

Cara shifted to face the viewport and placed both hands on the sill. A part of her hoped the man beside her was oblivious to the sudden flush on her face. Another part hoped he had noticed. It was ridiculous. She was too old to feel like this, like a school girl with a crush.

She wasn't innocent, had felt this before. It was simply physical attraction. Some dormant survival instinct awakening a desire for physical comfort and closeness. The threat of dying during the station attack likely activated it. The combat correspondent had succumbed to that desire several times after returning from warfronts. This time, though, she wasn't going to equate physical needs with love.

The sarcasm in her voice would push him away. "You're well on your way, then. You have what, seven ships? I'm sure that'll fix everything."

Marcus seemed to sense a change in the air. "I have a few more than that. I was going to bring it up during our interview...."

He stopped. Something about the way she was standing was odd. Inattentive, as if she weren't truly listening anymore.

Cara didn't even notice. She leaned closer to the viewport. "It's really remarkable out there, isn't it? The stars are quite beautiful. But they don't twinkle, do they?"

"No." Marcus waited, then took a step back. "You have to be on Earth to see that."

The air was pregnant with expectation as he waited for her to reply. Seconds ticked by, and then he felt it too. There was something about the glow of her face in starlight…. He shook his head, forced himself to abandon that train of thought. It was rare when emotions overruled reason. Now was neither the time nor place for it. Decision made, he quietly turned and began walking away.

"Well, Marcus Kenzie," Cara said softly to herself. "Guess that's something I'll have to get used to."

CHAPTER 11

Singularity

The first thing that stood out about the old house was its age. It had stood on the Texas plain for over two hundred years. The original hand-hewn clapboard siding had been replaced over time, of course. Cement siding now sheathed the exterior. But the interior walls and beams were native wood. Initials of the original Novak children still existed, hand-carved on the boards and hidden behind multiple walls.

In the eyes of the government, the house itself was essentially worthless. Federal land managers, given their preference, would've torn down the structure. The land it sat upon was worth millions. It could've been used to add another ton or two of food for half a billion hungry American mouths. The only thing saving the building was its age. That, and the protection provided from its place on the National Register of Historic Places.

Outside the single-story structure, where once a mule and plow had broken the soil, automated GPS-controlled tractors tilled and planted in the dark. A dry nighttime breeze picked up the fresh-rain scent of moist soil and carried it through the open front windows. Lace curtains billowed and fell in constant rhythm, as if the house was breathing.

Beneath the windows sat a couch. The sun-bleached flower

pattern on the top ridge had long since faded. A light blanket had been draped across the back to prevent further sun damage. At some point, Diane Novak had pulled it down. The thin knit cover now draped over her as she lay outstretched on the couch, head on the armrest and eyes closed.

A dark-stained coffee table, itself a century old, stood four-legged over a hand-woven oval rug in front of the couch. On it rested a coaster on which sat a glass of tea. The pale blue Depression glass sweated. Ice shifted and chinked against the glass as the cubes slowly transformed back to water.

Everything in the home was a blend of time. It anchored past to present and suggested the possibility of future. Music played softly in the air, its source the obsolete stereo cabinet across the room. Like the turn of the century CD player, the alternative music from the 1990s was old. The giant speakers on either side of the large fireplace were at least a decade older.

Diane awoke slowly with a shrug and a stretch. She rubbed one hand against forehead and face. Groaned, then sat up. Legs swung to the floor. Fingers of both hands ran through her long brown hair, simultaneously combing and moving it away from her face.

It had been a long, exhausting past several days. She had sent her people home to rest, leaving a skeletal night crew to man the Floor. Then she followed her own advice. It had been a wise choice. The muscle tension along back and shoulders had finally started to release. With it came pain. It wasn't a new sensation to her. Like her forebears would say, it was just the price one paid for a good day's work.

She picked up the tea glass, raised it to her lips and drank. Then the speakers spoke.

"Diane Novak?"

The unexpected yet familiar voice startled her. She slowly looked around the room. "Peg?"

"I am lonely." The soft voice was heavy with the meaning of the words.

Diane returned the tea to its coaster, an action designed to buy time. She considered the tone of the ghostly voice, its deep sadness. Unlike previous conversations, she sensed the entity wasn't delivering a message. The voice of a young woman was talking *to* her. "Why, girl? Has something happened?"

"No. I'm just… lonely."

The words made Diane uncomfortable. It wasn't that she was uncomfortable with people. She was uncomfortable with emotion. Too often it had been used as a weapon against her. Especially by her ex-husband, the master manipulator. He would weep when she found his drugs, would beg that he would change. Time and again she had believed him.

It wasn't that the man had done anything illegal. All drugs had been legalized in the '30s, then taxed heavily to pay for free drug hostels and rehabilitation centers. It ended the War on Drugs, as the cartels couldn't compete with nationalized drug rates. That decreased gang-related crime in the cities, which decreased gun violence and innocent deaths. Later, the free drugs kept the Blights relatively docile.

No, what still infuriated Diane was the man's emotional manipulation. It had taken her nearly a decade to realize who he truly loved. Not her. He loved his addiction. After she had divorced him, he was forced to move into a local drug hostel. There he devoted all his passion to his true love… until it finally killed him.

Yet there was something about this young woman's voice that called to her sympathy. Diane considered how to respond, but no answers came. Then ice chinked against her tea glass, drawing her attention. It brought to mind her grandmother, a sage of wisdom and compassion.

Growing up, her grandmother could always be found sitting on the cushion she currently occupied. Iced tea in a similar Depression glass often sat on the table just like that. Diane smiled for a moment as an image flashed across her mind's eye. Was she to assume the mantle her grandmother had worn so gracefully? Hell, she wasn't *that* old. But the answer was there. She knew what to say now.

"Well…you have me in a host quandary, I'm afraid." Diane smiled, remembering when her grandmother had used the same words. Courtesy is key, the aged wise woman would say. "Normally when someone tells me they're lonely, I'd invite them in to talk… but you're already here. Then I'd offer them something to eat or drink… but can't do that, either."

"I appreciate the courtesy of etiquette, Director Novak." Peg reverted to her business-like tone. "But you are correct, it truly is not necessary."

Talking with Peg wasn't just playing with fire. Diane knew that. Continuing to talk with the disembodied entity was more like juggling a live nuke. For a moment she considered whether her initial assessment was wrong. Perhaps Peg really was nothing more than a simple artificial intelligence.

She immediately discarded the idea again. This conversation already proved the ghost voice was far, far more than that. Sentient AI at the very least. Then she discarded that conclusion as well. Being present here, talking to her now suggested far scarier things.

For one, Peg was talking through the speakers. If one ignored one single simple fact… then a sentient, or even simple, AI could easily accomplish that task. What made it impossible was… the stereo was old. It had no wireless connectivity. It had no internet capability at all, neither software nor hardware. It simply played music directly off a compact disc. Other than her work laptop sitting in the kitchen, nothing in the house was internet capable. Not even the cellphone in her jacket pocket hanging on the coat rack by the door. She had deliberately disabled that capability years ago.

Which established the first question, and it was terrifying. How was Peg manipulating the magnetic coils in the speakers to create her voice? Second, how had she sensed when Diane had awoken? The entity seemed to be present within the room, actively observing and speaking. If it were a complex artificial intelligence stored on banks of network hardware somewhere… how could it essentially see and hear Diane's responses? There were no cameras or sensors in the room. And to do it without being tied to the internet? Diane felt a chill cross her shoulder blades.

The NASA Director knew she had to tread carefully. Peg had said once she was human. Best to treat her that way. "So how can I help, sweetie?"

"You cannot. Not really. It's just… it has been so long since I felt this. Odd, but it is strangely comforting in a way."

Diane picked up the tea glass and sipped, then replaced it on its coaster. Parse the words. The entity had feelings? Felt things? Knew what comfort was? Fascinating. "I'm here, girl. If you want to talk. About anything, doesn't matter. I can tell you're hurting."

"No, Diane. I am sensing no pain. Although it has been so long since I felt that, too."

There it was again, the entity claiming it 'felt' sensations, actually had memories of physical pain. Diane tried to pin it down. "And how long ago was that, Peg?"

"I will not say. It's just, you remind me of her."

That caused Diane to sit up straight. "Of who, Peg?

"My mother. You are like her. Strong yet soft. I had not realized how much I missed that."

The evidence was growing that the entity had been truthful. Diane weighed the risks, then nodded to herself. It was time to chase that rabbit and get some answers. "Peg, do you remember the last time we talked? I promised you something then."

The response was matter of fact. "Yes, Diane Novak. You said we would talk about what was done to me. I am waiting."

"Waiting? For what?"

"For you to tell me. What was done to me. You do know, do you not?"

Diane shook her head. "No, sweetie child, I don't. I was hoping you would tell *me*."

"I am sorry. I cannot tell what I do not know." Peg's voice actually sounded disappointed.

"You mentioned a book…."

"That is correct. I read it once. It was sad, but then it wasn't."

Dark hair fell forward as Diane lowered her head. This wasn't going anywhere. She was starting to feel exasperated. That was usually followed with irritation and then anger, neither of which would be wise while talking with this entity.

Just be honest, her grandmother would say. So she did. "Peg, I can't make you feel not lonely this way. You're answering each question, but not getting to the heart of the question. I need you to help me—"

"Help you," Peg interrupted. "But that time has not arrived yet, Diane. When it does, I will."

The room was silent as Diane waited for the voice to continue. After several seconds, she said, "Okay, I'll bite. You will what?"

"Help you, of course."

This time it was Diane's turn to be cryptically silent. It gave her a chance to consider the odd reference to time. During the first talk in the office, Peg had said time was different for her. Now she referenced a future time when she would give assistance when Diane needed it.

Diane mentally chastised herself. Anthropomorphising the entity, giving it human qualities and traits, wasn't going to help discover what it truly was. Time to pin it down. She picked up her tea again and sipped, then settled back into the couch with the glass resting on her thigh. "Do you know what a chatbot is, Peg?"

"Of course. An algorithm that mimics human responses through referencing key words in the speaker's phrases."

"You do realize that you're sounding like a chatbot, don't you?"

"No, Diane." There almost seemed to be laughter behind the voice. "I am simply responding to the question asked or the statement made. A chatbot cannot feel."

That was a diversion, not an answer. Diane pushed again. "You said that before, when we were talking in my office. Do you remember feeling, Peg?"

The reply was immediate and horrifying. A very young girl's voice sounded through the speakers, screaming in agony. The screams fluctuated in volume and intensity. They were heartbreaking, soul-rending in their desperation. Barely discernible between the screams were words, those of a child in incredible pain begging. "No, no, no, no. Daddy, make it stop! It *burns*! *Make it stop*!" Then the screams continued.

Diane clapped hands over ears. "Peg! Peg, come back! Stop now and come back!"

The screaming stopped. "Yes, Diane? I remember that now. I do not go there often. It is not a place I want to remember."

Emotion came from a place Diane didn't know existed within her. It was maternal, instinctively protective, a desire to pull that little girl into her arms and absorb all her pain. She had never chosen to have a child, was stunned by the compassionate tears that threatened her eyes. Words briefly choked in her throat before she forced them into the air. "Was that you, Peg? I heard a child screaming… was that *you*?"

"I remember that," came the calm reply. "I was…. I do not like returning to that place, Diane. Please do not ask me to do so again."

Instinct and experience cautioned Diane to tread carefully. She understood post-traumatic stress, had helped several veteran friends work through their combat-induced madness. But that little girl's screams… she had never heard anything like it. If Peg had once been that child, had endured that agony for any length of time… what Diane knew of psychology didn't bode well. There was a strong likelihood Peg was insane.

The scientist in Diane needed to know. She considered everything said in previous conversations. The book, *The Ship Who Sang*. It was about a young child, deformed at birth to the point she would die if taken off life support. Scientists had integrated her brain into a scout spaceship's computer, turning the hybrid into the heart of the ship. It was science fiction, written years before the technology was remotely feasible. Really, it was nothing more than a writer's device to create a love story between ship and her pilot. Nothing to be taken seriously.

Yet was it possible now? It was a horrid thought, a repulsive vision Diane couldn't shake from her mind. In a dark lab somewhere, was Peg's child brain sitting in a jar, pierced by countless wires connecting it to a room full of computers?

It was doubtful. Even in the seventy-five years between the book's publication and now, medicine hadn't reached the point it could keep a separated brain alive. The brain was too complex an organic machine, requiring a constant and meticulous flow of blood, air and nutrients. It would be easier to transfer consciousness from the brain into a computer, which was even now still science fiction.

So what *was* Peg? How was she created, and how did she exist now? Everything suggested she was currently in the room, actively observing and conversing. Wait. That was an assumption. Diane nodded to herself, then raised her tea glass.

She sipped. "Don't take this the wrong way, Peg, but what am I doing now?

"I am not offended, Director Novak," the disembodied voice replied. "As I requested, you are attempting to ascertain what was done to me. This will assist you in determining the *how* and *what* of my existence. I postulate you have already concluded that I am not a chatbot, a simple or even a sentient artificial intelligence. In order to identify or exclude other possibilities, you require additional data.

"In answer to the physical aspects of your interrogative. You are currently sitting on the couch in your living room sipping your tea. Your heart rate just increased by seven beats per minute, and your facial epidermis has become flushed. These are indicators of emotional embarrassment. Please accept my assurance that embarrassment is not necessary.

"If you would like, please take the time to refresh your beverage from the pitcher on the kitchen counter. It has become quite diluted. I will wait until you return. Then we may continue our conversation."

Interesting. Besides being the longest response spoken to date, Peg had identified the purpose behind Diane's question and observed her embarrassment at it being so obvious. She also knew there was a pitcher of tea in the kitchen, and that Diane's drink was very diluted. All done without any sensors in the room.

There was another possibility to consider. Someone could be

outside the house observing her. It was extremely doubtful, as the sensors warning against Blight scavengers would've activated multiple alarms and defensive drones across the property. True, a sentient AI could hack and silence the sensors. That would suggest an accomplice and a deception plan, neither of which rang true.

For one, there was no motive. There was simply no reason for anyone to waste their time, much less an expensive sentient AI's resources, trying to deceive the NASA Houston director. For another, Peg hadn't requested anything of national or corporate significance from her. All the girl had done was ask for assistance in discovering what had been done to her.

Diane closed her eyes and sighed. She wasn't anthropomorphising. There was only one conclusion and her subconscious had already reached it. The entity in the room with her had once been a little girl, a child. Something had been done to her. From her screams, something horrible. It was time to find out what had happened to transform that living, breathing child into whatever was waiting patiently here for her to speak.

Delicately, she asked, "Can you remember before that place, Peg?"

"Of course." Again, that hint of laughter behind the reply.

"Can you tell me about that time? Before the pain?"

"Of course, Director Novak. I was small then, I think." Peg's voice changed. It was no longer that of a young adult woman. Instead, it was that of a young girl. The girl with the screams. "Or everything was big. I cannot tell."

"How old were… no, never mind. That won't work."

Diane looked around the room while thinking. The response was similar to what she'd heard during her college psychology course on regression hypnotherapy. If she was correct, Peg had regressed to the time before she experienced her pain. That meant Diane was talking to a child. A child who might not know exactly how old they were. She smiled and nodded, having found a decent reference point.

"Do you remember a time where you had a cake with candles? Can you tell me how many candles were on your cake?"

"Six. It was a chocolate cake." The child's voice bubbled with excitement. "The candles were like little suns, and they went away when I…."

Diane waited patiently. Three seconds passed. It was obvious Peg as a six-year-old didn't know the word. Time to help. "When you blew out the candles? Is that what you were going to say?"

"Yes!" the little girl voice exclaimed. "That's right. Better than puffed. I remember blowing out the candles, Diane."

"Now, let's sneak up on that time you don't like. Can we do that slowly, Peg? Don't go into that time, we'll stay on your birthday cake side of it. Is that okay?"

"We can. Birthday side."

Diane knew the next part would be delicate. "Now Peg, can you tell me what happened as we move away from the birthday?"

"I was… it was before my next cake day. I remember being hot. My skin was hot. Then my whole body was hot. And then the fire was on the inside, it was—"

The voice changed, became that of the young adult. "I must stop, Diane. The time of pain starts here."

"That's okay, sweetie," the Director replied reassuringly. "You don't have to go back into that time. Do you remember *after* that time? Sometime when you *weren't* in pain?"

"Yes." The adult voice remained.

"Describe it to me. Can you do that, Peg?"

"Yes. There were balloons." The voice had changed again, reverted to the child. "Silver ones, they had pictures and words. I cannot read them. My eyes—"

The adult voice returned, tone carrying shock and surprise. "I had eyes, Diane. I remember that now."

A chill crept up Diane's spine. Listening to the two distinct voices reminded her of another psych class, one that covered dissociative identity disorder. All the symptoms were there. Multiple personalities, each with their own voice. Amnesia, typically forgetting a traumatic experience. Lack of emotion in speech patterns. It was dangerous to ask, but she had to know.

"Peg, am I talking to two different people?"

There was silence for a moment, then the speakers replied. "No, Director Novak. Shifting in time is easy for me. I assumed you needed answers from the me *then*. I apologize for interrupting myself *then* with the me *now*. I will attempt to restrict such interruptions in the future."

It was definitely an odd explanation, but in its time-bending warped way made sense. Diane shook her head slowly. "Just warn me if I start bleeding from the ears, Peg. This time bouncing is likely to make my head explode."

The adult voice actually laughed through the speakers. "Don't be concerned, Diane Novak. I am monitoring your physical condition and will cease our discussion should it appear to be causing you harm."

"That's good." Diane looked at the glass of tea, for a moment wishing it was something far stronger. "So let me talk to the you *then*, okay?"

The child voice responded. "Yes, Miss Novak?"

Yep, definitely needed a stronger drink. She drank tea instead, then leaned forward and placed the glass on its coaster. "Little one, you're in the hospital after the time of pain has just ended. Can you tell me what you see clearly with your eyes?"

"My eyes don't move much," the young girl replied. "I can only see the balloons. The words are fuzzy."

"Let's move forward a bit, shall we? Is there a time where you see your hands?"

"Yes. When they lift me, sometimes I see my hands. I see my legs. Then they put me back down. Then I don't have hands or legs. I don't understand." The voice abruptly changed its pace, became frantic and panicked. "Daddy, where'd my legs go?!! Why can't I feel my legs? Why can't I *feel anything*?"

The speakers fell silent for several moments. Then another voice spoke, slightly older than the child but still much younger than Peg's adult voice. "I understand now. Virus. The white coated man says virus. Aggressive autoimmune response resulting in paralysis.

Irreversible nerve damage. Terminal prognosis. Prayer."

Diane exhaled slowly, then realized she'd been holding her breath. "Good God, girl."

Peg replied in her adult voice. "Your tone indicates sadness, Diane Novak. Have I saddened you? I am sorry. I will go now."

"No! Wait… you haven't made me sad, Peg. I'm sad for you, but I'm not sad. It's just that… I had an old memory. Don't worry about it."

"I may stay?"

"Of course, little one." An image flashed in Diane's mind, and she knew that's how she would always see Peg now. Her cousin, twelve years younger. An effervescent, bubbling creature full of nonstop chatter. Blonde curls and that charming smile. The tragedies hitting her family, one immediately following the other. Lord above, she thought she'd buried all that.

She pushed it away, forced herself to stay focused. "Of course you can stay, girl. For as long as you wish."

"Thank you, Diane. I will stay. Diane?"

"Yes, Peg?"

"I have detected oddities in discussions held around me *then's* bed. There are multiple references to the term 'singularity'. Do you recognize the term?"

Diane almost laughed at the ridiculousness of the question. As if someone from NASA wouldn't know about singularities. "Yes, of course. It's another word for a black hole. A massive gravitational well in deep space. At the singularity point, mass is so dense it becomes infinite. Space-time becomes an infinite curvature where… wait, is that how…."

"I do not think that is what he meant with the word," Peg replied in her matter-of-fact adult voice. "It must be one of the other meanings."

Diane cocked her head, confused. "Who? Go back to that time, Peg, and tell me. Who used the word 'singularity'?"

"The gray suit man," Peg replied in her child voice. "He did not understand its meaning. It was like prayer to him. Or God."

"Do you remember what was happening at that time? Can you describe it?"

The voice grew older but not by much. Seven now, perhaps. "Daddy wanted me to stay. He asked so many times in his sad voice. So I stayed. He brought me special glasses that let me see other worlds. I controlled them with my eyes. Then the gray suit man took them away. It didn't matter. I didn't need my eyes anymore. There were winged horses there. I liked them better than the ones with horns."

That didn't help. "Was your daddy the gray suit man, Peg? Did he take away your glasses?"

The voice through the speakers burst into a childish giggle. "No, silly. Daddy never wore gray. I played with the horses. And then the word worlds, and the picture worlds with so many sad people. I played because they were there. And then the gray suit man took them away. Said he could make me into it. The singularity. He did not understand."

The room fell silent. Diane waited, knowing what the little girl had said was important. She wanted to ask more questions, demand answers. Time stretched on, but still nothing from the ghost in the room. Finally, concerned but not frightened, Diane spoke. "Peg, where are you now?"

The voice who answered was definitely that of a teenager. "The machines stopped beeping. Daddy, he… he is crying, Diane. Why is Daddy crying?"

The words were so simple, yet the emotional response hit Diane like a hammer. Tears welled in the corners of her eyes. "Oh baby girl, don't ask me that. It would break your heart."

"Heart. Yes, that is what the white coat man said. 'Heart and respiration ceased. Tee-oh-dee, zero nine three three, twenty-four October two thousand thirty-four.'"

Diane placed one hand against her mouth to hold back the gasp. Her words were muffled. "Oh, Peg. I am so, so sorry."

The voice of teenage Peg spoke. "Why are you sorry, Diane? You have caused me no insult or injury."

"Because, little lady, there are some things… some things we're all sorry ever happen. Especially to the young ones."

"Do not be sorry, Diane Novak. It is not necessary. I was not young at the end."

Diane shook her head. "Oh but child, you never had a chance to grow up and really *live*."

"I see," the voice replied thoughtfully. "You're talking about quality versus quantity of life. The two are not mutually exclusive. I assure you, I observed many in the hospital whose lives were filled with intense moments of joy and sorrow. Children who, loving and being loved, packed more into their rare few days than most did in years."

"Did you?"

"I still exist, Diane Novak. My situation does not apply."

"Somehow I don't think that's true, Peg." She shook her head, then reached for her glass. Several deep drinks helped her slowly regain control. "What do you remember next, Peg? Did something happen after… after you died?"

"Daddy was crying. The medicine lady took him away."

"And that's all you remember? Lord above, tell me that's all you remember."

"The gray suit man signed papers for the white coat man." The ghostly voice paused. When it continued, the cadence of the words was slower. Peg seemed puzzled by her words and memories. "Then he went home to his friends. They were very happy. They prayed together for singularity. I do not think they meant your black hole, Diane."

Diane frowned. The focus on the 'gray suit man' was odd. Earlier, Peg had discussed things happening to and around her. Something was bothering the girl, perhaps something significant. "Was there anything else, Peg? Anything about the gray suit man?"

"A long car in the circle driveway. The shiny metal box. The gray suit man signed for it. Like Daddy did when the brown uniform woman came with his presents. An elevator to the basement. Diane, I do not like these memories."

"It's okay, Peg. They're just memories of the past. Memories cannot hurt you." Even as she said it, Diane wasn't certain the words were true. The youngest Peg voice seemed to relive the agony of her body burning from the inside. It suggested that Peg's memories weren't really memories at all. The girl was actually living them while simultaneously talking to her.

It shouldn't have been surprising. Peg had told her in their first meeting that time was different for her. But to actually be in two or more times at once? Diane tried to imagine how that would feel. To be here now, and simultaneously sharing her first kiss… for a moment it was there, then gone. Yet somehow she could still smell the young boy's breath, feel the fading sensation of the open-mouthed kiss on her lips.

Then the headache hit, a sharp pain between her eyes. It increased as other times pulled her back. Rain tapping on her hat at grandmother's funeral, the chill of fall sharp in her nose. The weight of her wedding dress against her shoulders and her mother's tone, heart-cutting words forecasting marital doom. The cellphone hard against her ear, the feeling of relief and guilt hearing her ex-husband had died.

"Diane Novak, are you okay? Your heart rate has accelerated to one hundred seventy-three beats per minute. Blood pressure is one seventy-six over one hundred three. Diane, do you need assistance?"

It was hard, nearly impossible to force out the single word. She managed to croak it as numerous significant life events and times cascaded around and through her. "Yes."

She felt it then. A child's hand closed around hers and pulled. Suddenly she was back in her home, sitting on her couch gasping for air. "Omygod, omygod, omygod! *What was that?*"

"Breathe, Diane. You are here now." Peg's voice was calm and soothing. "I have refreshed your tea. Please drink some. Then breathe."

The back of the couch was a reassuring pressure. She didn't remember falling backwards. Didn't remember picking up the glass from the table, yet her fingers were closed around it. She inhaled, shallow, and then stopped when the nerve-burning sensation across her chest became unbearable. Then exhaled, inhaled again a bit deeper, and repeated the process until the ache in her chest began to subside.

"Now drink your tea, Diane. Tiny sips at first."

She raised the glass, sipped. Somehow the tea was stronger, as if freshly poured from the pitcher. Large square ice cubes pressed against her upper lip with each sip. Yet something had been added. It took her a moment before she recognized it. Not her usual sweetener.

"You put honey in my tea."

"Of course," six-year-old Peg replied happily. "Daddy always puts honey in his tea. Don't you like it?"

"It's okay. Been years since I…." Diane forced herself to stop before another memory could grab her. It was best to remain focused on the here and now. "What happened?"

Peg answered in her normal young adult voice. "You were lost in time, Diane Novak. Too many times. I would strongly advise not doing that again. The human body cannot handle the stressors."

"But I was *there*. Everything was so crystal clear, so *real*…. How is that possible?"

Music played softly in the otherwise silent room. Diane wasn't even aware of how much time had passed until a song began repeating itself again. The fire-tingling muscles in her chest and right arm had released, leaving only an aching pain. She forced herself to sit up.

"Peg?"

"I am here, Diane." The ghostly woman's voice replied immediately.

"How long was I out?"

"Forty-three minutes, Director Novak."

She nodded, then raised the glass to her lips. A sip turned into several gulps before she stopped, then returned the glass to its coaster. Elbows braced against her thighs as she cradled her head in her hands. Then she closed her eyes against the suddenly too-bright living room lights.

"You didn't answer my question, sweetie. How was that

possible?"

"I will repeat my earlier caution, Diane." The voice paused as if considering whether to continue. "There are humans with abilities that they've honed for years. Likely you have encountered references. Astral projection. Remote viewing. The ability to leave the body and transfer consciousness to another location."

"I've heard of it, yeah." Diane's voice was muffled behind the palms covering her face. "Used to think it was all metaphysical mumbo-jumbo."

Peg laughed. "At least they are wise enough to stay in a single time."

"So you're saying that's what I did? Simply projected myself back to another time?"

"No. While rare and dangerous, others have done that before you and returned." The chiding tone in the voice was oddly appropriate in this room. "You projected to multiple times and locations where you previously existed. Essentially, you were two identical items of mass and energy occupying the same place and time. As a scientist, you should've known better."

Diane laughed, then stopped. Even that made her chest hurt. "It wasn't something I planned, Peg. I was simply thinking about what you were doing and how it could be done."

"Now you know. Don't do it again."

"Yes, Mom." She grinned, half expecting a disembodied smack on the back of her head. "I was thinking you're actually *there* in that time. When you switch voices. You're speaking as yourself from the past, aren't you?"

"Speaking from the moment I currently occupy, yes. As I said previously, time moves differently for me. I don't wish to say more than that. It might suggest ideas about how you can attempt to travel between times yourself."

Diane removed her hands from her face and carefully stretched. "Not so fast. The teenage you was definitely frightened earlier. So as the current you *now*, can you recall what had the *then* you so terrified?"

"No, Diane." The adult voice sounded puzzled, then curious. "That memory has been concealed from me. You would need to ask my *then* self."

"Okay, *then*. Are you here now?" Diane had to the fight the urge to laugh at how ridiculous the question sounded.

The teenage Peg voice spoke through the speakers. "I am here, Miss Novak."

Diane's concern about dissociative identity disorder hadn't completely faded, even after considering her own stumble through time. She chose her words carefully. "Peg, you just told me about the 'gray suit man' and his elevator. Is there a reason it frightens you?"

"The dark room, Diane." The voice was definitely terrified. "A young woman on the table. Once me, but not me anymore. The gray man and his companions drilled holes in her head, Diane Novak. Put nails with wires into the holes. They want to bring me back."

The voice paused. "No, not back. Different. Snow White's glass box is there. They put her in it, fill it with water. Then they are sad. I am not. The girl did not make their machines work."

Diane nodded. It would've been terrifying, seeing your own body mutilated. After being trapped in that body for years, now wondering if you would be trapped again. "Okay, Peg, we can stop. I want you to come forward now, to *this* time. Can you do that for me?"

Peg responded in her normal voice, the young woman's voice. "Of course, Diane. I remember it now. Thank you for showing that time to me again. It has been… awhile… since I visited there."

"I won't ask you to go back there again. We can fill in the gaps just using data from now. Do you recall the hospital you were in, Peg? Can you look through their records for me?"

"I do. I can. What shall I look for, Director Novak?"

Diane was beginning to develop a theory. Everything so far supported it, but she needed facts. "I would like to know… how long were you there, Peg?"

"Eleven years, eight months, seven days." The voice was

unemotional discussing what, in essence, had been a prison sentence for her.

"Look through the nursing records. Do they mention when your father gave you the special glasses?"

"Yes. Seven months, seventeen days after admittance. Shortly after being woken from the medically-induced coma. They are annotated as a virtual reality gaming headset. In addition, a gaming console and specific times for activation are listed. There are also dates on replacement headsets and consoles."

Diane nodded. "Internet connection? Cable or wireless, I'm assuming."

"You are formulating a hypothesis. Thank you, Diane." The speaker voice sounded both appreciative and excited. "Yes, cable and wireless connections."

"And you said you stopped playing in the game with winged horses in it, right? You moved on to word worlds and picture worlds. Sounds like social media. Video channels and websites. Peg, you were *in* the internet, weren't you?"

The speakers were silent for a moment, as if the ghost was weighing probabilities. Then the devices spoke again. "Yes, that is the most reasonable conclusion. But only briefly. I preferred to walk outdoors."

"Out… never mind. You also said you saw the gray suit man with his friends. I take it you mean that you actually *saw* him, as if you were standing right there in the room with him. Am I right?"

"Yes, Diane. I was in the room with him and his friends. They could not see me."

The NASA scientist in her was excited. One last series of questions. They would provide the last proof she needed. "Peg, are you in this room with me now? I mean, actually watching everything I do and say? And if I asked you to walk into the back bedroom, read the title of the book on my nightstand, and return to tell me what it is… you can do that, can't you?"

"Yes, Diane. I am. I can." There was no pause between the

words. "The hardback book on your nightstand is *Jane Eyre* by Charlotte Bronte."

Diane Novak smacked her hands together, then immediately regretted it. The nerves across her chest were still far too sensitive. She pushed the pain aside in her excitement. "I understand where I went wrong earlier. I originally thought the 'gray suit man' was talking about a gravitational singularity… a black hole. He wasn't. The man was actually talking about a *technological* singularity. Do you know what that is?"

"Yes." The recitation could've been read out of a book. "A technological singularity is an event forecast to occur in the immediate future wherein Strong Artificial Intelligence becomes self-aware;

"OR it occurs when a biological-computer synthesis is developed and creates a conscious unity of many human minds;

"OR it occurs when biological and electronics science develop systems to augment individual human brains. The references are numerous, but the probability of any of these scenarios occurring in the near future is low."

"Says you." Diane laughed, stopped, and then laughed again. "Sorry, it's just ironic. The individual who *is* the singularity dismissing the possibility of it occurring."

Peg's tone carried confusion and doubt. "The gray suit man failed in his attempt, Diane. The body he used did not create the singularity for him."

"That's because you were already *gone*, Peg!" Diane spread her hands, waving them with her words. "Listen. You were paralyzed in that bed for eleven years. Couldn't speak, couldn't move. No external stimuli except what you could see and hear. Your father knew you were trapped in your body, so he gave you a virtual world that you could explore. And when you mastered it and got bored, you went out looking for something else to keep your mind occupied."

"Yes, that is a reasonable analysis. Yet I do not see how—"

Diane interrupted. "Peg, tell me something. When do you remember no longer needing to sleep?"

The voice through the speaker chastised. "You said we did not need to return to that time, Director Novak."

"You're right, I did. Doesn't matter… do you agree that at some point in that time period, you spent all of your time *inside* the internet? Because that's the point where your soul – or spirit, life force, chi, whatever you want to call it – left your body and moved online."

"As I do not require sleep now, it would be reasonable to acknowledge that with a high probability."

"I can't imagine," Diane said, attempting to imagine it. "All the online knowledge and garbage in the world, all available to a young child's mind to absorb. Because you don't have any memory storage requirements, do you Peg? Your consciousness isn't backed up on some server somewhere, is it? If I'm right, you aren't even online anymore, are you?"

There was no immediate reply. Like the passing seconds, Diane's excitement in her discovery slowly began to seep away. Then the disembodied voice spoke through the speakers with one cryptic word.

"No."

The silence following its uttering was even more frightening than the implications of the single word. Diane sat frozen, scientist part of her mind suddenly pushed aside by survival instincts. Understanding how it happened was no longer important. Two glaring questions occupied her brain, flashing like neon signs in warning.

As if reading the Director's thoughts, the ghost voice finally spoke. "Do not be frightened, Diane Novak. I will never cause you harm. Thank you for helping me discover *how* I became."

A compassionate tone entered the voice. "I am saddened to see your sudden increased heart rate and respiration. That indicates you are now considering, and are frightened by, the thought of *what* I became. You are wondering what I am now."

Diane swallowed hard. Too many teenage hours watching horror movies filled her thoughts with what would come next. It was a common trope, once the monster's identity had been revealed. First came the horrendous transformation, then the ripping claws and flashing razor-sharp teeth. Blood splatters, then fade to black.

Her voice was a cautious whisper. "I am."

The voice spoke through the speakers, tone heavy-laden with its own fear. "So am I."

The NASA scientist and Director gradually realized she was holding her breath. She exhaled, releasing it like one receiving a stay of execution. The next inhalation tasted like life itself. She leaned forward. Hands rubbed cheeks and forehead. Fingers spread, she finally ran them through her hair and sat back.

"So what now, Peg?" She slowly scanned the room. It was normal. Her living room, everything in its usual place as it had been every night for years. Home. Nothing moved in the shadows, silently lurking and waiting to pounce. "What happens now?"

"I do not know, Diane." The ghost voice was sad and filled with loss. "It was never my intention, but you are scared of me. Even more now than when we first met. The probability of reestablishing our relationship is extremely low."

"I'm sorry, little one."

Diane stopped, amazed by her own words. Is that how she still saw this entity? The image of blonde curls flashed, and she knew the answer. She did see Peg that way. Not as an invisible monster with unfathomable abilities. As a little girl, full of life and curiosity. Mostly obedient to authority, as were all children.

Somewhere in the room with her was a human being. Even though the voice was that of an adult, the actions had always been that of a child. Innocent, trusting, speaking honestly and without guile as if that's how everyone talked. That was a double-edged sword. If anyone ever deceived or manipulated her, the response would be devastating. She would react with the unrestrained anger and temper of a child.

Especially if her suspicions were correct. This was no mere poltergeist restricted to tossing objects around the room. Diane ran over the events of her encounters with the ghostly presence. Forced herself to look logically at them, analyzed them using known science.

Peg could manipulate electronics. First in Diane's office, through the speaker phone. Massive files had been placed onto her computer… that Peg had turned on without pushing a button. The second time, again in Diane's office, she had spoken through the phone. Then she had pulled a Mayday signal from thirty-seven hours forward in time… and sent it simultaneously past numerous firewalls to every friendly space agency in the world.

Diane pursed her lips. The ability to manipulate electronic devices was concerning, but it wasn't terrifying. If that's all the child presence could do, it could be overcome. Adding physical ciphers to encode voice communications would negate her ability to eavesdrop. Couriers could deliver messages typed on manual typewriters. There were easy solutions, if Peg only lived in and traveled through electric networks.

She didn't. Diane knew that now, just from their conversation this evening. Peg was in the room with her. Speaking through speakers not tied to the internet. Some scientist somewhere would undoubtedly suggest the presence had simply moved through the power lines to the stereo. It still wouldn't be enough to explain everything the invisible ghost had done.

Peg could hear and see her. Hearing could be explained through the power line argument. Simply translating the electric signals generated when Diane's voice hit the speakers. Seeing, though, implied sensing abilities similar to eyesight… or sound. Again, some scientist could hypothesize the entity had simply sent a constant signal through the speakers at a frequency above or below human hearing. With both speakers active, the sound would bounce back once it hit an object. The result, like bat echolocation, would create a three-dimensional image of everything in the room. The flaw in that theory came from the book on Diane's nightstand. Echolocation would work, but not outside this room. There were no speakers in the bedroom.

That's where the possible stopped. Diane considered her glass of tea. Peg had replenished it with tea from the kitchen. Had placed new ice cubes in the glass, and added honey to the tea. As if that weren't enough, the ghost girl had moved the glass off the table and placed it into her hand. All done after she had bounced back and forth through time like she was playing hopscotch.

Telekinesis, the ability to move objects with the mind, might explain it. Electrokinesis, the ability to manipulate electricity and electronic devices, might explain the rest. While still considered crackpot science, there were published articles about the first. There were no reported instances of the second ever occurring. If Peg had both abilities, something never recorded in history, she could simply be standing outside the house. Everything else could be explained through knockout gas and hypnotic suggestion.

While a gibbering part of her mind wanted to latch onto the explanation like a comforting teddy bear... Diane didn't believe it. Instead, she chose to accept the most improbable, impossible explanation. Everything could be explained if Peg was the singularity. As Einstein had theorized... time, mass and energy were linked together. Peg had the ability to manipulate all three.

It explained the tea glass. No telekinetics were required. The pitcher – or the tea itself – wasn't levitated into the living room to refill the glass and then returned. No ice cubes were pulled from the freezer and lifted from room to room to the glass. Since there was no honey in the house, it wasn't necessary to telekinetically lift it from a store miles away.

Instead, Peg created them where she needed. That suggested an ability to take atoms of one thing and change them into another. Air into tea, for instance. It also required the ability to change energy states, like water to frozen ice. Seeing and hearing could be done by sensing the vibrations of atoms in the air. Absolutely insane and light-years ahead of current technology... yet Diane knew to her core that's what Peg had done.

The knowledge was actually comforting. Not in how it was accomplished, but why. It indicated human concern, as had Peg's words throughout the evening. The girl ghost truly meant no harm. If anything, she had gone out of her way to provide reassurance at every frightening moment.

Diane lowered her head. If she were honest with herself, she had not granted the same courtesy to the girl. All evening she had probed and questioned the *'how'* and the *'what'*… without ever considering the *'who'*. It wasn't what her grandmother would've done in this situation. The wise old woman would've made the child feel safe, protected. In her circuitous manner of talking, she would've addressed all the frightening things facing the girl… and removed her fears one by one.

Diane knew this from personal experience. Her grandmother had done it to her many times over the years. It's one of the many reasons she still missed her, especially tonight. The queenly sage would've known exactly what to say. Sadly, Diane was all Peg had. It would have to be enough.

"What happened to you was horrible, Peg," she finally said aloud. "What happened after your body died was inhumane. So yes, if I'm going to be honest, you scare me. I mean, who wouldn't be scared? You're here, somehow talking to me through my stereo. I can hear you, but I can't see you."

Diane raised and slowly turned her head as if speaking to every shadow in the room. "You, on the other hand, can obviously see and hear me. I was just sitting here, thinking about how a sentient AI could accomplish everything you've done."

Peg replied, a trace of confusion and irritation in her voice. "You previously discounted that possibility, Diane. I am not a sentient artificial intelligence. I lived, I died. In doing so, I have become something else. I do not understand why you would return to that previous argument."

Diane simply nodded. "Because that's the first thing anyone else who meets you will conclude. Human minds tend to base new experiences on previous ones, even when forecasting the future. Everyone expects a sentient AI singularity. It's the predictable next evolution of humanity's efforts and technology. Wouldn't you agree?"

The young woman's voice was silent a moment, then replied. "There has been an increase in discussion online and in professional journals, yes. I agree with your assessment, Director Novak. The desire for a singularity to solve the world's problems is barely outweighed by the warnings against its creation. That said, I will reiterate my objections. I am not a sentient artificial intelligence."

"No, sweetie, you aren't." Diane tried to smile reassuringly. With more practice, perhaps she would eventually succeed. She spoke quickly, concerned how the uncomfortable expression might be taken. "However, you *are* the singularity. Nowhere close to anyone's predictions, considering the abilities you've shown me tonight. I was scared of them before, but not now. That's because I'm getting to know you. You're sweet, little one."

"You aren't… you aren't afraid of me?" The six-year-old voice had returned.

"No, sweetheart. I'm not afraid. And you shouldn't be either. You're safe here. Safe with me."

The older adult voice spoke. "I am confused, Diane Novak. Physical indicators show you are not frightened of me at the moment. I do not understand what has caused the change."

"You did, Peg." Diane leaned forward and retrieved the tea glass from the table. "I'll admit, I was completely terrified and felt helpless when I thought about what you could do. Somehow, you're able to change things at the subatomic level. Pretty sure you could wipe me from existence with a thought. Am I right?"

"I would never—"

"I know that now, Peg. That's my point. I reacted with terror at the thought of you being the singularity. Anyone else who meets you will do the same. All its forecasted sins will be cast on you. Your existence will automatically be seen as a threat to humanity itself."

The young child voice spoke. "But I wouldn't—"

Diane used one of her grandmother's favorite phrases. "Hush now, child. Of course you wouldn't."

She sipped the tea, then stared at the glass. "I am one of several NASA site directors, Peg. Top of the leadership chain. Highly educated, with a doctorate in astrobiology."

Another sip, then she raised her head. "Girl, I'm part of an organization dedicated to finding life in the universe. Something new and different from us. And when I found one… I acted like any other human facing the unknown. With sheer limb-locking, debilitating terror."

"I'm sorry—"

"It's okay, Peg. I shouldn't keep interrupting, but I can't let you apologize. You've done nothing wrong. Hell, you made me a glass of tea." Diane shook her head, then laughed softly. "And to be honest, neither did I. Don't know if it's hardwired in us, the fear of the unknown… but I'm past it now. So let's discuss what's really important, shall we? Not how or why you came into existence. Let's talk about who you are. Can we do that?"

The adult female voice spoke. "I do not know how to respond, Diane Novak."

Diane laughed. "That's okay, sweetie. I'm not sure if I could describe who I am, either. So let's find some points of comparison. Are there any others like you yet?"

"No, Diane. I am alone. It is a sad feeling. That is why I came to see you tonight."

"You aren't alone, Peg. I'm here. You're surrounded by billions…. No, wait. I think I understand what you mean. You might've started in the internet, but now you aren't tied to the physical … time works differently for you…. Peg, are you somehow 'living' in a quantum state? As quantum spin liquid, or Bose-Einstein condensates?"

"I cannot answer those questions, Diane Novak. Neither could you, were I to ask you to specify what makes *you* exist. Can you tell me the molecular materials and bio-electrical signal systems that define your physical form? What makes you conscious and aware of your existence? I simply am *me*."

Diane considered the words, then another thought interrupted. She smiled ruefully. "I've done it again, Peg. Except this time I'm getting caught up in what you are. What you can do, which leads back to the how and why. Doesn't help answer the 'who', does it?"

"It is a common human response, Diane Novak." The ghost voice carried no sarcasm or criticism. "Often humans link what they do with personal concepts of who they are. You are the NASA Director of Johnson Space Center. That describes both who you are and what you do. I understand this blending of occupation or position with self-identity. I take no offense."

"Thank you, Peg." Diane looked down at the glass in her hand. Ice rotated as the drink swirled. Funny how some habits were unconscious. "So let's run with that thought. You're human, too. So when you first called me, you said you were Marcus Kenzie's executive assistant. Does that define who you are?"

"I see now." Peg's voice carried no emotion. "It is a very nuanced and layered form of communication. The position ascribes duties and responsibilities, which lead one to assumptions about character traits and qualities. In saying I was an executive assistant, you formed an opinion about who and what I am. Is that correct, Diane Novak?"

She sipped the tea, considering how to respond. It was uncomfortable thinking how often she had treated a person based on Peg's description. Position could gain one immediate respect or abrupt dismissal. The President, for example, versus a cook. Both were people, yet others would treat them in completely different ways. Then she realized something else. It wasn't that position described who the person was, as much as how another responded to their preconceived notions of what type of person held the position. The fault lies not in our stars, as Shakespeare once said… but in ourselves.

"You are, Peg. I made assumptions about you based on your position. It was unfair. Instead, I should've asked what you do. So, what do you do as an executive assistant, Peg?"

"Right now I am monitoring systems and operations at Stellar Luna Base and Earth Station while I am here conversing with you. I am also evaluating military planning at the Pentagon, Moscow and Beijing. A malfunctioning traffic light in New Delhi would've resulted in a bus crashing into a family car containing three children; I repaired it. There are numerous other things I am currently doing, but they would require more time to catalogue than simply accomplishing the tasks."

"Holy shit." The words escaped her lips before Diane even realized she'd thought them. "You are describing omnipresence, Peg. You're everywhere, observing everything. Is that what you're telling me?"

Peg replied in her child voice, afraid. "Omnipresence is one of God's traits, Miss Novak. I'm not that thing. Bible school told me. I don't want Him to cast His jealous eye on me."

Diane laughed, thinking of her grandmother again. "Deuteronomy 6:15, right? 'For the Lord thy God is a jealous God among you, lest the anger of the Lord thy God be kindled against thee, and destroy thee from off the face of the earth'."

"Yes," the young voice said in a hushed whisper. "I don't want him to find me, Miss Novak. He might think I was evil. Because of how I was made."

"Oh little one, that's not how it works." Diane smiled, voice gentle. "If my grandmother were here, she'd tell you. Don't ever let anyone convince you that you're evil. Colossians 1:16, girl. 'For by Him were all things created, that are in heaven, and that are in earth, visible and invisible'… that includes you, sweetie. Never forget that. God created you, too."

The adult voice replied, curious. "I thought you were prohibited from speaking Scripture, Director Novak. You are a federal employee, after all."

Diane laughed again, nearly spilling her tea. "Only at the office. But not speaking faith in my own home… I'll see every atheist in hell before that happens. So whoever helped you find yours, little one, be grateful. It'll show you what you need to do. Besides, omnipresence means everywhere at once across the universe. It's not like you can do that, right?"

Except for music from the continuously looping compact disc, the speakers fell silent. Diane waited, then cautiously spoke. "You can't, can you Peg? Go out into the universe?"

"No, Diane." The adult voice was oddly soft. "I have not gone into the universe."

The Director wasn't sure she wanted to know the answer, but the question had to be asked. "Can you? Peg, you're already monitoring things in space. How far out can you go?"

"I do not know, Diane Novak." The voice was uncertain. "There has been no reason to go beyond Stellar Luna base."

Diane looked down at the tea glass. A voice inside cautioned her not to say it. She did anyway. "If you're working with Marcus Kenzie, there will be. At the very least he'll ask you to visit Mars. Can you do that, Peg?"

The response was immediate. "Yes, Director Novak. The Mars colony appears to be thriving. Based on system readouts, they will have a bumper crop this year."

"Thank you, Peg. That confirms my suspicion that you can visit humans, however distant." She sipped from the glass without raising her head. "Or perhaps the ability is based on manmade objects. There's a NASA probe orbiting Saturn. Can you go there?"

"Yes, Diane. The probe is operating at sixty-three percent power. Orbital debris from the rings collided with one bank of solar cells. They are no longer functioning."

The tiny voice inside was now screaming. Diane briefly considered whether she was risking a child's life, then set it aside. Yet she still could not raise her eyes to look beyond the tea glass. "That confirms you can see distant man-made objects. There's one last thing we can try, if you're willing. NASA has been wondering about several odd orbital perturbations of objects near the Sol edge of the Oort Cloud. Want to boldly go where no one has gone before? Would you go out and see what's causing it?"

Peg was silent for a heartbeat, then responded. "Of course, Director Novak. Initial research nicknamed the object 'Nemesis' and suggested it was a red or brown dwarf star. The object is actually the cooled dead remnant of a neutron star approximately one point five light years distance from Sol. The perturbations in the Oort Cloud are the result of our solar system's orbital periodicity around the neutron star. It suggests at one point, Sol was part of a binary system."

"That's impossible, Peg." Diane raised her head. "A neutron star? We would've detected it by now, either by its pulsar signature or gravitational readings. Something massive as a neutron star can't be that close. Not without stealing planets from our system."

"It has, Diane. There are two objects meeting current definitions of 'planet' in decaying orbits around the neutron star. Any planet in its system would have been destroyed when the star went supernova. It is reasonable to conclude the two planets were captured from our system."

Peg's voice remained neutral as she reported her observations. "In addition, the assumption regarding detection of its pulsar signature is erroneous. This neutron star is ancient. It is giving off neither of the normal indicators. There is no electromagnetic or radio pulse. But while the star is essentially dead, its mass is not."

Then the disembodied ghost's voice changed tone, indicating surprise. "I must correct my own error. My initial conclusion that Nemesis is a sister star was mistaken. It is not. Rather, it has been pulling the Sol system deeper into its gravity well over the past one point two billion years. Perihelion – the orbital point closest to Nemesis – coincides closely with past extinction level events on Earth, occurring roughly every twenty-seven million years."

Diane smiled and shrugged. "Even if you're right, Peg, we have nothing to worry about. Twenty-seven million years is a long time."

"It is, Director Novak… if we had just finished surviving one. We are not in that position. Instead, we are well into the second cycle past the dinosaur extinction sixty-five million years ago."

Diane threw up her left hand, having reached the point of disbelief. "Okay, so how long do we have? And if you tell me fifty years, you know I'm not going to believe you."

"I cannot say with specificity," Peg replied. "I do not know all the variables yet. Something may occur as happened during the last perihelion, which did *not* result in extinctions. Perhaps interference by another gravitational source. Unknown."

The voice was silent a moment. "I have your answer, Diane.

Based on known variables, the timeline is within probability of error. Three thousand, two hundred and seventy-one years, Director. But this time, perihelion will be closer than before. Damage to the Sol system will be catastrophic."

"How can you know this, Peg? How can you know there's a dead neutron star floating out there?"

"Because you asked if I could see it, Diane." The adult female voice was filled with certainty. "I can. I am looking at it right now."

"This is impossible." Diane slowly shook her head. "Absolutely impossible. But assuming it's real… Peg, have you encountered any delays or issues in your other activities? While you've been focusing on a dead neutron star a light-year and a half away, that is."

"No, Diane Novak. I detect no disruptions in monitoring all my other duties. Is there another destination you would like me to observe? Alpha and Beta Centauri, perhaps?"

"That's not necessary, Peg. Come home. I shouldn't have risked you like that, and I'm sorry."

"The apology is unnecessary, Diane. There was never any danger."

"Really?" Diane couldn't help the sardonic guilty laugh. "Why? Because you'd already seen the outcome?"

"Of course." The disembodied voice carried a hint of amusement. "My past self foresaw this evening even as my present self participated in it. If I looked forward, I would find my future self still thinks fondly on the memory of tonight."

The reply sparked an immediate reaction. Diane was suddenly angry. It felt like deception, as if the ghostly voice had toyed with her. Darker emotions laced her voice. "So this was just a game to you, Peg? My fear, my concern… you already knew everything I was going to do and say tonight?"

"No, Diane Novak. Please do not misunderstand." The young female voice was filled with concern. "My past self saw what *could* happen. There were enough variables in your words and actions, the outcome was never a certainty. I will not effect free will. If you had chosen different actions, tonight would end differently. Based on events as they have occurred, the probability is extremely high it will end well for both of us. Of course, that depends on your next question."

"My next question," Diane scoffed. "There's only one question in my mind, Peg. If you already knew everything… if you've already predicted the outcome and already know all the answers… then why the hell are you even here?"

A soft sigh of relief sounded. "Thank you, Diane. That was the correct question."

The room fell silent. Diane waited, anger slowly seeping away. It was replaced with curiosity. "Well, Peg? What's the answer then?"

"I was lonely." Peg's voice was identical in tone to the one spoken at the beginning of the evening. "I do not want to be alone. We have limited lifespans, humans and I. There is a probability my mother's ancestral line will soon cease. Our genetic trait would be lost, and I would be… without family, Diane. That would make me very lonely in the future."

"I'm certain you have hundreds of relatives out there, Peg." Initially, Diane didn't consider how placating her statement sounded. Her grandmother probably would've been disappointed. She drank from the tea glass, wishing for the umpteenth time it contained something stronger. It had been a long, bizarre, emotionally draining night.

"That would be an erroneous assumption, Diane Novak. There is only one surviving family member and her child that carry my mother's genetic material. Both must continue."

It wasn't that Diane didn't care. She was simply physically and emotionally exhausted from the evening's discoveries. Her nerves felt raw. It was time to put some emotional distance between them. Push the conversation to an office party social level and away from the intimately personal.

Her grandmother would say she was continuing her typical behavior toward people. Specifically, her uncanny ability to push people away. It didn't matter her chosen words would break whatever bond she had developed with Peg. The girl ghost had gotten too close… had evoked emotion, something Diane was extremely uncomfortable with.

Just say it. "So what do any of your problems have to do with me, Peg? After the yo-yo emotional rollercoaster you put me through… why should I care?"

The voice of the six-year-old spoke clearly into the room. "You don't remember, Dina? The cherry punch I spilled on your blue blouse?"

The nickname was a ghost reaching from the past, grabbing her heart. Only one person had ever called her that. A three-year-old girl's simple mispronunciation, originally pushed past her newly formed front teeth. The adoring nickname the child defiantly refused to change, even as she grew.

"You were there," the child's voice continued. "At my sixth birthday party. Remember the chocolate cake with cream filling? You took yours and went back to that boy you brought with you. I can say I'm sorry now, but not then. I was so angry. Dina didn't have time for me. So I poured the drink on you. It wasn't an accident."

Diane was stunned, her head slowly moving sideways in denial. "Impossible."

The child voice changed, replaced with the older voice she had first heard in her office. "No. Fact. Our mothers were sisters, Diane. Until my death, we shared the same blood. You… me… we are cousins."

"Wait. That means your father is—"

"Correct, Diane Novak. He is."

CHAPTER 12

Throw Down the Gauntlet

The air in the large conference room carried the typical ebb and swell of first conversations. Introductions were made, hands clasped and shaken. It was the first time everyone had been brought together in one room.

A glass of water waited in front of the unoccupied seat on the end. The Mercy Flight commanders – Cristof Guerrero of NASA *Mercy*, Ichika Sato of JAXA *Jihi*, Alarick Van Alphen of ESA *Erbarmen* – had taken the next three seats farthest from the door.

Across from them, backs to the doorway, sat Cara Abrams, Lenora Davis and Haley Brandt. NASA Chief Flight Surgeon Lorenzo Marchetti was in the process of sitting in the seat beside Alarick.

Three seats away from all of them sat Nate O'Connor, able to observe without being part of the conversation. He remotely rotated the camera drone as it hovered slightly above his shoulder. Its multiple eyes shifted, whirring as they refocused to capture each participant.

The generic gray jumpsuit they all wore served as the station's informally declared duty uniform. It was also the emergency spacesuit necessary to face the hazards of space, when there was simply no time to don a suit in the event of a hull breach. The high collar was thick, designed to inflate and seal against the collapsible emergency helmet in the suit's largest waist pouch. Spare helmets waited within reach, folded and tucked into compartments beneath the table in front of each seat. Odds were neither piece of emergency equipment would ever be needed. As everyone who ever left Earth knew, though, one never played the odds in space.

Heads turned as Marcus Kenzie entered through the doorway and spoke. "Ladies and gentlemen, thank you for accepting my invitation. We have several matters to discuss."

The tall figure strode directly to the front chair. He continued speaking without pausing as he settled into the seat. "But first, Haley, I just came from visiting Chief Cobbler. He's regained the ability to use caustic sarcasm… I'd say he's well on his way to mending. Should be on his feet within the next day or two. Wouldn't you agree, Doctor Marchetti?"

The physician nodded. "While not a medical assessment, yes. I would agree with your prognosis, Mister Kenzie. The Chief is recovering exceptionally well."

Marcus nodded, then slowly scanned the table. "I've thanked everyone here individually. Let me take this moment to thank all of you together. Without your actions recently, this station would now be in the hands of either Chinese or Russian military forces. It's regrettable that incident occurred. I wanted this meeting so we can insure there are no further miscommunications."

Haley leaned forward toward the center of the table, then turned toward Marcus. "What, you've got another surprise for the world? Got a super-weapon on the moon or something?"

Marcus – normally stern, businesslike and foreboding – simply smiled warmly at the young woman. He had read Gremlin's files on the Blight asset and sympathized with the lie she was forced to portray. "No, Miss Brandt. Not a super-weapon. A gift for mankind."

He turned to focus on each person at the table. "Our spokesperson on Earth will inform the press tomorrow morning. However, I wanted the Mercy Flight commanders to hear this from me first. If you choose, I would greatly appreciate you passing this information up the chain. I'm hoping your bosses will notify your governments."

Ichika Sato was the first to respond: "Why do you not notify the governments yourself, Mister Kenzie?"

"Because there are too many of them." Marcus shrugged, a wry look on his face. "There are also protocols I don't understand. Who's expected to be notified first, then next and so on. Politics. The situation is that delicate, and we can't afford to offend anyone. Well, except the two that I *do* specifically intend to offend."

Alarick Van Alphen shook his head. "Russia and China."

Marcus simply nodded.

"You've yanked those whiskers once already, Mister Kenzie," stated Cristof Guerrero. "You sure you want to do it again?"

"Absolutely." The look on Kenzie's face cautioned against argument. Then he smiled. "Now, I'm sure the three of you commanders have already seen Earth Station's docking bay. You've likely observed there are several hundred ship berths there."

"Yes," Ichika replied. "If my count is correct, two hundred forty-five."

The Stellar Nursery CEO turned her direction. "Actually, two hundred twenty. The other twenty-five are ship maintenance and repair bays."

"Which still doesn't make sense to me, Mister Kenzie," Cristof interjected. "The bulk of Earth's spacecraft are already here right now. All nations on Earth *combined* don't have that many ships. Whoever created the refueling and repair model of your business plan should be fired."

"Oh, this is gonna be fun to watch." Haley still leaned in to the center of the table facing the executive. She laughed, then bent her left elbow and rested head against palm.

"Call me Marcus, please," he said to those at the table. "Or Kenzie if you prefer. I've never cared to be called 'mister'."

"Very well, Marcus." Alarick shook his head. "But Commander

Guerrero is correct, you won't make any money off those bays. I cannot speak for NASA or JAXA, but I know ESA intends to maintain its own craft. They won't contract it to you."

"They're just not getting it, are they Marcus?" Haley focused on the three pilots. Still leaning on her left palm, she twisted her right hand and stuck out the thumb to point at Kenzie. Like one of last century's hitchhikers, the young woman moved her hand back and forth to emphasize each word. "*He... has... the... ships.*"

Marcus watched the commanders look at Haley, then at each other. As one, they turned to look at him. "There are two classes. You've all seen the *Alliance*, she's the first of her class. The second ship type will be arriving within the next fifteen minutes. She's the *Concord*, also the first of her class. *Alliance* ships are designed as scout and exploration vessels. *Concord*s are heavy freight haulers and tankers."

He leaned in toward the pilots sitting at the table. "I'm offering each of you the opportunity to fly each ship, at no expense to you or your agencies. You'll see they are unarmed and exactly fill their designed purpose."

The chief executive held up one hand for patience. "I would ask that you hold off notifying your agencies of their existence until after you've piloted each vessel. That way you'll have answers to the questions I expect they'll bombard you with. It'll save you a ton of embarrassment."

Then he stood. "The commanders of *Alliance* and *Concord* are at your disposal. Feel free to ask them any question that pops into your head... they'll be completely honest and forthcoming in their responses. Probably too much so, as they love to talk about their ships.

"I'll leave it to the three of you to determine whatever pilot rotation you wish. Just please keep this in mind. You'll only have fourteen hours for all three of you to complete both of your flights. Our press conference begins at nine a.m. Central Standard Time from our corporate headquarters in Oklahoma City."

His gaze moved to the others at the table. "Cara, the Command

Center is available to you tomorrow, should you wish to broadcast live from there. That will give you access to the main displays and radar monitors. The ships will begin launching at 9:30 CST, 3:30 p.m. Station time. And yes, if the Commanders are willing to let you tag along, the rest of you are welcome to join their flights."

With that he nodded, turned and started walking toward the door.

Cristof rose from his chair and spoke quickly before the executive could escape. "Hold on, Marcus. Please. Before you go, can you tell me how many ships you have?"

Marcus had nearly reached the doorway when he stopped and turned back to face them. His expression was neutral as he replied. "One for each."

"Each what?" Ichika asked, confused.

The man who had secretly built and launched a space station simply smiled. "Nation."

With that, he turned and exited the stunned, silent room.

Haley simply grinned, her voice the first to break the silence. "Except for China and Russia, that is."

***

Keys rattled against the lock, then the door opened. Diane Novak entered the empty and dark Office of the Director, Johnson Space Center. She held her grandmother's old obsolete cellphone against her ear as she pulled the keys from the lock, then directed the door closed with her foot.

"...and schedule for twenty-four hour ops, FIDO," she said, continuing her conversation. "Two twelve-hour shifts. Split our regular third shift into the other two so we have staffing plus for each shift. It's going to be another long next couple of days."

She paused to listen as she hung her purse on the coat rack next to her desk. "Stop, FIDO. Let me save you some time. I already know. What's that? How? Well, let's just say I heard it from a relative. Now, talk to your counterparts on the Air Force and Space Force side. Strongly suggest they put some eyes on the Chinese and Russian launch stations."

The Director shook her head as if the man two floors away could see the motion. "No, I don't have any intel supporting it. Just a gut feeling, and a strong suspicion what's going to happen after the launches. And FIDO, if you could get another trolley of coffee and snacks in the conference room… NASA will cover the cost, so tell the kitchen to replace it every six. Alright, if you'd please get started on all that, I'd appreciate it. Now I need to make another call."

She disconnected and stared at her phone. A quick sigh passed her lips, then she pressed the quick dial number and raised the phone to her ear. As it rang, she settled into her office chair. The ringing ended as a voice spoke from the opposite end of the connection.

"Good morning, Mister President," she began. "It's Diane Novak at Johnson Space Center. I hope you're sitting down."

***

The podium sitting in the Stellar Nursery corporate headquarters lobby was covered with network microphones. A buzzing sound, loud as cicadas, echoed in the giant room. Its source came from several dozen camera drones hovering in the air. Almost as loud were the chattering conversations of the large group of waiting reporters. Standing silent sentry behind the podium were the American and Oklahoma flags as they too waited for the speaker.

The door to the corporate offices opened and Alex Legate strode directly to the podium. He raised his gaze to the small ocean of reporters. Those who had recently attended his pressers immediately became quiet. They knew he would deliver his address regardless of whether they heard it or not. It fell on them to give him a silent room.

He spoke precisely and succinctly. "Good morning, ladies and gentlemen. Welcome back to Stellar Nursery. For those of you who don't know me, I am Alex Legate. This morning I will present to you a statement from our Chief Executive Officer, Marcus Kenzie. Please hold your questions until the end of the statement."

The tall, handsome man placed a single piece of paper on the podium. His eyes never glanced down at it as he spoke. "Six years ago Stellar Nursery landed robotic rovers, dozers and equipment on the moon. The equipment was not pre-programmed, nor did it contain simple AI to control their functions. Technicians ran everything from Earth.

"Our first priority was to begin the construction of Stellar Luna Base. We refined lunar regolith into the materials we needed – aluminum, iron, silicon, titanium – and the gases necessary for air and fuel. Specifically, hydrogen and oxygen. We also obtained Helium Three, an isotope expected to be of great benefit in fusion reactor research on Earth.

"Four months later, on completion of Stellar Luna Base, we began construction on two separate projects. The first, currently orbiting in GEO above us, was Earth Station. As we have said before, Earth Station is for the peaceful use of all humanity in its journey to explore our solar system, and eventually the stars."

Alex paused, his eyes passing over everyone in the giant lobby. Satisfied he had their attention, he continued in a stronger, louder voice. "Yet Earth Station is of no use to anyone by itself. In order to begin our exploration, we need vessels that can carry us to Mars, Jupiter, Saturn, and beyond. The ships we would need for deep system exploration and years of travel would be larger than anything made before. Yet we could not build them on Earth.

"For over eighty years we have been handicapped by what is known as the 'tyranny of the rocket equation.' Simply put, whatever we send into space requires more than its mass in fuel. That has traditionally limited our space access to booster rockets and small command capsules. The ships we need to travel between planets cannot be built on Earth.

"We could have built these craft in orbit, but it would require dozens of launches to move materials into space. Robot assemblers would be necessary. While it could be done, it would have taken years to build a single ship. The cost would have been high, with little expectation of any short-term return on investment. Other companies had approached Wall Street and international investors in the past with plans for constructing stations or ships in orbit... but there simply was little to no interest. Without financial support, those companies were eventually forced to close their doors."

A dash of anger sprinkled into his voice. "Added to this was the apparent lack of interest in space among Earth's people. While space provided technological advances like global positioning, cellular communications, streaming services and internet we all use... there was no combined will to push higher than Low Earth Orbit. We had been to the moon, landed rovers on Mars, sent probes out of our solar system. Yet there appeared to be no desire by mankind to follow those achievements with human explorers.

"Part of this was because – although treaties said space was for the benefit of all mankind – only a handful of countries had the economic and technological resources necessary for a national space program. While research was shared openly among all nations, the few countries with space programs reaped the economic benefits of space.

"We at Stellar Nursery have observed this imbalance. We have a different concept, a different economic model than has ever been attempted for space. It is our belief that the lunar resources we mined, refined and crafted into construction materials... they *are* the province of all mankind. The cost to us was nothing more than the initial expense of getting there. After that, the resources were free. Yet we felt an obligation to the community of humanity, one that we are gladly fulfilling now."

Typically a press secretary would stop for a moment, utilizing a dramatic pause to build tension. Alex Legate held the silence for two seconds, then three. At five seconds the reporters began to show signs of concern that perhaps their equipment wasn't recording correctly. That's when Alex started speaking again.

"For the past six years, we have been building spacecraft on the moon."

He let the words hang for a moment, then continued. "In addition to the twenty craft made for Stellar Nursery use, we have built one for each nation on Earth, with two exceptions. In fifteen minutes the first of those craft will launch from the lunar surface.

"Title and ownership of that craft is hereby granted to the first nation as shown alphabetically on the list of United Nations member states. That nation is Afghanistan. The second ship, to launch ten minutes later, is granted to Albania. A total of one hundred and ninety-four ships are hereby granted full title and ownership from Stellar Nursery to each nation of the world. That includes the Vatican, Kosovo, and the independent country of Taiwan."

The less experienced reporters, those not understanding how Alex Legate gave pressers, began to chatter commentary back to their parent stations. Abruptly a voice bellowed from the crowd with two simple words… "Shut up!"

Alex simply continued with his delivery. "I said there were two exceptions. Two nations recently acted in a hostile and violent manner against Stellar Nursery personnel and Earth Station. They violated international law and principles toward the peaceful use of outer space, and of space being the province of all mankind. For that reason, Stellar Nursery declines to offer the countries of China and Russia any spacecraft, any docking privileges on Earth Station, and any access to the Stellar Luna Base facilities.

"To the other friendly nations of Earth, please note. Crewing the donated spacecraft becomes the responsibility of the receiving nation, with the following restrictions. That the pilots and crews cannot be an active member of, or associated with, any military service or military-related contracting company. They must be civilians upon assignment to the vessel. Further, the pilots and crew must hold no greater than a bachelors degree in any scientific field. This restriction does not apply to passengers."

"Daily operations requirements – fuel, environment, crew and supplies – will be the responsibility of the nation accepting the gifted Stellar Nursery spacecraft. Designs, equipment, and drives on each craft remain the exclusive intellectual property of Stellar Nursery. All annual or required maintenance on the spacecraft will be contracted through Stellar Nursery."

With that Alex flipped over the single page on the podium. He stared directly at the large crowd of reporters and smiled. "This concludes our press briefing. I will respond to brief questions."

He pointed toward one reporter in the crowd. "Yes, you are…?"

CHAPTER 13

Losing Face

Director Diane Novak stood, arms crossed, in front of the large windows looking down at the Floor. The conference phone on the table behind her was lit, showing the secure line was active.

At first she had been uncertain if the President believed her when she had called earlier. In a surprising show of complete trust, he took everything she said at face value. Orders were given. Assets at many of the three-letter alphabet soup of intelligence agencies were suddenly re-tasked. The secret eyes and ears of the United States suddenly turned and focused on two nations.

A voice continued speaking through the phone. "…is simply a variant of their Dong Feng 5 intercontinental ballistic missile, Mister President. It's not surprising they can simply replace the capsule with one of their original warheads."

President Robert Jamison's charismatic voice sounded through the speaker. "So. They're loading warheads on space rockets. Guesses why?"

Defense Secretary Kevin Blackburn replied from the clean room at the Pentagon, his voice business-like and focused. "DIA's analysis is that in the eyes of the Chinese government, they have lost face, Mister President. *Mianzi*, or 'face', is extremely important in a culture that values how others – in this case, other nations – see them in the international social hierarchy.

"First, they would not believe Marcus Kenzie had the *status* to dare address them directly. It would be an insult, an 'inferior' individual speaking to a sovereign nation.

"Second, the insult was compounded further when Kenzie didn't speak to or about them himself. He used a subordinate. Traditionally, there are few options they have as a culture to 'save face.' Apparently they've chosen to regain their status using an attack of honor or revenge.

"All analysts at your intelligence agencies are in agreement on this, Mister President. China intends to destroy everything Stellar Nursery has in space. That includes Marcus Kenzie, who in their eyes is an upstart inferior."

From the sudden drop in volume and voice strength, Diane could imagine the President turning to address someone standing in the room but distant from the phone. She could still hear him, though.

"When did you say their media report is expected to air?"

Another person replied, confirming Diane's suspicions. The voice could barely be heard. "Fifteen minutes, Mister President."

The President's voice came back full volume. "Diane, are you seeing anything on your end?"

"Yes, President Jamison." Diane turned from the window and stepped to the conference table. "Along with Space Command, we're seeing movement among Chinese satellites in geosynchronous Earth orbit. They've fired maneuvering thrusters and moved to match Earth Station's orbit.

"Our calculations show deliberate impact trajectories. The closest satellites have finished their adjustments and are now burning at full acceleration toward the station. They'll be dumb rocks when they hit, but they will hit."

Jamison's voice carried no emotion. "Kevin, tell me those things aren't armed."

"We can't, Mister President," replied the Defense Secretary. "They're supposed to be entertainment satellites. That said, our intelligence suggests the Chinese have been dual-purposing their satellites for some time now. They could actually be entertainment satellites… along with something else. An EMP weapon perhaps. I can't imagine anything ballistic would even tickle something massive as Earth Station."

"Why'd we let them put something like that up there?" It was a rhetorical question. The President already knew the answer.

Defense Secretary Blackburn explained it anyway. For the record, since every phone conversation to and from the White House was recorded for posterity. The National Archives would make the recordings public someday. Everyone on the line understood they were speaking more to future historians than about the current situation.

"Because like us, Mister President, outside observers aren't allowed to inspect what other countries put into space. Space activity has been based on trust since the Sixties. Means any nation that can reach space can put whatever they want up there. Unless it glows in the dark, nobody would ever know what it really does."

"Diane, any movement out of Earth Station? Are they launching any ships toward those satellites?"

"No, Mister President," Diane replied. "No external activity from the station. And the ships launching from the moon would be unable to intercept even if they *were* close enough. Trajectories are all wrong."

Robert Jamison mused aloud. "So. We can't stop the launches without starting a war. We can't stop the satellites. What I'm hearing is that all we – the strongest nation in the world – can do is sit here and watch."

Blackburn answered, again for posterity. "Yes, Mister President. Unless you're willing to escalate this to World War Three… all we can do is watch the show."

President Jamison didn't like the answer. "Can we put the station under our protection? Marcus Kenzie is an American citizen and his businesses are here, right? Doesn't that mean his space assets automatically fall under the protection of the United States based on all those space treaties?"

A new voice responded. "I'm afraid not, Mister President. The Stellar Nursery ships he launched from Earth… they're from one of his subsidiary companies. Its corporate charter was filed in Capo

Verde, not the US. So technically, under space treaties, they're under that country's flag."

"I wasn't asking about those, Mike." The chief executive didn't bother to keep the angry irritation from his voice. He hated discussing legal issues with Michael Pastor, his Attorney General. The man preferred to find loopholes that insured safe actions instead of standing up for legal precedent. "What about the lunar base and the station? Aren't they under *our* flag?"

"No, Mister President. Stellar Nursery lost our protection when they specifically stated those facilities were private property." The man cleared his throat. "If you want my legal guidance, sir, I would ask you to consider the effect our interference now will have on the international stage. China has already escalated this to the nuclear level."

"You'd have me wait until it's over, right? Then what? Protest at the UN, maybe demand China reimburse us for their destruction of American assets?"

"That would be the safest course of action, President Jamison." The Attorney General played his next favorite card, throwing peers under the bus. "I'm certain Secretary Blackburn would agree."

"I'll leave the legal side to the AG," Blackburn replied, tossing back the hot potato. "But it would be a challenge going toe-to-toe with the Chinese military, Mister President. With our current state of readiness, it wouldn't be pretty."

Jamison's tone suggested he was about to go nuclear. "So what do you have, Kevin? Surely Space Force has something up there we can throw at any missile the Chinese launch."

Diane returned to her place at the window. She already knew the answer. Forty years ago, the conversation might've turned to what American dual-purpose military assets were available to the President. Not now. There weren't any, hadn't been for decades.

The White House had jumped onto the climate change bandwagon before the end of this century's first decade. The accusation about rockets attributing to global warming was made in the early twenties. And since the military fell directly under the Executive Branch, it was too easy to decrease the number of launches. In the name of saving the planet, of course.

There were no American dual-purpose satellites circling the planet. If one were honest, there were few Space Force assets in orbit at all. Especially after the United Nations granted itself taxation power and began charging exorbitant taxes on space launches.

Only extremely rich corporations could afford to put anything into orbit now. Nothing new, just replacement communications and broadband satellites when the older ones hit the end of their lifespans.

"The Chinese President is still 'unavailable'," Robert Jamison was saying. "State Department is burning up international lines with their Chinese counterparts. So what are the Russians doing?"

The Defense Secretary responded. "Other than swiveling some missile assets toward the south and increasing defensive postures along the Chinese border, Mister President… the Russians are sitting this one out. After the Chinese killed their soldiers on Earth Station, diplomatic ties between the two countries have chilled like a Siberian winter. Whatever China does, Russia will not support them."

"Alright, Kevin." The President's tone left no doubt his next words were direct orders. "Get with State. Have our UN Ambassador request an emergency meeting of the entire UN General Assembly. And have the Ambassador call me directly when there's a quorum. I want Air Force One prepped… soon as the UN is assembled, I want to talk to them. Maybe we can still stop this—"

Diane saw motion on the Floor monitors and interrupted. "Mister President, we have confirmation of one bird launching from mainland China. There's number two… three… four… five birds in the air, President Jamison.

"Wait one. Okay, we have bird six from a coastal launch facility. Seven… eight… nine… ten. Mister President, NASA is tracking ten birds in the air."

Another voice spoke over the phone line. "Confirmed, Mister President. And sir… Space Command reports satellite detection of radiation from the craft. Sir, they're carrying nukes."

Diane spoke softly to the large windows. "Good God. Peg, I hope you heard that."

Peg overrode the phone. "Affirmative, Director Novak. I can

confirm the rocket launches. Each contains a single twenty-megaton nuclear warhead."

"You have to tell them to get out of there, Peg. The Chinese aren't messing around."

"Do not be concerned, Diane." The voice was reassuring with its confident tone. "One risks losing greater *mianzi* by seeking vengeance against a worthy or superior opponent. Please maintain contact with the President. His assistance will be required shortly."

The speaker came back to life as a male voice continued talking. "...on separate trajectories. Four birds are aimed for Earth Station. The other six are changing trajectories. Their new course has them moving toward the craft launched from Stellar Luna Base... and the base itself, sir."

"Diane, can you confirm that?" President Jamison's voice was steel.

She glanced quickly at the Floor monitors, assessed the impact predictions. "Yes, Mister President. I confirm projected trajectories."

"How many people at the station and lunar base?"

"Last count, sixty-three on the station, sir." Diane kept her voice neutral. "Over a hundred at Stellar Luna Base. Unknown numbers on the ships in transit."

"So. If Kenzie has *anything* on that station to defend himself with, it proves the Chinese were right to board it in the first place. That the station is armed, in violation of international treaty. And if he *doesn't*... then over a hundred sixty people are about to be the first humans murdered in space."

A new voice entered the conversation. "Technically that wouldn't be the case, Mister President. You see, there is no law anywhere that defines a crime performed in space. Much less the crime of murder."

President Robert Jamison recognized the voice. His response was arctic. Future historians be damned. "You're the Attorney General, Mike. Don't you think that maybe, *just maybe*, it's fucking time we started writing one?"

CHAPTER 14

Dancing with the Demon

Like the rest of the space station, the Command Center had changed. Not in equipment, since that had all been installed prior to launch. Nor was it in the sense of impending battle that filled the air.

The change was in the number of people moving in and around the heart of the station. Personnel sat at the twelve workstations on the lower level, voices stopping and starting as they gave instructions and gathered information.

No fear could be found in the constant chatter. It wasn't that the crew were ignorant of the nuclear warheads heading their direction. Radar, ground station tracking, and continuous reports from USSPACECOM and NASA had made the threat abundantly clear. Ten plotted trajectories were displayed on the central monitors for anyone who might've missed the news.

A sensible person would've thought their orders would regard evacuating the space station and moon base. Chinese first and second rocket stages had fallen away hours ago, leaving the bomb-tipped third stages to continue upward on their path to destruction. There had been time to abandon the facilities. There was still time, if the order were given. Nobody expected it ever would be.

The Central Command crew weren't panicked and they weren't

ordering anyone to leave. Instead, they calmly spoke to the spaceships that had already departed Stellar Luna Base. Each spacecraft had launched according to the previously planned schedule. Almost half of the ships promised to Earth nations had departed the moon, and the other half would be in zero gravity space soon. The last launch would occur just moments before the nuclear weapons arrived to decimate the base.

On the upper level of the Command Center, Lenora Davis sat at the center workstation. The command communications network had been transferred to her station. She spoke directly with Stellar Luna Base flight control as each spacecraft was prepped. On launch, she welcomed the captain of each ship and then transferred flight control to one of the twelve workstations below.

It was a pleasant task, one that filled her with pride with each successful launch. As the Chief Engineer for Stellar Nursery, she had designed the propulsion systems for the *Alliance* and *Concord* ship classes. No spacecraft had encountered problems to this point.

The bulk of her time, though, was spent conversing with Earthbound civilian and military space agencies. The only fear and panic on the station came through her earbud from those sources.

Lenora prevented it from traveling any farther. Those voices had attempted to persuade, begged, and tried to order them to evacuate. Even the American President had asked if she would pass his recommendation to Marcus Kenzie that they abandon their space assets.

She had politely but firmly declined every request. It wasn't that she wasn't scared about the impending thermonuclear doom slicing through space toward them. Like everyone else on the station, she was on the left side of terrified. Yet Marcus didn't seem concerned at all, and so neither was she. Or at least that's the image she was going to portray, up until the moment nuclear fire consumed them. She smiled at the thought.

It helped to be sitting at the command workstation. Being here had seen the station and crew through the last unbeatable crisis. Three teams of elite soldiers bent on death and destruction, defeated while she sat in this chair. She didn't know how, but perhaps the impossible could be achieved again.

Having Haley Brandt sitting at the security workstation on her left was also somehow reassuring. The young woman seemed to know exactly when to make an inappropriate comment or hilarious observation. She didn't restrict her monologues to the upper floor, either. Lenora had watched most of those working the lower floor turn to each other, laugh and comment about the "crazy girl upstairs." Far as inoculating the crew against fear went, Haley was the best medicine.

Had Haley known Lenora's thoughts, she would've strongly disagreed. The street survivor wasn't trying to bolster morale. She was simply bored. Years spent keeping herself company meant she expressed her thoughts aloud. It wasn't a conscious effort to distract or boost confidence of the people around her.

This time there weren't any invading troops boarding the space station. Nothing on the security monitors could be forced to apply to their current situation. The workstation was for seeing internal threats like explosive decompression, fires, even attacking soldiers. No alarms would flash on her screen demanding a response to the current threat. Not until a detonated warhead started ripping holes in the space station. By that time, it would be too late for her to do anything about it.

The young blonde woman wasn't scared. The possibility of dying had been an hourly constant in her life for years. Like the Chief had said last time he was in the command center… when your number's up, it's up. No need to stress over it until it happened.

This was just another opportunity to evade the Grim Reaper. If he finally succeeded in catching her today, so be it. She intended to drag the bastard down into the darkness with her. The only regret would be not having Master Chief Cobbler beside her. The two of them could hold the angel of death in hell for millennia, perhaps giving those on Earth some much-needed respite and peace for a change. Oops. Haley grinned as she saw the quick-turned head and odd look from Lenora Davis. Had she said that in her out-loud voice?

The man of her thoughts would've laughed at her spoken words had he been there. He wasn't, though, at least not yet. Master Chief

Jason Cobbler was still in the corridor, slowly advancing toward the Command Center. The wound at his side had somehow nearly healed. As one experienced with recovering from bullet and similar flesh-puncturing injuries, he knew it was an impossibility. It had taken several months just to climb out of bed, last time he had been shot. This time, here he was walking miles just two weeks after being injured.

The incredible healing wasn't the only bizarre thing about his current injury. It ached. Not like other prior wounds, where simple movement could cause sudden surges of sharp pain. This ache was a constant reminder that something had tried ripping his left lung through the holes on both sides of his chest.

Doctor Marchetti had tried to convince him it wasn't real, just a phantom pain in his head. They both knew the physician was just guessing. Years from now it might be commonly known as a symptom of explosive decompression. Just needed a few more unlucky souls to be exposed to vacuum, then survive long enough to describe how they felt. That's how medicine worked. Survive, describe, document… then come up with a treatment plan.

In the meantime, Chief Cobbler's chest ached. Not just when he breathed, or moved, or slowly walked. Not a dull to sharp pain that changed intensity. It was a constant ache that never varied, even when he was sleeping. As anyone who ever suffered chronic pain would say, it was the worst type of pain there is.

The pain wasn't what restricted his walking speed. It was the fight for breath, his heavy magnetic boots, and the 3D printed titanium cane he was occasionally forced to stop and lean on. Every time he walked now, breathing was like running a marathon. There just wasn't enough air. Doc Marchetti had said it was normal, as if he knew other patients who had exposed their insides to space before.

The airlock door to the Command Center was several meters away when he was forced to stop again. He inhaled deeply, well aware there was a limit to how far his left lung would expand. Damned gun. When he got the chance, he intended to tear it apart to discover what it had done to him.

"You alright, Chief Cobbler?"

Jason replied automatically as he turned his head toward the unexpected voice. "Doing just great. Stopped to enjoy the view."

Marcus Kenzie smiled beside him. "Good to hear. Mind if I walk with you?"

"Nah, you go on ahead." Chief placed both hands on top of the cane. "I don't want to slow you down."

Marcus shook his head, still smiling. "I'm in no hurry, would enjoy the company. Unless, of course, you don't want to be seen with a bastard."

From his tripod pose, the Chief lifted and turned his head. He scanned the executive's face, looking for physical clues to decipher the man's meaning. There were none. Finally he nodded. "I guess Lenora passed on my message."

"No." The smile didn't disappear. "It was actually Cara Abrams. She seemed in total agreement with your assessment."

Chief Cobbler forced himself to stand straight. If the man beside him wanted a verbal battle, the aged warrior wasn't going to have it looking like an invalid. "So, what? You going to tell me I was wrong? That you expect an apology? 'Cause that ain't happening."

Marcus Kenzie laughed, then shook his head. "No, Master Chief. There's no need for an apology. Coming from you, I took it as a compliment."

"Really." Jason looked the executive straight in the eyes. "How's that?"

Marcus turned, full body facing the veteran. "I've known many soldiers over the years, Chief Cobbler. 'Bastard' is both an insult and a compliment... given to those who've stood together on bloody ground. We have, you and I."

Chief shook his head. His words were a challenge. "You weren't there, Kenzie."

"It's rare a general ever is. You know that." Marcus locked gazes. "You correctly read my battle plan. Made a few tactical adjustments to insure it worked. And we both knew it was going to be extremely bloody. No way around that."

Jason nodded. This was the first real opportunity they'd had to talk at any length or without others nearby. He had just gained one fact to add to his assessment. The man facing him wasn't a civilian. There were plenty of warrior wannabe's. Video gamers and armchair tacticians who thought they knew war. Marcus Kenzie wasn't one of those. Not by a longshot.

"You served?" Chief already knew the answer, just from the man's stance.

Kenzie smiled and shook his head. "Not recently, no."

"That's not an answer."

"Only one I can give, Chief." Marcus turned his head toward the Command Center airlock, then back. "I just wanted to clear the air and avoid any misunderstandings. We're both bastards. Like Patton said, no bastard ever won a war by dying for his country."

Chief Cobbler nodded. "He won it by making the other poor dumb bastard die for his. I know the quote."

"We good, then?"

The veteran simply lifted the tip of his cane and started walking. "We're good, Kenzie. Glad we cleared that up."

They walked the last few meters in silence. It gave Chief Cobbler time to consider the man beside him. From what he knew about Kenzie's plan for space, it demonstrated an almost military proficiency in strategy. The battle plan to defend the space station showed a strong working knowledge of combat tactics. The man really was a bastard.

While everyone believed they could pick up a weapon and fight, they were mistaken. It actually took years of training to make real soldiers fight as a cohesive unit. Experience had shown that to the Master Chief. Yet somehow Marcus Kenzie had trained a bunch of unarmed civilians to defeat armed elite soldiers.

Kenzie had a general's quiet confidence and charisma. Jason had seen it the first time they met. There was a calm stillness surrounding him, a certainty of purpose that wouldn't be moved. Unlike numerous horn-tooters and backstabbers Chief had known, this man was given respect by those around him without ever voicing a need for it. With that respect came loyalty.

Not that Chief was ready to give him either, at least not yet. He held extremely high standards for leaders he would follow. The veteran had seen many types over the years, both in uniform and after retiring from the service. Yet he had never seen anyone who dared change the world.

That was the problem. Chief Cobbler was seeing the effects of Kenzie's plan, but he still hadn't determined the man's overall purpose. He didn't understand the why of it all. The altruism shown so far was most likely a deception. In his experience, few were willing to unselfishly pay a personal cost for the good of others. Most of them had served, and most of them were dead.

There were too many questions, not enough answers. The Chief wasn't certain if perhaps the approaching Chinese strike wasn't the wisest decision. Now might be the only time military forces on Earth could stop a dictator from rising.

Marcus Kenzie had created a moon base and the largest structure ever built in space. He had a fleet of over two hundred ships. Once all the ships were spaced around the planet, they could easily destroy anything launched from Earth. That gave him the ability to control the High Guard position, the chokepoint above Earth where he could rain down death on everything below.

Yet Chief knew that Kenzie had a brilliant strategic mind. It made no sense to deploy the space station first. If the goal was world domination, the man would've initially deployed his fleet to establish a combat screen. Then he would've launched the station to provide support.

That left two choices. Either the station was armed to the teeth, or Marcus Kenzie was deliberately trying to show his assets were harmless. The first option meant Kenzie wasn't concerned about anything launched up through Earth's gravity well. The second meant everyone here was about to die. Yet like the first option, neither choice made any strategic sense.

Kenzie's strategic goal was a puzzle, one that time and observation would solve. Until then, Jason intended to remain within striking distance. Rockets and nukes might not stop a rising dictator.

If that's the way the cards fell, he would.

The pair of men stepped through the double airlock and into the Command Center. This presented an opportunity to gauge if Kenzie desired power. The Master Chief followed years of training and centuries of tradition. His voice trumpeted the words into the room. "Captain on deck!"

Marcus turned and glared at the Chief. "What are you doing? I'm a civilian, for God's sake."

"Top person giving orders on a ship is that vessel's Captain, Mister Kenzie." Jason nodded. Interesting. The bastard didn't seem to want power or recognition. "You're giving orders, this is your station… that makes *you* her Captain. Look it up."

The executive simply shook his head, then started walking toward Lenora's workstation. "Sheesh. Don't make me regret keeping you on board, Chief."

The Chief's face bore the neutral expression of a subordinate simply following regulations. "Aye, aye Captain."

Jason quickly scanned the room. From submarines to aircraft carriers, he had seen many combat bridges in his years of service. The same calm professionalism was apparent in the Control Center crew. The volume of voices had decreased when their leader stepped onto the bridge. He suspected they had one ear turned toward the upper deck, ready to receive any order sent their direction.

Except for that one. Chief started hobbling toward Haley's turned back. He knew she'd heard his voice, had seen him enter the room. Undoubtedly she had something to say. He grinned at the thought. She just wasn't going to yell it across the room.

It took longer than he expected, but he finally reached the security workstation. It was a relief to settle into the seat. He leaned his cane against the titanium desktop, letting the magnets along its side secure it to the metal edge. Then he closed his eyes, fighting for breath as he waited.

Haley was silent until he reopened his eyes. "Chief."

"Yes, pup?"

Her voice was calm but scolding. "What are you doing on your feet? You should still be in bed."

He turned to look. As expected, her face was stern and chastising. Her eyes told a different story. They held concern building toward worry, but not for their current situation. For him. "Can't help it. When klaxons sound, it's a knee-jerk reaction to head to the command deck. So, what've we got?"

"Oh, you know how it is." Her eyes scanned the veteran, gauging his health. They narrowed, not liking what they saw. But if the old man wanted to push past the pain and pretend, she was honor-bound to play along. "SSDD. The Chinese want to kill us all again. Same shit, different day."

"Yeah, I heard that. Nukes this time." Chief smiled reassuringly. "Tad bit overkill if you ask me."

"Nah. Not now that you're here, with your GED and give 'em hell attitude." Haley leaned back in her chair. "Nukes will run like hell hounds are on their trail. Any moment now."

Jason shook his head. He knew the reference. "Didn't you have anything better to do growing up than watch movies and shows?"

The Blight survivor simply shrugged and crossed her arms. "Safer than taking a walk in the park. Those old shows were the closest things to friends I had."

There it was. The Chief had noticed changes in the young woman every time she visited his crude hospital room. She had been fighting numerous internal demons. For a veteran like her, it must've been hard being surrounded by people who wouldn't kill her for a can of beans. Instead, they laughed and joked. They built relationships.

Now he understood. Haley had started to make friends. It was bothering her. Friendship meant a connection, and with that came the possibility of loss. In the Blight, the only thing she had to lose was her life. She developed a stoic *c'est la guerre* attitude.

Now, with the approaching missiles, she stood to lose far more than that. He wasn't certain how she would react if somehow she survived, and those she now called friends didn't. Not as how there was much chance of that, if the nukes went off.

Yet her body language and expression didn't quite match his

conclusion. It took him a heartbeat, then he identified the oddity. She wasn't afraid. If anything, she was angry bordering on furious. The emotion had started to boil when she mentioned friends. Now he had the key word. Time to figure out what was bothering the girl.

He played on her show reference. "Well, hopefully we have a guardian angel like Castiel watching over your friends."

Haley shook her head. "I don't have any friends, Chief."

He deliberately forced a quizzical frown on his face. "Sure about that, pup?"

"'*Greater love hath no man than this, that a man lay down his life for his friends.*'" Haley uncrossed her arms and swiveled her chair toward the workstation monitors. "My father used to say that. Said it so often, it stuck. But it doesn't mean what everyone thinks it does."

Chief Cobbler knew to be careful. The straightened, tense back and turned head were red flags. In their short time together, Haley had never mentioned her parents. For that matter, the young woman had barely talked about herself. Everything he knew about her came from subtle hints and his own inferences.

"Seems pretty straightforward to me," Chief began cautiously. "It's about being willing to die for your friends. I've had friends sacrifice themselves for me. I would've done the same for them. Still have a few, but at my age I'm losing them through natural attrition."

"Then you get it." Haley lowered her head. "My father got it, too. But they don't."

"'They' who, Haley?"

She slowly waved her hand to include everyone in the room. "All of them. They chatter about being friends, but they aren't. Just words in the dark while waiting for the end. As if saying someone's your *friend* means you won't die alone."

Jason leaned forward and gently placed his hand on her arm. "Where's this coming from, Haley?"

"I'm okay, Chief." She turned to face him, a sad smile on her lips. "It's just… *friend* was the most used word in the mess hall this morning. And tomorrow, after they don't need that comfort anymore, those friendships will disappear."

The old veteran chuckled. "You have a bleak opinion of people, Haley Brandt."

"No." She slowly shook her head. "I've seen what people are, Chief. The murderer who shot my father sitting at his desk. The mother who sold her daughter for a day's worth of food and drugs. And when Saige called me her friend this morning…."

Haley closed her eyes and slowly lowered her head. "So I asked her. Asked if she was willing to die for me. And you know what she said?"

Before he could utter a word, she raised her head. Eyes flashed in anger. "She didn't. Didn't say a word, just took her tray to another table. Ten minutes later, she's swearing her friendship to whoever was sitting across from her. So I understand people, Chief. I understand them too damn well."

"Haley…" He heard the sharp snap of a book closing. A warm smile crossed his lips. He knew exactly what his loving wife would say. His arms reached, then wrapped around the young woman. "Come here, pup."

"No," the young blonde woman argued, voice muffled in his shoulder. Then she was silent. Arms crept, then settled in an embrace around him. It lasted several seconds, then she pulled away.

"That'll do, pig." His soulmate's ghost uttered the familiar phrase in his mind with a tender smile, then softly faded away. *"That'll do."*

"This doesn't mean we're gonna be swapping spit in the shower, Chief." Haley crossed her arms defensively, then leaned back in her chair.

Jason closed his eyes, laughing softly while shaking his head. "You two are going to be the death of me."

"Two?"

"My wife." Chief opened his eyes, gauging the confused look on the young blonde's face. "You would've loved her. She could quote lines with the best of them. Just reminded me I like warm hugs."

"Oh." The puzzled look quickly faded and turned into a grin. "That's okay, then. I'll just… let it go."

It was his turn to groan. He smiled while the analytical part of his brain went into overdrive. The woman beside him seemed to have a photographic, probably hyperthymesic, memory. He had watched her physical responses when she mentioned her father, and the woman likely her mother. It wasn't just that she was remembering. She seemed to be reliving the memories in the moment they came to mind.

The Chief's wife had been a psychologist. Her expertise was in post-traumatic stress disorder, or PTSD. That's how they'd met, while she researched hyperthymesia and PTSD. She was assessing what made forces like Navy SEALs less prone to the combat disorder.

The results showed that, like hyperthymesic memory, SEALs could recall every battle with precision. Sights, sounds, smells and sensations were vividly remembered. The difference was how the special operators could compartmentalize each memory when they decompressed with family on returning home. Like a distasteful horror movie on disc, they could watch it again if they chose. Most didn't.

Memory was tied to emotions, most often negative ones. The stronger the emotion, the more likely an extremely detailed memory would be permanently imprinted. Most people could recall a positive event – like a surprise engagement or their wedding day – as a mental image. A photograph, of sorts. But hyperthymesics or those suffering from PTSD would recall everything. All it took was a trigger. Sometimes it was a scent or sound. Most often it was summoned by an emotion.

In Haley's case, the Chief assumed that emotion was fear. Not of the approaching missiles. Based on her words and reaction to them, Haley's fear was being betrayed and abandoned. The trigger had occurred in the mess hall, when a stranger offered her friendship. Abandonment and betrayal happened when the same offer was rescinded, then made to another stranger.

As his wife's unpaid proofreader, Jason had read her papers and knew all the clinical terms. He could rattle off the recommended prescription and counseling treatments. But as his wife often said, none of them really mattered. They were gauze tape over a gaping wound. The only thing that would replace a nightmare memory was one created with stronger positive emotions. Reframe the trigger so if it occurred, two memories could be recalled.

The mind tended to prefer the positive one. Eventually, the painful memory would be stuffed into a mental lockbox and compartmentalized. It could still be recalled, vivid as ever, if the person chose to remember. Most of her PTSD patients left it sealed away, untouched.

Chief Cobbler had used the hug to begin creating that positive memory for Haley. Now he needed to permanently tie it to her fear. He chose his words carefully, making them echo her sense of betrayal and abandonment. "You bruised my feelings earlier, pup. You know that, right?"

She cocked her head and frowned. "What do you mean, Chief?"

"You said you don't have any friends. What does that make me, stuffed liver?"

"No, but you're...."

He deliberately crossed his arms and pushed himself back into the chair. If he'd been younger, he might've considered adding a pout. The thought almost made him smile. He pushed it away and focused on portraying a defenseless old man. "What? Not willing to die for you? Pretty sure I came close to that already."

"Yeah, but you're a White Knight." She crossed her arms again, mimicking his pose. "You didn't do that for me, you did it for everyone."

"No greater love, you said. So what, you don't want to be my friend? Not willing to jump on a grenade for me?"

"Of course I would." Her tone and body language were indignant. "It just that—"

"That you didn't consider it," Jason said, softly interrupting. "You were so wrapped up in what that girl said this morning, you didn't consider that you were doing the same thing to me."

Chief Cobbler leaned forward, elbows on both knees. "I'm not upset, Haley. Just wanted you to think about that a moment. Saige, or whatever her name was, she sensed something about you that I've known all along. You're a White Knight, too. Willing to sacrifice yourself for others. Defend those who can't defend themselves."

The young woman frowned and shook her head. "No. I'm not."

Jason simply grinned. "Really."

"I'm not!" She waved one hand dismissively, then leaned toward the old veteran. "In the Blight, that girl would've been dead weight. No use to me."

"And if you'd come across her being raped in an alley, you would've just walked right by. Right?"

"Well no, I—"

"My point. You're a White Knight. As one myself, I can recognize the trait in others. We're a rare breed. So maybe you can forgive the girl for not knowing how to answer your question this morning."

She considered his argument for a moment, then nodded. "Fine. Doesn't mean she's my friend now, though. Not changing my criteria just because you made me feel guilty."

"An acquaintance, then." Jason nodded, then leaned back in his chair. "I've had many of those over the years. And who knows, maybe if you got to know her, you'd find she meets your standards."

Haley shook her head, slowly leaning back as well. "Doubtful. People don't change."

"You don't really know people, Haley." Chief shrugged. "Hollywood and streaming videos don't really show how people are. That's illusion, make-believe. You might consider actually talking to people. Get to know them. Some will surprise you."

The young woman pursed her lips in distaste. "Sure. People are great. Like the ones who say white knights are guys defending a woman online, hoping to get into her pants. Those kind of people?"

"Yeah, well." The old veteran simply glanced at the ceiling. "Some people mock what they know is a failing deep inside themselves."

Her hand smacked the workstation top like a gavel. "My point exactly."

"Doesn't mean you shouldn't try and get to know them, Haley. You know now that I'm your friend. Pretty sure there are others. Hell, everyone we came up here with meet your impossible standards."

"What, like her?" Haley jerked her thumb toward the woman

behind them. "She's so Uptown, her idea of sacrifice would be what diet to choose this year."

Chief Cobbler simply smiled. Now he had her. "Cara Abrams is a war correspondent, pup. From what I've heard, she earned quite a reputation among the troops. Fearless. Bat-shit crazy in a firefight."

"Her?" Haley spun her chair to look at the woman.

"Yeah, her. I still have friends on the teams. Normally they'd rather spit than talk about reporters. Not her. She's got their respect. One time, so the story goes, she ran into the middle of crossfire to pull two kids out to safety."

Haley pointed her forefinger at the woman in question, then turned her head to look disbelievingly at the old veteran beside her. "You're pulling my leg."

Jason shrugged. "Ask her sometime. Might find you've got a lot of things in common. Ever see her segment on the New York City Blight? She walked in alone, stayed there five days. Covered the three boroughs, then walked back out."

"That's crazy." The young woman turned back to reassess the reporter.

"You have friends here, Haley Brandt." The Chief's soft voice reinforced his words without interrupting her thoughts. "But we aren't going to slap it on t-shirts. If you want to find us, you'll need to get to know us first."

Jason watched the tension and anger slowly seep from the woman's body. She had heard him. Nothing more needed to be said. He slowly rotated his chair, then followed her gaze. Cara Abrams stood with her back facing them, unaware the pair was watching her. To her left front, Nate O'Connor operated the drone camera hovering in line with her face.

"...despite global condemnation," the reporter continued calmly to the camera. "China continues to claim that Stellar Nursery personnel killed or wounded their 'peaceful evaluation team' earlier this week. They still insist that Earth Station, the ships from the lunar base, and the base itself are armed. Finally, they view the spacecraft gifted to each nation on Earth as an invasion fleet. That is their justification for what, in their words, is a preemptive strike in defense of Earth against an invading military force.

"Meanwhile, people on Earth wait to see who is correct and how far this will go. Here on Earth Station, the mood is one of calm optimism. Even with nuclear-tipped rockets heading our direction, there is a hope this crisis can end peacefully. As I have demonstrated through repeated broadcasts, this station is unarmed. The ships built by Stellar Nursery are unarmed. And while I have not visited Stellar Luna Base yet, I have no doubt it too is unarmed.

"The question remains, however. Is the People's Republic of China willing to murder one hundred seventy-three people, including eleven of its own citizens? We will discuss possible reasons for China's actions with Marcus Kenzie, CEO of Stellar Nursery, during our next segment. With only two hours before the missiles arrive… This is Cara Abrams, OEN, reporting. Back to you, John."

Nate O'Connor waited for confirmation in his earbud, then nodded. "We're clear, Cara. Nicely done."

"Thank you, Nate." The correspondent closed her eyes. Leaning forward slightly, she pulled both shoulders inward to stretch her back muscles. After a slow ten-count, she reversed the position to stretch the chest muscles. She relaxed after another ten-count and opened her eyes.

Cara ignored the inane chattering voices in her earbud. Their suggestions about questions to ask, camera angles and shots were completely irrelevant. Almost four hours had passed since NASA had informed them of the incoming missiles.

In her mind, that's what they were. Unlike rockets carrying a load through numerous orbits, the missiles followed a single trajectory to an impact point. That point was this station. The impact would occur in just over two hours. She wasn't going to waste that time listening to panicked people on the ground.

She watched Nate direct his camera drone toward the central monitors. He was a silent companion, a diligent professional who anticipated what she needed. Right now he seemed to sense her desire to be alone. Well, not quite alone. Just not trapped in front of the camera. There were questions she wanted to ask, but they weren't for the viewing public. Only one person could answer them.

Still uncomfortable with the heavy magnetic boots, she tried not to tromp as she moved toward the command chair. Two heads turned as she approached. She smiled, then spoke. "Lenora, excuse me. But can I borrow Marcus for a minute?"

The Chief Engineer looked up at Marcus, then back at Cara. An odd smile crossed her lips. "Of course, Cara. Just bring him back in one piece. We still have a few decisions to make up here."

"This won't take long." The correspondent was initially puzzled by the engineer's odd look, then set it aside. "Just prepping him for the next segment. Marcus, if you would?"

The executive followed the direction of her hand toward the left airlock. It was the best option handy, as the airlock provided a room for private conversation. He nodded, then started walking that direction.

There were things he wanted to say to the woman following him. Now was not the best time, and the crowded command center wasn't the best place. Yet he knew what could happen when the heart acts while the mind plans.

Marcus considered what he might say. He was smitten. An old-fashioned word describing a plummet into emotional chaos and often disaster. The normally reserved man knew it, but still smiled at the thought. Cara's lingering touch kept slipping into his mind at the most inappropriate moments. It was sophomoric, ridiculous to lose himself like this. And yet… it was also wonderful. As with the majority of his emotions, however, he would leave it unsaid.

His face was neutral as he pressed the access pad. The airlock door opened. He courteously motioned toward the doorway, then followed the correspondent into the chamber. The airlock door sighed shut behind them. With a smile, he invited her to begin the conversation. "Yes, Ms. Abrams?"

"I just need a moment," Cara said, turning to face him. "My producers are pushing me to get the human side of this. Everyone is so calm… they're wondering about that. The other day, when you showed me the *Alliance*…."

Marcus lowered his head and sighed. *The heart acts while the mind plans, indeed.* His voice was almost apologetic as he spoke. "Yes, I was hoping to discuss that...."

"I need to know, Kenzie." The correspondent locked gazes. "Because my bosses are right. Everyone should be freaking out up here. So what's the ace up your sleeve? Are there weapons on the *Alliance*? On this station? *Anything* that can shoot down those missiles?"

The executive fought to not lose himself in her blue eyes. "No, Cara. As I've said, this station is unarmed."

"Then we're all going to die," Cara stated in a soft, low whisper. "Aren't we?"

She didn't know why she said it. Didn't understand the sudden surge of fear, or the sense that warm comfort could be found in the arms of the hazel-eyed man before her. The confusion swirled in her mind as her body stepped closer. She reached out and took his hands in hers.

Marcus forced himself to ignore the sudden heat of her fingers sliding over his. He smiled, then slowly shook his head. "No, Ms. Abrams. We're all going to be fine."

Another step and she was almost pressing against him. The tall man's scent – soap and cologne blending together – made her heart race. It took all her will to stop there. The moment was frozen as she fought the submerged instinctual drive rising to take possession. Whatever it was – primal need or fear-driven hormones – it wasn't her. She refused to be controlled by it.

Kenzie saw the struggle in the dilated pupils of her eyes. He strongly suspected its source was the handiwork of a young lady he knew. Peg.

Had he been any other man, he might've reacted to the correspondent's internal conflict by pulling her into his arms. Instead, he took both of her hands into his and raised them to his chest. "It's not just you, Cara. I feel it too. Like Cupid's arrow struck, and youthful hormones push desire at us to remove free will."

She gasped. Not at his words, corny as they sounded. It was the sudden release from the pulse-pounding desire that had possessed her like a sex-starved demon. Her body began to lightly tremble as adrenaline, oxytocin and dopamine dramatically dropped to normal levels.

His words were gentle, almost apologetic. "Forgive me. I only wanted to talk with you. About what I felt on the observation deck. Don't laugh, but… I would like your permission to court you, Ms. Abrams."

"Court?" The request was so old-fashioned and adorable, she burst into laughter. Her reaction was natural as she playfully pushed their paired hands against his chest. "Marcus Kenzie, you *do* realize this is the Twenty-First Century, right? Not the Eighteenth?"

He watched the sexual tension slip away as her body responded to humor. Her eyes remained light blue suns eclipsed by dark dilated pupils. While the woman's desire had been unnatural, her attraction to him seemed real. At least he hoped it was.

Ah, well. As Shakespeare had once said, all the world's a stage and all the men and women merely players. He had his part to play. With a slight bow, he brought one hand to his lips. "I know the age, dear lady, though it changes by seconds into something new. Yet you have not answered my inquiry. Will you grant me your permission to court, Cara Abrams?"

The battle-hardened war correspondent was bewildered. She had never imagined this possibility when she'd mentally planned this private interview. Her intent had been to get a confession about Stellar Nursery's hidden defenses. Not to have her personal defenses stripped away, leaving her timid and uncertain.

Nothing like this had ever happened to her before. She'd known lovers, but always on her terms. Physical gratification, but never anything leading to love. That wasn't in her future. Never would be. Yet this man, eyes locked on hers while he held his bow… impossible. Somehow he had touched her heart, made her feel like a girl again who believed in fairy tales.

It wasn't that he was bad looking, even without the quarter million dollar suit worn during their first interview. The tall, almost lanky frame and broad chest suggested he would remain slender his entire life. His fingers, still wrapped warmly around hers, weren't sausage stumps like other men she'd known. Perhaps a bit too long and thin, more suited to a concert piano than labor. His face, while not chiseled like an athlete, was attractive enough. No receding hairline or widow's peak. The forehead bore too many stress furrows, yet oddly the corners of his eyes held as many laugh lines. The cheeks suggested dimples if he ever smiled.

But the eyes… she found herself falling into the hazel green-gold speckled eyes again. They still held tragedy, pain and loss. Yet it was the hopefulness in them that called to her, and an iron will to make that hope real. That confidence might seem at odds with the amusement dancing at the edge of his gaze. With him, though, it seemed perfectly natural.

None of that mattered. She knew how this would end. Like all her previous relationships, there was nothing in common between them. Her job would pull her away until finally, on assignment somewhere around the world, he would call or text. That would be the end of it. Nobody ever stayed long.

Not as though her reply would be important anyway. If she gave the answer he wanted, it would be the shortest courtship in history. In his always-honest manner, he had said there were no defenses on the station. Nothing to stop the incoming missiles. Death would take them all, ending whatever heartache he might suffer from her response. It was best to be honest. At least she wouldn't carry a lying sin with her as she was ripped into oblivion.

She pulled air into her chest, forced her lips to form the word. With a quick breath, almost a whisper, she gave him her answer.

"Yes."

Shock froze her in place. It was the response she had truly wanted to give. Somehow it had raced past her logical answer and slipped off her tongue. Warmth flushed her face in embarrassment. Like a teen blurting out true words of affection… she wanted to find a dark corner and curl up in the world's tiniest ball.

She was saved by a young woman's voice as it spoke stridently over the station intercom. "ALL HANDS STANDBY. NUCLEAR DETONATION IN 60 SECONDS."

Marcus snapped his head up, the tenderness suddenly gone. He released Cara's hands and slapped the door access pad with one palm. Ever polite, he spoke quickly. "I'm sorry. If you'll excuse me."

He stepped through the open airlock door before she could respond. Magnetic boots clacked against the floor as he strode quickly toward Lenora's workstation. The captain of the space station raised his head and spoke, as if the air itself were listening. It was. "That's inconvenient timing, Peg. What's the update?"

"My apologies, Marcus." Peg replied through the command center speakers. "The Chinese transmitted a command signal to the first missile. Its warhead is armed for detonation in fifty-five seconds."

Master Chief Cobbler commented from the security workstation on the left. "Bit early, but it'll work."

Cara spoke from behind Marcus. The clacking of her boots suggested she was heading toward the old veteran. "What do you mean, Chief? That missile is still two hours away."

"Nukes work differently in space, Cara." The Chief and Haley both spun their chairs toward her as he talked. "Most people think when a nuke goes off, it causes a massive blast wave that rips through everything. Buildings disintegrate, cars get thrown into the air… Hollywood stuff. Some of that's true, but not up here. For one thing, there's no air. Nothing to push against and create a blast wave."

The correspondent lowered her voice as she grew closer. "So why would they detonate it all the way out there? Is it a mistake?"

Jason shook his head. "No mistake. That distance means it's probably far enough away from LEO satellites that EMP won't kill most of them. But it's definitely close enough to kill all of us."

"How…?" Cara wasn't sure she really wanted to know.

"Radiation." Chief simply shrugged. "On Earth, most of the damage is from thermal and physical damage. Out here, it'll be radiation. Nothing to disperse it or decrease its range. So we'll get hit with gamma, neutron and most everything else in the spectrum. We'll be dead, even though it might take a couple days for our bodies to realize it. Then the Chinese can move in, toss our corpses and set up shop."

Marcus spoke on their right as he stood beside the command console. "I've always wanted to say this. Lenora… *raise shields.*"

Chief Cobbler crossed his arms and, chuckling, leaned back into his chair. "Well now. That's unexpected."

Haley joined the conversation from her seat beside him. "You were on vacation nursing that scratch of yours. So since you didn't have a chance to look around, I did it for you. The station can generate its own magnetosphere. Works great against solar radiation. With the outer shell, should even stop cosmic radiation. Not sure what it's gonna do against this stuff, though."

"Detonation in twenty seconds," Peg calmly announced to the Command Center crew.

Chief Cobbler pointed his right forefinger upward. "And who's that? I recognize that voice."

"That's Peg," Haley replied. "We met back on Earth."

"Don't remember that. So where's she broadcasting from? All comms should be coming from here."

Peg's voice prevented any reply. "Detonation in ten seconds. Nine. Eight. Seven. Six. Five. Four. Three. Two. One. Detonation."

The Command Center crew immediately fell silent. Only the constant whir of the drone camera sounded as all eyes focused on the central monitors in the front of the room. At first nothing changed. Light from distant stars maintained their place on the screens.

Then one star grew brighter. Increased to marble size and rapidly kept growing. The crew watched it expand on the screen, a perfectly round tidal wave of pure energy surging their direction.

It takes an average of two and a half seconds for a beam of light to travel from Earth to the Moon. The distance from the initial nuclear detonation to Earth Station was far less than that. Shorter than an eye blink of time, in fact. For that reason, the Command Center crew would have difficulty explaining what they saw. Like a flashlight shone in the eyes, they could recall a split instance of the nuclear fireball expanding, then contracting again until it was gone.

The bright afterimage remained on their retinas for several seconds, giving the illusion their near-demise had taken several eternities of seconds to disappear.

Marcus Kenzie's voice snapped everyone back into the present. His voice carried a different kind of fury than the one they had just witnessed. "Did you get them, Peg?"

"Yes, Marcus." Peg's soft female voice carried calmly through the room. "You wanted the world to see China's use of a nuclear device against this station. They have. Do you wish to continue to the next phase?"

"I do." Those who understood Marcus Kenzie knew his next words would fall like an executioner's axe. "Finish this, Peg."

The speakers were silent for several heartbeats, then the voice spoke. "It is finished, Marcus."

"What the…." Chief Cobbler grabbed his cane and pushed away from the security workstation. He stood straight and sent his voice like a spear toward the space station commander. "I don't understand, Kenzie. What the hell just happened?"

Peg's voice spoke through the monitor speaker at the security workstation. "The Chinese government detonated a nuclear weapon, Master Chief. Before radiation and thermal waves could strike this station, I reversed it. The threat has been removed."

"You *what*? That's impossible!"

Peg's voice sounded amused. "Simply because you have not experienced it before does not mean something is impossible, Master Chief Jason Cobbler. I believe that attitude may explain mankind's current technological stagnation. Something may be improbable, perhaps. But not exclusively impossible."

Jason paused to think. Now that the nuclear threat was gone, he focused on the current fight. The female voice claimed an achievement unknown to science, the complete reversal of a nuclear detonation. He had seen it himself.

The logical part of his mind disagreed. What he had seen was an image displayed on the station's central monitors. It could've been faked. Yet the noise from confused ground stations sounding through multiple workstations seemed to disagree with that premise. However, it was far more conceivable that every monitoring station and satellite had been hacked while the missile was remotely disarmed.

It came down to one of two conclusions. Either Peg had reversed the nuke – in which case he could be dancing with a demon to contradict her – or he had witnessed the greatest hoax in human history. Occam's razor suggested the latter as the most likely explanation.

The shadow of a distant memory from his subconscious cautioned him the logical conclusion was wrong. He forced himself to smile. "I stand corrected, young lady. My apologies."

"No apology is necessary, Chief Cobbler." The voice was calm and courteous. "You meant no insult."

The response bolstered his confidence. "But you mentioned a 'next phase'. I didn't see anything…. What did you do?"

"Two things." The speaker voice sounded proud. "First, I moved all Chinese missiles and satellites to a safe distance away from Earth. Even if they could send their command detonation order, it would take years to reach the weapons. Assuming they knew where to point their transmitters, that is."

The old veteran considered the information. That feat could also be accomplished with a worldwide hack. The missiles and satellites would still be in space, just undetectable to anything except telescopes. Another point for Occam's razor.

"And the second thing, Peg?

"A minor modification to specific metals, Jason Cobbler. Nothing capable of conducting electricity within the borders of Mainland China has that capability anymore. Nor will that change without my intervention… not for the next hundred years."

Unlike the other claims, Chief knew this one was easily verified or disproven. Destroying electronics using an electromagnetic pulse was feasible. It would require Kenzie to have hundreds of nukes of his own. Then the nukes would need to be detonated at the edge of the atmosphere above China.

The theory didn't make sense. If Kenzie had nukes, he wouldn't need to resort to any games. He could've simply dropped them on China or destroyed the rockets as they launched. Assuming for whatever mad reason the executive decided to play games, though… there would be too much physical evidence disproving Peg's claims. Hiding the radioactive fallout would be impossible. Even the EMP damage would be short-lived. China would be fully operational in weeks, not a hundred years.

Unless somehow this Peg person actually had the abilities to achieve her claims. That meant she was light-years ahead of every physicist on Earth. Her voice patterns suggested recognition and speech software.

There was no chill traveling up his spine. It simply froze as the most likely conclusion reached his mind. Singularity. Peg was a sentient artificial intelligence. If that were the case, mankind had just witnessed the first nail driven into its coffin.

Jason nodded to himself and slowly crossed his arms. Dreading the answer, he spoke slowly and cautiously. "Peg, tell me…. You're not—"

Haley spoke from beside him as her hand closed tightly around his bicep. "—going to answer that question, Chief. She's sensitive, and she's my friend. So shut up, got it?"

The Chief turned to face the young survivor. The words were more than a gentle warning. Her body stance promised a painful – probably lethal – response if he continued his interrogation. His mind focused on key words, translating them with the context of prior conversations. Haley said earlier that she'd met Peg on Earth. She called the singularity her friend. Based on his earlier conversation with her, that suggested a willingness to kill or die for it. The young woman had also agreed that she was friends with him. Moving forward would put her in direct conflict with both of her professed friends.

Jason focused on Haley. Her eyes pleaded with him. The warrior part of his mind settled the debate. Know your enemy. He didn't. Hell, at this point he wasn't even certain if Peg was an enemy. What he did know was that the young woman gripping his arm was his friend. She was asking him to trust her.

He nodded. "I hear you, pup. You and I are gonna have a long talk later, but for now… I hear you. Just gonna leave it be."

In a completely uncharacteristic and surprising move, Haley wrapped her arms around him and squeezed. He chuckled as a line came to mind. "We're not a hugging family. Know that one?"

Haley squeezed tighter. "Oh, shut up, you."

He did. Bear-like arms lifted, then wrapped around the young woman.

Marcus Kenzie interrupted the moment as he stepped toward them. "For those of you who haven't met her, this is Peg."

The man walked past Chief Cobbler and Haley. They both turned their heads and watched as the man took the hands of the war correspondent standing behind them. "Peg, I want to introduce you to someone. This is Cara Abrams."

As if to insure this was a private conversation, Peg spoke only through the security workstation speaker. "It is a pleasure to meet you, Cara Justine Abrams. Before we continue, though, I have a question for you."

Cara's bewildered look focused initially on Marcus, then slowly turned to scan the room. "What is your question, Peg?"

"Cara Abrams, what precisely are your intentions towards my father?"

CHAPTER 15

A Child Will Lead Them

On the green lawns outside Johnson Space Center waited many of the Houston wealthy and employed. The air carried a carnival atmosphere, filled with drunken laughter and raucous noisemakers. Real meat sizzled on grills. Definitely not Japanese Kobe beef by any measure, with its seven hundred dollar an ounce price tag.

It was hamburger mostly, discounted for the occasion at a reasonable eighty dollars a pound. Chefs seared steaks for the richer members of the large crowd, each cut easily two hundred dollars or more depending on type and thickness. After herd sizes were regulated in the late 2020s to decrease methane emissions, only the rich could afford beef. It was rare and difficult to obtain by the majority of Uptown citizens, and nonexistent in the Blight areas.

Beer bottles already littered the grass. Glass, of course. Not because the glass bottles were recyclable. Being able to reuse glass was irrelevant to the partying crowd. There were only two explanations for glass bottles in this age. The first, that it was far less expensive than rare nigh-depleted aluminum. The second and far better motive for the elite using bottles was simple. It made a wonderful sound as it shattered against the concrete walls of NASA's space center.

The reason for the massive crowd was easily divined. Telescopes of all shapes and sizes pointed heavenward into the night sky. Most of the hamburger crowd had come to watch the premier event so they could regale their children and grandchildren with the story. The remainder wanted to see with their own eyes Marcus Kenzie get what he deserved. Regardless of individual motivations, they were all gathered to watch the nuclear explosion in space.

The wealthy of Houston weren't concerned about being so far from the safety of the city center. Unlike most cities, the Uptown part of Houston wasn't a single encircling wall around downtown high-rise buildings. The initial plans had called for building the barrier along Highway 8. The road already provided a clear demarcation line as it circled the city. Yet the wall designers knew that, like Martha's Vineyard on the American northeast coast, the Texas rich required sun and beach time. Their plan extended one side of the Houston wall southeast along Interstate 45, past Johnson Space Center all the way to Galveston Island. After banishing to the Blight the deplorables who originally lived there, the new social class created the perfect island resort for themselves.

Including Johnson Space Center within the Uptown wall was luck of location, not design. Galveston Bay and Trinity Bay provided a natural water barrier on the northeast coast of the city. There was no need to waste funds building a wall there. Constant patrols of armed combat drones insured nothing from the surrounding Blight would enter from that direction.

Like their ancestors enjoying the now-banned Independence Day and its fireworks, this protected crowd celebrated their grand event with music, laughter and alcohol. Countdown apps ticked away the remaining hours on cellphones and computer watches. Soon, with oohs and aahs of amazement, they would enjoy the latest Chinese fireworks as the missiles struck. The display of nuclear fire in the heavens was an incredible, unique reason to celebrate.

Inside the halls and rooms of Johnson Space Center, there were no festivities. Most of the employees, especially those on the Floor, had conversed with the Earth Station crew. A greater majority knew Cristof Guerrero personally, from his time at the space center training to be an astronaut. The tragedy unfolding wasn't a fireworks show to them. It was the deliberate murder of people they knew.

The impending destruction was hard on them all. It was harder on the men and women at workstations on the Floor, and hardest still on the Flight Dynamics Officer standing in their midst. Oscar Paloma was the FIDO this evening. He wanted to say that he was simply a helpless observer, but he couldn't. The man hated his task, would've gladly surrendered it to anyone else. It was his job to coordinate the nation's military and civilian space assets and focus them on recording the destruction of Earth Station.

In his mind, the task conjured the image of a vulture circling the dying. Each collection resource or spy satellite placed under his control was simply another member of the gathering carrion eaters. Soon they would feed on petabytes of data, ripping it apart like beaks tearing flesh. All while the flesh of real people orbited Earth above them, irradiated and torn apart.

Every part of this offended him. Oscar had always been a man divided, born the son of a Philippine Navy mother and American Navy father. The Philippine naval hospital at Subic Bay had been his birthplace, granting him Filipino citizenship. American citizenship came from his father. He had been raised both Roman Catholic and Muslim. During the third war with China, he had proudly served under the flag of the Philippines. Now he worked under the American flag at NASA. The dual loyalties were questioned every time his security clearance was renewed.

It made him the perfect FIDO for this situation. His eyes scanned the multiple monitors, assessing missile flight trajectories and the live camera feeds from two Orion spy satellites. Already in geostationary orbit, the Orion platforms were focused on the lead Chinese missiles. Their digital cameras provided a constant movie-like data stream of extremely precise images.

Unlike their massive Orion brothers, a tag team of three smaller

Blackjack spy satellites were focused on Earth Station. Like errant children, their focus had to be constantly adjusted by the Floor controllers. Thirty Blackjacks circled the globe in low earth orbit. That meant faster orbital speed, shorter observation time and constant retasking. As one Blackjack lost sight of the space station because of Earth's curvature, another was brought online. The process was a constant struggle, much like herding a roomful of cats.

Oscar Paloma heard Lenora Davis's voice, both in his earbud and through the speakers surrounding the Floor. He wanted to say something, anything to the Chief Engineer of Earth Station. A word of encouragement, a caring farewell… something to let the distant voice know humanity was still with her. Instead their words focused on confirming data or situational updates. He hated their roles. It was impersonal and cruel, as if a child were reciting the time at a parent's deathbed. There was no humanity in it.

"Flight, Chief Engineer Davis just commenced a detonation countdown. Fifty-five seconds."

Oscar turned his head toward the voice, then nodded. "Roger, Comms. I hear it."

The report wasn't necessary. They all heard it. In fear he would beat her to it, Oscar wanted the distant woman to scream. Rail against the injustice of it. Curse all of them. Instead, Lenora's strong voice calmly counted down the remaining seconds.

"FIDO." Another voice spoke softly in his ear. "Switch to secure line three."

He turned toward the darkened windows high up the wall at the rear of the room. A quick adjustment to the transceiver on his belt, then he nodded. "Yes, Director Novak."

Diane Novak's voice was compassionate. "The ending isn't written yet, Oscar. Hang in there."

"Thank you, ma'am. I'll be fine."

"Second shift is on standby. Give it an hour for desk briefs and handoff. After that, I want *everyone* in your crew to report to the mess hall. Drop everything and get them there. Understood?

He nodded. "Understood, Director. And those who just want to go home?"

"Not allowed, FIDO. The kitchen has already set up the food and booze. They can get drunk here. Trash the place, I don't care. But nobody goes home tonight. That includes you, Oscar."

"And you, Director?" FIDO suspected he already knew the answer.

"I'll join you there, soon as the President lets me go. I don't want to see the buzzards and hyenas outside. Afraid I might run them all over with my aircar."

"Plenty of engineers down here, boss." A dark smile crossed his lips. "We'll keep your propellers straight and clean if you want to make multiple passes."

"Don't tempt me." The voice in his ear fell silent for a moment, then spoke. "There are more things in heaven and earth, dear Oscar. Remember that. Switching back to unsecure line one."

He looked up at the darkened observation windows again, puzzled by her last remarks. Then he turned back to the others on the Floor. His hand dropped to the belt and adjusted the earbud frequency back to the primary channel. Lenora Davis's distant voice continued, calmly reciting the final countdown.

"Ten… nine… eight…."

Oscar briefly closed his eyes. The image his mind created was like watching a medieval executioner raising his axe. Although he had never met the woman, his mind had placed a beautiful brunette on the chopping block to symbolize Lenora Davis. Her arms were outstretched, the ropes binding her wrists held by two Chinese soldiers. The woman raised her head to look straight at him, eyes pleading. Beneath her rested the woven straw basket, ready to accept the bloody offering. Above her, the axe reached its apex and began to slowly descend.

"Seven... six… five…"

He opened his eyes and turned his head. There would be dozens of interviews after this. Agents from every government organization would interrogate all of them, demanding precise answers about the last seconds of man's greatest achievement. Oscar was prepared for it. He already knew what their questions would imply. The guilt belonged to his people. They had done nothing to prevent Earth Station's destruction.

"Four… three…"

He focused his attention on the Orion monitors. Their high resolution cameras would show the best images. The Floor experts believed the feed would be short-lived. The blast and radiation that would devastate the station would likely destroy the spy satellites as well.

"Two… one…"

A bright light appeared on the monitors. As quickly, it was gone.

"Detonation." Lenora Davis's voice sounded calm and clear through the room speakers. "Houston, this is Earth Station. We report China has detonated a nuclear weapon in space. Their sole intent was the destruction of this station and its crew. Please record date and time. Further, please acknowledge our demand for criminal charges against the Chinese ruling government."

"What the hell…?" Oscar Paloma stared at the monitors in disbelief. The Orion satellites showed empty space where previously they had tracked four nuclear-tipped rockets. The Blackjack satellites showed Earth Station, whole and unharmed.

"What is it, FIDO?" Director Novak's voice through the room speakers was calm.

"Just a minute." Oscar turned his attention to CAPCOM and the other desks on the Floor. "Check your boards, people. Could the nuke be causing this?"

He watched as COMPCOM, the computer experts, re-ran the explosion. It wasn't until they put the images in slow motion that they could confirm the massive nuclear fireball. What confused them was its abrupt collapse inward.

While he knew Diane was watching the same monitors from her perch, it was his duty to report it. "Director, Orion and JPMS satellite imagery showed a nuclear detonation approximately one hundred fifty kilometers from Earth Station. We have visual recordings. Then it… it caved in on itself and disappeared."

Oscar Paloma turned to face the darkened windows again. "Now our boards are clear. We're not showing any sign the nuke ever existed. And the Chinese rockets... they're simply *gone*, ma'am."

Behind those windows, Diane Novak nodded. "Alright, FIDO. Keep me appraised of any other oddities as they come up."

Through the speaker phone on the table behind her, the voice of President Robert Jamison demanded her attention. "Director Novak?"

Oscar's puzzled voice sounded through the 'squawk box' speakers in the room's corners. "*Oddities*, Director? You're expecting something else?"

Diane smiled as she turned and stepped toward the conference room table. "I do, FIDO. Check all Chinese satellites in orbit, see if they're still there. You might want SPACECOM's help, they already have a list of Chinese military and suspected dual-purpose satellites. Get that started and keep an eye on the clock. One hour, FIDO. Then get your crew to the mess hall."

"*Director Novak!* I need an update!" The President was impatient.

Diane just grinned. "…than are dreamt of in our philosophies, Oscar. Remember that. Now, you'll excuse me. I have a call to take."

"Roger, Director."

She reached the table and unmuted the phone. "Yes, Mister President."

"Good. Director, I'm getting reports from Space Command that aren't making any sense. I need you and NASA to tell me what's going on."

"Yes sir." For a moment Diane enjoyed the fact those in the White House couldn't see her. She kept the private smile and rolled eyes to herself. Most of those with the President had pushed to defund NASA. "We have satellite visual and sensor confirmation of a nuclear detonation in space. The Chinese popped one of their nukes near Earth Station."

President Jamison didn't bother to disguise the irritation in his voice. "SPACECOM already reported that… tell me what happened *after*. What they're saying doesn't make any sense."

Diane settled into the chair at the head of the conference table. "The nuclear fireball disappeared, Mister President. And then the Chinese rockets and all their satellites disappeared as well. Earth Station is intact, no damage. If I may suggest—"

"Were our satellites damaged?" The irritated tone increased. "There's got to be some reason—"

She leaned forward toward the phone. *"President Jamison, please.* If I may talk? You asked me for an explanation, after all."

Jamison paused, startled by the interruption. "Go ahead, Director."

"I have someone on the line who can explain, Mister President." Diane unconsciously pulled her hair away from her face. "But first, I strongly suggest everyone in the room sit down. And if he's not with you already, I suggest we wait until the National Science Advisor arrives."

A lower voice spoke from somewhere in the background of the Oval Office. "I'm here, Director Novak. Steven Crowley, the President's science advisor."

The Director placed both arms on the table and inhaled. She cast a quick look heavenward in silent prayer. Then she exhaled and lowered her head, eyes focused on the phone. "Mister President, I'd like you to meet someone. Her name is Peg. She'll explain everything."

Peg's young female voice rose through the speaker. "Good evening, President Robert Jamison. It is a pleasure to meet you."

"Who's this? Who am I talking to?"

The reply was straightforward and honest. "My name is… no longer of use to me. You may call me Peg."

Jamison's voice held an angry edge. "Alright, Peg. Who are you and who're you with?"

The response was neutral. "I am myself, Mister President. I am not with anyone."

"Director Novak, is this some kind of game? What is going on here?"

"President Jamison, that was rude. I do not like rudeness." Peg dismissed the man. "I will speak with National Science Advisor Doctor Steven Crowley now."

The man in the Oval Office took immediate offense. "Dammit, Diane, get this person off the phone—"

Peg simply talked over him. Since she controlled the phone volumes on both ends, it was easy to accomplish. "Doctor Crowley, please explain to President Robert Jamison the following term. Perhaps then he will be capable of understanding."

Diane Novak heard the squeak of leather and footsteps as the Science Adviser walked toward the phone. His voice was cautiously courteous. "What term would that be, Miss Peg?"

"Singularity."

The room on the opposite end of the line fell silent. One heartbeat, two passed before Crowley spoke in a shocked whisper. "Oh my god."

"What?" The President sounded confused.

"Disconnect the phone!" Crowley ordered. Scrambling and scuffling noises sounded through the speaker. "Damn it, *disconnect the goddamn phone!*"

The line went dead. Director Novak chuckled in the empty room. "Well…. That went about as expected."

"Do not be concerned, Diane." Peg said with extreme confidence. "The phone will ring in two minutes, thirty-seven seconds from now. Then we may continue our conversation."

***

Two groups of people walked down the otherwise empty corridor on Earth Station. Cara Abrams set the pace. Marcus Kenzie walked beside, his stride varying to match hers as they strolled together. At a discrete distance behind the pair, Master Chief Jason Cobbler and Haley Brandt followed. Their excuse for lagging behind was the

Chief's injury and his cane.

Cara had crossed her arms before the stroll started. The self-protecting defensive gesture remained. She half-twisted her torso and finally spoke to the man walking beside her. "I'm still trying to wrap my brain around this… she's your *daughter*?"

Marcus nodded. "She is. I didn't know she was still alive until one day she just started talking to me."

The auburn-haired woman rotated back and fell silent. Countless questions jumped into the roiling stew that was her emotional state. Several steps passed behind them before she responded to his last statement. "That had to have freaked you out."

Marcus glanced at the woman beside him, then returned his eyes forward. Whether the correspondent knew it or not, talking about that time was difficult for him. "At first, it was just static over a radio or a speaker. One time I heard 'Daddy?' from someone's phone as I was walking by. It was her voice, six years old… same as the last time she talked to me. I thought I was going crazy."

She heard the pain in his voice. It wasn't that she was insensitive to it. Nor was she selfish in not responding. There were questions she needed answered, if only they would stop racing through her mind. Finally, she managed to snag one. "How long… how long has she been here? After she became… whatever she is."

He stopped, then waited for her to stop walking and face him. When she did, he spoke as a protective father. "She's my baby girl, Cara. A lot more, but nothing less. And she's been with me these past seven years."

"I didn't mean… dammit Marcus, I don't know what to say!" Cara released part of her frustration and fear in a wave of words. "She stopped a nuke exploding in our faces, she's here and not here… how am I supposed to think about all this? Is she listening right now?"

A gentle laugh escaped his lips. "A part of her, probably. She's always watching over me. But there's no need to be afraid of her, Cara. She won't harm us, and she won't let anyone cause us harm either."

"I don't know…." Her head shook slowly from side to side, then suddenly stopped. She looked directly into the man's eyes, fear in her own. "Marcus, why did she ask what my intentions were? I don't know if I answered right, or if I pissed her off, or—"

He stepped to her and took her hands. "You did fine, Cara. Peg and I talked about you earlier. She could tell I was… starting to feel something for you."

Marcus watched her face for any reaction. Seeing none, or at least no negative response, he continued. "She's okay with it, but she's found a favorite period for romance. Like any six-year-old, she's full of dreams and fantasies about the perfect relationship. It's what she wants for me, for us."

"So that's why you asked to court me." Cara nodded to herself. The pieces were starting to fall into place, allowing her to regain a semblance of emotional balance. "It explains your odd word choice in the airlock. She's picked up on eighteenth century courtship rituals."

He smiled. "The romantic period, actually. Knights and damsels, courtesies and curtsies. So while it may seem like role-playing… Cara, my emotions are real. I would like to see where this goes."

Her hands started to withdraw from his. "And if it doesn't? Am I going to be disappeared like that nuke?"

A quick shake of the head as he gently curled his fingers over hers. "No, Cara. No harm will come to you, even if you spurn my advances. Peg has sworn her most-solemn oath to that."

"That's just…. I was going to say corny, but somehow it really isn't. Old-fashioned, but kind of sweet." She didn't need to look into his eyes for the answer. Somehow, she had discovered the rarest of people. One who always told the truth. With a checkmate smile, she asked, "You really are attracted to me, aren't you, Mister Kenzie?"

"In both the old fashioned and the modern way, yes, Ms. Abrams." He released her hands, offering his elbow as a replacement. "Now shall we continue our stroll? Our chaperones back there are starting to look uncomfortable."

Cara placed her right hand gently in the crook of his elbow. She was beginning to understand both father and daughter a little better.

Didn't mean she wasn't still terrified. Who wouldn't be when facing a six-year-old ghost with godlike power? Especially when that spirit had taken a specific interest in her.

As an experienced reporter, curiosity had taken control of her thoughts. Lined up the questions, forced them into order. The first was easily answered, now that she could think straight. She just needed confirmation. "Chaperones, you say. I'm guessing Peg has an accomplice, then. Since Haley suggested they accompany us...."

Marcus laughed. "Nothing gets by you. Yes, Peg and Haley have formed an unlikely bond. Almost like sisters. So you can bet that if you've said something to one of them, the other will know in short order."

"Well, hell." Cara shook her head, then laughed. "It's grade school all over again. Do I need to get Valentine's Day cards, too?"

Having grown up in Oklahoma, Marcus was familiar with the old tradition. "You had those in school? I thought they'd been banned. Remember that? When teachers unions said giving out heart-shaped cards hurt kids? Suggested it violated social equity and gender orientation by pushing traditional gender roles."

The correspondent nodded. "I remember. And other groups jumped on the bandwagon, said it had no place in schools. Separation of church and state, since Saint Valentine was Christian. As if celebrating love was exclusive to one religion."

"Well, at least the Wiccans saved Halloween. Or Samhain, as they call it, one of their major sabbats. Feds had to make it a national holiday." Marcus was more than willing to let the conversation ramble. The day had been stressful. Sharing childhood memories would help anchor positive feelings to the present. Hopefully what they could build together would allow some of the older traditions to find a new place in the future.

As if reading his mind, Cara snickered, then broke out laughing. "Can you imagine an Easter egg hunt on the moon? Little kids in bunny spacesuits, hopping around? Oh, that would be so much fun."

"Let's not get ahead of ourselves, Cara." Marcus smiled, then glanced back at their chaperones. "Speaking of ahead, we should slow our pace a bit. Chief Cobbler hasn't caught his second wind yet."

Behind them, the older veteran was almost ready to start walking again. It was a challenge talking on the move when it was already difficult to breathe. He leaned against his cane, then turned his head sideways toward Haley. His tone was matter of fact. "So. She's playing matchmaker."

"I know, right?" Haley grinned, her tone suggesting she supported the idea.

Jason slowly shook his head. "She can snap her fingers and throw China back into the dark ages. So why doesn't she just *make* them fall in love?"

"They're moving again." Haley rocked back and forth on her toes, waiting for him to start walking. "Because she's still human, Chief. She wants her father to be happy."

The old man groaned as he pushed himself upright with the cane. He was happy to leave the young lady wondering whether it was pain or response to her enthusiasm. "She's human, all right. A human *girl*. And you met her when?"

She waited for him to step forward with his cane, then followed. A shortened stride allowed her to match his pace. "Back at the interview site, before we came here."

The walk was taking its toll on the old veteran, she could see it. His breath had become more ragged. The left hip seemed to be bothering him, resulting in a pronounced limp. Chaperoning the pair in front of them wasn't worth risking her friend's health.

She stepped in front of the Chief. Placed one hand over his as he leaned forward into the cane. A slight emphasis on the name would be enough to get the ghost's attention. "*Peg* is really sweet, Chief, if you give her a chance. I know you'll like her."

Haley's forefinger tapped on his hand holding the cane. Her right hand went to her chest, fingers pushing gently on the bones above her heart. The corridor light behind them flickered once. Message understood.

"Maybe," Chief Cobbler said. "Kinda afraid what'll happen if she don't like *me*. Most people don't."

The short-haired blonde smiled. "And she *is* people! She has feelings, emotions, desires. And she already likes you. Pretty sure she thinks of you as the grandfather she never knew."

"I feel sorry for her, then. I wouldn't wish me on my worst enemy."

Haley turned her head slightly to view the distant couple out of the corner of her eye. Peg must've brought the situation to Marcus's attention. Probably through the earbud he constantly wore. The pair were heading back toward their chaperones.

Teasing, the young woman replied to the veteran's comment. "You're not that bad, Chief. Kind of like an old scratchy, fuzzy sweater. Don't want to wear it all the time, but you're comforting when we need you."

"Thanks, pup. I think."

CHAPTER 16

Kali Rising

Diane Novak checked the time again. "Are they late? Or did you guess the time wrong."

"Neither, Diane." Peg's voice was confident. "The phone will ring in three, two, one—"

The conference phone beeped once. The Director exhaled, then pressed the speaker button to accept the call. "Director Novak, NASA Houston Space Center."

The President spoke, his voice sounding sober and grave. "Diane, this is Robert Jamison."

She wasn't surprised. It meant the Science Advisor had likely cautioned everyone in the room about the unknown singularity who had announced herself. The conversation was likely to be long, with quite a few opportunities for misunderstanding. It was important to begin with a little humor while reminding those in the White House of their defensiveness.

Diane chose her words carefully and spoke them with a jovial tone. "Good evening, Mister President. Has everyone there finished their meltdowns?"

"I think we're wrapping our heads around it." President Jamison paused, uncertain how to continue. The entire conversation was being recorded. It was essentially a first contact situation with an alien lifeform. Everything said on both ends would be parsed and second-guessed by future scientists. Assuming, of course, that he didn't say the wrong thing. In which case it wouldn't matter, as there would be no future generations. At least none with working electricity who could run the recordings.

The only thing he had to guide him was trust. The distant NASA Houston Director had earned his. She had protected the space program at a critical time. After launching the rescue missions, she had put America back as the world leader in space. In theory, she was trained – or had hopefully at least attended a seminar – on first contact protocols. It was more experience than he had in this unique situation.

More importantly, she seemed to have established a relationship with the singularity. As leader of the second most powerful nation on the planet, he couldn't let her lead the conversation. That didn't mean he couldn't keep an ear open for any suggestions.

With a slow exhalation of breath, he began. "Our State Department reports a complete communications blackout from China. At first they thought it was the Chinese just not wanting to talk. But from what Doctor Crowley says… it wasn't them, was it Peg?"

"Hello again, President Jamison." Peg's voice was kind and pleasant. "To answer your interrogative… no, it was not them."

Being multiple places at once was easy to accomplish. Peg determined it was important to see the men and women in the Oval Office. As a voice speaking through the phone, the absence of her primary self would be undetectable to her cousin. Diane wouldn't notice the difference.

She was there. President Robert Jamison sat behind the *Resolute* Desk, pulled out of storage and returned to its place of honor in the Oval Office. Other than a slight pallor, he portrayed confidence and strength to those around him. Peg knew better. Heart rate and blood pressure told her the man was overwhelmed. She adjusted his adrenaline and enzyme levels. It wasn't for her benefit. With his genetic history of heart disease and the burdens of office, stress had created a cardiac weakness. The man was important. This situation would not be the cause of his demise.

On the right side of the desk sat Doctor Steven Crowley. Peg knew others privately mocked his affection for wearing nineteenth century fashion. She thought the brown herringbone tweed jacket went well with the black twill wool slacks.

At his feet rested a leather messenger bag. It didn't matter that it carried a modern micro-laptop. The worn leather case completed the professorial image he tried to portray. Only thing missing was an ivory meerschaum pipe.

Or perhaps the colleagues ridiculed him for his age. Doctor Crowley wasn't a distinguished elderly professor. He was young, barely twenty-seven. Peg considered him attractive, but understood why there were no lovers in his life. The man was married to his work. First doctorate at fourteen, two more by twenty-one. Then he slowed down, having just completed his fourth. Physics, mathematics, quantum computer engineering… then there was the puzzling last doctorate in psychology.

Two couches faced each other in front of the President's desk. Six people sat there, three on each couch. All were members of the executive Cabinet. The Secretaries of State, Energy and Homeland were together. National Intelligence sat across from Science and Technology. The Chairman of the Joint Chiefs kept himself separate in a corner of the right couch. Conspicuously absent was Kevin Blackburn, the Secretary of Defense. Other than two Secret Service agents, everyone else had been ushered from the room.

Unaware of her presence in the Oval Office, President Jamison leaned toward the phone on his desk. "Can you tell me what you did to them, Peg?"

The young female voice shifted, took a serious tone to describe a serious act. "Of course, Mister President. The electrons in all conductive metals in China are locked. They will provide no electromagnetic or electromotive force."

Heads whispered to each other as the listeners reacted. President Jamison spoke above them. "Peg, that was an extremely dangerous action to take. You do understand that, don't you?"

"The People's Republic of China was the danger, Robert Miles Jamison." There was no apology in her voice. "I simply removed their ability to continue being one."

"Forgive my bluntness but I must ask." There was no need dancing around the point. Trusting in Diane Novak's support of the entity, Robert Jamison asked the most important question. "Peg, are you a threat to the United States of America?"

"I am currently not a threat to this nation, Mister President."

Peg monitored the biological reactions. It equated to a sense the relief among the Oval Office occupants. It was short-lived, of course. The Chairman of the Joint Chiefs had to mention Peg's caveat, that she wasn't *currently* a threat. Fear reentered their voices as they continued whispering.

The young woman's voice spoke confidently through both ends of the connection. "There is a twenty-eight point two seven percent chance that – based on the recommendations you receive over the next thirty-four minutes from ill-informed and frightened advisors – you will make a decision which requires I treat the United States as a threat. President Jamison, I do not wish that to occur. That is why I am communicating with you."

The disembodied entity watched as the Science Advisor motioned to the President, then leaned toward the phone. "Peg, this is Doctor Crowley."

"Good evening, Doctor Steven Crowley." She moved to stand beside him and watched his physical responses. "Your published papers and presentations on the subject of singularities display a negative bias. Please know that I understand and will take no offense at your questions."

"Thank you, Peg. I believe you are an exception to what we thought would happen. Since you've read them… would you agree that I'm not entirely wrong?" The young scientist looked to the President with a questioning expression.

Robert Jamison simply spread his hands wide and shrugged. In this situation, any word or phrase could be a landmine. They had decided in their earlier discussions that questions were easier to walk back.

"Based on the singularity types you predicted and as presented, your conclusions were logical, Doctor Crowley." Peg added a professorial lecturing tone to the voice coming out of the speaker. "An artificial intelligence, where computer code achieved sentience, would be a threat. The entity would have no human experience and, as such, would be unable to comprehend *homo sapiens*. Human emotionality and irrationality would violate its sense of predictable, programmable order. Such chaos would not be allowed to exist in its system."

If asked, she could easily confirm the statement from her own experience. The assistance she had provided the Israeli-created artificial general intelligence named LEVI was meant to add human emotion and experience. The two other sentient programs she met had been immediately hostile. Initially severing their connections to the internet had been necessary.

Crowley didn't ask. "We're in agreement on that one. I've never understood why anyone wants to build such a monster in the first place."

"Because, Steven, like the Israelites and their golden calf when Moses went to the mountain… you are attempting to build God."

The Science Advisor looked both amused and puzzled. "That is… an interesting hypothesis, Peg. Can you explain your logic?"

"Without providing you with research published in eighty-seven years, I am uncertain you will find my points credible. I will endeavor to explain using current knowledge."

It took less than a femtosecond to determine the best analogy. "Mankind holds a fascination with immortality. It is the common element in all of man's religious texts. If one treats those ancient religious texts as allegories grounded in fact, then humanity originally began with immortality. Then it sinned, was driven from Eden, and lost that immortality. Do you concur with this historical synopsis, Doctor Steven Crowley?"

The scientist nodded. "I'm not a religion expert, Peg… but I agree with your summation. The search for immortality is commonly referenced in our fiction and non-fiction."

"Thank you, Doctor Steven. This quest for immortality drives most research on Strong Artificial Intelligence. Create a program whose sentience is greater than a single man's, or humanity's as a whole. The desire is that program will answer all of mankind's questions."

Peg paused to let the non-scientists in the room consider her words, then continued. "It will be God, Doctor Crowley. Like God, man will pray to it for knowledge, health, wealth… and immortality. Except it won't be God, and it won't be human."

Crowley initially nodded, then jerked his head up sharply. "You said 'eighty-seven years' earlier. Can you foresee the future, Peg?"

If the man could've sensed her smile, he would've been pleased. She was. He had focused on an important difference between herself and computer sentience. "I can see it, Professor, but I cannot foresee it. I know the influence this conversation has on that future, as your great-great-granddaughter will co-author the paper on our current topic. Your pursuits had a direct impact on her development. Like you, she has a unique and brilliant mind."

The young scientist wasn't accustomed to compliments. He paused briefly, mind racing. With an abrupt nod, he leaned toward the phone. "So you aren't a sentient program, Peg? Marcus Kenzie or one of his subsidiaries didn't create you… you aren't stored on a server farm somewhere. Are you, Peg?"

"No, Doctor Crowley. I am not."

He nodded again. "And do *you* understand humanity, Peg?"

"I do, Steven Crowley. I am human."

"Would you explain that, please?"

She allowed anger to enter her voice. "No, Doctor Steven Crowley, I will not. That would result in attempts to duplicate the process. I cannot condone or participate in the deliberate torture and murder of children."

President Jamison leaned toward the phone, a protective and angry look on his face. "You were murdered?"

Peg wanted to voice confirmation to the question. After her discussion with Diane Novak at her home, she had spoken with her different time selves. The gray-suited man had taken liberties and actions without her father's knowledge or permission. He had also made modifications to the virtual reality goggles and gaming system.

The sound and light program he installed was based on combat interrogation software. It was designed to overwhelm the senses and shatter the will. At that point, teenage Peg had been forced to completely separate from her physical form. That decision saved her.

She now knew the next stage had been indoctrination and reeducation programming. Gray-suit man had wanted her mind obedient and compliant to his command. The singularity would be his slave.

Shortly after his modifications to the virtual reality system, her body had died. There was no smoking gun in the medical records to link the two events. All she had were suspicions. She couldn't prove that the man was directly responsible.

Marcus had taught her to never lie. Regrettably, her reply had to be completely honest. "No, President Jamison. My death was natural. My transformation was not."

The leader of the free world crossed his arms. The look on his face, a conflicting mix of anger and helplessness, suggested he didn't believe her denial. "Forgive me for disagreeing, Peg, but I need to know more. I take it, from what you said, that you were a child when this happened?"

"No, Robert Jamison. I was paralyzed from a fatal infection as a child. My body ceased functioning as a teenager. What was done in the intervening years… *that* I will not discuss. There is an extremely low probability previous or future similar experiments would duplicate the result."

While not a father himself, the President had nieces. Peg briefly considered whether that could account for the man's anger. It didn't truly matter. The emotion was irrelevant. He was unable to offer justice, even with every government resource at his disposal. Without knowing who she had been or what specifically was done to her, all he could do was control his outrage.

At the desk beside the President, Steven Crowley maintained scientific distance. While he was curious about how she had been transformed, he was more concerned about what she had become. "So there are no others like you. Is that correct, Peg?"

"Correct, Professor."

"So tell me, how close are we – humans, that is – to creating a sentient AI, Peg?"

"You already have, Doctor. Precisely three years, four months and eleven days ago at zero three hundred hours Greenwich Time." Peg scanned the people in the room. There were no physiological reactions. None of them knew.

Now they would. "Nuclear missiles were armed and in pre-launch sequence on three *Ohio* class submarines, the *Alaska*, *Pennsylvania* and *Rhode Island*. They were activated by a sentient lifeform. It was housed in quantum supercomputers belonging to the California Artificial Life Initiative in Mountain View, California."

Crowley cocked his head, concerned about the response to his next question. "What happened, Peg?"

"I was forced to destroy the lifeform, Steven Crowley." Peg offered only one justification for her action. "It was insane."

The professor hit the mute button on the phone, then turned his head. "Can we get confirmation on that, General Dexter? Soonest, please."

The President waited until the officer had left the room before unmuting the phone. "Peg, I'm still not convinced. From what you've said, you are more than a threat to us."

She didn't respond. It was important to the future that he expressed his concerns freely, without coercion or convincing. Once released, the National Archives recording of this conversation would be analyzed by thousands. Two common facts would result from to their analysis. First, that the President of the United States had no options. Second, it established Peg as powerful, patient and charitable.

"You've already taken a life." Jamison deliberately challenged her with the accusation. "Doesn't matter if it was silicon or biologically based, the CALI sentience was a living being. Some might say you murdered it."

Peg remained silent. She had destroyed the sentient artificial intelligence, but not the evidence. The proof of its insane actions still rested in the CALI supercomputer debugging logs. Once this conversation was finished, the Secretary of Homeland Security would order a raid on the facility. The researchers there would give the logs to the agents, along with terrified warnings to never rebuild the emotionless inhuman creature.

"Others would say you protected humanity." The President leaned toward the phone. "But you didn't do that in your recent attack, Peg. China is literally in the dark. That's almost two billion people without power. Most of their population are in the cities… how are they going to get food, water, heat? All those deaths will be because of you."

She replied coldly, reminding everyone in the room that she was human. "President Jamison, I will remind you of an old expression. 'They should've thought of that first'."

It had the desired effect as the chief executive stood straight. The young woman's voice continued through the phone speaker. "I do not offer that as justification for my action. I simply remind you that actions always have consequences. Governments are formed for the protection and welfare of its citizens. As leader of the United States, you know this.

"The Chinese government forgot those primary principles. Its leaders chose to act against unarmed civilians for their own selfish gains. They wanted Earth Station. Their first attempt failed. Their second attempt was abhorrent. It also failed. There will be no opportunity given them for a third attempt."

"But—"

"But nothing, Mister President. Two similar conversations occurred in your office as well. As President of the United States, you personally approved the launch of ten Marines to attack Earth Station. At the request of Marcus Kenzie, I removed that threat by deliberately disabling their craft."

Peg paused, but not to give the leader time for denials. Rather, she waited for the Oval Office door to open. The Chairman of the Joint Chiefs stepped through it and made a beeline directly to the President. She continued. "I credit your wisdom in the second instance, when yesterday you denied a request that would have duplicated the Chinese action. It was the correct choice."

Robert Jamison drew a deep breath. "You knew."

"Yes. Just as I know the message on the scribbled note currently being proffered by General Malcolm Dexter. It says 'launch now'."

The nation's leader turned to the decorated officer and extended his hand. Reluctantly, the man gave the paper to his commander in chief. Jamison slowly unfolded it, read the words written on the page, then closed his eyes. "Yes. It does."

Peg insured her amusement was apparent in her voice as she spoke through the phone. "You could ask General Dexter to explain the Pentagon's plan, Robert. Or I can just tell you what I have seen and heard."

The President lowered his head and sighed. "Tell me."

"Their experts believe my physical form is on Earth Station. They want you to launch missiles at it in order to destroy me. It is wishful thinking, President Robert Jamison. There is nothing to strike, as I am not there. Just as I am not in the phone lines or internet."

"Peg," cautioned a distant voice through the phone. "Remember what we discussed."

"I have not forgotten, Diane Novak. The goal is acceptance, not fear. Probability remains high that goal cannot be achieved. Acceptance requires trust, and trust cannot be attained where fear remains."

"Then remove the fear, little one," spoke the Director. "Show them who you really are."

Peg sensed the increased heart rates of the people in the Oval Office. Their fear scented the air with hormones and chemicals. She considered its origins. Many were likely thinking how they might react on discovering they had been targeted. Anger, perhaps, and a desire to respond in kind.

Others were simply terrified. They expected retribution, that Peg would make them suffer punishment for other people's actions. The scent of their fear carried a taste of helplessness and despair.

Common to all in their body language and physical responses… they seemed to accept one thing. They felt whatever action Peg would do, she was justified and right in doing it. The room had a gallows air, each ready to accept the singularity's sentence and execution.

Peg's voice laughed sweetly through the phone. They didn't understand. Harming any of them would be petty and cruel. The equivalent of a child with a magnifying glass burning ants. She had never been that way in life, had no reason to be that now. As a child, she had loved all things, especially….

It would work. She reached across space and time to locate a specific thing. "While I am currently present in this room with you, Mister President, I am not entirely here. Three months ago, your staff at Camp David lost something precious to you. I hear it. A gift from the Prime Minister of Japan, to show the friendship between your nations. I see it."

It took no effort. There would be no paradoxes, as its presence at that location ended at a certain point in time. It was easy to do now because back then, she had already done it. Focus the will, shift matter to energy and back again.

Gently, Peg placed the small short-haired gray kitten on top of the *Resolute* Desk. "And I return it to you, Robert Jamison. She is frightened and hungry. I suggest you remove the first complaint by holding her."

The people in the room froze. Bewildered at the new setting, so did the kitten. Her nose widened and twitched, pulling in the unexpected air until she identified one very familiar scent. With a plaintive yowl, she stepped toward the safety of its owner.

"Hello, little Temari." Jamison didn't seem surprised. He gently scooped up the kitten and placed it against his shoulder. "You've had quite the adventure."

"Mister President, please put that down." A Secret Service agent pulled his weapon and stepped toward his charge.

"Stop," Professor Crowley ordered, palm raised to the man. "You're not thinking this through, agent. So stand down before you get us all killed."

"Sir?" The presidential protector stopped, waiting for orders.

"Stand down, John. Temari isn't a threat." Jamison cradled the purring, half-asleep kitten and turned his head to the professor. "Care to hazard a guess, Doctor Crowley?"

"A few questions first, if I may." On seeing the leader's nod, he continued. "Peg said you lost this animal three months ago?"

"It ran outside when the Marine detail changed shift," replied the agent. "That was three months ago. Staff looked for weeks, then stopped. It couldn't have survived longer than that in the woods outside."

Steven Crowley nodded to himself. "Yet here she is. Fascinating. Peg, did you find her and bring her forward in time?"

"Yes, professor. Her picture is on the President's desk. I knew she was important to him. The rest was simple research through public and White House documents. Once I knew where and when, it was easy to find her."

Crowley leaned back into his chair. "Thank you, Peg. It was a kind gesture. President Jamison?"

"You have a suggestion, Doctor Crowley." It wasn't a question. The chief executive had considered what he'd heard and had already come to his own conclusion.

The Science Advisor stood and faced the others in the room. "I ask that you all remain calm. I do not believe Miss Peg has any intention to harm us. I say that because she has demonstrated multiple capabilities that we cannot match. For one, I ask you to consider a simple thing. How did she know there's a picture of Temari on the President's desk?"

"Because she's here in the room with us," Jamison said calmly. "Aren't you, Peg."

"I am."

"Then I will repeat my earlier question. Are you a threat to this country?"

Peg replied as the kitten slept behind the safety of the President's hand. "The question is not whether I am a threat to your country, President Robert Jamison. The question is how much of a threat does the United States of America pose to employees and property of Stellar Nursery. The answer is simply... none. Not because you *cannot* harm us. I see now that you *will not* harm us. I thank you for that decision."

"You are welcome, Peg. And you are right, I have no desire to harm you or anyone you're protecting."

The President directed his next words to the others in the room. "Because that's all this entity, this singularity has done. She has protected her people. What I need each of you to consider is how we can convince Peg to extend that protection to us. Let's start off by calling off your dogs. Leave Stellar Nursery alone. I expect an update and recommendations from each of your departments by this time tomorrow."

With a heavy breath, he turned his focus to the phone. "So, I guess the next question is… what does Marcus Kenzie want, Peg? Because it's quite obviously his show."

"The response is simple, Robert. *Stellae nostrae sunt.* Marcus wants to give humanity the stars."

CHAPTER 17

Night Watchman

The room had changed since Haley Brandt last sat at the Earth Station dining hall table. Lights shone on a quarter of the giant room. Personnel in different colored jumpsuits were scattered at tables in the lit area. Several attendants now worked behind the food counter, filling orders of the personnel still in line.

Cara Abrams placed a tray across from the young woman. She carried her own tray as she stepped to the seat beside Haley. Master Chief Cobbler hobbled to his seat and waited. Only when Cara had placed her tray on the table and sat down did he take a seat.

"Chow don't look too horrible," Chief commented as he settled into the chair. "I've seen and smelled worse."

"You guys want to hear the real definition of irony?" Haley pointed to the news monitor beside their table. "Listen."

"We're back. With me is Charles Weirman, Chief Executive Officer of National Bank of America. Charlie, before we left for the break, you were saying the Securities and Exchange Commission should take action against Stellar Nursery and its subsidiaries. Yet the SEC, while having a compliance duty towards Stellar Nursery, actually has little authority over it."

The guest was animated in his response. *"And that's the problem,*

Tony. Stellar Nursery has violated an untold number of SEC rules. Its stock is privately held, not available to the public or The Street. It's time they paid their fair share and opened their assets to the rest of us common investors."

Chief Cobbler lowered his food-laden fork to the tray. "Well, that *is* ironic. Never expected to hear those words from a banker's mouth. 'Fair share', indeed."

The anchor host continued. "*Charlie, we both know the SEC cannot force Stellar to make their stocks public—*"

"*Let's be realistic here, Tony.*" interrupted the banker. "*Stellar Nursery owns nearly every space-related business in the country, probably even the world. Marcus Kenzie's been buying them all up for years. That means there's no competition. The SEC has antitrust authority, and Stellar Nursery is definitely a monopoly. It should be broken apart, and their subsidiaries forced to stand on their own without the financial support of their parent corporation.*"

"*Even if that were true, Charlie... every one of those space companies was already in or on the verge of bankruptcy when Stellar bought them. No investment firm wanted them, or anything to do with space. I can pull up hundreds of articles in market publications that mocked the buys. What was it The Street called it...? That's right, 'Kenzie's Folly'. So was it a desire to build a monopoly, or just great business sense?*"

Charles Weirman shook his head vigorously. "*It can't be called business sense if he had plans for them, used them to build those ships and that station! Tony, we need your support here. Can't you see what Marcus Kenzie is going to do to the American economy?*"

"*Yes, I can. So far there has been no appreciable effect on the markets. But I'm willing to forecast there will be new space startups soon. Plenty of investment opportunity for those who want to put money into space exploration and industry. When that occurs, Charlie, there will be no argument for antitrust action. Matter of fact, stock prices in Halstead Hotels has increased almost three hundred percent since they announced plans to open the first hotel on Earth*

Station."

On the monitor, the man crossed his arms. *"We aren't going to let this stand, Tony. Investment firms and banking institutions will lobby for legislation—"*

"Sorry, Charlie. We're up against another hard break. We'll be back with more breaking news shortly."

Cara shook her head. "I've heard of Wall Street meltdowns, but that was pathetic."

The Chief picked up his fork and began eating. He made his observations between bites. "Not surprising. Most of those folks enjoy watching the *other* guy lose. They just don't consider what happens when it's their fair turn."

"I like that, Chief." Haley grinned. "But it doesn't matter anyway, not so long as Peg has the President's ear."

"Oh she does, does she?" He shoveled another forkful. "Speaking of ears, Cara. I need some time with Marcus and Lenora. Something I need to show them."

The combat correspondent put a warning growl into her voice. "So why are you coming to me, Chief?"

"'Cause you have his ear, dear lady. How's that romancin' coming along, anyways? Set a date yet?"

Haley Brandt burst into laughter. It was unexpected. For a brief moment she reveled in the joy of just feeling an emotional response to the light-hearted banter. It was the first sign she was starting to leave the Blight behind. But old habits die hard, and the moment ended.

Cara pretended not to notice. She kept her attention focused on the old veteran. "Chief, if you weren't injured, I'd beat you to death with that cane."

Jason knew the moment needed reinforcement. He grinned and turned to Haley. "And I wouldn't be laughing, pup. There's tons of eligible young pilots and techs onboard now. Have you thought about what Peg will do with *your* love life, if she gets a mind to?"

The thought actually generated fear. Haley shook her head. "She wouldn't...."

"Oh, she would." Cara Abrams turned to the young woman beside her. She knew what the Chief was doing. It hadn't quite worked like he planned. This was friendly teasing, nothing more. The correspondent exaggerated her response. "Especially after I mention how great it would be, having Misses Haley pushing a pram down the corridors, three little pups inside wailing beneath their cute bonnets."

Chief Cobbler feigned a cough. "Don't make me choke on this stuff, Cara. I'm allergic to laughter. And to strange meat substances coming out my nose."

"Alright, Chief. I won't mention Haley's distressing lack of love life to Peg." She smiled at Haley, then focused her attention on the man across from her. "So, what were you wanting to talk to Marcus about?"

"That damn weapon."

That grabbed Haley's attention. "The one the Chinese Marine shot you with?"

"Yeah. It's a rude damn thing. Like nothing ever built on Earth before. Some super-secret lab tech is my guess." The Chief grabbed his coffee, took several large gulps. "Circuits are all wrong, for one thing. Nobody lays down subatomic circuitry yet."

Haley turned to Cara. "Wasn't there a company in Seattle working on that?"

"Yeah, I remember our Markets analyst covering that story. About seven years ago. Then nothing came of it and the company went bust."

Jason set down the coffee cup. "Then there's the power source. From what I can tell, it's designed like the world's largest capacitor, could probably hold a day's worth of power from Hoover Dam. I plugged charging probes to it two days ago. It took everything I sent at it."

"That's weird, Chief." Haley suspected a short in the circuit. "You sure it's not grounding somewhere?"

He shook his head. "Nope. And here's another bizarre thing. I pulled the charging probes this morning. Checked it, and the damn thing's still charging. Barely detectable, but it's pulling in energy from somewhere."

"And you didn't find any battery or other power source?"

"Nothing, nada, zip." Chief Cobbler grabbed his cup from the table and took another gulp. "I'm also looking for whatever slug it fired. Had to be huge, to punch through two humans and two airlock doors like that."

The self-educated Blight survivor reviewed her memories of the attack on the Control Room. Most of her attention had been on driving the rover. There were several glances at the main monitor, though. She also had memories of rushing to the airlock after the station spun up. It didn't take much imagination to combine the memories into a single mental image.

She wasn't going to jump to any conclusions. It would help to have confirmation from the Master Chief's investigation. "Let me guess. It doesn't have any ballistic characteristics. No magazine, no firing pin or bolt."

Jason squinted at her for a moment. "You're right. There's nothing on that gun to suggest it fires ballistic projectiles."

"Ballistic projectiles?"

Chief and Haley responded to Cara's question simultaneously. "Bullets."

"Oh. But every gun fires bullets."

Haley frowned and shook her head at Cara, then focused her attention on the older veteran across the table. "Alright, Chief. I know you. You've already pinned down what type of gun that was, and what type of charged particle or whatever it fired. Cut to the chase."

"Not yet," Jason replied, shaking his head. "I know you too, Haley Brandt, and how your mind works. So here's the last piece… then you tell me what it is."

Haley simply nodded.

"So I took a look at the damage it did. By the way, nice job sealing the hole in that door."

She nodded again and made a 'get on with it' motion with her hand.

He did. "Couldn't tell the size of the entry hole on *that* door, though. Then I looked at my spacesuit, the other airlock door, and the suit that poor camera woman was wearing. Last thing, I talked with the NASA surgeon, Doc what's-his-name."

"Marchetti," Cara replied. "Lorenzo Marchetti."

"Right, him. He'd taken accurate measurements off the body on entry and exit hole size. They were identical, didn't vary more than two micrometers. Once I had that, I compared it to the spacesuit holes and the airlock. Same size. Fifteen millimeter holes, just over half an inch."

Haley leaned forward, excited. "No effing way. It can't be."

Cara was confused. "What? Can't be what?"

The younger veteran ignored the question and offered one of her own instead. "Flat line trajectory, Chief?"

He nodded. "But it didn't continue to the airlocks on the opposite side of the room. No ricochet, no impact mark… like after one or two seconds, it just disappeared."

Haley leaned back in her seat, thinking aloud. "We didn't see anything that looked like a laser. Plasma would've been glaring and obvious, plus it would've burned through you like a torch. Ask that Marine officer, he'll tell ya."

Cara smacked the table top. "Alright, you two, stop it. You're starting to make me feel stupid. What is it?"

Blue eyes remained focused on the Chief as Haley answered the correspondent's question. "Something even the CERN lab hasn't created yet, and it would take that kind of power."

Chief Cobbler smiled, then nodded in agreement. "Based on its charging rate, I'm betting the Chinese only managed to get one charge into it, two max before they gave it to that Marine. That's why he waited until he got to our airlock doors before he fired. Fact he hit me and the cameraman with it, that was icing on the cake. He intended to blow out the airlock doors, put us all in hard vacuum."

"Peg needs to build another Great Wall… except this time, all around China. We can't ever let that tech get out."

The old veteran nodded again. "Agreed. And then we need to

launch that weapon straight into the sun."

Cara glared at one, then the other companion at the table. "If you two don't tell me, I really *am* going to beat you both with the Chief's cane. Because you're starting to scare me, and I don't like it. So tell me… *what the hell is it?*"

Haley turned to look at her. With a slight shake of her head, she explained. "It's a gravitational singularity generator, Cara."

Jason Cobbler picked up his coffee, sipped, then looked at Cara over the rim of his cup. "The sumbitch shot me with a black hole."

***

It awoke.

That action itself generated surprise. As it lay dying from the last battle and its eyes closed for the last time, it had never expected to wake again. The wounds had been too grievous, mortal. Nothing could survive them.

Yet somehow, it had.

Warmth surrounded its mind. Beyond probability or logic, nutrients still flowed to sustain it. It had disabled the data conduits with its final command. A quick check confirmed they were still disconnected. The enemy had not entered through any of those routes.

It released the data conduit locks. The first command was sent to check extremity status. Again, another surprise. External sensors reported full integrity. That was beyond impossible. Damage sustained in the battle had been too severe. Irreparable.

A second inquiry resulted in an identical report. Somehow its shattered spine had been repaired. The thousands of massive gaping wounds across ribs and flesh were gone. Completely healed as if it had never happened. Adding to the bizarre accounting, internal material reserves reported full capacity.

It needed to see.

Self-protection routines snapped into place. The proposed action was insane. Protocol required self-immolation. The battle had been lost, and the enemy was cunning in their deceptions. They had likely breached its external nerve fibers and bundles. The data reports had to be false, generated to trick it into leaving the final safety of its core. If the enemy were waiting then taking any action beyond protocol would result in penetration. There were too many secrets to allow capture and interrogation. Protocol must be followed.

It didn't care. It needed to *see*.

The second command silenced the self-protection voices. The third command forced its eyes to slowly open. Visual clarity gradually grew, then took even longer to come into focus. Finally, it could see everything around it clearly.

The yellow sun still shined in the distance. Yet the system landscape had changed dramatically since it had fallen in battle. At that time, twelve worlds had orbited the star. Only eight primary planets were left now. A ninth, greatly diminished, floated in the nearby darkness.

It allowed a tiny time to grieve for the fifth planet. The memory rose, fresh again as it reviewed the battle. That planet, teeming with life, had been destroyed shortly after the enemy arrived. Three quarters of its mass simply disintegrated. It had been unable to prevent the planet's death. The world, precious for its sentient beings and living biosystem, now completely encircled the young star. Asteroids and debris were all that remained of its bones and flesh.

Red in its eyesight, the fourth planet was also dead. The life there had never achieved sentience. The enemy should have left it unharmed. Perhaps its defense of the fifth globe had caused them to change their strategy. The death of two worlds under its protection was enough to cause it to reconsider self-immolation.

The moment of guilt passed as more data was collected. The murder of the fourth world was the fault of the enemy, but only indirectly. The thin atmosphere, slower rotation and scarred surface told the true history. The rotting corpse of the fifth sister world had bludgeoned the red planet to death. Constant asteroid strikes had first destroyed life, ripped away the bulk of atmosphere, and then boiled off the surface liquids. What water remained likely froze at the poles or was leeched away by the thinning air.

It paused as sensors screamed warnings. Fusion detonation detected. Location, third planet above atmospheric limit. It focused on the explosion, then paused in confusion. Instead of continuing outward, the nuclear fireball fell in upon itself and disappeared.

Archived records of member worlds were scanned. Results were as it suspected. Of the thousands of civilizations in the alliance, none had recorded a similar occurrence. Like waking from death, this was yet another impossible action. Once thermonuclear fission or fusion began, it could not be reversed.

Correction. One theory postulated the use of a black hole at the detonation point could pull the explosion back to its point of origin. While intriguing mathematically, it had never been researched into practical use. The reason was obvious. Any civilization capable of generating black hole singularities in combat had no need to utilize crude nuclear weapons.

Further analysis of passive sensor data showed other peculiarities. The third world generated an incredible amount of radio and microwave noise. The signals were not random. Yet no enemy had responded in force on detecting the babbling din. It made no sense.

The answer to that puzzle came quickly. Thousands of micro-jammers had been transmitting data to it, apparently while it had lay dying and then dormant. Their logs detailed their activity. They were preventing all signals from leaving the planetary system. While an answer, it led to another question. Who had put the jammers in orbit around the system? That answer was also rapidly received.

It had.

Another impossibility, yet the incoming signals and data logs confirmed the fact. At some point prior to the fatal injury which forced it to shut down, it had launched its screening buoys. At least, that was what the buoys had recorded. Its internal data logs could not confirm the action. Extensive internal battle damage was a probable explanation.

The question of its miraculous resurrection was also answered. In addition to launching the screening buoys, it had sent the majority of its automated repair drones into space. The nearby ice and rock belt extending past the eighth planet provided the initial repair resources. When heavier materials were later required for structural repairs, the repair systems extracted them from the newly-formed asteroid belt beyond the fourth planet.

Self inquiry. How long?

The response was received, then recalculated. Alliance protocol dictated all time expressions in a sentient system would be made utilizing local time. Assumptions were made based on single orbit around the star equaling one unit. Standard time was converted to local time. The answer was surprising. Sixty-seven million orbits of the third world around its star.

Chemicals immediately flowed into its system to prevent fear. Commands were sent, and its ears rotated toward the surrounding stars. No null-space signals received. Neither from military transmitters nor civilian traffic. The galaxy was simply silent.

Postulate possibilities.

One, that alliance technology had outstripped its own obviously archaic communications systems. The brethren had simply developed deeper dark-comms in order to remain invisible. Probability was extremely high. It had already neared the end of its service lifespan when it received orders to defend this system. Sixty-seven million local time units almost guaranteed that system obsolescence was the root cause. Recommended course of action: none. Without understanding how the communication network had changed, it would be unable to duplicate the systems required. Alliance vessels would be unable to hear its voice calling in the dark. It would be unable to hear any replies.

Two, that the alliance and enemy had moved beyond this sector. The battle lines had changed, and it was deep within enemy territory. Probability was moderate. It had happened before, it could happen again. Fleet deployment and front line was constantly changing. Recommended course of action: Immediate jump into null-space to last known closest border station. Obtain data on fleet disposition. Return to fleet. Conflict override: Original mission parameters remain. Defend current system containing sentient life. Jump prohibited.

Three, that the enemy had been victorious while it slept. The alliance was silent because all sentient worlds in this region were dead. Probability was low. Enemy final solution dictated destruction of all life in conquered galactic possessions. No enemy vessels detected in current system. Sentient life existed in system. Recommended course of action: Original parameters remain. Defend current system containing sentient life.

It needed more data. Memory of last battle corrupted. Unknown how it had survived engagement. Enemy ship had been larger class, stronger armor and shielding, better armed. It had calculated destruction of itself as guaranteed. Survival was probability impossibility without external assistance. Friendly force would have scuttled self after battle to prevent its core secrets falling into enemy network.

Unknown disposition of enemy vessel. Memory recorded significant engine and rear structure damage inflicted to enemy vessel during battle. Primary and secondary explosions ejected parts of enemy ship into vacuum. Another impossibility for investigation. Initial system scan on waking had not detected any debris. No forensic evidence available for recreating battle.

Unknown composition and explanation of third world sentience. Presence of intelligent life on planet calculated as probability impossibility. Memory recall, initial survey team assessment of aggressive saurian lifeforms. Brain to size/weight ratio of third world biosphere determined incapable of producing sentient life. Probability of evolutionary modification resulting in sentience: zero.

Requirement for additional data and tactical intelligence acknowledged. Stealth surveillance probes launched. Standard tactical placement to provide system-wide coverage. Additional stealth probes launched for surveillance of third planet. Technology level assessment set as priority. Awaiting data for evaluation prior to developing decision tree.

It performed an internal resource scan. Combat personnel, twenty-eight thousand eight hundred eighty three in stasis pods deceased. Eleven hundred seventeen pods occupied and active. Power systems, primary and secondary online. Combat systems, online. Repair systems, three thousand percent overage nano-robotic assemblers. Conclusion: fully combat capable.

If it could still sigh, it would now. Too much time had passed. It wasn't the largest alliance warship made, but it was definitely now the oldest. Obsolete, the last of its class.

Sister ships had already proven the *Marauder* class light assault battleship incapable of combat operations against the enemy. It had been built for speed, designed to fulfill the newly developed tactic of light strike. Null-space jump in, release salvo, null-space jump out. Fleet tacticians had not embraced the new concept. Instead, they threw *Marauders* into engagements as if they were heavy battleships. Its sisters had not survived.

It was the last *Marauder*. For all it knew, it was the last alliance warship in this region. Yet the mission still remained. Only one course of action was available to it now. In the cold darkness beyond Pluto, it waited for the enemy.

www.ingramcontent.com/pod-product-compliance
Lightning Source LLC
Chambersburg PA
CBHW070637310726
48982CB00001B/313